The Paper Boy by James A Lyons

www.jamesalyons.co.uk

Cover Art and Design by Numan Ahmed

ISBN: 9798829196264

AUTHOR NOTE

This book was self-published with a minimal marketing budget. Authors such as myself rely on word of mouth to get our stories out there to as many people as possible. If you enjoy this book, please recommend it to friends, leave a review on GoodReads or Amazon, or share on your social media channels!

Naturally, there may be a few minor spelling and grammar mistakes. If you spot something, or just want to provide any feedback or say hello, feel free to email me on james.a.lyons@outlook.com.

Cheers for reading!

James.

FIND JAMES ONLINE:

twitter.com/jalwrites
facebook.com/jalwrites
goodreads.com/jamesalyons

THE PAPER BOY

DEDICATED TO ANY KID
WHO HAS EVER FELT OUT OF
SYNC.

MONDAY

ONE

They always say that today should be the first day of the rest of your life. This is true, unless today happens to be a Monday, in which case maybe wait until tomorrow.

It was 6am on a strangely dark morning. It was summer, but a Monday is a Monday, and the thin curtains in the square box bedroom blocked a weak morning sun. Tim Johnson woke up suddenly to the sound of Saint Monique belting out her latest single from the robot-shaped clock radio that he had been given by his Grandma and Grandad Johnson this past Christmas. The bright red numerical display made him feel as if he was undergoing laser eye surgery as he looked at it with a squint. It was the mechanical voice stuttering *wake up, wake up* that it shouted four times before Fox FM kicked in that had stirred him from a deep sleep less than ten minutes ago. Tim shuffled in his single bed and turned onto his left-hand side. Saint Monique was one of his favourite singers, in fact he would call himself borderline obsessed with her, however at six in the morning he wasn't as appreciative of her slickly produced pop music. He sat up slightly and hit the snooze button with more force than necessary, forcing the robot to fall onto its face. Pulling his duvet up over his head, he buried himself hoping that the extra ten minutes of hibernation would somehow stir some enthusiasm within him.

Despite a similar routine being played out nearly every morning for two years, Tim still hated waking up this early. Winter was usually the worst time, with the darkness of the morning seemingly lasting forever, but even in July, as it was now, it was always bad on a Monday. The only saving grace was that it was so close to the end of term. There were just one-and-a-half days of lessons to struggle through before six weeks of freedom arrived. Year Ten had followed the generic pattern of the previous three secondary academic years, and he had seemed to float around unnoticed amongst most of the other people in his year. Everything about Tim was average so it was easy to camouflage himself in-between the other one hundred or so students in his year at Greenwood Secondary.

Tim would have been less tired this morning had he not stayed up longer than his mum had realised last night, quietly watching an episode of *Choose That Guy* on the television. *Choose That Guy* was dreadful television, and everyone knew it, but it had been the most watched programme for the eighth week in a row. It was one of those types of programme that somehow made you less intelligent the more you watched it. As with all reality shows though, it was addictive, and he knew that finding out the latest gossip from it would allow him to join in all the conversations with his classmates at break times later. Chloe, the sole female contestant, had whittled down the contenders for the prize of 'a holiday of a lifetime' from a dozen to just four. Tim was disappointed that his favourite, Jay, had been voted off. According to the postcard biography that popped up during the first episode, Jay was six-feet tall, an Aries, and came from some place called Tenby, wherever that was. Tim had text his friend Lydia with anger when it was announced that Jay had lost the public vote. He was angry that he was gone, and angry that he spent a whole hour texting in votes for him, all for nothing. At the end of the day though, it didn't matter. Next year there would be a new bunch of identikit humans going through the same old routine. He'd probably end up watching it again.

Underneath the covers, Tim slipped back into a deep sleep quickly, and thoughts of being chased across a courtyard entered his dreams. He had snuck inside a small dark room when there was a thump at the door, presumably by whatever he was running from. The banging got louder and louder until the door was finally broken down, at which point, he woke up with a start. He blinked open his eyes back into reality and saw the figure of his own mum entering his bedroom.

"Get up," she said briskly. "I've knocked a few times, but you chose to ignore me."

Tim let out a small 'urgh' before stretching and picking up the clock. It had now somehow passed six-thirty. Realising that he must have turned his alarm off rather than snoozing it, he leapt out of bed and began to dress rapidly.

"Why didn't you wake me up earlier, mum?" he complained, blaming her for his inefficiency as he pulled on his socks whilst she gazed over the garden.

"I was getting up late," she replied. "Anyway, you're fifteen and a half now so you shouldn't have to rely on me for everything." Her voice was sounding more hoarse than usual. It was as if she had been eating gravel.

"Why are you speaking like that?" he enquired.

"Like what?" she said back croakily.

"Like...well...like you've been shouting."

"Oh, Saturday night's karaoke was a good one. I think it's a delayed reaction from that."

He had forgotten that she had been there. He had been at his best friend Leo's house for a sleepover that night. On the second Saturday of each month his mum would meet up with some of her friends and head to the local snooker club for a 'Tombola and Karaoke' evening. The snooker club had been doing them for years and used it as an opportunity to raise money for a local hospice. Regardless of whether the money was going to a worthy cause or not, Tim was at the age now where he could feel embarrassed on her behalf, mainly as she never showed any embarrassment herself. He prayed that no parents of his school friends were present this time as he wasn't sure he could deal with more tragic stories about what she had sung. News in the small town of Greenwood travelled fast and the jokes about her were a monthly feature in the Year 10 Mars form room. He still wasn't over last month's tales. Apparently, his mum had duetted with a young, terrified looking, German bartender on his first ever shift singing 'Don't Go Breaking My Heart', before doing a Cher number that was described by at least three people as 'borderline offensive to all'. He secretly wished that they would ban her but sadly there was no such luck.

His mum, Katherine, was forty years old, which, from what he had heard other people say, is old enough to know better. In her mind she still thought that she was a teenager though, and on a night out she still dressed that way. Her hair was short and dyed platinum blonde. From what he could remember, it hadn't been its natural colour since he had started school a decade ago. Tim had thought that she would be more normal if his dad, Cameron, was about. His parents were very much still married, however his dad worked overseas a lot. He had been a Navy man when he had met the young Katherine whilst on shore leave down in Portsmouth. She was working in The Ship and Castle pub that sat just inland from the harbour, and he just happened to stumble in, quite literally. She helped him up after he fell over a table within seconds of stepping inside. Cameron had always enjoyed his job and was currently halfway through an eight-week expedition somewhere in the middle of an ocean. He was due to be home at the end of July, and the family planned to go away together once he was back. Tim wanted to go somewhere exotic and far away and had been led into a false sense of excitement when he had spotted brochures from the travel agent listing holidays in Japan, the Caribbean, and beyond on the coffee table a few months back. When he was told that they would be heading to Clacton-on-Sea for a week he was bitterly disappointed. There wasn't anything wrong with Clacton of course, it's just that this would be the sixth year in a row that they had gone there. He would have to keep himself busy in the amusements by the beach again, putting endless two pence coins into the machines.

Needing to leave for his paper round quickly, Tim pulled on some black jogging bottoms and threw an oversized hoodie over his torso. He checked the mirror, and his tired mousey looking hair was jutting out at all angles, as if he had been given a fright. He poked at his cheeks and watched as the ice white finger marks slowly returned to their original pinkish colour. He put on a blue baseball cap and headed down the stairs. There would be no time for breakfast just yet. He was already ten minutes late and it would be a real push to finish work and have time to shower before school.

Greenwood was a funny old town. It was separated into two parts, split right down the middle by the small but fast flowing river. Tim lived on the eastern side, in a three-bedroom semi-detached house at 247 Oak Tree Crescent with his parents and older brother Marty. They had moved in here when Tim was only a year old, however he was now outgrowing the size of his bedroom. He liked the name Oak Tree Crescent, but it did make it sound much nicer than it really was. There wasn't even an oak tree along the whole of the estate. The house was in a block of four, with the gardens of each set of two backing on to each other. The neighbours were okay, but Tim didn't really speak to them much, other than to say hello. They were all slightly older than his parents, and either had no children, or children who had grown up and left home.

The east was the best side of the town. Those living in the west would claim otherwise, and there was no love lost between the two. Everything Tim needed was on this side of the river anyway. His school was here, his friends lived here, the good shops were near, and of course, the newsagents from where he worked. If each side kept to themselves, the town would remain in harmony.

The paper round that Tim had held for two years saw him look after the deliveries on six of the housing estates in the east. Although they were small estates, there were still over sixty to deliver each morning. He'd got quite good at it by now though, and having tried and tested every different possible route, he had the art of it worked out so that he could get everything completed in just over an hour (his current personal best was sixty-four minutes and twenty-three seconds). He tried to leave the house at 6.10am every day, except on a Friday where he would leave a little earlier as this was the day where he dropped off the bills to the customers, and in return he would get a fair few pounds in tips. He always made sure that he was at his politest towards the end of the week. Those living in Ash Street, Pine Close and Birch Avenue often slipped him a couple of coins, but it was at the richer estates where the big tips would roll in. Those in Elm Meadow and Beech Close lived in large, detached houses, some with electric gates, crunchy gravel driveways and double garages. It was rare when at least one of those residents didn't pass over a five-pound note to him whilst disguising the transaction in a handshake. Tim was mostly well liked amongst the adults, and many people often referred to him as 'Singh's Boy' when they saw him in public. The Singh in question was Mr Mahmood Singh the newsagent. He had owned the shop on Bridge Street for many years and everyone was a friend to him. Tim had always got on well with him too, and Mr Singh often told him to help himself to a chocolate bar at the beginning of each round (he chose a Wispa every time). His only gripe was the name of the newsagents. It was currently called Singh Stars, which was a pun that worked about ten years ago maybe. Most locals just called it Singh's, so it shouldn't really be important but the jagged font and the large cartoon microphone on the shop front just made it look a bit dated. It was a good enough job for Tim to have though and would save him having to do the washing up in one of the many local restaurants for money instead.

Tim turned the key in the back door and was greeted by rain pouring down heavily. It was mid-July; the weather shouldn't be like this. Feeling a bit deflated, he headed to the cupboard near the front door to swap his hoodie for a luminous and oversized waterproof jacket, and was caught by his mum as he slung it on. She was bounding down the stairs in fluffy slippers, with a white towel wrapped around her body, and a pink one tied up around her hair. He had tried to escape the house before she had come down as he knew what she wanted even before she opened her mouth.

"I've got the leaflets for you to take today, Timothy," she said as if on cue.

Tim groaned and fell back against the hallway wall. "Can I do them tomorrow? It's raining, and I haven't got time today."

"Time will cost us money young man. You know that Monday is when my customers expect to find out what I have for them this week."

Tim wanted to argue, but he knew that it would prove pointless. His mum always made it sound as if she was the head of a really important business, but the truth was that her schemes just added more ammunition to those at school who wanted to mock him. For the half of his school year who didn't know her from the karaoke, Katherine Johnson was well known for her business adventures. She worked from home and seemingly had an endless supply of job-lot items to sell. Each week was something different, and she used Tim's paper round to help with the advertising. She had always encouraged him to get a round, and the leafleting for her goods started within a fortnight of him beginning the job. He didn't know for sure if Mr Singh knew it was happening, but Tim would have been surprised if he wasn't just turning a blind eye.

Each Monday morning his mum would leave a stack of leaflets on the pine kitchen table, which he would then deliver to all those who had newspapers. Any remaining ones would be delivered after school to the houses nearby. There must be a million employment laws being broken, but his mum always bought him magazines and clothes in return for his help. Tim was easily bribed. He had tried talking to his dad about it once, but he was very much from the 'I'm staying out of this' camp. Tim was dreading what he would have to advertise today. Last week it had been Tamagotchi's, small keyring sized devices with an old style screen where you had to feed and pet an imaginary animal in order for it not to die. His mum had said that they had been popular in the nineties and hoped their time would come around again. In fairness, a lot of people did buy them for their children, probably for their own nostalgia rather than the child's amusement. Tim kept one for himself, but the novelty wore off after his had died within forty-eight hours because he didn't take it for some form of electronic exercise.

"Would Marty be able to deliver them today instead?" Tim asked in a last attempt to get out of it for the week.

"He's got karate after college today so won't be about," came the reply. "Also, if you don't do it, I won't take you on holiday with us." Tim didn't let on that this was not even a mild threat, and either way there was no chance that his parents would trust him at home alone. They didn't even leave him at home if they did their big shop on a Saturday afternoon, not unless Marty was home anyway.

Marty was Tim's older brother by two-and-a-bit years. He never had a paper round. He had left Greenwood Secondary last summer and was currently coming to the end of his first year on an apprentice carpentry course at Windrush College. The two used to argue quite a lot when younger, but things had settled now.

Admitting defeat, Tim took his paper bag and scooped up the leaflets from the kitchen table, before heading to get his bike.

"Don't forget to close the back door," he whispered to himself as he stepped outside. It was like his mums very own catchphrase. Sure enough, a second later, she croaked the phrase at him before he was even fully through the door. He waved a leaflet over his shoulder and slammed it shut. He darted down the central path of their small square garden, and towards the cover of the shed, rain finding its way down his neck as he fumbled with the lock. Once sheltered inside, he hunched over and discovered what it would be that he would be advertising today. He took a leaflet off the pile.

*******SPECIAL OFFER*******
BISCUIT PARTY MIX PACKS AVAILABLE NOW

SELECTION BOXES OF MIXED BISCUITS AVAILABLE. IDEAL AS SMALL GIFTS FOR TEACHERS, COLLEAGUES, FRIENDS OR NEIGHBOURS, OR JUST TO SAY THANK YOU TO A SPECIAL SOMEONE.

IF YOU WOULD LIKE TO TAKE UP THIS OPPORTUNITY, PLEASE FILL IN THE ORDER FORM OVERLEAF

This was worse than normal, he thought. Who wants to buy their biscuits from a strange woman down the road? And what is a party mix of biscuits? It would literally be cheaper for people to get their own from the shops. The ones from the shops would be in date too, unlike the ones that were being stored presumably in his parents' bedroom. He sighed, put the leaflet back with the others in the bag and jumped on his bike to Singh Stars.

TWO

"Morning, Mr Singh," Tim said cheerfully as he entered the newsagents, the small bell near the door clanging above him. He was feeling partially upbeat still, despite being soaked to the skin from the weather already. His waterproof coat was proving to be anything but.

"Good morning, Tim," came the reply, accompanied by a wide smile from the centre of Mr Singh's bright white short beard. "I thought you'd got lost," he said, but without any hint of annoyance.

"I overslept by accident. Mum was sleeping in so didn't notice," Tim replied.

"Oh yes. Your mum was out on Saturday so she may need the rest."

"...were you there?" Tim asked, his heart racing through embarrassment.

"I was."

"Did she embarrass herself?"

"It depends how easily embarrassed you get, son."

Tim was worried.

"It doesn't take much when it involves mum, Mr Singh."

"Every mother is embarrassing."

"Not to the same level though. Do I want to know what she did this time?"

"I am not one to judge or to divulge my thoughts," said Mr Singh, smiling.

Tim would have to wait until school to see if any stories came up in the gossip before the morning register in the form room. He knew that whatever she had done would not reflect well on him or make his life easier. Whilst Mr Singh started doing a final count of the newspapers into his bag, Tim browsed the shelves.

"Help yourself to a chocolate bar," said Mr Singh as usual, without looking up, so Tim slipped a Wispa into his inside pocket. He perused the magazines, seeking out the sports section. Tim was not the sportiest of people but enjoyed watching them on television. He secretly stayed awake for most of the night during the Tokyo Olympics, watching with his television in his room on mute so not to cause suspicion. He was much more into sport than anything else. His brother had tried to get him into music, lending him his magazines after he had finished reading them, but they hadn't really been of any interest, so he had stored them in the shed to use for the guinea pig hutches last year.

Of course, sport was still a big part of the school curriculum, but Tim seemed to be bad at nearly all that Greenwood Secondary had to offer.

In fact, he had reasons to dislike all the sports the school selected for a variety of reasons.

1. **Football**
   The most popular sport. No eye-to-foot coordination. The ball stings your thigh if hit against it in winter. Big pitch so it's tiring.

2. **Rugby**
   Same as above, but with more confusing rules. Too small so thrown around like a ragdoll by the bigger kids. Scrum smells of sweaty boys.

3. **Cross Country Running**
   TIRING! Shoes hurt the feet. Have to rub Vaseline on yourself in unspeakable places to avoid chaffing. Chances of getting lost in the woods quite high.

4. **Gym**
   No upper body strength. Equipment very dated. Balance beam too thin, ropes hard to climb, can't do a front or back flip.

5. **Athletics**
   (See Cross Country Running). Also, hurdles are too high, long jump makes you have sand in your shoes for WEEKS, discus less fun than frisbee.

6. **Tennis**
   BORING.

7. **Cricket**
   Apparently there are numerous ways to get 'out' in cricket, but only four seem understandable. Told to stand in positions like *mid-off, gully* and *third man* like some secret code that we are meant to understand. Also, the boundary rope is literally miles away (okay not *literally* miles away but it looks it). The ball is also hard and that would hurt if it hit you in the head, helmet or no helmet.

8. **Basketball**
   The net is too high, and too small.

9. **Hockey**
The least worst of the sports but Greenwood is behind the times and only really lets girls do this whilst boys do rugby.

Games at primary school were always much more fun. There was one called King Penguin which had two teams, with team one trying to throw a spongeball over the other team, where it was caught by someone stood on a wooden bench. If the other team caught your throw, you were out. It was a game that everyone could be good at. They should actually make it an Olympic sport.

Ever since the London Olympics had taken place when he was small, Tim had been into a lot of the less popular sports. For the last couple of years though, he had wanted to give diving a go. There was something about diving that he connected with, although when he first had these thoughts last summer, he hadn't even been able to swim, which is kind of a fundamental element to being allowed to join the local club. He had finally taken courses at Greenwood Leisure Centre and could comfortably do twenty-five metres, albeit with his head out the water as much as possible, and only breaststroke. Not only this, but he was also scared of heights. He was further away from being able to dive off a ten-metre board into a deep pool than anyone else. He assumed that the fear of heights would ease as he got older, but if anything, it had got worse. He was trying to understand why it was diving in particular that appealed so much to him. Whenever it was on, he would have to watch it.

It was during the last Christmas holidays that his mum had agreed to pay for him to have swimming lessons. It took a bit of time to become confident, including many lessons where he clung onto a float so hard that his knuckles turned white. After ten lessons however, he was comfortable to swim ten metres unaided across the shallow end of the local pool. Since learning to swim, he had started to go to the pool with his best friends Leo and Lydia (or 'Lyds' as she was called by the group). With them he felt comfortable treading water and splashing about, but rarely ventured towards the deep end. He often looked at the diving pool, and the top board towered over him like a skyscraper. Maybe he was kidding himself thinking that he would ever be able to get up there.

Tim was halfway through an article about one of Britain's top divers in an Olympic Review magazine when he was interrupted by Mr Singh, ready to hand his heavy bag of papers across.

"Um, Mr Singh, can you keep this magazine for me please? I'll buy it with my wages on Friday if that's okay?"

"Not a problem. I'll put it under the counter."

"Many thanks. Righty-o, see you later!"

Tim heaved the fluorescent yellow bag over his shoulder and walked out the door, the bell clanging gleefully again as he swung it open. He took the leaflets out of his pockets, where he had stored them out of sight of Mr Singh, and struggled on his bike down the road.

Although the rain slowed him somewhat, he still made it home for 8am, and happily had just enough time to have some cereal after his shower. He was feeling more alert and felt that this Monday wouldn't be so bad after all. This soon changed when he remembered that today was the annual inter-class football tournament. As there were only twelve boys in his class he was automatically included in the squad, but he had neither the desire nor the required skills to be of any use. Add to the fact that he was too scared to head the ball in case it knocked him out, him being on the team would be more of a hinderance than any help.

Being the last couple of days of school, he would much rather be doing literally anything else. He wanted to hang around with Lydia and Leo, but they would be off with their own classes doing football or hockey. Tim would have preferred to be playing hockey instead, easily. Lydia and Leo were the two people who were most like him, and they had formed a bond on their first visit to the secondary school a few weeks before finishing at primary. They always stuck together as a threesome during Years Seven, Eight and Nine, and had been disappointed when the school had split them between three separate form groups when moving to Year Ten.

Tim would have to do his usual during today's tournament. This meant standing in short shorts and long socks on the touchline, whilst those who could play better than he could (as in, everyone) kicked the ball around on the pitch. His form tutor, Mr Stephenson, would always try to make Tim play in one match in order for all children to have their chance and not feel left out, but Tim was perfectly happy not being included. In fact, last year he had run away to hide in the changing rooms so that he wouldn't be dragged into the starting eleven. This was the only problem with the end of term; all these 'fun' social activities were more of a hassle for most involved rather than resulting in anything positive. On top of the football tournament, there was also the end of term disco in the school hall which was due to take place tomorrow. When the idea had originally been floated, Tim had been asked to sit in on the student committee in charge of organising the event, but only lasted two short meetings before being told that he was 'anti-fun', and that his negative attitude was causing alarm for the other, more eager, members.

“Oh, you’re back,” said his mum as she entered the kitchen as he poured a cereal cocktail of cornflakes and chocolate crisp into a bowl. She was dressed now finally.

“Would you be kind and help me after school please?”

“I was going to see Leo and Lyds,” he said, through a mouthful of food.

“It won’t be for long; you can see them when you’re done.”

“Done with what?”

“It’s the biscuits. We need to pack them up into boxes for people who buy them,” she said gesturing at non-existent boxes to her left.

“I only took the leaflets this morning though. What if no one buys them?”

“We have to be prepared for when they do. If you have spare leaflets, I’ll deliver them for you as compensation. These could be a winner. You saw how well those tamathingys went last week.”

“Tamagotchi’s. But yeah, an out-of-date biscuit isn’t going to keep a kid occupied for long.”

“It will only be ‘til four-thirty, I promise. I’ll pay for you to have food out or something for tea. Leo and Lydia can help pack the biscuits if you like?”

“I don’t want them anywhere near here whilst I’m doing it,” he pleaded, “I don’t want anyone to know how weird you are.”

“It’s normal.”

“No mum, it’s not. It’s weird. Anyway, they probably have better things to do.”

“You said they were going to hang around with you, so that’s a lie,” she joked, before kissing him on the forehead and heading to make a coffee.

She had recently been given a new fancy and professional looking coffee machine that promised to make better coffee than at a café, but she hadn’t mastered the skill. Last week the frothy milk had fired directly at her instead of her cup, and most coffees seemed to be a bit lumpy at the bottom, for reasons unknown. Tim pulled himself onto the countertop and ate the remainder of his cereal quickly, before dumping his bowl in the sink and grabbing his hoodie before setting off to school.

“See ya later, mum,” he shouted as he bolted outside.

“Don’t forget to close the back door!” came a cry from inside.

THREE

The entire day at school was a disaster. The three lessons were dull (physics, religious studies and woodwork), and the 'end of year activities' that the teachers had planned for each were quickly redesigned for indoors due to the rain lasting up until lunchtime. Tim hoped that the bad weather would continue until home time so that football was cancelled, but sadly it came to a stop during his lunch (tuna and sweetcorn sandwiches, Wotsits and a Wispa). The brighter weather meant that the football tournament had to go ahead. Tim had found himself to be more useful than normal during this year's games though. Mr Stephenson had given in to his whinging and said he didn't have to play if he didn't want to, which suited Tim fine. Instead of spending anytime chasing a ball on the pitch, he had been given the role of 'ball fetcher'. This involved climbing over a gate into the farmers field that neighboured the sports field and retrieving any stray ball that was hoofed or sliced over the hedge. The appalling accuracy level of some Year Tens meant that he was called into action frequently, and there was hardly any time to just sit around. Whilst standing on the sidelines he had discussed his plans to become a diver with his science teacher Mr Stephenson, who had been fairly encouraging back and said that if he worked hard then it might happen one day. Tim explained that he had been looking at the divers in a magazine and that he wanted to become toned like them so that he was strong enough to do a handstand at the top of a ten-metre board before falling gracefully and acrobatically into the water. Tim often daydreamed about being in an Olympic final, going for gold for Team GB in somewhere like Los Angeles, Paris or Rome. He wondered if anyone would ever be reading about his life in a magazine in the future.

"Remember you are only fifteen Tim," Mr Stephenson had said. "You still have a few years of natural growth yet."

Tim hated waiting. Waiting years seemed an eternity at his age. By now he should really be part of a diving school. He had asked for some weights for his birthday or Christmas last year (they fell on the same day) but was told that it was of no use whilst he was still developing. Despite all his efforts in swimming lessons and being shown endless videos on YouTube by his PE teacher Ms Trafford, he could still not get to grips with front crawl and ended up swallowing a litre of water with each attempt. Mr Stephenson explained to Tim that the school would never agree to lead diving classes. Swimming itself was also ruled out at Greenwood Secondary since they had filled in the pool and built a new geography block on top of it two years ago.

As the school day came to a close, Tim's form group hadn't won football. In fact, Form 10 Mars lost every game. Their best result came when they managed to finally score once against Form 10 Jupiter, even though it was an own goal. The high of scoring was small as the opposing team had scored nine. Not bad for a game which only lasted twenty minutes. The other two games saw so many goals conceded that the score may have even reached double figures. In the second game Tim had lost count completely. He was certain that this tournament was run so that the science teachers didn't have to do any planning for the last week before summer. The heads of each year acted as referees, including Mr Hines, who was a bit wobbly on his feet. He had been at the school for about thirty-five years and watching him stutter around blowing a whistle had led to Tim eyeballing the nearby buildings for a defibrillator in case it was needed urgently. No one properly cared for the football, but everyone felt obliged to help make it happen.

After the matches, Tim walked back to the squalid changing rooms and showered quickly so that he could escape the school as swiftly as possible. He disliked the changing room experience. He was not confident in his own body and wished to be more developed like most other boys in his form. Tim always struggled to get dressed whilst under his towel, cowered as far into the corner as possible. The whole experience made him too nervous to talk to anyone. He barely even looked up.

After the horrendous usual changing experiences, Tim made his way to the front gates of the school grounds, where he bumped into Lydia and Leo. They were still dressed in their green and gold PE kits. Living on the same side of town was handy as it meant that they could walk towards home together most days.

"We still hanging out this evening?" Lydia asked.

"Yeah, won't be for a bit though as gotta help mum with some stuff," Tim replied.

"What is she selling now?" Leo chimed in.

"Um, I dunno. She just asked me to help."

Tim was happy to tell Lydia and Leo all the weird stuff that his mum did, and they found it quite sweet in its own unique way. Even so, he thought that they would think selling out-of-date biscuits would be strange. They would find out though when a leaflet was stuck through their door but delaying the inevitable was easier.

"Give me a text when ya ready and I'll let you know where we are," said Leo.

"Will do. How was your football by the way, and the hockey, Lyds?"

"Rubbish," they both replied in unison.

"I had to go in goal," complained Leo.

"But you're like four foot tall!" laughed Tim.

"I'm taller than you."

"Barely."

"Did you save any?"

"I saved one, but only because it hit me in the face. I have a bruise and everything, look!"

Leo turned his head and showed the side of his face to Tim. His black skin was considerably darker around his left eye, with slight swelling, and the eyeball looked a bit bloodshot. Tim instinctively poked at his face with a finger.

"Does it hurt?"

"Well, it does when you do that," said Leo, wincing and batting Tim's hand away. Tim laughed, which made him choke on his chewing gum.

"What about you Lyds, did you score any...hockey goals?"

"I scored one. It came off my foot, but no one noticed."

"You not allowed to kick it in?"

"No," she said bluntly, "It's no wonder you were told to stick to football."

"Waste of time that was too. Spent most of it in the farm," complained Tim.

"That'll explain the smell," said Leo.

"Yeah, yeah, whatever."

"Katie was talking about your mum by the way Tim," said Lydia.

"What was she saying?"

"How your mum's a scruff for selling dodgy stuff to idiot people."

"I hope you told her to shut up."

"I would if she didn't always bully me for being bigger than her," said Lydia quietly.

"You aren't even big. Want me to say anything to her for you?" Leo asked.

"Nah. When I left, she was feeding her Tamagotchi."

"Brilliant," said Tim, happy at the irony.

The trio walked down the hill and onto the High Street, and along towards the estates. Mr Singh was outside cleaning the shop windows as they passed.

"Your mum has your magazine, son," he called out as they waved hello from across the road.

"Oh, thank you," Tim replied.

"Is it a dirty magazine?" asked Lydia.

"Urgh, don't be disgusting Lyds, it's just an Olympics one."

"Does it have the divers in?" asked Leo

"Not everything I buy has to be about divers, mate," Tim said defensively.

"I wasn't being horrible; I like that you like diving."

"Hmm. Whatever. It does have them in though as it happens. It's telling you about their training and what they eat and things."

"You still going to give it a try?" asked Lydia.

"Eventually. Might see if I can convince Mum to let me start over the summer."

"Can I borrow the magazine after you?" begged Leo.

"What for?"

"I'm just interested. I like things. Sports things, y'know."

"I'll bring it with me later and you can have a look. I thought you preferred athletics anyway."

"Well yeah, I do, but the diving is good too. You know I loved it at the Olympics."

"Would you dive? You can join at the same time as me and we can train together and everything. It'd be quite cool."

"I dunno," replied Leo sadly, "I don't think you get black divers."

"There are *definitely* black divers," said Tim encouragingly.

"Name one," said Leo quicky before realising he may have sounded aggressive. "Sorry, all I am saying is that I haven't ever seen one."

"I'll find some clips for you on YouTube and text them to you later," Tim replied, understanding the frustration.

"Cool, thanks."

"And then you can come diving with me."

"Ah, why not. If I drown on the first lesson, I'd still get points for trying."

"What is it with you two and diving?" asked Lydia. "Everyone else at school is into football and rugby and things."

"It's good fun to watch," said Tim, slightly hurt. "Plus, it's really skilful."

"It's just the same thing over and over again though," she replied.

"Nah it's decent enough," said Leo.

Tim was happy that Leo was into diving too. It made him feel much less weird about his choice of sports. For the rest of the journey the three discussed the latest episode of *Choose That Guy*, dissecting who were the ones who should be voted off, Tim still defending Jay as much as possible. He hoped that he could somehow come back and win the trophy. It still had another three weeks to run though so it was possible that they would be too bored to care by the time the final came around.

FOUR

Tim arrived home via the back garden and slung his backpack on the kitchen chair. He tried to close the back door before his Mum had the chance to remind him.

"Don't forget to close-"

SLAM

"You don't have to break the back door either," she said as she walked past carrying a self-created latté. She had even attempted to do a leaf pattern with the foam but had failed.

"I'm meeting Leo and Lydia soon so can we do these biscuits quickly?" begged Tim.

"It shouldn't take long. They're all in the front room. Marty is in there too, so it will be even quicker."

"I thought he had karate?"

"Oh, it got cancelled. His instructor fell off a ladder and landed on his dog's kennel."

"Oh no, is he ok?"

"Yeah, he's fine, just a sprain."

"I meant the dog."

"Yes, Tim, I am sure he's fine too."

"Cool."

Tim left the kitchen, slung his green school jumper over the bannisters and entered the small living room. The room was at the front of the house, but the outside view was obscured by net curtains. It was all very Neighbourhood Watch. Nothing in the Johnson's front room matched. There was a sofa and two armchairs, their patterns and colours clashing. The wall was filled with pictures of the two boys taken yearly at school, all complete with matching clothes and bad haircuts. Even though they were separated by over two years in age, their mum had dressed them the same for photo day. The television was on mute in the corner. It was surrounded by hundreds of DVD cases, most of which hadn't been opened for many years. The green wallpapered walls looked tired with the odd scuff, and the white deep rug in the centre of the room was fraying around the edges. Marty was sat, cross-legged, in the middle of the rug, leaning back on his arms.

"Hey Mart," said Tim as he sat on his heels on the floor opposite him.

"Have you seen this lot?" Marty replied, gesturing towards the back wall with a nod.

The entire back wall was hidden by box upon box of biscuits. There were boxes of Bourbons, Custard Creams, Jammie Dodgers, Pink Wafers, Rich Tea, Chocolate Hobnobs, Party Rings and shortbread everywhere. There must have been at least sixty large boxes in total.

"Jesus Christ!" exclaimed Tim.

"Yep."

"And we have to pack all of these?"

"Yep."

"And it won't take long?"

"Nope."

"Hmm. How did they store all these upstairs?"

"They didn't. They had about ten boxes up there. Mum thinks that they are going to sell well though, so she bought a load more at lunchtime today."

"I ain't packing all of these," exclaimed Tim.

"That's what I said. I also said I wouldn't help carry them into the house, but she caught me, and I couldn't escape. My arms are knackered."

"Urgh," sighed Tim.

"I know. Anyway, how was football?"

"Same as always."

"Did you win?"

Tim laughed instead of giving an actual answer.

Katherine Johnson entered the room in full businesswoman mode. Both children hated her like this. She had a notepad, stickers, gift boxes and a clipboard. The whole dodgy biscuit business would soon be like a military operation.

"Right, this is how we are going to do this," she said, as if addressing a large corporate workforce and not her two teenage sons. "Marty, you will be in here, packing a selection of each of the biscuits into small bags, then you pass them through the serving hatch to Tim, who will be set up in the kitchen. Tim, in there you will then put them in boxes, fold down the lids and seal them with one of these cute stickers. Then, once that is done, you put them into the cardboard boxes, with twenty boxes in each."

"How many boxes have we got to make up?" asked Marty, a bit desperately.

"We shall start with two hundred, and then see what the time is."

"Two hundred?! TWO HUNDRED?!" shouted Tim. "I only delivered about sixty leaflets."

"And I delivered a load more," replied his mum. "They'll sell, trust me. Any that your paper people don't buy can be taken down the car boot with us on Sunday."

Their mum loved a car boot. It would be rare for her not to travel down to the car park of the local Cash 'n' Carry on a Sunday morning and set up her wobbly table stacked with random junk alongside her friend Sue, who had a licence to sell everything due to her owning a catering supplies business. It was another way that all the kids at school found out what she was wasting her time with.

"When you say 'us', you don't mean me and Marty do you? I don't want to do the car boot this weekend."

"No, you don't have to do it this week as Pat and Pet are coming to help instead," replied their mum. "They're popping over in about half an hour to check out the goods."

Pat and Pet, or Patricia and Petunia to give them their full first names, lived opposite the Johnson's. They always went everywhere in a pair and were the type of people who were very huggy and over-affectionate. Tim didn't enjoy their company very much, although Marty was a bit more relaxed around them now that he was older. Katherine Johnson was both of their best friends, and they would have been present at the karaoke session on Saturday. They always did a rousing rendition of 'I Know Him So Well' from the musical Chess. Tim had heard them sing this multiple times as they often performed it at the house parties on New Years' Eve. He actually enjoyed it as Pat had been in The Greenwood Town Choir for a number of years and could actually hold a note. Tim wasn't in the mood to talk to them today though, and even though they were due at 4pm, there was a high chance that they would be around at any moment. It wasn't unusual that they'd randomly burst through the backdoor and stay for an hour or two.

"Let's get started then," said Tim's mum, as she picked up the gift boxes and took them into the kitchen. Tim was unenthusiastic but jumped into action when the kitchen hatch opened, and his full name was called loudly. He trudged into the kitchen and sat on one of the four wooden chairs around the kitchen table.

"So, these are your gift boxes," she said, pointing at said boxes in case Tim had suddenly somehow forgotten the English language, "and these are the stickers." She passed him a large roll of green and white striped stickers, each with the word 'cookies' written across the middle in a blue comic sans font. "Marty will start packing biscuits now into little plastic bags and when he passes them through, box them up, put the sticker on, and put them in the cardboard tray over there," she continued, nodding towards a pile of banana boxes that she had stolen from the service yard of a supermarket. They were stacked taller than his head height in front of the washing machine. "Got it?"

“Yes mum,” he replied slowly. “You’ve literally told us twice in the space of a minute.”

“Good.”

He had just over an hour before he wanted to leave and meet Lydia and Leo, and hoped Marty got his act together so that this painful process could be completed in time. Marty had changed a bit in the last couple of years and was slowly coming out of the other side of his grumpy teenager phase caused by puberty. The brothers got on well, although there were times when he was thrown aside by Marty in the past, when he was told he couldn’t join in with his cricket games on the fields behind the house. Marty was influenced a lot by music and was often seen with his bass guitar. He had asked for an instrument for his fifteenth birthday and was lucky that his parents had agreed on a decent instrument and not a trumpet or similar. Each new type of music that Marty got into was reflected in his dress sense. He briefly dabbled with techno music when he had been Tim’s age and spent that summer wearing hideous shirts and flashes of neon. These days it was all about rock, and as he sat in the front room, he was wearing blue denim skinny jeans, and a black denim jacket. The names of some of his current favourite bands adorned this jacket in the form of patches, all hand-sewn on by their mum. Very rock and roll.

Tim did recognise that his older brother was considered cool though and was subtly copying a few of his techniques to appear the same. He had one pair of skinny jeans, which almost cut off the blood to his feet the first time he had worn them, but he thought that they did look good on him. Marty currently had cropped hair around the side, with the front flicked up in a lazy quiff. Tim wanted to have the same hairstyle, however each time he lifted his fringe he became paranoid at how large his forehead appeared. He had always had a high hairline, but panicked that he was already receding, something which internet search engines told him was either impossible for a kid of his age, or a sign that he should go to A&E immediately, depending on which site you clicked on. Instead, he had to make do with his floppy dark brown hair that mushroomed in shape when it went past it’s due date for a cut. Tim’s hair was halfway down his ears, with the left side wavier than the right. The lack of symmetry made him look wonky.

Not wanting to sit in silence, he connected his phone to the small stereo in the kitchen and put his current favourite playlist on shuffle. The first song was one of his favourites by Saint Monique. Again poppy, it was an upbeat song called ‘Glove Puppet’. It was throwaway pop, but Tim liked it all the same. He had learnt the words within hours of it being released, and secretly practiced the dance in the privacy of his own room. He felt good until he had seen his reflection and realised that he was all limbs, making him look a bit like a drunken Pinocchio. His mum entered the kitchen almost immediately and turned it down a notch. "Tim," she started, "I forgot to get the little thank you cards for the inside of the boxes, can you be a darling and grab them please?"

"Where are they?"

"In the shed, on the right, near the gardening gloves."

"Do they have to go in?"

"The nicer the boxes, the more we will sell."

"This isn't The Apprentice mum; it's selling stale biscuits to weird neighbours."

"If you don't get them then you won't get your magazine."

Tim's mum knew how to blackmail him. Admitting defeat, he stood, grabbed the keys from the hook over the sink, and headed outside.

"Don't forget to close the back door."

Tim threw the door back behind him and trudged down the path to the shed, trying his best to avoid the puddles that still remained along the way. The day was now much brighter, the sky becoming a palette of gold and lilac, and the mugginess of summer had returned. He struggled again to open the rusted lock of the shed, finally opening it with a quick yank. Inside he saw the cards immediately, however he had to shift all three mountain bikes out of the way to be able to reach them. There was also a spider hanging from a web, dangling off the wooden supports for the roof, and he jumped back when he spotted it. There were only three things that he didn't like, and spiders were even worse than heights and deep water. Why did it have to be diving he was most keen on? How could he stand so high up in tiny swimwear and stare into the abyss of a deep pool below?

Needing to get to the cards, he picked up a trowel and hit at the spider. It remained on his web, swinging away from him, before pausing and coming back towards his face like an eight-legged Tarzan. Having made the situation worse, he made a grab for the cards readying for a quick escape. He stuffed them into his pockets and then picked up a can of spray oil from the floor to ease up the lock later. He felt itchy at the thought of the creature and felt as though there was something climbing up his back all the way until he had reached the kitchen again.

Back at the table, he restarted 'Glove Puppet' and readied himself for the task. Marty was being very efficient with his packing, and before long Tim was causing the flow of biscuits-to-table-to-banana-boxes to get clogged up in the middle. He quickened the pace and decided that his sticker placement didn't need to be quite so accurate. The main trouble that he was having was with the pop-up gift boxes, which were flimsy and occasionally tore along the side when he tried closing the lid. Time ticked along quickly though, and before 4pm the two boys had managed to complete about sixty packs. Still ahead of the game, Marty came into the kitchen, chewing loudly on some gum.

"Want anything from the shop?" he asked.

"How come you're going? We have to finish these."

"I've done a load and I'll be back in ten minutes. Mum's on the phone upstairs so she won't even notice."

"Fine. I'll have a Wispa please."

"Cool," said Marty as he went to leave. He was cool. Tim was furtively envious of how cool his brother appeared. He moved over to the counter and looked at his reflection in the dark door of the microwave. He lifted his hair into a quiff, before deciding that it was too long to do so and that his forehead was definitely too big. "I wonder if I'll ever grow into it," he thought.

Tim spent the next five minutes racing to see how many boxes he could do, snaffling a Party Ring or two from a couple to keep his energy up. Party Rings, like Skips, were the taste of children's parties. Each birthday as a kid he would have a few friends over between Christmas and new year, and they would sit around a large picnic blanket on the living room floor. In the middle were sandwiches and cocktail sausages on sticks, and then Skips and biscuits piled high in large, coloured, plastic bowls. A cake would then be bought into the room by his mum with an ever-increasing number of candles on to match his age, and in the style of whatever fad he was currently in. There were dinosaurs, volcanoes, pirate ships, dragons and even more dinosaurs. Although only sponge cake, jam and icing, his mum's cakes always tasted the best. Those parties had stopped when he moved to secondary school, and his birthday cakes these days always doubled up as the family Christmas Cake. Fruit cake was never as good, and was never shaped like a dinosaur, although the inch-thick layer of marzipan that his mum put around it on all sides was appreciated.

By the time Marty had returned, Tim had managed to catch up. His brother tossed the bar of chocolate in front of him. Marty left the door to the garden open, and Tim decided not to shut it on this occasion as the slight breeze that came through was welcoming. Tim could hear his brother back in the front room, and the rustle of plastic meant that more biscuits would soon be on their way across.

Tim was nearly out of the thank you cards, so paused his music and headed down to the shed to get some more. The lock seemed even tighter this time, so he sprayed it with oil until it was dripping down the metal and staining one of the mismatched paving slabs at his feet. He wiggled the key about, and it opened up. He tested it a few times to make sure that it wouldn't stick for a few days and headed back into the shed, opening the door slowly and peeking around to try and catch the spiders' whereabouts. The smell of the oil made him feel a bit weird, and the fact his hands were covered in it didn't help matters. He decided to perch on the seat of one of the bikes to regain his composure. He'd never really noticed how cluttered the shed had become, including the old magazines. The guinea pigs (Bubble and Squeak) had met untimely deaths during a cold snap last winter, so the magazines had no reason to be here. Tim manoeuvred his way to the piles of papers and picked up a couple of the music magazines that had belonged to Marty. He scanned the pages and didn't recognise any of the bands that were featured, but it was clear to see where his older brother had gotten his current style from. Some of the guitarists in the pictures would definitely show up if you searched for the word 'cool' online.

Feeling an urge to start gathering some tips on how to dress and act, he tore some of the pages out and folded them into his school trousers. There were six weeks of no school approaching, and he knew that this could be the right amount of time to reinvent himself before returning in September. By the time he was sixteen he would be one of the coolest kids at school, if only in appearance. Flicking through more pages, it wasn't just the guitarists' coolness that Tim liked. There was something about them that made him feel different. A few of them looked as if they had been placed in the magazines, in this shed, for Tim to discover. He didn't know who had set this chain of events up, but he wanted to thank them. Why did they stand out to him so much? He would keep these torn images in the drawer beside his bed as a reference point for when he went clothes shopping or to the barbers next. Everything about them just seemed *right*.

He picked up another magazine after discarding the first two on the floor and searched for more. He became lost in a world of young men with styled dark hair and perfectly fitting t-shirts as if he had just discovered the holy grail. He decided that he would come back in the evening and take as many of the magazines as possible back in so that no inspiration could be missed. Noticing that he was running out of time before meeting his friends, he stuffed everything back on the shelves and turned to leave. The spider was now hanging in the doorway. He was trapped. He searched for something to hit it with, and the only thing long enough was a bamboo cane that once had held up his dad's runner bean plants. He swung it like a lightsaber and hit the spider first time. He searched for where it landed, until he saw that it was now attached to the cane and moving back towards him. In a blind panic he ran out the shed and threw the cane over the wall like a javelin into the garden of number 249. He felt itchier than ever now.

He changed his mind once more and went back into the shed to find more magazines to calm his nerves and forget about the whole thing, gently tearing out more pages to study later. His journey into this new cool world was suddenly burst by a loud scream in the distance. He knew it belonged to his mum, so quickly flung the magazines aside and darted out of the shed. He looked up the garden path and saw his mum in the kitchen waving a wooden broom around frantically.

FIVE

"Timothy Johnson, get here NOW!" Katherine shouted at him. He ran up to the back door to be greeted by a scene out of a horror film. There must have been half a dozen pigeons flying around inside the kitchen, all scared, having been interrupted whilst destroying box after box of biscuits. Marty was pinned to the kitchen door, wanting to help but frozen by fear. Tim could see that his brothers jacket had been splashed by at least three direct hits from the backside of a pigeon and would most likely be ruined if it wasn't thrown in the washing machine immediately.

"How many times have I told you to close the back door when you leave this house?" his mum continued.

"Marty left it open. I only went to get more of your cards," he argued, knowing that this wouldn't let him off the hook.

"Well, it's too late now. All these will have to be thrown away," she said, gesturing with the bristles of a broom like an angry medieval jouster towards the boxes that had been knocked across the floor.

Tim picked up as many boxes as he could, but it was true, the majority of his hard work over the previous forty-five minutes had been wasted. The biscuits were bad enough before, let alone when they were covered in feathers and dirt. The more that they tried to clear the birds, the more destruction it seemed to cause. One was perched cooing from on top of the fridge, another flapping wildly along the counters, knocking everything in its wake onto the floor. The new coffee machine was now also a temporary perch. It was a complete and utter disaster.

Tim picked up a tea towel and threw it over one of the birds. Picking it up, he took it to the door and shook it outside. He turned around and picked up another. As he went back towards the door, the first pigeon jumped back inside. He aimed a kick at it and missed it spectacularly, resulting in him slipping and ending up on his back staring at the ceiling. Marty's fear of birds would not be cured by this incident, and he was still in the same position against the door, no ounce of coolness left. His face was whitened, and he couldn't move his legs to escape.

Pat and Pet had entered the garden via the side gate, but once they reached the kitchen door they shrieked and left quicker than they had arrived. Tim grabbed at a chair and levered himself up, tossing custard creams out on to the patio in the hope that this would somehow tempt the pigeons outside. The entire kitchen floor was now covered in a layer of crumbs and Tim knew that there would be some severe punishment for this. It would be a while until he could get his hands on the magazine with the divers, that's for sure, so the musicians folded in his trouser pockets would soon become like gold dust. He pushed them deeper into his pockets to make sure that these valuable pages of glossy magazine Gods would not be lost in the conflict.

For the next few minutes, the family (with the exception of the statuesque Marty) battered, swiped and swatted at the animals in the kitchen, before eventually, the last one left. Surveying the damage, Tim sat on the chair briefly before starting to sweep broken boxes into a black bin liner. His mum wasn't talking to him and was more concerned with stripping Marty of any piece of clothing that needed to be washed. He ended up stood in the kitchen in just his boxers, still with a terrified look plastered across his face. Tim hadn't seen him blink for five minutes.

After order had been restored, Tim was in his bedroom, and had stored the magazine pages in his top drawer. Having showered and changed out of his clothes (due to the fear that spiders were still crawling over him, or that the smell of bird mess was lingering on his school shirt), he had text Lydia and Leo and arranged to meet them in fifteen minutes by Singh Stars. Surprisingly, he hadn't been grounded because of him ruining the biscuit production line, but this was more to do with the fact that his mum didn't want him anywhere near her, rather than her being relaxed about everything. He had promised that he would help to get as many orders as possible, and do all the boxes himself, but she had replied only with a "Well, obviously" before walking off in the other direction. Marty wasn't best pleased with him either, so avoiding the house completely for a couple of hours would be in everyone's best interest. He would meet the other two and maybe get some food, giving them an opportunity to plan how they would survive the fast-approaching school disco. As he sat on his bed, he took a Stegosaurus covered notebook and made some notes whilst studying the pages of the music magazines. He made a list of the things he wanted to get over the summer so that by the time the new school year came around, he could be seen to have gone through a Doctor Who style regeneration. Looking different, being cool, but the same Tim.

THE COOL LIST

Denim jacket (or leather?)
More skinny jeans
Converse shoes
One of those belts with metal studs on

~~An ear piercing~~ (would hurt. Probs too young?)

Good headphones

Hair gel

Headband?

The list wasn't extensive, granted, but it was a start. He needed to think of a way to try and afford any of this. He wished that he had been born in the summer so that he could get stuff for his birthday. Having a Christmas birthday was rubbish as you didn't get twice as many presents like everyone thought. Sometimes his birthday cards even had a robin or Jesus on the front as well, especially from the lazier people in his family. He would need Marty's help and wished that he hadn't ruined his clothes a few minutes earlier. What he needed to do was deliver more papers for Mr Singh, and therefore allow more opportunities to hand out leaflets for his mum. It might mean having to get up even earlier each morning, but in the end it would be worth it. He'd ask Mr Singh if there were other estates that he could take on, even in the west of Greenwood if necessary. He just hoped that he wouldn't inadvertently cause any more catastrophes over the next few weeks.

SIX

Sat around a table at a café on Bridge Street, Lydia and Leo found Tim's situation hysterical, despite him telling them that it wasn't funny. Maybe one day he could look back on it all and laugh. It would probably take his mum and brother much longer to see it that way though sadly. The three friends had headed into the café to start to discuss tomorrow's school disco. They weren't the most popular at the school but were seen as better than a lot of people. They hated the hierarchy of popularity at school but were happy to just exist in the weird middle ground. The theme for the disco was 'American Prom', which none of them were keen on.

"If you didn't get kicked off the committee Tim, we could have had something better," said Leo, before taking a sip of his iced coffee.

"I would have been outvoted from whatever I put forward anyway," Tim replied.

"What would you have gone for?"

"I'unno, maybe rock music?"

"Rock music?" questioned Lydia. "You hate rock music."

"Nah, my brother has got me into it. They wear cool clothes and have cool hair and things. It's way better than American prom."

"Anything would be better. Anyway, your brother just wears denim and slicks his hair back."

"Even so, it can look cool if you do it right. I took some pages out of his magazines and made a list. I'll show you later."

"Like a mood board?" asked Lydia.

"Nah, more of a visual list of what I want to look like," Tim responded.

"That, Tim, is literally a mood board," laughed Lydia. "I have one for what I want my future house and my wedding to look like."

"None of us have ever kissed anyone so what's the point in planning a wedding? My list is much cooler."

"You can't just become cool by clothes, you have to just, well, be cool, and we're not, are we?" sighed Lydia.

"We could be?" Tim said stubbornly.

"How?"

"I'unno. I just think a nice jacket would help."

The three sat in silence for a short while whilst finishing their drinks. Lydia wiped cappuccino foam off her top lip and broke the silence.

"What are you two gonna wear tomorrow then? I'm borrowing one of my cousins' dresses. It's like a Cinderella one, a lovely sea blue with long white gloves."

“Ain’t that uncomfortable? And I thought you hated the theme,” said Tim.

“I do hate the theme, but there’s nothing we can do about it.”

“I’m gonna wear THE suit,” said Leo, excitedly.

“Oh God, the purple one?” Tim had seen this suit before.

“It’s not purple, it’s maroon. And the collar and lapels are black felt.”

“Nice! I love that suit,” said Lydia encouragingly.

“Thanks, Lyds,” he said, genuinely happy. “Tim, what are your options?”

“Option. Singular. I only have one suit. I’ll have to wear that black one that I wore for my Grandads funeral last year.”

“Wow, a suit for every occasion,” Leo joked.

“Shut up, I only have the one.”

“Can you borrow one of your brothers?” asked Lydia, more helpful than Leo had been.

“Nah, he’s like a foot taller so it’d look ridiculous. Plus, he won’t lend me anything for a while after pigeon-gate.”

Tim’s two friends laughed again.

“It is not funny!” Tim said, almost begging them into sympathy.

“It is a bit,” said Leo.

“Quite a bit, actually,” added Lydia.

Tim wasn’t feeling very chipper, even after his drink had been paid for by the others to cheer him up. They had walked around town for a bit and sat on the bridge over the river in the centre of town, throwing bits of stale bread to the ducks that swam around oblivious to everything else. For a short while they discussed venturing to the west side of the town but decided their lives didn’t need to be filled with avoiding kids from the other school. Compton High and Greenwood had a fierce rivalry in all sports, and many of the pupils from each would not be seen dead hanging around with anyone from the opposite school.

Tim had seen enough trouble for one day and decided he would head home and hide back in his bedroom again. He might try and fill some more biscuit boxes if he was allowed on the ground floor of the house.

As the evening panned out, Marty became more friendly again, and even came into Tim’s bedroom to see if he was okay.

"You forgot your Wispa," he said, tossing the chocolate bar at his younger brother. Tim failed to catch it and it caught him on the end of the nose. Rather than complain, he split open the purple wrapper and took a big bite before putting the rest to one side.

"Marty, can you help me with something?" he asked whilst chewing.

"Depends on what it is."

"Well, how do I become cool?" he asked, partly embarrassed.

"You'll never be cool," came the short response.

"But I mean, you're cool and I want to be cool too."

Tim knew that complimenting his brother would make him open up more. Marty puffed his chest out and was glad to have been called cool, even if it was his slightly awkward little brother who had said it. A compliment was a compliment at the end of the day, however annoying the person who gave it was.

"What about me do you think is cool?" asked Marty.

"You dress good...and you have good hair."

Marty ran his fingers through his dark hair whilst looking in the mirror on the wall. After having stood in the kitchen in his boxers for twenty minutes, he had changed back into a black band t-shirt, and had black denim jeans that were torn across both knees. A chunky metal chain was attached to one of the side pockets for no apparent reason. In fact, the whole outfit would have been great if it weren't for the red and white polka dot socks that he had on his feet. It was rare to see Marty not in a black t-shirt these days. His wardrobe was darker than an undertaker's tie rack.

"Who you trying to impress?" he asked finally, looking at Tim via the reflection in the mirror.

"No one," replied Tim, "I just don't want to wear knitted jumpers and stuff anymore."

"None of my clothes would fit you," said the older brother.

"I don't want hand-me-downs anymore either," said Tim quickly. "If I get some money, can you take me shopping with you?"

"Not a chance. That would affect my coolness wouldn't it."

"I like the boys in your magazines," said Tim.

"You what?"

"I mean, your music magazines, the people in there are what I want to look like."

"Stop taking my magazines."

"I didn't, I got your older ones from the shed."

"They're still down there?"

"Yep. I took some pages out though."

"That's weird."

"Why?"

"I'unno, just is. Anyway, show me."

Tim opened the draw of his bedside cabinet and handed the folded-up pages to his brother. Marty folded them out to their original size, giving a plain yet stern look towards Tim when a feather floated out and fell almost sarcastically to the floor. Marty came towards the bed and sat next to Tim. Looking at the top page, he jammed a finger onto the guitarist in the picture towards the bottom right-hand corner.

"Him, that's Pistol Pete," he said, "He writes the songs for Mirror Ball. They're playing at Reading Festival this year. Can't wait to see them."

"You're going to Reading?" questioned Tim.

"Yeah, mum said I could as long as I get good results in my woodwork exams."

"Can I come with you?" pleaded Tim.

"One hundred percent no," came the expected reply. "Anyway, Mirror Ball are good, you might not like them but pretending you do might be a start."

"I'll get some of their music."

"Yeah, check out their album called Head Rush. It's great. Much better than that crap you currently listen to."

"Hey, Saint Monique is good!" said Tim.

"Uncool, Tim, uncool."

"I don't care that you hate her."

"And I don't care that you like her, but if you want my help we need to compromise."

Tim made a mental note to scale down his outpouring of love for Saint Monique's music in public.

"Who else is good?"

"There's loads. Just start with Mirror Ball and let me know what you think yeah?"

"Righty-O!" Tim replied chirpily.

"Oh, and stop saying 'righty-o'."

"Uncool?"

"Very."

Tim was glad that his brother had softened quickly after the incident earlier. Marty mumbled that he had somewhere to be and left the room before heading out the front door soon after. Tim pulled his notepad out and added "Mirror Ball CD" to the cool list.

TUESDAY

SEVEN

Unlike the day before, Tim woke up on time on the Tuesday morning, ensuring that he didn't attempt to snooze his alarm for a change. He had to get out on his paper round and try and convince his customers to buy some of his mum's biscuit boxes. It would be weird trying to actively encourage people to engage with this rubbish, but he had to otherwise he may spend the entire summer holidays inside. Today was also the day of the school disco (or *prom* if he was forced to use the ridiculous wording of the bright posters) and he wanted the rest of the day to be as drama free as possible, knowing that the disco/prom itself would be a car crash from start to finish.

He stood from his bed and opened his wardrobe, taking out his suit so that it was ready to change into quickly after school. It definitely still looked like a funeral suit. The black tie didn't help with that, so he made a mental note to run to town on the way home from school and get one that was slightly more cheerful. On his way to the bathroom, he caught a glimpse of himself in the mirror and noticed a large brown stain on the back of his dinosaur pyjama bottoms. He reluctantly reached down and swiped a finger across the patch slowly, before bringing it up to his nose to give it a sniff, retching as he did so. He was relieved to smell a sweet sugary scent rather than anything unpleasant and went back to his bed and pulled the covers back in one swift movement.

The first day of the new cool Tim had started off as well as the previous day had ended. The half-eaten Wispa was ground into the sheets, and although still not fully convinced he knew what cool was, he knew it wasn't wearing pale blue clothes which had cartoon dinosaur faces on it, obscured by milk chocolate. He pulled the bed sheets off and threw them in the wash basket along with his bottoms and left a note on top of the lid saying "Sorry (it's chocolate btw)" for when his mum made the gruesome discovery.

He looked around his room. In ways it was becoming that of a proper teenager. GCSE workbooks sat on the shelf above his white desk, and polaroid photos of himself with Leo and Lydia taken at different places were pinned into a rectangular corkboard. Some parts of the room remained just as it had been when younger. It hadn't been repapered for about a decade, and the childlike wallpaper was still visible in the gaps between his posters of a world map and the periodic table.

Down at Singh Stars he refused the offer of more chocolate, still troubled by the morning's events. Mr Singh enquired about his Monday, but he decided to just say all was fine rather than go into the full feathered horror story.

"Mr Singh?" he said shortly after, remembering his plan. Mr Singh was looking down at some paperwork and didn't answer specifically, but made a '*hmmm*' noise from behind the counter. Tim assumed this meant that he was listening, so continued. "I was wondering if there were more houses that I could take on?"

"More? Whatever for?" he said, now looking up, surprised.

"I usually finish within time and thought you might want the help."

"Let me have a check."

Mr Singh pulled out a ring binder and started flicking through the dog-eared pages, each slightly too large for the folder. It seemed that he still did everything by hand rather than a computer. He tapped a pen between his teeth for a few moments.

"It doesn't look like I do, sorry."

"That's okay," said Tim, disappointed. "I was just curious. If anything comes up, let me know."

"I shall, thank you. I wish the other paper kids were as eager as you."

Tim smiled at the owner and went back to browsing the magazines whilst he waited to be given the daily round. Not wanting to waste any time, he dashed out the shop as soon as Mr Singh had loaded his bag.

He visited the houses in Ash Street and Pine Close first as always and made a rule that if he saw a light on downstairs, or any movement through the glass of the front doors, he would gently tap, put on a cheerful smile, and ask if they were interested in any biscuits. This was the most practical, and probably only, way to get the orders in. He had brought a new notepad with him and was ready to make a list of all the orders that he would get.

Things started off well, and the first three houses alone saw ten boxes ordered in total. He avoided a couple of the following houses as he could hear dogs barking inside and didn't have the energy to outrun the beasts. Instead, he flung the paper through the letter box and then ran back to the path so he could jump on his bike quickly. The weather was the best it had been so far that summer, warm on the skin despite the earliness, and all of yesterday's rain had now evaporated. Leaving on time gave Tim all the opportunities to make sales and he was happy with how well he had done so far. As he completed Pine Close, he had reached thirty sales, and this increased to nearly fifty before the end of Birch Avenue. The weather must have put everyone in a good mood, he thought, as he cycled to the next house, letting out a cheerful yet out-of-tune whistle as he went. He hoped that all the orders would make his mum cool her temperament a bit and hoped that he would be close to a hundred by the time he had finished the round completely.

He passed across into Elm Meadow, entering via an alleyway at its southern end. The rich, green trees in the large gardens shaded him from the early morning sun and he took his time to trundle to his next stop. The people in these houses tended to get the heavier papers, and on Tuesdays many of them came wrapped in plastic with an additional magazine all about the financial comings and goings of London and the like. He'd learnt a bit about that kind of thing in Tutor Time at school, but even the headlines in these big papers made no sense to him. He didn't know what FTSE stood for, and he didn't know who Dow Jones was (he sounded Welsh maybe?), but Tim feigned interest with the customers where necessary to keep in their good books and get some good tips.

The first house he approached had a slick navy sports car on the drive, sat with the engine running. A pigeon had deposited some of its previous dinner from a nearby tree right on to the middle of the windscreen. It was as if the birds were deliberately mocking him now. He laid his bike on its side and the gravel driveway crunched like crisps underfoot as he made his way to the front door. The wooden door was slightly ajar. Tim tapped on it gently, but no one came to respond. He tapped again, slightly louder, which caused the door to open three quarters of the way towards its maximum.

He could see down a white painted corridor to a shiny kitchen at the far end, all black cupboard doors and chrome fittings. A lady was stood facing away from Tim, a ruby silk dressing gown with matching-coloured slippers forming her outfit. He didn't know whether to tap again, afraid it might startle her and cause her to drop her breakfast into the sink. Deciding not to knock, he reached forward and grabbed the door handle, attempting to pull it back to its original position unnoticed. He didn't want to step inside the house and had to stretch quite far from the welcome mat to reach it. When his body was at full length, gravity caused his paper bag to swing around his neck and topple him off balance. With nothing to grip onto other than the handle, he fell face first towards the ground. He ended in a pile half inside the house, and half out, his eyes around an inch from the marble tiled floor. The newspaper in his other hand flew forward and clattered into a small telephone table, which wobbled and then deposited a jar of pens onto the ground.

"Um, can I help you?" came a male voice from the staircase on the left. A tall man with greased, neat hair was looking down at him, his hands motionless halfway through putting on a tie.

"Biscuits!" said Tim in a panic.

"Pardon?"

"Sorry. Your paper. I have your paper. I am the paper boy."

"Thank you," said the gentleman, confused, as he helped Tim to his feet.

Tim stood in the doorway and brushed himself down. The man just stared back at him.

"Is there anything else I can help you with?" said the man, slightly confused by the mannequin-esque child in front of him.

"Would you like a biscuit?"

"Biscuit? What are you talking about? Have you banged your head?"

The man shouted "Cynthia" down the hallway.

After a moments pause, the lady with the dressing gown turned her head and stared at her husband. "Cynthia, could you bring a glass of water for the boy please? Maybe a cold flannel too. I think he must have banged his head."

Without a reply, she took a glass out of a cupboard, filled it from the tap, and brought it to Tim. He wasn't thirsty, but as potential customers he accepted with thanks.

"Little lad fell through the door," said the man to his wife quietly. "He keeps talking about biscuits."

"I told you that you should keep the door closed," she replied.

"My mum says the same!" said Tim, joining in.

"Are you okay?" she asked.

"Yes fine, thank you. And thanks for the water. Would you like some biscuits?"

"Biscuits?" said the lady, looking confused.

"See. I told you he kept saying it," added the husband, happy at his point being proven.

"I put a leaflet through your door yesterday. My mum is a biscuit seller."

"I thought it was a leaflet for some kind of children's toy?"

"Oh, that was last week. This week we have biscuits."

"I'm sorry, yes of course, we are fine for biscuits this week. Thank you though. It's like I said to your friend earlier, it's nice that you think of the residents, but the pack we got from you earlier will be more than enough for my coffee morning."

“This morning? I didn’t come this morning?”

It was Tim’s turn to be confused.

“Not you, but another boy. I picked up a packet from him.”

“I don’t have a friend?”

The man put his hand on Tim’s shoulder, before saying “I think that bang to your head has done you no favours. Make sure you get home and rest before school if you can. We don’t want you losing your memory there as well, do we?”

Tim wasn’t sure how to respond to this. He hadn’t banged his head, and definitely didn’t have a friend selling the biscuits either. It couldn’t have been his brother as he would have still been in bed. Slightly befuddled, Tim returned to his bike and went to the next house.

Many other houses on Elm Meadow appeared to still be sleeping, and the orders had dried up substantially. He still couldn’t get the thoughts of the couple out of his mind and couldn’t understand why they thought that they had bought biscuits already. Thinking that they must just have been using it as an excuse, he was shocked that the very same thing happened again as he delivered to the first house in Beech Close. It then happened at the second house. And then the third. All three households told Tim that they had already got some biscuits from his friend earlier that morning. “Maybe I did bang my head?” he thought as he cycled back home.

EIGHT

Back at home, Tim threw his bike into the shed, and went into the kitchen, closing and locking the back door behind him to be on the safe side. His mum was sat at the kitchen table with a gold mug of coffee and was flicking through a copy of 'Live Your Life' magazine. His mum loved that magazine. It was one of those that had stories headlined by things that were either horrific sounding (My Ex-Husband is a now my stalker!) or somewhat bizarre (Haunted by my dead budgie) all written in big fonts using primary colours. It was well known that his mum also wrote in regularly to the 'Your Tips' section, with each one being weirder than the last. His friends knew it was her despite her using the not-very-coded code name of Kitty from Greenwood. Her last one had been about making a scarecrow out of old CD's and his friends recognised his paper bag in the back of the photo. He wished that she would stop but she got a feeling of excitement from the fame it bought, using the term fame extremely loosely of course.

"You haven't written in again, have you?" Tim asked as he kicked his trainers into the hallway.

"Nah, they didn't print mine this week."

"Oh, that *is* a shame."

"Hey, I get vouchers each time I'm in there. And anyway, I'm still not talking to you."

"Would it help if I told you I got some orders?"

She relented. "It would a bit. How many?"

Tim pulled out his notepad. "62," he said. "Although, it was a bit weird."

"Weird how?"

"Well, the people in the posh houses kept telling me they had already bought some today."

"But you hadn't taken any with you?"

"Exactly."

"Did they tell you where they got them from?"

"They just kept saying that they got them from my friend."

"Leo?"

"No, not specifically, just a friend."

Katherine took another swig of coffee, swilled it around her mouth a bit, and then swallowed.

"And it definitely wasn't you?" she asked.

"Of course not, I've not touched the biscuits since, well, since the pigeons."

"Leave it with me and I'll find out what's going on. When Marty is back later, we will make up some boxes and you can deliver them after school."

"I can't tonight mum, it's the disco ain't it."

"Okay you can do them tomorrow. Have you got your suit ready?"

"Yeah, it's hanging up. Oh, mum?"

"Yeah?"

"Can I have my Olympics magazine now please?"

"Not yet, you're still not forgiven. I'll let you have it if you come to the car boot with me on Sunday."

"Fine."

Disappointed but not surprised, Tim headed upstairs to get ready for school. He really didn't want to go to the car boot sale but knew that he had to get on the good side of the family again. As his round had been more leisurely than normal, he decided to skip a shower and instead spent the ten minutes laying on his bed looking at the musicians again. He would see if he could save enough change from his earnings this week to get the Mirror Ball album. If he worked hard enough for his mum, he might be able to afford the belt as well. He had no idea what she would be selling next week, but with school over he could spend some more time taking orders without being judged by others.

The morning at school went by in a flash, (Double Maths and then English Lit – Macbeth. Urgh), and the topic of the disco was all that everyone seemed to be talking about. Even Lydia and Leo were excited, despite them saying that they thought the whole thing was stupid yesterday. As soon as the lunch bell had rung, each student ran off home to prepare for the evening. They would need to be back for it to start at 6pm, which gave enough time for Tim to get home and change out of his uniform, have some toast and marmalade, and then head out and get his new tie.

He hadn't ever bought anything formal for himself, and first tried the old tailor shop on Corn Street. It was a small and dark shop, about half the size of a badminton court (or a third of a tennis court). It had low ceilings, and the sunlight through the windows reflected off the dust that hung in the air, forming a spacey-galaxy effect. They had a load of different colours and designs of tie, but nothing that really suited what he wanted. He didn't want to look like a shrunken down version of a banker. He wanted something plain, something bright, but most importantly, something *cool*. The prices in the tailors also put him off. He never knew that they were so expensive. He feigned interest for long enough as the elderly shopworker held up a variety of options, before thanking him and saying that he would come back with his mum, knowing full well that he wouldn't. The money he would spend on a tie in there would easily cover the cost of half of the things on the cool list.

Feeling a bit deflated, he walked past other shops at speed, peering through their large window displays to see if there were any hints of a cheaper tie. With his preferred options exhausted, he defeatedly had to cross over to the western part of the town as a last resort. He went into a moderately sized clothing store and was happy to see a line of ties along the back wall, next to the boxers and beanies. They were only £5 each as well, easily within his budget. He picked up at least ten different colours and stood in front of the floor-to-ceiling mirror, holding each one up to his neck to see if they clashed with his eyes or his hair, both of which looked pale from the over-enthusiastic strip lighting. He wished that he had worn a plain white t-shirt instead of the garish colourful one he had chosen.

"Nice ties," came a voice from behind in a sarcastic tone. Katie from school appeared behind him in the mirror. Katie never had time for Tim. She never had time for most people and often tried to talk down to anyone to make herself feel better.

"Go away," Tim said, holding up an orange tie to his throat.

"Why?"

"I'm busy."

"Don't you want a friend's help?" she enquired.

"You're not my friend. You're always horrible so you'll probably pick the stupidest one for me."

"You'll do that yourself anyway."

Tim turned around to continue to argue when he noticed that she was sticking a biscuit into her mouth. He turned back to the mirror, still being watched, and held up three more colours (red, mustard and green). None of them suited.

"You going with Lydia?" she asked.

"No, well, yes. But also, no."

"What does that mean?"

"I'm going with her, but not *with* her."

"And Leo?"

"Him as well."

"You can't go as a three. Couldn't you get a date?"

"I didn't want a date."

"Why not?"

The question took Tim by surprise. He didn't have an answer for this. The other boys went out their way to try and take a popular girl with them to the disco, but for Tim he didn't really care for that at all.

"Didn't want to," Tim replied eventually.

"Why not though?"

Katie was persistent if nothing else.

"I don't really like discos and it's too much hassle."

"Everyone else has dates."

"Do you?"

"I do actually."

"Who?"

"I'm not telling you that. I think it's odd that you three would rather hang around together than actually do the prom properly. You probably haven't even spoken to a girl properly before."

"I'm talking to you now."

"Well, yeah, but what I mean is that it's odd that you don't want to take a date."

"Well, I don't. And nor does Lydia. Or Leo."

He was getting frustrated now.

"You're all as weird as each other."

"We aren't weird."

"You really are."

"Anyway, where did you get those biscuits?"

Katie moved the box behind her back. "You're not having one."

"I don't want one. And that's not what I asked. I asked where you got them."

"I'unno," said Katie, sticking a bourbon into her mouth, before adding "Mum got 'em," all whilst spitting crumbs out.

"Who from?"

"Some kid dropped them off, from down the road."

"Where is the road?"

"Why are you so interested?"

"I just need to know, Katie."

Tim put all the ties over a clothes rail and turned to face her. He stared until she had swallowed.

"There's a woman from the west who was selling them, okay?" she said finally.

"Do you know which street or house?"

"Nah. Mum sorted it. I think it's odd. I mean, which freak would go around houses selling old biscuits to people?"

Tim knew that this was a deliberate dig at his own family. He noticed Katie still had her Tamagotchi though, and it was pinned to the belt around her dress. Tim decided to stop his enquiries and turned his attention back to the mirror.

"See you later...weirdo," Katie said as she trudged off towards the escalator. Tim didn't respond. Wanting to tell his mum about a possible rival, he quickly decided on a sky-blue tie, paid for it and then walked home as quick as possible.

When he got home, he ran around the house and garden in search of his mum, but she was out. Marty was in, so he told him to pass on the information. He said that he would leave her a note as well. It was now just past four thirty and Tim had little time to get ready for the prom. He showered quickly and then changed into his suit. Although promised that he would one day grow into it, the sleeves and trousers were still a few inches too long. It was all he had though, so it had to make do. He tucked the trouser legs a little inside themselves, tied on the tie and pulled his shirt collar straight.

He headed back into the bathroom and wiped the steam off the mirror with toilet roll. This left it streaky and covered in white fluff marks but was good enough so that he could see his face fully reflected. His hair was untidy and definitely not disco ready.

"Marty!" he shouted downstairs. There was no answer. He called again but he still didn't reply. He needed some hair wax to make himself look presentable and had wanted to borrow his brothers. Taking no reply as a positive, he unscrewed the lid of the small, blue tin of wax from his brother's shelf and plunged his right index finger into the gooey contents. He had watched his brother do this before and copied his action by rubbing his hands together to spread the wax. He then ran them both through his hair rapidly. He lifted his head up to the mirror. It looked greasy and messy. It was stuck up in the air, forehead fully exposed. He flattened it down. It now looked even worse. He should be heading out the door now to Leo's, but there was no way he could be seen like this. For the next ten minutes he tried his best to fix it, but with each attempt it kept getting worse. In the end he settled for it to just lay sort of flat. Having wasted valuable time on something unproductive, he bounded down the stairs, put on his school shoes and ran the three streets away to Leo's, holding his oversized trousers up by the sides so that they didn't fall to his ankles.

NINE

Tim banged on the black door at Leo's. He lived at Number 10, and it had always reminded him of Downing Street. It was opened immediately by his mum.

"Oh, hey, Mrs Gardner," said Tim cheerfully, looking a little sweaty. He loved Leo's mum.

"Hi Tim. You look great. Want a drink?"

"Thank you, although my hair is rubbish. And no, thank you, I don't drink."

"I wasn't offering you alcohol, you're fifteen. I meant a coke or something."

"Oh sorry, yes please, can I have an orange squash?"

Mrs Gardner held the door open and motioned for Tim to come in, telling him to keep his shoes on. Leo came down the stairs to meet him. He looked great in his maroon blazer, checked trousers and shiny shoes.

"You look amazing!" said Tim.

"Thanks mate. You do too. Hold on though."

Leo ran his hands through Tim's hair and finished with a few flicks of the wrist. "There ya go."

In fifteen seconds, Leo had made Tim's hair a million times better than what he had managed himself. It was smooth around the edges, tucked back behind his ears, and with a small but subtle quiff at the front.

"Cheers, Leo," said Tim, staring at the mirror from close range. "I tried to do that myself but I just looked like an electrocuted hamster."

"I've never seen one of those," replied Leo.

"Okay, that was a bad metaphor, but you know what I mean."

Tim took his phone out of his pocket and snapped a picture in the mirror for Instagram. He then texted Marty along with the words "Cool, eh?" Marty replied instantly with "for you", which as compliments go, is a good one from him. It would definitely be a suitable new profile picture for all his social media.

Tim followed Mrs Gardner into the kitchen, who told him to take a seat at the breakfast bar. He swiveled on the tall stool as she poured the drink, before placing it down in front of him. The kitchen smelled of baking and he scanned the counters for anything sweet. He couldn't spot anything though, which was a shame as he was dying to have something. The time he spent rushing around town looking for a tie had meant that he hadn't had time to eat since the toast. He thought he would have been able to last until they got back to the school, but the thought of American style hotdogs and nachos wasn't really appealing to him anymore. It would have been cooked by the school kitchen staff, and he knew from experience that the hot snacks that they made were either underdone or burnt. Their pizza was notorious for being awful. The pepperoni was one step away from still being able to walk, not that the meat content was above ten percent.

Leo came into the kitchen smiling widely. He was looking even slicker than normal, and his bruised eye from the footballing incident could not be seen. He moved closer to Tim and leant in towards him, grinning.

"What do you think?"

"Your hair looks good."

"Number two all over. Got to be smooth and look your best," he replied, doing an odd little jig.

"It's only the school disco."

"Even so, got to look your best. You're looking good too by the way."

"Thanks to you. My hair was awful."

"Hey, don't worry, that's what I'm here for."

"How did you sort your eye out?"

"Mum helped me use her foundation. Our skin tones are nearly identical, so it was quite easy," he responded, his voice trailing off as he bounded back down the hall to have another look in the big mirror.

Tim didn't know why he had to keep checking the mirror, he would easily be one of the sharpest dressed people there tonight. It was true what he said about the sharing of skin tones. Leo, his mum, his dad and his younger sister too, all had perfect skin. Tim's wasn't too bad but there were occasions when his forehead broke out in spots. He tried his best to combat this by keeping hydrated and smearing splatterings of his mum's hand cream over his face, but it didn't seem to work. In fact, all that happened when he did this was that he ended up smelling of mandarin or whatever scent she had got in bulk during one of the skincare weeks of her scheme.

Leo's parents, Flo and John, had been married for just over twenty years. They had held an anniversary party last month in the gardens of the local museum and had booked an area of Minster Hall in August to renew their vows. Their actual marriage had taken place in Barbados, the country where they both had been born. To try and create a similar atmosphere at the anniversary party they had hired dancers, and a chef had prepared an authentic Caribbean cuisine buffet with baked chicken, fried prawns and sweet potato pie, with sides of steamed vegetables, fried plantains and a variety of salads. Tim had never eaten food so good before and had asked the Gardener's if he could come around regularly to try more of these different things. He had been round a few times so far and was looking forward to more visits during the summer holidays. The event had also been soundtracked by a steel band playing a mixture of traditional calypso tunes, and the whole evening had seemed like the greatest party that had ever been held (it was at least a billion times better than the *American Prom* would be, that's for certain).

Leo's dad was always kind to Tim and often provided advice when his own dad was working overseas, which sadly was for three-quarters of the year. Tim felt guilty that his own dad would be missing these moments in his life. His dad loved him, and wrote and called where possible, but it must have been hard for him not being able to help his sons prepare for special occasions, or to go to parents evening, to kick a ball in the park or to just see his sons grow every day. John Gardner was a big man, standing at about six foot five tall. Leo had yet to see these genes pass down to him and looked tiny when stood next to his father. John always seemed to be cheerful and was well liked by everyone on the estate. Tim could hear him laughing through the ceiling, something which was noticed by Flo as well.

Flo swept her long jet-black hair over her shoulders and put it in a loose ponytail using an elastic band. "He's just getting himself ready to take you boys to the disco," she said smiling.

"Oh, we will be happy to walk, honestly, we don't mind," said Tim, not wanting to make him go out of his way.

"You've got to arrive in style to these things Tim, and besides, he said that he would pick up Lydia on the way too."

Tim took a swig of his drink and was secretly glad that he didn't have to walk across town in his oversized suit. It was warm outside, and he didn't want to look sweaty in all the photos that would be taken throughout the evening. Leo came back into the kitchen and grabbed Tim on both shoulders, before giving him a little shake.

"You seem more enthusiastic than earlier, L," Tim said to him, noticing the bouncy nature of his friend. He only ever called him L when being super casual, and he did the same to Lydia, which just made everything confusing if they were all together.

"Yeah, I thought it would be better to embrace the ridiculousness of it rather than act all awkward."

"It's going to be awful though."

"Nah, me, you and Lyds can make our own fun. It's better than hanging around in a café and stuff like we normally do."

"True."

"And anyway, I love having an excuse to dress up."

"You never need an excuse."

Tim wasn't envious of Leo and loved that he always seemed to be so positive, but he did wish that he could have even just half the confidence that his friend emitted. Tim used to assume that Leo was like this because he was one of 'the drama kids'. It's like you see in all those American films, where all the kids in the school plays have endless energy and the ability to do anything without fear of being mocked. Tim had watched Leo as Dandy Dan in Bugsy Malone and some background soldier in Oh! What a Lovely War. Life was one long musical for some of them. This idea was dismissed when Tim had realised that half the drama students at Greenwood were reclusive, and...well just a bit odd really. No, Leo's confidence was another trait inherited from his parents, his dad in particular. John Gardner was the life and soul of any party, and always one of the first on the dancefloor. You never saw John in clothes that weren't smart. He wasn't one of those dads who would clean their car in a vest and jogging bottoms, the type of bottoms that would endanger public decency whenever the occupier bent over to wet his sponge. No, John always had shirt on, tucked into chinos. Leo was the same, every day was smart casual even outside of school and the only time you saw him out of a shirt or his favourite red-and-white-striped t-shirt was when they had to do PE, and even his PE polo was always brilliant white, not the faded grey-cream like Tim's. In an alternate world, Leo was too good to hang around with people like him, so Tim was glad that this was the reality in which they had been found.

"So, Timbo, Dad said he will give us a lift."

"Yeah, your mum said. Thanks."

"No problem, daddio."

"Why are you talking like that?"

"Like what?" he said, grinning knowing full well what Tim had meant. Before Tim could respond to this rhetorical question, Leo continued, "I'm just excited. Once tonight is out the way we have six whole weeks of doing whatever we like."

"Not whatever you want," interjected Flo. "You're helping do the summer house."

"You have a summer house now?" asked Tim.

"Not yet. That's what she means."

"She?" questioned his mum.

"Sorry, that's what mum means. I'm helping dad build one. We want it to be finished by August, so we can use it for shade during barbecues and stuff."

"Is there anything your dad can't do?"

"Not embarrass me in public?"

"Mate, you know my mum. Your dad is nothing in comparison."

"Hey, your mum is fine. How's the biscuits?"

"Meh, she's not fully over the pigeons still but she is getting there."

"That was funny, man."

"Yeah. Hilarious. Text Marty and ask how much he enjoyed it."

"Ah they'll get over it. Anyway, she will forget about it once the dog walking starts. All that fresh summer air is enough to calm anyone down ain't it?"

"Dog walking?"

"Oh....um...yeah. I thought you knew."

"No...." replied Tim nervously, still swinging on the stool.

Flo rummaged around in a small stack of letters that were pinned against the wall by a chicken shaped porcelain egg storer. With a quick "a-ha!" she pulled a slip of paper out and put it on the table in front of Tim.

*******DOG WALKER FOR HIRE*******

BUSY SCHEDULE? FEELING ILL? CAN'T BE BOTHERED?

**IF YOU ARE UNABLE TO WALK YOUR DOG, GIVE "WALKIES AND TALKIES" A CALL
ON 07700 900 222**

**NO DOG TOO BIG. NO DOG TOO SMALL.
AVAILABLE TO FIT YOUR SCHEDULE
COMPETITIVE RATES FROM JUST £10 PER HOUR**

The name Katherine Johnson wasn't present, and there were no written clues at all about who was behind the scheme, but the phone number was clearly his mums, and it was the same font as all her other flyers. Tim looked up from the leaflet towards Leo, and then across to Flo. Both were just looking at him, not saying a word.

"My friend is going back to work after finishing maternity leave," Flo started. "She has a little terrier, lovely little white thing it is. She was saying to me that she felt guilty about leaving it all day, so when I saw this leaflet, I thought I would text the number to see if they would help out."

"I can see where this is going..." said Tim awkwardly.

"Once I had typed in the number and hit send, I realised that I had sent the message to your mum. Thinking I had made a mistake, I got Leo to read the number out and I sent it again."

"And it was my mum again, right?"

"Yeah. I thought you must have known about this though, sorry."

"She hasn't mentioned it at all. And anyway, she normally uses me to deliver the leaflets."

"I got this one off the noticeboard in town. They're everywhere."

"Oh."

"It's a good idea I think, Tim," said Leo, trying his best to be encouraging.

"Something will go wrong. You know it will. I know it will. Everyone knows it will. And you know that when it does, I will be right in the middle of all of it."

Tim had muttered the last sentence very slowly and matter-of-factly. He knew it. This news wasn't something that he needed before trying to enjoy himself. He made a mental note to speak to his mum about it later. Before anyone in the kitchen could discuss this anymore, they were interrupted by a loud shout from a short distance away.

"YEEEEEEEEEEEEEEEEEEEEEEEEEEEEEEEEEEEE-HAAAAAAAAAAAAAAAAAA"

"That'll be dad," said Leo, as if it needed clarification.

John Gardner danced into the kitchen, pretending to lasso his wife across the room. She joined in with the charade and allowed herself to be caught by the fake rope, and the boys watched in part-astonishment and part-horror as Flo was reeled in across the wooden floor, ending with her being pulled into a full embrace. The pair then started a small line-dancing display, which was cut-short by Leo.

"Did...did you practice that? You're not doing this outside the house," Leo said, before starting to laugh. Tim just sat bewildered. When John got into a role, he got into it fully. There were never any half measures. He had an American-flag style red, white, and blue shirt, blue denim jeans, cowboy boots and a Stetson hat.

"Are you boys ready for the rodeoooo?" John said, flicking his car keys into the air before catching them with a spin.

"It's best that we get this over with quickly," replied Leo.

"He bought a whole outfit just for this?"

"It was in the loft. I don't know why, but unfortunately for us he had it if needed."

John kissed Flo, as did Leo, before Flo gave Tim a hug.

"Enjoy yourselves boys. Take lots of pictures!" she said from behind as they walked out the front door.

"We will," they replied in unison as they dashed across the drive to the people carrier, hoping not to be seen.

TEN

The drive to Greenwood Secondary only took ten minutes, and Lydia looked incredible in her long, shimmering blue dress. Tim told her this as she had got into the car, and she was really happy with the compliment. "You don't think it's a bit over the top?" she had asked, but both boys reassured her that it looked great. Her blonde hair had been made wavy, and hairpins had been put in place to ensure it stayed looking glamorous.

John drove the car into the school grounds and parked a few feet away from the main entrance, where a long, slightly shabby looking red carpet was laid. Tim was certain it was the one that had been rolled up in the storeroom of the school gym ever since he had started there. The theme of the disco was very prominent, and banners with stars and stripes were hanging along the tops of most windows in the foyer. What was known as Greenwood Secondary a few hours ago, was now to be known as Greenwood Valley High for the rest of the evening, and although the committee had meant well, it made Tim cringe a little bit inside. They had tried their best to make things seem as authentic as possible, but they had clearly not done any actual research other than teen movies, and the whole thing relied on poor American clichés. 'What was wrong with just having a normal disco?' he thought as he entered the lobby and made his way towards the main hall with his friends.

As they turned the final corner, they were stopped in their tracks by the *Greenwood Cheer Squad*, who were in fact a few of the annoying popular Year Eleven girls. Lydia knew some of them from the hockey team. The only one who Tim didn't mind was Evie, who was strong, independent and took no hassle from anyone. The rest of the cheer squad always had to be the centre of attention though. Tim, Leo and Lydia not being seen as cool by the other students meant that the 'cheer squad' put on a slightly less than enthusiastic rendition of the pre-planned chants for the three new arrivals, half-heartedly shaking silver pom-poms with expressionless faces. This suited Leo, Lydia, and Tim fine. The three of them quickened their pace and entered the hall, free from the glares of the cheerleaders.

To give the school some credit, the hall itself did look better than the outside, although that wasn't hard. The lack of proper daylight coming into the room meant the poor decoration was less noticeable in here. It was amazing what could be done with some crepe paper, balloons and poster paint. The DJ in the far corner had begun playing a selection of pop music, and those pupils who were experiencing a sugar high had taken to the dancefloor already.

"I'm not up for dancing yet," said Tim as they walked around the edge of the room, trying to find a quiet trio of chairs. The others felt the same and they headed to one of the tables in the corner, away from the eyes of their peers.

"I might get some food," said Leo. "Want anything?"

"It's going to be awful though," replied Tim, thinking about the hotdogs again.

"I'll pick you something up anyway. Lyds, want anything?"

"Yeah, just get me anything. I'm not fussy."

With that Leo left the other two and headed to the serving area. Tim realised that the cooks hadn't made any effort with fitting into the theme and looked disinterested in their green school staff canteen overalls, aprons or tabards. If he was still on the committee, he would have made them wear roller-skates, just to punish them for speaking bluntly to all the students each day. It would have been particularly good to see Derek, the grumpiest of all grumpy kitchen staff, whizzing around on skates with a hot dog in each hand. To hell with health and safety. Tim turned to watch Leo. He was the most eager of the three and broke out into mini-dance breaks at various points as he crossed the dancefloor. A couple of students high-fived him as he bopped past, and he did a spin after each, also taking photos along the way.

"Hey, Tim, has Leo spoken to you?" asked Lydia.

"About what?"

"I've no idea. He was being really coy earlier but wouldn't tell me what it was that was bothering him."

"Nah, he ain't said anything. He seemed happy enough before we picked you up. Just look at him now."

Tim could see him dancing as he poured mustard and ketchup onto his food from large, tired looking plastic bottles.

"Maybe it's something about his parents?"

"Nah, it can't be. They were the same as always too. You saw what his dad was like in the car."

"True. I can't believe John kept that hat on for the whole journey."

"And that music. He loves trying to embarrass us."

"We don't even have to try and embarrass ourselves, so him adding another level almost makes it so embarrassing that it's actually funny."

"Those ladies at the traffic lights didn't appreciate him shouting at them though."

"He shouted 'right on' to them out the window so I'm not surprised."

There was a brief pause whilst the two took a sip of cola.

“I think you should speak to him,” Lydia said.

“Nah, he will always be like that. We should just learn to enjoy it.”

“I meant speak to Leo, not his dad.”

“I can’t do that. He’ll know we were chatting about him then.”

“I guess. I could leave you both alone and then he might say it then?”

“Nah. Let’s just leave it. If it’s that important he’ll tell us eventually.”

Leo approached the table again, carrying three paper plates covered in mini-hotdogs, mac ‘n’ cheese and nachos. “Got ketchup on my shoe, didn’t I,” he said laughing and holding his leg in the air. “Thought I’d get you a mixture. I’ll eat whatever you don’t want.”

He put the plates on the table and ate quickly without looking up or even seeming to breathe. Lydia had removed her gloves to eat, not wanting to stain them with the nuclear-yellow mustard that formed a puddle on her plate. Once they were all done, Leo suggested they go and dance. Nervously agreeing, Tim joined him on the dancefloor whilst Lydia headed to the toilets. Since the Saint Monique bedroom display, Tim hated his dancing. He had an okay rhythm with his arms, and an okay rhythm with his legs. The only problem was that he couldn’t do the arms and legs together. It narrowed his dancing options down to either shuffling his feet around with his arms rigid or keeping his feet still and flailing his arms about his head like one of those inflatable mascots you sometimes saw at car salesrooms. Deciding that arms would be more noticeable than legs, he started punching the air and waving them from side to side. It would never win awards, but Leo kept encouraging him to keep going. Leo was a good dancer. He just had it. Tim didn’t know exactly what *it* was, but regardless, he had it. It must have been all those drama club lessons.

“I wish I could dance like you,” shouted Tim over the thumping music.

“Y’what?” shouted Leo back.

Tim cupped his hand around Leo’s ear and said it again. Leo smiled and moved around until he was behind Tim. He put one arm on Tim’s bicep, and another on his thigh. When the chorus of the song came back around, Leo moved Tim in time with the music. It felt weird, but Tim didn’t mind, and he started laughing and enjoying it. No one else seemed to be caring either. Normally this would have made him feel awkward, but he would barely see these people for a few weeks and when he did, he will be in his cool rock star phase, so nothing mattered tonight. Once Lydia had returned, the three stuck to the centre of the hall and danced and sang to all the songs they knew, and some of the ancient ones from the nineties that they were less familiar with. An hour passed by in an all-American flash. The highlight was when the DJ played Glove Puppet. Tim was high on excitement (and presumably the chemicals in the hot dogs) so sang along loud and even attempted a few of the dance moves. He failed, but it was as flamboyant as he'd ever been in public. The flashing lights and heavy noise made Tim lose track of time, and in his mind, it could easily have been near midnight, however in reality it started to die down just after 8.30pm. The head teacher was due to do a talk at 8.45 so Tim headed off to the toilets whilst he had the chance. As he went to push the door, he fell forward as it was opened from the inside. He almost crashed straight into Leo.

"Easy there," he laughed and held it open.

"I'll be back in a minute, L. Meet you by the table."

Tim went into the toilets, did what he needed to do, and then went to wash his hands. He had forgotten about the faulty taps in this bathroom though, and water spurted out directly over his crotch. He tried to jump out of the way quickly, but it soaked through. Even though the suit was dark, it was still obviously drenched, and he didn't want to face going back into the hall with his lower half glistening. He tried at first to cock his leg up so that he could use the hand dryer but had been interrupted just after he started. Gary, one of the oldest kids in his year, had asked what he was doing, but Tim couldn't think of a suitable excuse. In hindsight he should have just admitted the truth. Gary mumbled 'weirdo' under his breath. Tim gave up and shuffled back towards the hall. He was surprised to see Leo still stood there when he came out.

"You took your time," he said, his eyes slowly moving down from Tim's from face to his crotch. Water was dripping and leaving small blotches on the brown carpet-tiled floor beneath his feet.

"Taps," said Tim and gave a small smile.

"I'll believe you," joked Leo.

They started walking down towards the hall, but when they reached the doors, Leo pulled Tim towards the right, dragging him outside the main entrance. The cheer squad had gone so that was something at least

"What are we doing?" Tim questioned as they moved across the car park.

"I want to talk to you."

"Have I done something?"

"No, no, no. No. I just wanna ask you something."

Tim was confused but followed him regardless. It was a perfect summer evening now. The sun was still warm, and he could smell the scent of a bonfire nearby. He loved this smell as it reminded him of the burners on the narrow boats that moored on the canals near his grandparents' old house in Lincolnshire. The smell made him miss them both. On the far side of the car park was a small wall that formed a border for the wildflower garden that the Year Seven's had created to save the bees. Leo sat on it, and tapped the bricks with his palm, silently asking Tim to join him. Ensuring there was no chance of being stung by the insects, and eager to find out what the problem was, Tim sat next to him apprehensively.

"Tim, you know the diving thing."

"Yeah, you're gonna train with me, aren't you?" said Tim, worried that Leo had changed his mind.

"Oh yeah, yeah, of course. I meant the divers, rather than the diving."

"Which ones? Did you get the videos I sent?"

"Yeah, it's not that. Just the divers in general."

"Which ones?" questioned Tim again.

"Well...most of them."

"Like the ones in the magazines?"

"*Exactly* like the ones in the magazines."

"What about them?"

"Well, I dunno. I like the diving stuff."

"Me too."

"Let me finish."

"Sorry Leo."

"I like the diving thing, right, but do you just like the diving thing?"

"I like the diving thing."

"But I mean, is it just the diving thing?" pushed Leo.

"I like the athletics thing too. And the cycling thing."

"No, you're not getting what I'm saying."

Leo was getting flustered.

"Because you're not really saying anything. You just keep asking if I like diving."

"It's more about the divers themselves."

"What about them?"

There was a small pause. Tim noticed Leo looking over to the distance. He didn't turn back to him before continuing to explain what he was trying to say.

"Well, they make me feel weird. Good weird. Like, it's not just the diving bit that I like. I like the divers who dive as well as just the diving."

"Stop saying diving."

"Stop, I am being serious. I'm trying my best. I think what I mean is that I sort of have a crush on them."

"Oh," said Tim quietly.

"I don't want to make you feel awkward Tim, sorry."

Tim sat there quietly. He could feel his stomach starting to knot.

"I can't really explain it properly," Leo continued. "It's not like I only like the divers. I sort of have a crush on Lydia too."

"Wow, right okay."

"That's a thing though, isn't it?"

"Yeah obviously, Lydia is nice. She looks amazing tonight."

"You're so cute when you're confused," Leo said as he nudged his shoulder against Tim's.

"Eh?"

"What I mean is, I have a crush on girls *and* boys. That's a thing, right?"

"Yeah definitely. Someone on Choose That Guy was bi, remember?"

"So, I'm not weird."

"Nah, definitely not."

"And you don't think I'm weird and you're not going to laugh, and you're not going to run away and stop speaking to me?"

"Of course not."

Leo smiled and put his arm around Tim and gave him a hug.

"Tim, I was so scared to tell you. When you went into the toilet earlier, I just needed to say something."

"What made you realise this?" Tim asked, once Leo had dropped his arm. He was starting to feel a little sick with nerves.

"I just became a bit obsessed, I guess," he said, before pausing for a few seconds. "I couldn't stop looking at them and even when I try to think of just girls, I still think of boys too."

"I'm no expert, but it sounds like you definitely fancy both, but it's cool."

"Are you sure it's cool?" asked Leo, desperately trying to make sure Tim was okay with it.

Tim could feel himself becoming red, with nerves and fear. He swallowed a couple of times and rubbed his sweaty palms together. He turned to Leo and put his hand on his in order to both be reassuring and to steady himself.

"Leo, of course I'm sure. It is totally and utterly cool that you like boys and that you like girls," said Tim, before looking his best friend in the eyes, "In fact you liking boys is amazing ...because I think I do too."

ELEVEN

After Tim had got home from the disco, he had said to his mum that he was going straight to bed to watch TV before sleeping, tired out from all the dancing. The reality was that he just wanted time to think. She had kissed him goodnight on the top of his head and said he looked like he needed the sleep, which he found a bit rude. He thought he looked as alert as normal.

Once upstairs he switched the television on, changing channel until it landed on the latest episode of *Choose That Guy,* but he didn't take in anything that was being shown. Now that Jay had gone his interest in the programme had waned. He turned the television down and laid on the bed, staring at the ceiling, trying to take in everything that had been discussed with Leo. The light from the TV changed the mood of the room constantly.

He'd read stories in the paper about people who had been beaten up because of their sexuality and he didn't have much confidence in the people of Greenwood to understand what it was like. How could they understand when he had no clue what he was himself? This whole thing had somehow clicked up to the next gear only an hour or so before. From what he knew, he didn't know anybody who was gay or bisexual or anything *unstraight*, not counting Leo of course, and Leo was probably lying in bed thinking the exact same things as he was.

He definitely hadn't told Leo to make things easier for his friend. It was something that had been sat mainly dormant at the back of his mind whilst the more conscious thoughts were thinking it was just wanting to dress like a rock star or be better at sports. He hated trying to figure it out and his teeth ached from subconsciously grinding them together whenever he thought about it. Even saying the word gay to himself in his head made him scared about how people would react. He thought back to when he told Mr Stephenson that he wanted to be toned like the divers in the magazine. He then also wondered if his brother thought he was weird for becoming immediately obsessed with the picture of Pistol Pete from the music magazine. He suddenly wanted to tell more people how he felt just to help himself understand, but then quickly decided that it may not be that simple.

It could be his and Leo's secret, although he would still like to talk to Lydia soon. Being one of his closest friends, she knew nearly everything about him already, and vice versa. Tim sat up and opened his window to allow some fresh air into the room. He looked into the final stages of the sunset, before pulling out his phone to text Leo.

“Hey Leo. You awake?”
“Yeah. You?”
“Yeah, obviously. I text you”
“Shh I’m tired. Thanks for tonight though”
“Thank you too”
“I hope it wasn’t weird?”
“Nah it’s not at all”
“And you didn’t say you felt the same to make me feel normal?”
“No. And it’s not abnormal. Is it?”
“I don’t think so”
“Me neither. Do we need to tell Lyds?”
“I was thinking that. I think we should speak to Lyds, but maybe not yet. Like, I’m confused about things”
“Me too. I just thought the divers and things were cool, but they make me feel different too”
“Can I ask something?”
“Sure!”
“When you said you like boys, do you just like boys? Or, like, is it girls too?”
“I’m pretty certain it’s just boys”
“That’s cool. I like how I’ve now got a gay best friend”
“Me too”
“Bisexual!”
“Sorry”
“Ha it’s cool. Urgh why is everything so confusing”
“Because we’ve only both said it aloud for the first time just now”
“’True. Do you feel like this about anyone at school?”
“Definitely not. Is that weird? Should I?”
“I dunno. I sort of also have a tiny mini crush on someone else too”
“Yeah, Lydia.”
“No, someone else as well!”
“OMG who?!?”
“LOL I am not telling you that. I’ve told you enough tonight haha”
“Fair. I’ll ask again tomorrow. Unless it’s me?”
“‘LOL you wish”
“:D”
“’I’m glad I told you”
“I’m glad I told you too”
“x”
“x”

At some point shortly after texting Leo, he had fallen asleep, waking past midnight with rolling news displayed on the television and his phone in his left hand. He checked the screen and had no messages or notifications. He was still fully clothed so stripped off and tried getting straight back to sleep. An hour later he was still awake so pulled out his phone again. He texted Lydia and Leo separately asking if they were awake. He didn't expect a reply and didn't receive one. He turned on his bedside lamp, opened his drawer and took out an old diving magazine. Looking at the divers, he knew that what he had told Leo had been true. They made him feel weird. Good weird.

WEDNESDAY

TWELVE

Wednesday morning, Tim was up and ready for his paper round. He had decided to get up and leave as quick as possible, nervous that he would be asked awkward questions by his mum, despite there being no reason for her to know anything about how he felt. The whole thing had been playing on his mind and he had slept awfully as a result, waking nearly every hour. As much as he didn't want to think about it, it was a pretty major thing. In fact, in his head it was a massive giant solar-system sized ball of worry. Wanting to take his mind away from it, he planned to focus on his paper round, trying to get a few more orders on his way, although after yesterday morning's confusion of people having already bought biscuits, his hopes weren't too high.

Tim managed to leave his house without seeing his mum, his brother still asleep as always too. He headed to Singh Stars, took a Wispa for a post-round treat, and headed on his way.

"Morning paper boy," came voices from the other side of Bridge Street. He looked across and saw Pat and Pet on one of their power walks. It was their new fitness regime after the trampoline fitness class they had joined didn't work out. They had matching blue coats on. Tim thought they were too overdressed for the bright morning but gave them a cheerful wave without slowing down, thinking it was odd that they didn't actually use his name despite knowing him basically his whole life.

"See you this afternoon," they shouted from behind.

Tim couldn't remember any event planned for the afternoon and was worried that he had agreed to do something a while ago and forgotten about it. It wouldn't have been the first time that this would have happened. It was actually quite frequent. Each time he made a mental note to add things to the calendar on his phone, before never getting around to doing so. He once completely missed a birthday meal for Marty as he forgot the date that his brother had been born on. For some reason he had it in his head that his birthday was on the second of May, and it was only on the second of April that he realised his mistake. He'd turned up at home (after hanging out in town) without a present or card, and the family were already onto their Eton Mess by the time he finally joined them for his chicken curry. His phone had run of battery whilst out, so his mum had been unable to get hold of him.

The first half of Tim's round was uneventful, and no more orders were placed. As he moved to Elm Meadow and Beech Close, he knocked on doors twice, rather than the usual once, in a last ditch attempt to secure more biscuit sales. All his efforts resulted in a grand total of four new orders. He had noticed that the couple whose house he had fallen into yesterday were avoiding him. He could see a shadow behind the net curtains as he knocked. After they failed to answer the door, he gave up, staring at the figure behind the curtains over his shoulder as he made his way down the drive. He was pleased to see that the pigeons had excreted on the man's car windscreen again.

Back at home, he slung his bike and bag into the shed and went into the kitchen. His mum was now up and making coffee, asking if he would like a cup. He declined, and always would until she had learnt how to master the machine. It also meant that he could avoid all potential for awkward questions, however she did ask how the disco had been last night.

"Yeah good, thank you."

"Oh, that's nice," she responded. Surprisingly and luckily she didn't dig for any more information.

Tim just wanted the morning to rush past so that he could head into town and look for things from his list. He had sat on the sofa for less than five minutes watching repeats of old gameshows before he was dragged into the kitchen to pack more biscuits, this time with the door locked and the key safely hidden away. In town he was planning to get the Mirror Ball CD and a belt at the weekend. He wanted them sooner but there would be no way that Mr Singh would give him an advance on his wages. Instead, he would need to do more tasks for his mum, and be nice to his brother, so that he could get some bonus money from the biscuit sales. He had noticed that the living room now contained a high number of banana boxes stacked with the biscuit collections and gathered that mum and Marty had redone all the work whilst he was out last night. It was probably safer for all involved that Tim wasn't present after the disaster on Monday, so he was just sat in the kitchen tying up their loose ends.

After a quick shower his thoughts had turned to going back to school in the autumn. He felt like he was going as a new person regardless of any new clothes, but no one could know this. Leo had said the previous night that he wouldn't tell anyone anything because as long as Tim knew, he would be happy. It was made easier after Tim had told him that he felt the same. Lydia would probably probe a bit into what was so important for Leo to say to Tim, but with her birthday falling in a weeks' time they could form a cover story, pretending that they had a big surprise for her and then tell her that she would find out very soon. This would mean that they would actually have to plan something, but that was something which they could sort at the end of the week.

Shortly after he had finished with the biscuits, he spotted Lydia outside the house walking down the road. He said hi to her out of the living room window, the net curtain covering his rear, making him look like he was in a wedding dress.

"What were you two chatting about last night?" she shouted, as expected.

"You'll find out soon enough," he replied, tapping his nose with a finger, something which he had seen people on television do.

"Is it a party?" she asked.

Tim hadn't prepared for this level of interrogation and he panicked, before blurting "Yes. No. I dunno," in quick succession.

"That's a yes then," she said with a smile, before heading off towards the fields.

This week was panning out to be busy enough as it was, and now he would have to arrange a party too so that Lydia wouldn't be offended. He texted Leo to see if he could meet him during the afternoon away from Lydia, and he agreed to come across to his house at 2pm, oddly signing the text off with 'au revoir'. Leo was not the most gifted with languages, so it made him chuckle.

Tim was more into German. His language skills were not brilliant, but he was already better at this than he had been in French. He was forced to do French in the first two years at Greenwood Secondary, but always complained that the French have too many vowels. The only thing that he could remember from those two years was how to say "I would like a loaf of bread and to call an ambulance please," which would be useless unless there was an emergency in a Parisian bakery.

On the first day of the school holidays, it was a tradition for a big football game to happen between as many pupils as possible, but he'd had enough of his peers for one year. From his bedroom window he could see a small playing field, and in the distance, he spotted many from his school walking across the grass in groups of four or five, kicking a football high into the air when they reached the centre. They'd likely be there for hours so he made a mental note to not head that way later.

Tim had stripped off his paper round clothes and threw them in the wash basket, happy that there was a month and a half before he'd have to pull on the awful green school jumper and gold tie combination that sat on the top of the basket. It was now just past one o'clock, so he tidied his room a bit by throwing books under his bed and cleared his clothes off the fold down chair so that it would be ready for his meeting with Leo.

There was a gentle tap at his bedroom door.

"Hullo?" he said.

"Can I come in?" came his mum's voice.

Tim looked around as he answered, making sure there were no magazine articles lying around. He was terrified that everything would cause some kind of suspicion now. Safe in the knowledge that no evidence of his sexuality was on show, he said that she could enter. His mum probably wouldn't have noticed if he had left evidence everywhere, she was hardly Sherlock Holmes.

"Hi Tim," she said, as she walked across the room and sat on the bed. "I think you can have this now," she continued, as she passed him his Olympic magazine.

"Thanks mum," Tim replied, "sorry about the other day."

"Hey, it happens. I bought too many biscuits anyway so in the end it was an easy way to get rid of a load of them. Just don't make it a regular thing though."

"I won't."

"Now, are you free this afternoon? I think we need a talk."

Tim froze. Did she know? Had Leo said something to Flo who had then text mum? His palms got sweaty again immediately.

"Leo is coming over at two. We have to plan a party for Lydia."

"A party?"

"Don't ask."

"Can I come?"

"Yes. We need the numbers."

"You know how to make people feel special, don't you."

Tim just smiled and let the words hang in the air. Katherine soon continued. "Pat and Pet are coming across this afternoon as we have some information that I think may be of importance."

She was sat tapping a pen on her teeth.

"What about?"

"Those people who said that they'd already bought our biscuits."

"Oh," said Tim, relaxing a little. "Do you know who sold them?"

"We think so. We just need to do some more digging."

"Like spying?"

"If you want to call it something exciting, then yes, spying."

"Awesome."

"You need to leave it to the adults though, okay?"

"So why do you need me?"

"Well, that's the thing. I've agreed to walk a dog this afternoon for one of Flo's friends."

Tim had forgotten all about the flyers. "I'm not doing it."

"It's only a small dog, and it only needs to be a short walk."

"But I'm meeting Leo."

"He can help you. Will do you two good to get some fresh air."

Tim kicked the edge of the bed gently. "I don't trust myself with animals."

"You'll be fine. Just collect it, take it to The Rec, let it run around, bring it back and collect the money."

'The Rec', or The Recreation Ground to give it the full name, was the largest and most popular park in Greenwood.

"What's my share of the goods?"

"The goods? You've been watching too many dramas. If you mean how much you'll earn, I'll let you keep the lot."

"How much is it?"

"£20."

Tim knew that doing this would mean that he could get the CD today.

"What time do I need to pick the dog up?"

"Two thirty. The lady said she'll give you it's favourite ball to play fetch with, and she has the bags to pick up its mess."

"Urgh. Can we not just teach it to clench?"

"Not really possible. It's quite a placid dog so you'll be fine with everything, I'm sure. I'm going to do this regularly whilst she starts returning to work slowly."

"Does she know I'm coming and not you?"

"I've given her a text and she said it's fine. I'll take it out on Friday. Now, I must get downstairs ready before the others arrive."

Tim waited for his mum to leave before jumping on his bed and texting Leo to tell him there was a slight change of plan. He was hoping that Leo liked dogs, but unfortunately the response was not positive. Apparently, Leo had been chased by a Great Dane as a kid and he ended up trapped at the end of an alleyway while the dog knocked him to the floor and licked his face. It looked like he would have to face the task alone and meet Leo later.

Once he was changed, he headed downstairs and saw cakes and biscuits in the kitchen and had already taken half of a mini Battenberg into his mouth before he was told not to touch them. His mum said that she would fill him in on the details of the meeting with Pat and Pet when he returned. She handed him a slip of paper with the name and address of the client on and ushered him out of the back door. Tim wanted the event to be over as quick as possible yet scuffed his trainers along the floor as he trudged down the road. He was given instructions to meet Maggie Ellis at her house at 27a Pine Close. He couldn't recall ever meeting her before but imagined she would be okay considering she was a friend of Flo's. Pine Close was made up of houses built during the 1960's, and the majority were identikit and generic. Much like the oak tree of Oak Tree Crescent, there were no pine trees on Pine Close either. All the streets were given these names to just make them sound nicer.

Number 27a was the ground floor flat in a block of three, made slightly larger by having access to the basement level below. Tim had seen enough films to fear the basement already. He approached the door and pressed the buzzer stating the name of Ellis and waited. After a few seconds it buzzed and a stressed, echoey female voice said, "Is that Timothy?" through the intercom. Once he had confirmed that it was, she told him to push the door and take the first turning on the left inside. He entered the flat and was greeted by Mrs Ellis who had her dark hair pulled back over her shoulders, being held by a gold, plastic clip. Her hands full of rattles and picture books.

"Sorry for the mess," she said as she half offered a hand forward to be shaken. Tim grabbed her fingers and waved them about a bit in a poor attempt at formality. Her hands were strangely cold and bony.

"I'm just getting ready to take the baby to my mother's so I can pop into the office for an hour or so. I start back there next week and need to sign a few documents and have a back to work meeting."

"It must be nice to have a routine back," said Tim, not knowing what else to say.

"It will be, yes. Not that this year has been bad. It's such a joy to watch a child grow, learning to crawl and smile."

"I can imagine," he replied.

"I've just got to put these downstairs and then I will be back. Head through to the lounge if you like and get to know Snowy before he goes out."

Obliging, Tim walked into a very cluttered front room and saw the baby laying on its back, punching at a colourful farmyard themed mobile that hung just above his face. He felt quite harsh in thinking it, but Tim didn't really like babies. They all looked the same and smelt weird. He stepped across a multi-coloured playmat which squeaked on certain panels, and towards the corner, where there was a chair with a white West Highland Terrier laying across the red cushions. Tim was better with dogs than babies so perched on the arm and gave the dogs belly a rub. "Hello Snowy," he said in a high-pitched childlike voice he'd never heard himself use before. "Who's going for a walk? You are. Yes, you are. You're coming to the park Snowy, aren't you?"

"Timothy," said Mrs Ellis from the hall, "I have the lead, his ball and the poo-bags here for you."

The thought of picking up the dog mess was already making him feel a little queasy. He walked back across the room and found Mrs Ellis with a travel bag over her shoulder. She passed him the items required for the afternoon, and then a crisp £20 note. He placed it in the pocket of his shorts and zipped it tight and asked if she needed any help before she had to go.

"All fine thanks, everything is in here as far as I know. Now, your mother knows about doing this again on Friday, doesn't she?"

"Yep. She told me about that before I left."

"Excellent. I have to go back for another meeting at work then also. Have you met Snowy yet?"

"I have yes. Very cute. He likes being tickled doesn't he."

"Oh, he does. He's not always as cheerful as this though," she said smiling widely.

"That's common though, I guess," said Tim presumptuously.

"Yeah, it will always be like that, I guess. I think he'll start talking soon."

"Talking?"

"Yeah. He is making lots of sounds and almost forming a few words."

"Snowy is? Are you sure?"

"Completely. Come and listen."

Tim followed her into the room, wondering if the lack of sleep from having a baby had started to send her mad. He knew people treated animals like part of the family, but even so, this was strange. He followed her into the room amazed and watched her crouch over her son.

"Are you going to speak for Timmy, Snowy?" she said as she squeezed the baby's rosy cheeks.

Tim looked across to the dog who was staring straight back at him. Having dawned on him, all he could mutter was "The baby is Snowy."

"Yep, my little Snow Snow. Clever kid he'll be."

"And the dog?"

"Oh, I've had Adam for five years now. He's not so clever." She laughed quite loud at this.

Tim looked across to the dog and mouthed Adam out of the eyeline of Mrs Ellis. 'Who calls their dog Adam but their baby Snowy?' he thought to himself. Feeling awkward, he stretched out the lead and Adam jumped immediately off of the chair and sat at his feet. “Coming for a walk then, mate?” he muttered as he clipped the lead onto the dog’s black collar. The dog didn’t answer, unsurprisingly. A minutes ago he was almost shocked to hear it was about to utter its first word.

“Lovely to meet you Mrs Ellis. What time should I bring him back?”

“Is four okay? I’'ll be back by then easily.”

“No problem, see ya later.”

THIRTEEN

Tim had left Mrs Ellis' house, still muttering to himself about how the names seemed to have been given to the wrong things. Adam immediately pulled on the lead, wanting to drag Tim to the park as quick as possible. The sun was now very strong, but the temperature bearable, as he walked the length of Pine Close and towards the fields that were laid out behind the residential areas. The field behind his home was closer to The Rec but as the football was still likely ongoing, he would settle for a small park at the end of the street instead. It was an ideal spot to waste five minutes and to hopefully tire the dog out a little before heading to The Rec.

Having had Adam with him for only a few minutes, he realised that one day he needed to own a dog. How had he let himself be won over so easily? Adam was sat in front of him, staring with his tongue out. Tim pulled out a half-bare tennis ball from his pocket and threw it overarm into the distance. That was the idea anyway. In reality, his scrawny arms meant that the ball travelled about fifteen metres. Off his lead, Adam collected the ball and had it back at his feet in a matter of seconds. He tried again, but not much more distance was found. Adam bought it back. At this rate Tim would be tired out before the dog. Trying a new technique. He lobbed the ball gently into the air and volleyed it with his right foot. He caught it imperfectly however it somehow flew off into the distance. He took his phone out of his pocket and texted Leo.

"Her dog is called Adam but her baby is called Snowy"
"That's not normal."
"THANK YOU! I made a right idiot of myself"

Adam was back at Tim's feet again already. He kicked and threw the ball a couple more times before his arm and leg started to twinge so he decided to give up, clipping the lead back on and setting off towards The Rec. What should have been quick progress was hampered by Adam's need to sniff and then urinate against every post that they passed. The poo bags were called into action as the pair were outside the children's play area just inside The Rec. Six pairs of parents' eyes immediately locked on him as the dog crouched down. Tim took a bag and waved it at them to confirm that he wasn't going to leave it. They continued to watch as he bent over, retching, and taking the mess inside his bag-gloved right hand. The warmth made him feel sicker than the smell did. He decided there and then that actually he'd never ever own a dog. He carried the bag at a full arm's length to the red bin towards the footpath and made a dramatic action to lift the lid so that those parents still watching would be happy in the knowledge that the excrement was now in its rightful place.

The Rec was large and contained two football pitches in its centre, as well as a couple of basketball courts whose nets had vanished a long time ago. On the far side was a small, wooded area, and a dirty brook meandered along the eastern section. Already bored of the walking, Tim took a seat on the grass and Adam laid down beside him. He'd been thinking about the talk with Leo at the disco and wanted to tell Lydia how he was feeling. He sent her a message asking if she was free. He realised that she hadn't responded to his text during the night yet. Once sent, he laid back on the grass and let the sun hit his face. His phone started ringing. Glove Puppet was at full volume and hearing it as his ringtone made him realise that this was another thing that needed to be changed to become cool.

"Alright Lyds," he said after swiping to answer.

"Alright? What you up to?"

"In the park with Adam, you?"

"Who's Adam?" she questioned quickly.

"Oh, it's that dog that mum was meant to walk."

"You mean Mrs Ellis' dog?"

"You know her?"

"Yeah, she works with dad."

"Do you know her son is called Snowy?"

"Yeah, why?" – *Why didn't this seem strange to her?* Tim thought.

"Well, it's weird. Why has the dog got a boy's name and the baby got a dog's name?"

"Snowy can be a boy's name too."

"But Adam is more appropriate."

"Well, you can't have a dog and a baby called Adam, can you?" said Lydia, matter-of-factly.

"That's not what I meant. Like, call your baby something normal."

"There's probably lots of people called Snowy."

"I give up."

Tim left a short silence, thinking how to start.

"Anyway, what did you want?" said Lydia before he could.

"Just to say hello and catch up."

"We saw each other yesterday so unless you have any gossip, we can't have much to catch up on"

"Um, no, it's okay. I'm just bored in the park."

"Are you sure there isn't anything?"

"What have you heard?" Tim was getting nervous again.

"About?"

"Nothing." Too late.

"So, there is something?"

"No, it's cool...just..." he tailed off.

"You're sounding very weird Tim" she said after a short silence. "I've got to help mum do some cleaning so call me back later if you like."

"Righty-o."

"Laters, Tim."

"Wait!" he shouted hoping that he had caught her before she had hung up. There was silence. The call was still showing as connected though.

"Well?" came her voice again finally.

"Can I talk to you?"

"We're already talking."

"Are you alone?"

"You're making this sound like one of those creepy calls we were warned about in Tutor Time," she said flatly.

"I'm serious. Are you alone?"

"Yeah, hang on." Tim heard the door of her bedroom close on the line. "Are you alright Tim?" she asked, now sounding more concerned.

"I think so, it's just, well I can trust you, can't I?"

"Of course. What have you done?"

"I haven't *done* anything. It's just, I was speaking to Leo last night and I have to tell you too. I think I'm gay, Lydia."

He blurted it out quicker than he wanted to. The plaster had been well and truly ripped off.

"Oh," said Lydia, before silence returned. Tim waited a moment nervously before continuing.

"Lydia?"

"Hi, sorry."

"No, sorry," he apologized. "I shouldn't have said anything."

"Thank you for telling me."

Tim wished this was a video call instead so he could try and gauge her reaction better.

"Please don't think I'm weird," he said softly, as fragile as glass.

"I don't, sorry, I just wasn't expecting it."

"Okay."

"No honestly, it is fine."

He felt that she had realised that she wasn't sounding the most supportive but let her continue. "You just took me by surprise. You sure though, yeah?"

"Pretty certain. Well, not pretty certain. Not certain at all. I definitely fancy boys, let's just say that." He was questioning himself again. Why was this so confusing? "Lydia, I don't know exactly the right terms but gay seems right? I'm so sorry."

He wasn't upset, but the confusion was making his heart race, and he could feel sweat behind his ears.

"Don't say sorry, you idiot. It's cool of you to tell me. Thank you."

Lydia was sounding her usual self again.

"Please don't tell anyone I've told you."

"I won't."

"Promise?"

"I promise."

"Thank you."

"Is this what you were discussing with Leo at the disco?"

Tim said it was, before realising that she might remember that it was Leo who had wanted to speak to him, and not the other way around. He told her that they had been talking about her birthday, but he had decided to tell Leo. Telling Lydia took a weight off his shoulders, but there was a nervousness still inside him. He was worried that the wrong people might find out and cause him trouble. He'd heard about a Greenwood kid who was a few years older who got bullied out of school for being gay.

The pair continued to talk on the phone for a few minutes, with Lydia changing the subject quite quickly. Tim assumed that this was because she wasn't wanting to dwell on what he had said. She wanted to show that it didn't change anything between the pair. Tim hoped that this wasn't because she didn't care, and that thought was pushed back out of his head. He didn't need voices telling him that one of his friends would desert him.

He dragged his foot up and down the grass until a small bare patch of mud appeared in front of him. He wished that everyone would be as cool as Lydia and Leo about it, although he knew that wouldn't be the case. After promising him again that she wouldn't tell anyone, they arranged to meet on the following day.

FOURTEEN

The phone call to Lydia had only taken about ten minutes, although about half of that was filled with heavy, awkward silences. Arms no longer in pain, it was only when he pulled the tennis ball from his pocket to throw again that he noticed Adam had disappeared. He glanced around in all directions but couldn't see him. Panicking, he jumped up and started shouting Adam as loud as possible. Despite The Rec being fairly open, it easily had enough hiding places for a dog to run to. He ran towards the play area and asked the parents if they had seen him, all of them confirming that they hadn't. One parent pushed a baby in a swing whilst staring back, not blinking or saying a word. Looking around, he decided his best option was to start at the entrance and work his way around the perimeter of the fields. Every few steps he shouted Adam at the top of his voice, throwing the ball in front of him in a desperate attempt to lure him back.

So busy with shouting, he became careless with his stride and hadn't noticed how close to the small brook he had gotten. One stumble over a loose branch later, he bounced down the small muddy slope on his backside and landed feet first in the water. The muddy brown liquid came up to his hips, leaving his head and arms thankfully dry. The bottom of the stream was boggy, and his feet had sunken into the mud, leaving him stuck. He could just see over the top of the bank and spotted a woman running. Her neon top was blinding in the sunshine. She was listening to something on her headphones so had failed to hear him shout for help as she dashed past him. He watched her as she headed towards the exit of the park but was glad to see that she had turned just before the gate to set off on a second lap. He waited and waited as she went off into the distance before turning a corner and back towards him. When she was a few metres away he shouted again, louder this time. Again, she dashed past.

It took two more laps for Tim to get her attention. Shouting had proven to be useless, and not having much to work with, he decided to throw some algae at her. He didn't see exactly where it landed but was close enough to make her come to a stop after a couple of strides and investigate where it had come from. She pulled a small bottle off her running belt and drank it as she looked towards Tim.

She swallowed her drink and immediately started to shout "HELP! HELP!" at the top of her voice. She was shouting so much that Tim couldn't tell her to stop. As the seconds ticked by, more and more of the public gathered on the bank. His feet were sunken so far into the bed of the stream that it felt like he was set in concrete.

"CALL THE FIRE BRIGADE!" shouted the woman.

"Really, it's fine, honestly," replied Tim, trying to counterbalance her panic, but someone was already on the phone to the emergency services.

"Are you okay, are you okay?" someone said quickly without a pause.

"Yeah, I'm alright thanks," said Tim glumly. "Honestly, I'm fine. It's not that deep."

"We don't want you to get pulled away," another onlooker said.

"It's hardly the Nile, is it?" said Tim sarcastically. "Look, if someone could give me their hand that would be magic."

Three people edged slowly down the bank and held out their arms. He grabbed onto the strongest looking limb and attempted to pull himself free. He managed to get one foot unstuck but had no way of pulling the other out of the mud. He let go and returned to his original position. He wanted to have another attempt, but the small crowd that were now watching said that it wouldn't be worth it. He felt as if he was in a zoo. To his alarm, a few minutes later, sirens could be heard in the distance, getting closer by the second. He prayed that they wouldn't be for him, but within moments the blue flashing lights of a fire engine were skirting around the edge of the park. He peeked over the top of the bank at full stretch and watched in slow motion as the engine manoeuvred its way through the gates, slowly bumping across the grass towards him. The arrival of the fire engine caused more people to come and watch, and a few were taking photos on their phone. Tim knew that these would make their way online before he was even set free.

He stood in silence as he watched three firefighters jump out of the vehicle. One of them came across to him whilst the other two busied themselves pulling a ladder off the side of the engine.

"Hi kiddo." came a northern voice of the first firefighter. "I'm Julia and I'm the sub-officer. How did you end up in here then?"

"Hi. I'm Tim. I was looking for a dog and wasn't really looking where I was going."

"And where is your dog now?"

"I'm not sure," he said as he started worrying that he would never see him again.

He gave a description to Julia and the large crowd, and they promised that they would find Adam. Two of Julia's colleagues had shifted to the edge of the bank and laid the ladder across the stream. One of them hopped to the other side and they shifted the ladder until it was just above Tim's right shoulder. Then, they laid on it from either side, reaching down and grabbing an arm each. Tim tried kicking his legs to help speed up the rescue, and his legs soon became loose, although sadly this was helped by the fact that his trainers remained lost in the mud. The firefighters moved into a half-standing half-sitting position, still holding on, and then pulled as hard as they could. Tim popped out the mud like a stuntman from a cannon and was plonked down on the ladder. He crawled across the final metre back to dry land and laid on the grass, thanking the team for their help, wishing he could disappear from the embarrassment. His clothes were soaked, and small bits of algae clung to his calves. Checking his pockets, he was glad to see his phone was still with him, although he would need to put it in rice when he got home to stop any damage. He had no idea if this would work, but he'd seen Marty do it last year.

He sat helplessly, tired on the grass, as he watched the crowd disperse around the park in search for the dog. Julia crouched next to him and reminded him of the importance of water safety. He assured her that he was going to be a diver one day and that he was an okay swimmer. They offered him a lift home in their engine, but he didn't want to be seen being taken home in a vehicle that would alert everybody on Oak Tree Crescent that he'd done something stupid again. Julia was satisfied that he would get home safely, especially with it only being a few minutes' walk, and instructed her colleagues to put the ladder back on the engine.

He wanted to text Leo about it all, but with his phone working intermittently he gave up. He was glad that he still had the £20 note in his pocket too, as a trip to town was definitely needed after the events of the last twenty minutes. He'd have to try and get the Converse shoes as a priority. Tim pushed himself to his knees and looked around the nearby area for Adam. He wouldn't know how he would explain to Mrs Ellis that he had lost her dog within an hour of picking him up. An even higher level of panic had just started to set in when a man in cricket whites started jogging towards him.

"Hey, son," said the man as he got within earshot. "We've got your dog." He was slightly overweight, and his face was red, his speech broken up by quick bursts of heavy breathing. Tim jumped up so quick he became lightheaded and had to spend a moment steadying himself.

"Where is he?" asked Tim. The man was still out of breath, and pointed towards his right as he doubled over, left hand on his knee. With a quick thanks, Tim jogged down the grass in the direction that he had been told, his feet squelching inside his socks with each stride. He caught sight of a group of four people bringing Adam back across the park, with a makeshift lead being held by the leader of the group. As they got closer,

Tim noticed that the previously white dog was now covered in mud up to his neck too, looking like he had been dipped in chocolate.

"Thank you," said Tim, as he clipped Adam's damp lead onto his collar. "Where was he?"

"He got into the pond on the far side," said a tall thin man. "He was chasing ducks when we spotted him. Had to tempt him out with biscuits."

Tim wanted to ask where the man had bought the biscuits but thought better of it. There wasn't much time until he had said that he would return Adam home, and instead of a relaxing stroll around the rest of the park, he now had to take him home and bathe him.

As he walked down his garden path, he noticed that the curtains in the front room had been drawn across. His mum loved the sunshine, so for these to be closed on one of the brightest days of the year was strange. Rather than drag the dog, and himself, through a clean kitchen, he tapped on the front door sharply with his knuckles. Some of the green paint flaked away as he did so. He'd have to remind Marty that he still had to repaint the door as he had promised he'd do it at the start of the year. After waiting a few seconds, he tapped the door again, and then the window leading to the front room. He heard movement and could see a figure moving towards him through the frosted glass. The door opened, and he was surprised to see the safety chain on. Rather than it being his mum, Pat squeezed her face into the small gap.

"Oh. Hi Tim. You can come in," she said, before looking down at the dog, and then his legs, and finally the puddle forming on the driveway at his feet. Her eyes widened when she noticed the mud. "Do you want a towel?" she said rhetorically, not waiting for the answer, instead closing the door and going back inside the house. The curtains to the right twitched, and then closed again quickly. Eventually, his mum opened the door, and Pat and Pet were stood behind her, resembling bouncers at a nightclub.

"What's happened to you?" his mum asked, horrified at the state of his clothes, which were clearly ruined. Tim explained the whole situation.

"You can't come in the house with those on," she said. "Take them off and I'll get some newspapers on the floor."

"I can't get undressed here, mum." Tim begged, but she had already gone inside. Pet had quickly nipped to the kitchen and returned holding a black bin liner at arm's length.

"Put them in here," Pet said, smiling kindly.

Pat and Pet had lived opposite the Johnson's for the best part of a decade now, and Tim could always remember them being a part of his life. Pet was much smaller with shoulder length light-brown hair which fell straight. Her thin face was hidden behind round glasses and her cheekbones were prominent. Tim didn't know her age, but if he had to guess he would have said mid-forties at most. Pet worked at Greenwood library and was likely responsible for all the books that lined the living room of her and Pat's house. There must have been at least six big full bookcases in their front room alone. Pet was always encouraging Tim to read, and often leant him books on various topics that he needed to use for homework.

Pat on the other hand was slightly larger, her face rounded and glassless. She liked to wear silk scarves over knitwear. Pat's hair was also very different to Pet's, and was bright blonde, curling down to just past her ears. Again, Tim would have put her in her mid-forties also so was unsure which of the two was the eldest. Maybe as Tim and Marty got older there would be confusion as to who was the oldest also, but for now it was obviously Marty.

Pet stood at the door of the Johnson's, arms still outstretched holding the bag open. Tim looked around to make sure no one could see him and slipped his t-shirt off over his head and threw it into the sack. He felt weird being watched by Pet, but the quicker he stripped, the quicker he could get inside and hide. He used his feet to remove his socks, and then removed his shorts. His shorts were still dripping, and he could smell the stale water on them. Once all bagged, Pet placed the bag down and looked over her shoulder. Noting that the newspaper wasn't yet present, she asked Tim to stay on the doorstep. He felt exposed in only his boxer shorts, and the hot weather was causing them to steam.

"Alright mate?" came the voice of Marty from behind him. "What are you doing out here like that?"

"I'll tell you later, just get me inside."

"The doors open."

"I know, but I'm waiting for mum to put some paper down."

"Why have you got a dog?" Marty asked, pointing towards Adam who was now laying in the sun behind the green recycling bin, the mud on his fur quickly turning clay-like.

"It's the one mum made me walk. We fell in the river."

"Want help cleaning him?"

"Would be good thanks. Where have you been anyway?"

"Just to town. I was told to go outside whilst they had their meeting."

"What was it about?"

"The 'rivals' apparently."

Tim was confused as to what was going on now. All he did know was that he was stood outside in bright yellow boxer shorts, a muddy dog nearby and starting to feel a bit self-conscious. He was thankful that Marty had offered to clean the dog. He didn't think it could get any worse until the door reopened fully, but instead of Pat, Pet or his mum, Leo stood there.

"What are you doing here?" Tim asked.

"Got here early and your mum said I could come in and wait," he replied, smiling.

FIFTEEN

In the Johnson's hall, old newspapers now formed a path towards the stairs, and then up towards the bathroom. Tim ran past everyone and switched on the warm shower. He stood there and let the water hit his neck and fall down his back. He hoped that much of the dirt would come off without scrubbing but had to rub his legs quite hard with a flannel to get them clean, with the hairs on his legs being painfully tweaked as the mud came loose.

Once clean and smelling of pineapple and mango bodywash, he got dressed and came downstairs, letting Marty take Adam up for his turn at getting washed. Tim took a can of coke out of the fridge, slipped a bourbon biscuit into his mouth, and headed into the front room. The chairs had been pushed aside and it now resembled the headquarters of MI5 rather than the cosy front room, albeit on a tight budget.

"What's happening?" he asked as he walked in and stood in the middle of the room, "and why did you get Leo involved?"

"We know who has been selling the biscuits," said Katherine, not waiting for a reaction before continuing. She had a large piece of paper pinned to the wall and pulled out a wooden spoon to use as a pointer. "You got orders from here, here and here," she said, pointing towards Ash Street, Pine Close and Birch Avenue, "and only a few from here," whilst moving the spoon over Elm Meadow. "You said that the ones in Elm Meadow claimed to have already bought biscuits, which would be impossible, right?"

"Right," confirmed Tim, perching onto one of the kitchen chairs that had been brought through.

"Now," his mum continued, "when you said this yesterday, I asked Pat and Pet to keep an eye out this morning."

"That's why you saw us out so early," said Pet, reminding Tim that they had been opposite Singh Star's as he left for his deliveries.

"Ladies, show him what you saw."

Tim was impressed, and only slightly bemused, at the length that they had gone to in order to get to the bottom of this not-actually-that-big-of-a-problem. Pat pulled out a digital camera and came and crouched next to him by the chair. She turned on the display and pointed the screen at Tim. It was a picture of Pet sitting on a donkey.

"Um, I'm not sure I follow," said Tim.

"This is from earlier today. It is important in terms of the biscuits," replied Pat.

"A donkey?"

Pat pulled the camera back around, before flicking forward a few images.

"Sorry, that was us in Blackpool in June. I mean this photo here."

On the screen now was a figure in the distance, someone he didn't know.

"What are the blurry bits?" Tim asked, noticing that only the middle was in focus.

"I was hiding in a bush," she said, as if that was perfectly normal.

"And who is that woman?" Tim said, turning his attention to the lady in the centre of the image, her back to the camera.

"A-ha!" Pat responded, who then flicked to the next picture, and then the next, and then the next. Tim hadn't seen her before. With the number of photos that had been taken, and with the speed that Pat was flicking through them, it was like Tim was watching a bad stop-motion animation of someone posting leaflets.

"Just after these were taken, she noticed me, so I had to break cover. I pretended I was doing some weeding."

"At 7am?"

"People have done stranger things at that time," said Pet from across the room, before letting Pat continue. "I asked her what she was doing, and she told me she was newish to the estate and was selling things as a way to get to know more people."

"That's fair enough, I guess?" said Tim, genuinely thinking so.

"No, it is not," said his mum quite loudly. "She is deliberately selling the same things as me, to the same people, in order to ruin my business."

"Seriously?"

"This is war, Tim," she responded much more intensely than Tim was expecting.

"Just ask her not to."

"Oh, don't you worry, we will."

"Good. Anyway, I'm gonna head out. Leo, you wanna come to town?"

"Wait a second," his mum said, stopping anyone from leaving. "This is where you two come in"

"Don't bring me into it, please," he pleaded, but it fell on deaf ears.

"Pat and Pet know this lady to be called Anna!" she said, pointing to the digital camera to indicate who she meant. "She lives on the western side of the town and has a son. We don't know his name yet, but we want you two to befriend him, and try and get some inside information. From what we know, the son delivers newspapers too, and is roughly your age. He works for Paul's Newsagents."

"How do you know all this already?" Tim said amazed.

"We have our ways. Now, try and get a message to the boy for me."

Tim looked across at Leo, and he stared back, defeated.

Twenty minutes later, the two boys had left the house, and were dragging Adam back to Mrs Ellis. The temperature had dropped slightly, but it was still warm enough to just be in a t-shirt. Leo was keeping his distance away from the newly cleaned dog. Tim hoped that Mrs Ellis wouldn't ask too many questions.

"You OK Tim, after last night and that?" Leo asked once they were away from the house.

"Yes, I actually am. Surprisingly so. You?"

"Yeh I'm ok thanks. I keep thinking that everybody knows and is judging me though," he said quietly.

"Yeah, same. Although, I kinda told Lydia today."

"Lyds? Really? Was she okay?"

"I think so. She was quiet but said it was just because it was a surprise."

"Did you tell her I'm the same?"

"Nah, that's for you to tell her. Also, we aren't *the same* the same, are we?"

"When should I tell her, d'ya think?" he asked Tim.

"When you feel you want to."

"I might do it today."

"Really? Well, let me know before you do. I mean, or if you don't. Like, just text or summat. I don't know why."

Why did he feel so flustered every time he thought about it?

"Will do, thanks Tim."

The two walked in silence for the rest of the journey. It didn't take long until they had reached Mrs Ellis'. Tim tapped the door, and it was answered almost immediately.

"Hi Mrs Ellis. Hi Snowy. I have your dog," he said almost too confidently, thrusting the lead in her direction. She took hold of Adam who immediately tried running away, glad to escape the crazy people. Mrs Ellis dropped the lead and let him disappear. She thanked Tim and said that he must have enjoyed meeting Adam, having been out for nearly an hour longer than planned.

"I shall see your mum on Friday, Tim, thanks again," Mrs Ellis said, none the wiser as to what had happened that afternoon. "Adam hopes to see you again soon!"

Tim smiled and muttered "not a chance" under his breath as he headed back to the road towards Leo. As they reached the corner, Lydia turned up. Leo had text her to tell her about the dog, and she said that she would like to come to town with them. After a moment Leo's phone rang and he walked ahead as he answered.

"Are you okay Tim?" asked Lydia a few moments later.

"Yeah, fine," he replied.

"I mean, with what you told me earlier."

"Yeah. It's fine. I don't really have anything else to say about it to be honest." He was being genuine. It was too exhausting. He wished he had someone older who could help.

They remained silent until Leo had returned to them, and he started filling Lydia in on the plan that Katherine Johnson had put together with Pat and Pet. She thought it was intriguing and Tim couldn't understand why they both thought it was normal. They say you can't choose your family, but you can choose your friends, and Tim wondered how he had ended up with family and friends who were so out of the ordinary. When they reached town, they headed for the music shop.

"Since when have you liked Mirror Ball?" asked Leo as he was flicking through the big posters nearby. Tim was queuing to buy the Head Rush album.

"I'unno. My brother told me I might like them."

"I thought you liked Saint Monique and pop stuff?" asked Lydia.

"I do, but I'm going to branch out a bit."

"You're turning into your brother."

"No, I'm not," Tim protested, "it's just I want to be a bit cooler."

"You are cool."

"To you two maybe, but to everyone else I'm not."

The trio wandered around town for half an hour, looking at, but not buying, various clothes, before walking back towards their estates. As they did so, Tim brought up the topic of his mum's rival.

"So, are you going to help?"

"I don't think so sorry," said Leo. "I don't see it as a big deal."

"Nor do I," said Tim, "but mum won't let me not do it."

"Like, if you need anything let us know," said Lydia.

"You're not helping either?"

"Nah, I don't like conflict," she confirmed.

"But you two were really into it on the way down here?"

"Oh, I am," said Leo, "but I'd rather just watch it from a distance."

"Me too," added Lydia.

"Cheers guys," said Tim sarcastically.

Tim was disappointed, and trudged back home, shutting himself in his bedroom as soon as he got in. He laid on his bed and put in the Mirror Ball CD and listened from start to finish whilst flicking through the Olympic magazine. The day had tired him, and he only resurfaced briefly to have some chips from Mr Smart's Fish Bar that his mum had picked up from town. His legs were aching and heavy, and his right ankle was sore from the rescue in the park. He fell asleep fully clothed before 9pm.

THURSDAY

SIXTEEN

Tim woke the following morning to a cup of tea on his bedside table. Whilst reaching across to pick it up, he spotted his mum staring out of his bedroom window.

"Hi mum," he said croakily.

"Good, you're awake."

"What time is it?"

"6am. Paper round time," she replied, clapping her hands together.

"There's no school today so I'll go later."

"I need you to go as soon as possible really."

"Why?" he asked, offended that his lay in had been disrupted. Katherine Johnson walked across to his bed and slipped a bit of paper into his hand.

'Johann Johannsen' were the only two words written on it.

"Is this a person?" he asked.

"Yes. That," she said, tapping her finger onto the paper, "That is the boy you need to see. He has a sister too we believe. I want you to befriend him and get some information."

"But who is he?"

"He is the son of Anna, the lady stealing the business from me. He works down Paul's."

Tim let out a frustrated long grunt. "Why have we got to be friends though? I barely get on with people I've known for years," he pleaded.

"You don't have *be* friends; you just need to *pretend* that you're his friend. Do whatever you can so that we can have a word with his mother and sort all this out."

"You make yourselves sound like gangsters," he replied, barely believing the level his mum had risen to.

"No, not at all. We just can't have anyone moving into our territory. We just need you to get his mother to speak to me.

"Fine," Tim said wearily. "Leave it with me."

As he cycled towards Singh Stars, he decided on his plan. After his round, he would head to Paul's Newsagents and leave a note to be passed on to Johann. He'd leave him his phone number and ask for a meeting to be arranged. He wasn't sure if it'd work, and even if it did, he wasn't convinced the children would be able to bring peace to the situation. Johann would probably throw the number in the bin. Tim knew he would if someone randomly gave their number to him. Tim was happy for his round to be over as quick as possible, and there were no leaflets to be given out or any other delays that could be foreseen.

All went to plan until he got Paul's Newsagents to deliver the note. He put his bike against a lamppost and turned to head inside when Adam the Terrier ran up to him and started begging for attention. Tim was already sick of this dog and knew that he would haunt him every time that he had something to do. He had to think of a way to get out of having to walk him again on Friday. Even though it was his mums turn to take him out, all the havoc that was being caused with Anna led him to believe that he would be burdened with him again.

"Hello Tim," said Mrs Ellis cheerfully.

"Hi," he responded, flatly.

"Look how excited Adam is to see you!" she said as Adam stood on his hind legs and pawed at Tim's knees. Tim just smiled back.

"Are you excited to see Timmy, Adam? You are, aren't you. Do you want to wait with Timmy whilst mummy gets her magazines?" she continued, leaving Tim with no choice but to hold onto Adam's lead as she headed into the shop. She was still being very friendly, so it was clear that Marty had managed to get the dog cleaned well enough after the impromptu pond swim, so that was a small victory, he thought.

Tim sat with Adam for a few minutes watching a seagull eat a sausage from the rubbish left from last night. The bird was probably having a more substantial meal than Tim had at the prom. It wasn't long before Mrs Ellis came out the shop and took Adam back, before saying goodbye and walking off. Once gone, Tim entered the newsagents, and was strangely nervous. He wanted to appear like a normal customer and ended up spending a while browsing the birthday cards whilst he assessed the situation. Remembering Lydia's birthday was coming, he chose a cheap card with flowers on and took it to the lady at the counter. She had a grumpy face and seemed cold and unapproachable. She took the card without looking up, bashing some numbers into her till.

"Fifty-nine pence please," she said, bored, as she slipped the card into a small paper bag. She wouldn't win *Britain's Best Customer Service Award* that was for sure, if such an award existed. Tim rifled through his pocket for some change and poured shrapnel on the glass counter, making a long clattering sound. He waited until she had selected the correct amount from the pile and then he slipped her the note in a way that resembled the passing of secret information in drama films that he had seen. He felt like a mini version of a bank robber demanding money from a cashier. She opened the note out, read it, and looked at him.

"I'll make sure I pass it on," the lady said dryly, folding it back up after seeing how little information was on it.

"Cheers," Tim replied, and quickly ran out of the shop towards his bike. Tim didn't think for one minute that he'd ever hear from Johann, so biked home and gave an update to his mum. It was weird to finally be away from school, and he wished that he had made some plans with Lydia or Leo. As it stood, he had a whole day to waste. He could always go shopping and do more for his transformation, but when he emptied and counted his coin jar the change didn't even add up to eight pounds. Added to the ten pounds he had left from the dog walking, it wasn't enough for anything really. Throwing the money back into its container, he went and knocked on Marty's door.

"What?" came the short response.

"Can I come in?" he asked, opening the door before he'd had a positive response. Marty was sat on his bed playing bass guitar, failing to stop when Tim started to talk. Eventually Tim moved across the room and took Marty's headphones from him.

"I'm busy," he said, moving the headphones back over his ears. Trying a new approach Tim pulled the lead out from the amplifier. Suddenly feedback and white noise filled the room at full volume. Tim hadn't got the first clue at what all the buttons did that ran across the top of the amplifier, so rather and do anything useful, he put his fingers in his ears and started screaming. Once Marty had restored peace, he asked Tim to leave.

"I'm bored," Tim said.

"You're annoying," Marty responded.

"Can you teach me more things? More bands, more cool things?"

"Have you bought the CD?"

"Yeah."

"Well go and listen to that and leave me alone."

Tim wanted to argue but his brother had already plugged his bass back in and had started to aggressively pluck at its four strings. Tim retreated to his bedroom and looked out the window. He could see his mum at the bottom of the garden, and Pat and Pet were back as always. They were stood around a cardboard box that said "Jones Cheese & Onion" across the side. Tim watched, half hidden behind his curtain, to see what they were doing. He thought Pet caught him staring, despite his attempts to duck down out of sight. He knew they were up to something, but he didn't know what. Crouching so that only his eyes and the top of his head were on show, he continued watching. Every time one of them moved their head, he would dive on the floor hoping not to be spotted. He was up and down relentlessly. Whatever it was that was being discussed in the garden, Tim knew that he would end up being involved somewhere down the line. He scrambled on his hands and knees across his bedroom floor, before slipping out of the door and down the stairs, making sure that he didn't step on any of the creaky floorboards that could be found on the fifth and seventh steps down. He passed through the kitchen quietly before jerking the back door open quickly and jumping into the garden. He looked at his mum and her friends, all of whom were staring back at him.

"What's in the box?" he asked whilst approaching them.

"What box?" asked his mum innocently.

"That box," he said, pointing towards the rear of Pat and Pet. He suddenly noticed that there was no box there. "Where have you put it? I saw you with a box. What have you done with it?" he said, getting frustrated.

"We didn't have a box. Now why don't you be a darling and pop the kettle on."

Tim knew they were hiding something and was so agitated that he couldn't even form words. All he could do was let out a growl and storm back into the house. He didn't bother to put the kettle on and instead went back to his room, slamming the door behind him. He glanced out the window and saw Pat and Pet hurriedly leaving via the side gate, sure that they had the box with them. He would find out what was in there whether they liked it or not.

He hated this family at times and wished that his dad would be home more. He hated how he had to wait for so long to speak to him. Sending a letter was possible, but it often took over a month for a reply. It seemed ages before he would get back ashore. His dad was much more placid than his mum and he would have sorted the stupid rival situation before he'd even had his cornflakes. Tim was in a bad mood, and even turning up his new CD did nothing to brighten this. He stopped it on track three and left the house. His mum text him almost straight away telling him that he had to be home by midday as she needed him, but he didn't even bother with a reply.

He walked around to Leo's and banged the door. Noticing that the car was off the drive, he wasn't surprised when nobody answered. He then walked to Lydia's and did the same, but it was the same situation. He walked along the road and towards the river, kicking an old can ahead of him. He was bored and angry and it was only 11am. How was he going to survive the other forty days or so of summer? At the river he sat on the bank and swung his legs over so that they dangled above the water. He picked at the weeds that were growing out of the dry mud and threw them into the water. After a few minutes, his phone beeped loudly, which almost made him fall in. Ever since he had submerged it in the brook yesterday it had been temperamental. He'd left it in rice overnight, and although it was working, the volume had a mind of its own, regardless of how often he put it on silent. Ready to send an angry text to his mum, he was surprised to see it was a message from an unknown number.

"Hi. It's Johann. We need 2 meet"

This was an unexpected turn. Maybe Johann's mum was as crazy as his own. Maybe she was smuggling things around with the help of her neighbours too.

"Hi Johann. OK. Where?"
"Mine?"
"When?"
"5pm. Tonight."
"I'll be there."
"Cool. We must be quiet. Mum does not like visitors"

He slipped the phone back in his pocket, before immediately pulling it out again.

"Don't know where you live Johann."
"446 Buttercross Road."

This was the western side of town for sure. Although it was a path rarely ventured, Tim did know of the estate as it had a large adventure playground that he'd been to when younger, and the best hill in Greenwood for sledging when it snowed. He assumed it wouldn't be so hard to find the right house when he got there. He was worried about being caught by Anna. What if she kidnapped him?

"See you @ 5."
"Don't tell anyone."
"On it."

Tim suddenly felt like a cop in a BBC drama, arranging secret meetings with unknown figures. Okay, so it wasn't in an underpass or in a church doorway, but it was still exciting all the same. It would never make the most dramatic of shows but at least he now had something to do. With a purpose, he felt a lot calmer, even to the point of feeling a bit guilty about storming out the house. Hopefully his mum wouldn't have minded though.

He decided that if he helped her make lunch or something, all would be back to normal by the afternoon.

He swung his legs back from the bank, stood and moved to the path and walked with a spring in his step. The sun was already at the level where he would burn easily, and he was a bit dehydrated, so he stopped by an ice cream van for a cornetto and a small bottle of ice-cold water. The van had a large white sign with blue writing stating the name 'Mr Creams' but he doubted that this was the ice cream man's real name. He had six hours to kill before he had to make his way west and strangely hoped that it would pass quickly.

He got home and was surprised to see Marty had finally started to redo the front door. He was still in his trademark black t-shirt despite the heat, but his jeans had been replaced by running shorts. The outfit didn't match at all, and without shoes his white ankle socks were darkened with dirt along the bottom. He was currently sanding the old green paint off and a cloud of dust surrounded him.

"Hey Mart," he said as he walked towards him

"Alright," he replied without looking up. "Mum still wants you by the way."

"Yeah, any idea why?"

"Nope. Something for her schemes probably."

"Probably."

Tim stepped past his brother and into the house, trying not to knock into the door and cover his clothes with dust. His mum was on the phone at the end of the hall and made a 'get me a pen' motion with her hand when she spotted him. He passed her the pad and pen that was on the side table, and she mouthed her thanks as he left for the kitchen. He jumped up to sit on the kitchen side and took the biscuit tin from the counter and got through three party rings rapidly. The yellow ones were his favourite despite knowing that each colour tasted the same.

"Hey Tim," said his mum as she entered the kitchen. "Get off the side."

Tim obliged. "What did you need me for?"

"You seem cheerful again."

"Yeah, sorry," he said, and he mostly meant it.

"Have you got any plans today?"

Tim wasn't sure if he should mention that he was seeing Johann or not. He decided that it might be better if he kept it a secret for himself as he didn't want any more interference from his mum, so instead told her that he was seeing Leo in the evening. She seemed satisfied with this, and then picked up two large envelopes from the table and brought them across to him. He was waiting for her to ask him to take Adam out, but surprisingly this never came.

"I need you to deliver these for me. They have to get there before half twelve."

Tim looked at the clock, the deadline was less than thirty minutes away. He asked what was inside.

"A girl I know has been up all night being sick. You know Sarah from down the road?"

"The party planner woman?"

"Yeah her. She's meant to finalise two events today and needs to get the instruction across. All you need to do is put these through the letterboxes and then come back."

"And they're expecting them yeah?"

"Yep. A make-up artist is heading to each house, and they will know what to do then."

"What kinda parties?"

"Well, only one is a party, I guess. One is a surprise. A couple are having their engagement photos taken and the husband has arranged everything for his fiancé. She doesn't know the theme yet. It's quite sweet if you think about it isn't it?"

"Meh. I guess. Grown-ups are weird. What's the other?"

"A boy's birthday party. They're both on Langdale Oval. Do you know it? Numbers thirty-two and fifty-six."

"Argh not the west side again."

"It's not *that* far. You'll be there and back within twenty minutes if you leave on your bike now."

"Fiiiiine," he sighed as he ran upstairs to collect his rucksack. He threw the envelopes inside and biked quickly back through town, over the river before making the deliveries. It only took him eight minutes and thirty-two seconds. On the way back he tried racing himself and was pleased when he got home in seven minutes and fifty-four seconds.

He noticed that his brother hadn't made much progress with the front door. It was still green, but now with one strip of bare wood on the right. Back inside, he saw his mum moving biscuit boxes into his grans old shopping cart.

"Are you taking them to be delivered?" he asked.

"Nope. *We* are."

"But mum I've already helped today, and I don't want to be seen with that thing," he said as he pointed at the rickety tartan trolley.

"Oh, it's fine come on. You'll get some of the money remember."

Blackmailed again, he agreed to help. If they were quick, he might be able to have some time for shopping.

SEVENTEEN

The biscuit delivery went better than expected. All orders were dropped off, and most people paid. In total they had bought home over £80. Due to him remaining quiet, and for delivering the envelopes earlier, his mum rewarded him with £40. With the change remaining from the dog walking and paper round, he now had £57.36 saved up towards his transformation. He checked the clock on the microwave and saw he had two hours still before needing to bike to Johann's. In his head this was enough time to do some shopping and get home, so he went up to his bedroom and pulled out his list. Converse shoes were what he really needed, so would go to the shoe shop first. If they were too much he would concentrate on jeans and headphones instead. He wanted the kind of headphones that his brother had been wearing when playing guitar earlier that morning, but when he enquired about where to get them from, he was annoyed to hear that they had cost over £150. He had no idea where Marty got the money from. He never had to help do his mums dirty work other than the front door, which was one of the longest running tasks of all time.

As he put the list back in the drawer, he took out the picture of Pistol Pete and studied it more in case there were any details that he might have missed. He was now utterly convinced that it wasn't just his cool style that he wanted to copy. He wanted to actually be him. He wanted the look. He wanted his biceps. He wanted his incredible jawline. Since speaking to Leo, he thought a lot about what it was that made him feel *good weird*, and it was definitely his looks as well as his style. He took his list back out and added everything that he needed to think about at the bottom. Maybe he would tell Marty how he felt. That would be *weird* weird, but he had ages so there was no rush. Pistol's hair was straight, and Tim looked in the mirror and grabbed his straggly hair and pulled it until it hurt. He let go and it pinged back to its original position. Maybe he would ask Lydia for tips on this as if he tried to straighten it himself, he would probably end up with scorch marks across his big forehead. Lydia always had unbelievably straight hair. Sometimes she would straighten it in the corridor of school before registration if she had got up late, something that she had gotten detention for at least three times.

The other thing that Tim noticed in the picture of Pistol Pete was the make-up. It wasn't much, but around his eyes had been darkened. He'd like to give this a go too, but that would be at the very end after everything else was done. After studying the picture in depth, he added to his list.

Denim jacket (or leather?)
More skinny jeans
Converse shoes
One of those belts with metal studs on
~~An ear piercing~~ (would hurt. Probs too young?)
Good headphones (£150!!!!)
Hair gel
Headband?
~~Mirror Ball CD~~
Hair straighteners (Ask Lydia)
Eye liner
Tell Marty I'm gay (not yet)

Whilst he had been updating the list, he hadn't kept an eye on time. It was now somehow closer to 4pm than he would have wanted so would have to go to town on his way to Johann's, but not come home first as he had originally planned. As he was tipping his larger rucksack upside down to rid it of schoolbooks, Marty tapped on the door. Just like Tim had done himself earlier, he hadn't waited for a reply before entering. Tim quickly threw his list and magazine pages in his drawer.

"What you got there?" he asked. Tim hadn't been quick enough.

"Oh, I was just writing some things down I wanted to buy," he said, unable to think of a lie and act natural at the same time. "I mean, things I might need for diving."

"You still gonna do that?"

"Yeah. Me and Leo are going to sign up for some lessons."

"Cool."

"Is it?"

"Well, not really, but you do whatever you want."

"You'll want to be my friend when I go to the Olympics."

"Yeah, never know, I guess. Weirder things have happened."

"What do you want anyway?"

"Just wondered if you want to do some of the front door."

"No way. That's your job. I have to do everything else. And anyway, I'm off to see Leo."

"Was worth a shot I guess," he said as he turned around and walked away, leaving the door open.

Tim's trip to town wasn't very successful, mainly as Converse were much more expensive than he thought. He did try a few pairs of jeans on though, but none were as skinny as he wanted. Shopping for jeans really wasn't the ideal activity in the heat, and once he had a pair on, he struggled to get them back down his legs. The only thing from his list that he did manage to buy was the belt, and he stuffed this in his backpack. He texted Johann to tell him that he would be arriving in fifteen minutes and headed into a supermarket to get a snack whilst waiting for a reply before heading off. He settled on a pack of walnuts, going against the usual Wispa as he didn't want his back to be covered in chocolate like his sheets had been. It took five minutes for the reply text to come through.

"Tim, text me when you're close"
"No probs"
"Are you alone?"
"Yes. You?"
"Mum is here. Remember she can't see you here"
"Cool. See you in 10"

Tim felt uneasy about Anna being there too. The meeting was meant to be secret without either parent knowing. Even though his own mum had forced him to get in touch with Johann, if she knew when they were meeting, she would give him a long list of questions to ask, and he didn't need the hassle. Buttercross Road was the last estate before the edge of town and was much longer than those on the east of Greenwood. Tim cycled slowly up from the bridge, and it wasn't long until he had reached the street. He cycled uphill along the pavement checking the house numbers. When he had found 446, he turned and cycled towards the end of the road again before texting Johann.

"Here"
"K. Mum is upstairs so come now. Quick!!!!"
"I have my bike"
"Lock it away from the house"
"OK"
"Text me when you're at the end of the garden"
"*thumbs up emoji*"

Tim locked his bike to some railings that led towards the primary school and sneaked slowly along the pavement. He didn't even know what Johann looked like so was paranoid that he could be being watched from any of the side alleys that led away from the street. He reached 446 again. It was large and perfectly symmetrical, resembling the house that all children would draw. The windows were wood-framed, and the brickwork was clean. He stood a short distance away from it.

"What now?"
"Wait outside"
"I am"
"When the light in the front window flashes, run down the side of the house"
"Righty-O"

Tim crouched by the wall and tried his best to act casual. He was so nervous that he had started to sweat, and he put his arms out straight on either side so that wet patches didn't form around the armpits of his light blue t-shirt. He hoped no one was looking at him out of the window as it must have been a strange sight.

After what seemed like an age, the downstairs light flashed twice. Tim looked over his shoulder and darted along the side path, trying not to clatter into the three wheelie bins. He gently tapped the door at the end.

"Quick, come in," came the male voice from inside. The door was pulled open just enough for Tim to squeeze through. Inside, the thick curtains of the back room were closed, and even though the sun was still beating down outside, the room felt dark and cool.

"Nice to meet you Johann," said Tim.

"Nice to meet you too," came the reply. Tim detected a slight accent to the voice, especially around the word 'meet'. It sounded more like he was saying mate.

"Now Tim, I have to discuss things with you. It is very serious now, you understand?"

"Um, yes, I think so."

"Good. You wait here. I will open the curtains otherwise mum will know we are up to something. You will need to sit with your back against the wall, okay?"

"Okay," said Tim, finding the whole situation bizarre. Johann pointed to the wall, urging Tim to sit quicker, and once he had followed the instructions, Johann pulled the curtains open, and darted out the room immediately. The sun filled the room, and Tim took in his surroundings.

The room he was in appeared to be acting as a second lounge. It wasn't as homely as your normal front room, and there were no family photographs on the mantelpiece or the walls like there were back at his. Two floral armchairs sat facing a flatscreen television, and the walls were painted duck egg blue. To his right, a small electric piano was set up, with a few books of what looked like sheet music laying across the small leather-topped stool. The houses on Buttercross Road were larger than Oak Tree Crescent for sure. It was one of the reasons why those on Elm Meadow and Beech Close in the east felt slightly out of place. The ones on Oak Tree Crescent were all the same as Tim's. Three bedrooms, a small front room that backed onto a kitchen at the back of the property, which then led out to a modestly sized garden. Pat and Pet had knocked the wall down between their kitchen and front room to allow for their long bookshelves. When they had done so shortly after moving in, Tim's parents had considered doing the same, however the cost could not be justified whilst the children were still so young. They still often discussed carrying out the project eventually, but it never seemed to get any closer to being done.

Around five minutes had passed with no movement into the room. Tim remained sitting against the wall, waiting for something to happen. He could hear voices through the wall, but however much he tried, he could not make out anything being spoken clearly enough. The sound was muffled, as if he was underwater. He pulled out his phone and text Leo, telling him the address in case he didn't make it back home. That was unlikely, but the film he had watched last week involved an abduction, so he didn't want to take any chances. He was disappointed at not receiving a reply within a few seconds like normal.

EIGHTEEN

It was ten minutes before the chrome doorhandle to the clean white door was finally pulled down. Johann entered slowly. It was the first chance Tim had been given to see Johann properly. All he could do was stare at him. The discussion with Leo must have opened up the part of his brain that dealt with feelings because he developed an immediate fascination with him. He was maybe a year older, maybe the same age. It was hard to tell. He was a little bit taller than Tim, which was certain. Probably somewhere between himself and Marty in that respect. Tim started to stand, but Johann told him to remain still. There was definitely a hint of an accent in his voice, and his tone was very calming, despite him being quite direct. Johann moved closer and sat crossed-legged opposite him, and then proceeded to pass Tim an A4 sized envelope. Tim watched as Johann brushed his left hand through his mid-length straw coloured hair, noticing that it was naturally this perfect colour. His cheeks had light freckles, and his eyes were a bottle green. He couldn't help but stare right into them. He was waiting for Johann to start the conversation, so just sat smiling at him.

"Nice to meet you properly. Do not open the envelope yet. I want you to open it alone in case mum sees," Johann said eventually.

"You too, and I won't," replied Tim, sticking his hand out for a handshake. His heart beat a little faster when Johann took hold of it. Tim held on a little too long by accident and was eventually shaken off.

"Now, there is some trouble," said Johann, sounding a bit more concerned.

"Is it about your mum?" Tim asked.

"Well, yes and no. It's more about your mum."

"But she hasn't done anything," pleaded Tim, not sure whether he even believed himself.

"I go from the start."

"Will."

"Sorry?"

"I *will* go from the start. You missed out the word 'will'."

"I did? My English is not yet good."

"Your English is fine! I just get pedantic when people say things wrong sometimes."

"Pedantic, pedantic, pedantic," said Johann.

"Like scrupulous, I mean, like, I get caught up in minor things that aren't important."

"I see. Anyway, this is not a minor thing. It is a big thing."

"Is it about the biscuits?"

"I don't know the details of biscuits. All I know is your mum has done something bad."

"What is it?" Tim asked. He couldn't imagine her doing anything *actually* bad at all so hoped it was a misunderstanding.

"Wait here and keep quiet," said Johann. "I must make sure no one will come in. My mum sometimes comes in here if she thinks I am up to something. When I am up to something I make sure I sit near my piano so that I can use it as the excuse."

"Up to what kind of things?" asked Tim.

"It doesn't matter."

As he said this, he switched on the power and played a small tune that Tim didn't recognise. Johann being able to play piano made Tim like him even more. Having been instructed to remain sitting, he watched Johann open the window above his head, and hated himself for trying to catch a glimpse of his midriff as he stretched across. His new acquaintance put his fingers to his lips to remind Tim to stay quiet, and then he headed back towards the door.

"Wait!" said Tim in a kind of whisper-shout, just as he was about to leave.

"What?"

"Can I stand up please?" Tim asked, "I have sore knees," he added, gesturing to his knees with both hands to confirm this fact in case Johann didn't understand.

"Yes, okay, if you must, but if you hear a noise, hide behind the chair," he replied, pointing at one of the armchairs towards the far wall of the room.

Tim stood up and looked out the window carefully. The part of the garden that he could see was huge. It must have been about five times bigger than his own and was full of trees. He could see a pond at the rear, and a neatly trimmed lawn. In the middle of the garden stood a bird table, with bread and nuts hanging down in feeders from all sides. Johann caught him looking.

"My mum is a gardener," he said, Tim unaware that he was still in the room. "It is the main reason she chose to move here."

"It's nice. Nicer than mine."

"Yeah, it isn't bad. I like it because I can sunbathe, and no one could see in."

The thought of Johann sunbathing made Tim feel very giddy.

"How old are you?" asked Johann as he moved across to stand next to him.

"Fifteen. And you?"

"Fifteen also. In September I become sixteen."

"Ah cool. My birthday is on Christmas Day," said Tim.

"Oh, you are like Santa Claus," laughed Johann.

"I don't think he has that birthday to be honest. Would be pretty bad for him if he did as he would have to work on his birthday every year, wouldn't he?"

Johann let out a slight chuckle. Changing the subject back to his mission, Johann told Tim to be quiet again and reiterated to him that the envelope must remain closed. This time Johann promised he would be back in a moment. Tim wandered around the room once he had gone, examining the small number of materials that were scattered around. There was a magazine about gardens, one about films, and an old copy of "Live Your Life" that was dated from the middle of June. Tim turned to the tips pages and wondered if his mum featured during that week.

'Instead of throwing out stale bread, blend it up and keep it in the freezer for when you make scotch eggs. Kitty, Greenwood'

He remembered when his mum went through the phase of blending up the old bread, however he hadn't seen one scotch egg being made in the last month. He wouldn't be surprised if those breadcrumbs were still in the freezer. He tossed the magazine aside and went back to the window. There were no voices to be heard and he listened to the birds and the gentle running of the water from the feature in the pond. He jumped momentarily when there was a clunky noise towards the right, ending up sat back on the floor. He rose slowly and peered gently around the curtain and saw a squirrel sat on top of the fence post. He watched as it cleaned itself, before it jumped down and sat on the bird table, scaring all the winged creatures away. Tim felt this was unfair so made a quick clap before realising how loud it had come out and fell to the floor again in case anyone was alerted. He stayed still, and when he was sure no one had heard, crept back up and looked out the window.

The squirrel had stopped and was staring back at him. Remembering he had some walnuts leftover in his pocket, he maintained eye-contact and tipped a few into his hand. He placed a few on the windowsill too in an attempt to entice it across. Not sure how to speak to squirrels, he made a clicking sound with his mouth quietly, a bit like how he had seen people call horses. To his surprise it worked, and the animal moved onto the back of a deckchair a few feet away. He continued to click, and the squirrel moved even closer. After leaping on to the windowsill he picked up the loose nuts and then sat patiently for more. Tim wondered how tame it could be and tried to feed it from his hand.

He took a half-step back for safety and shook his hand about to show the animal that more food was available. The squirrel remained still. He gave it some whispered encouragement and shook his hand again. This time the squirrel went for it, and flung itself at Tim. It took Tim by surprise and in a panic, he dropped the nuts inside the house and dived on to the floor to one side. He was horrified to see that the squirrel was now a few feet away on the carpet. Tim shuffled on his backside towards the wall, which alarmed the squirrel more, scared at being trapped in the room. It started to try and escape and began running forward and back at speed along the rear of one of the chairs. Tim tried to grab it when near, but this just made it more frightened, and it started doing complete laps of the room. It bounced from one chair to the next, off the wall, along the mantelpiece and finally across the piano.

DONG DONG DONG DONG filled the room as it scurried along the black and white keys, before starting on a second lap. Two thuds on the chairs, a tapping across the mantelpiece and finally another DONG DONG DONG DONG across the piano. To Tim's horror he started on a third lap, and the same thing happened again. DONG DONG DONG DONG. Rather than go round for a fourth trip, it found the open window and escaped back out into its natural habitat. At this very moment the door swung open, and Johann ran back in.

"What are you doing?" he cried, quite forcefully.

"It was the squirrel," pleaded Tim.

"What squirrel?" came the response. It did sound ridiculously unbelievable.

"A squirrel came in," said Tim, trying to make Johann believe him.

"But he played piano."

"No, he ran across it."

"Three times?"

"Nearly four, actually."

"Hmm," said Johann doubtfully.

Without the guilty party present, things didn't look good for Tim. Johann was wide-eyed (yet still beautiful) and grabbed hold of Tim's arm, forced the envelope into his hand and pushed him behind the chair. Tim was unsure about hiding there, so instead opted to conceal himself behind the curtains.

A female voice shouted into the room in a foreign language. It was an older female voice, which Tim assumed was his mum, Anna. Johann replied but Tim didn't understand.

"I said that I think the wind blew something onto the piano," Johann said to Tim, sensing his confusion. "I think she is coming. Please hide."

Tim pulled the curtain tight around himself. He could hear Anna stalking the room and he wondered if he could slip out of the window too. He held his breath and made himself as thin as possible. She was so close to him that he could hear her just by the curtain. Tim was sweating now. He was wishing for her to go, but before he could think of an excuse as to why he was there if discovered, his phone beeped loudly. It was clearly still having issues after he took it for an accidental swim.

Tim froze. The curtain was pulled back and Tim got his first glance of Anna. She was tall, at least a foot and a half taller than he was, and she looked incredibly angry. He wasn't sure just what she was thinking and didn't intend to find out. He shouted bye to Johann and leapt over the nearby chair and bounded out the room. He reached the side door within seconds and struggled briefly to get it open, escaping just before he was caught. He ran down the street and unlocked his bike in record time, before cycling all the way to the bridge before stopping to take a breath.

NINETEEN

Tim's shins and thighs were burning from cycling so fast, and he was thankful when he finally reached home. He pulled into the drive just in time, as when he jumped off his bike, Leo was just about to ring the doorbell. His cover was so close to being blown. The front door was now fully sandpapered, and he was impressed with the amount of work Marty had managed to do over the last few hours. Tim hoped he remained keen so that he would paint it tomorrow as the dishevelled door made their house look much shabbier than the others surrounding it.

"Hey Leo," Tim said, leaning his bike against the bins.

"Alright. Where have you been?"

"I'll explain later. If anyone asks, you have been with me. What are you here for?"

"I was bored. Mum and Dad are off to a salsa class, and my sister is at my aunts until Monday, and apparently, I'm not allowed to be home alone."

"Mum says the same about me. I didn't know your parents did salsa."

"It's their first time tonight. They wanted to bring some *spice* to their lives. Their words."

"And that works?"

"We'll see."

"Would you have had to have gone with them?"

"Yeah, it was either that or my aunts, but that would have been boring. I told them that I was seeing you."

"Quite handy actually. I need your help," said Tim.

"Why?"

"Just come in."

Tim opened the door and took Leo into the kitchen. There were still a few boxes of biscuits around that would have to be shifted at the car boot on Sunday. Leo took a seat whilst Tim headed upstairs to get changed. In his bedroom he got undressed and checked out his reflection in the mirror. He desperately wanted to be less scrawny and hoped that the rest of puberty would be kind to him. He lifted his arm and was happy to see that there was definitely more hair growth than when he last took the time to check properly. Marty went through a really awkward stage when he was around Tim's age, and in photographs from that time it looked like his head was slightly too large for his body. He'd grown into it however, and as much as he hated to admit it, he guessed that his brother wasn't the worst looking kid in his year, so that was a good sign for himself. Tim brushed his hair, and this reminded him to text Lydia about the straighteners.

There was a tap at the door and Leo entered. He looked at Tim and was surprised to see him in just his boxer shorts for the second time in two days.

"Do you just not wear clothes these days?" Leo asked as he went to sit on the bed.

Feeling suddenly exposed, Tim pulled on a t-shirt and shorts and sat next to his friend.

"You good?" Leo asked him.

"I am actually yeah. I keep thinking I should be more weirded out about everything but it's yet to happen. In fact, I am thinking of telling Marty."

"Woah, that's a big step."

"Is it?"

"Well, I dunno," replied Leo. "Just felt like that's what I should say. If you think he will be fine, then why not. I don't feel ready to tell anyone else yet. Just don't want anything to give fire to others y'know?"

"I think most people would be okay with it," said Tim hopefully.

"Maybe yeah, but I don't want to take the risk," said Leo. "Being bi won't go down well with everyone, and it's probably worse for me being black too."

"Do you get bullied for that at school?"

"Not so much here, but I'm lucky. Some people have it much worse than I do, like in different places. I don't know if its cos my dad is well known with most people or not, or if Greenwood is actually progressive. Occasionally though you do notice some people treat you differently, even if they don't realise they are doing it. They just make assumptions."

"Let me know if you need any help."

"I've spoken to mum about it before. It's been nothing major at all so far luckily, but just little things where you are stereotyped. Like, I'm never picked first in rugby, but nearly always picked first in basketball despite being rubbish at it. Some kids just assume I must be good at basketball because I'm black."

"I feel bad for choosing you first the other day now," said Tim, worried.

"But you always pick me first for everything because we can both be rubbish on the same team, you don't pick me first for other reasons."

"If you're happy to be on my team I'll continue to pick you."

"Sounds fair to me. Anyway, you still haven't told me where you've been yet."

"Oh yeah, mum made me try and help with stopping that other woman stealing our business."

Tim explained that he had left the note for Johann and that they had arranged to meet. He then had to explain who Johann was as Leo was confused. He then told him about going up to Buttercross Road and the piano and the squirrel. Leo asked him what Johann was like, and Tim tried to remain nonchalant when talking about him, but whatever he tried, he failed to do so. Leo soon caught on to the excitement in Tim's voice and stopped him from continuing.

"You're unstoppable now mate," he said, laughing. "It's like, now that you've told me that you're gay, the floodgates have been opened."

"Hey, it's only because I hadn't really understood it. I always thought it was weird that I was obsessed with certain people, but just assumed it was just something everyone goes through," replied Tim.

"I was the same to be honest. I only realised when someone on the television was talking about it, and I realised that they were representing me. It's a weird feeling ain't it?" Leo said.

"It is, yeah, and I still don't know everything about what I am. I feel a bit like a fraud?" replied Tim, questioning himself. "I feel like I should know but why don't I know?"

"It'll sort itself," said Leo. Tim was not sure if or when that would be. Although the two boys had known each other all through secondary school, Tim still felt a little uncomfortable speaking out loud about this. He needed a distraction and had the perfect excuse to change the subject.

"Chuck us my bag, L," said Tim, pointing to the rucksack. Leo grabbed it and flung it into Tim's stomach accidentally with too much force. "Cheers. I've got an envelope from Johann."

"What's in it?"

"Dunno yet. I'm sort of a bit worried to open it. I don't want any more hassle this week, and you just know it's going to be trouble."

"The way your week is going, you're probably right, but I still want to see."

"I do too. He just said not to open it in front of his mum. He didn't say about opening it in front of other people though, and anyway, you don't count."

Leo narrowed his eyes and looked at him. "Thanks Tim, I think."

Tim pulled out the envelope but delayed the opening by showing Leo his new belt that was pulled out the bag with it. Leo said he liked it, and Tim explained how it would fit with the rest of his new wardrobe. Finally, though, no further delays could be made and he held the envelope in his hands. It wasn't heavy, and assumed it was just a note of some sort.

After spending a moment building up the courage to do so, he slid his finger along the seal and pulled it open. He held it by the bottom and tipped the contents onto the space between the two of them on the bed. On top of the pile was a photo, and out of context it made no sense. It was just a picture of a tortoise. He waved it towards Leo, who couldn't add anything of use. Underneath was a small, typed note. He pulled it open.

"What does it say?" asked Leo, noticing the blank expression on Tim's face.

"Hi Tim. Our mums have fallen out. They had a row this morning where your mum said she will make my mum pay for stealing her business. I was told it was nothing but now my tortoise Barnaby has been stolen. Mum thinks your mum has taken it. We want to have it back as soon as is possible or mum will go to the newspaper. You have 24 hours. Johann"

"Woah," said Leo. "This is all a bit over the top isn't it."

"Just a bit," said Tim as he was re-reading the note slowly. His mum hadn't mentioned the argument, but he believed that it had happened. She must have done it whilst he was away doing his papers in the morning.

"Do you think your mum did it?"

"Um, I don't think she would have, that's the thing. The argument, yes, stealing a pet? No."

"Then just ask her. If she didn't then there's nothing to worry about."

"It'd be nice to help though wouldn't it. I'd like to find out what's happened and help get him Barnaby back."

"It could be anywhere, what's the point?"

"I just want to help," said Tim, trying to get Leo onside.

"Is this because you fancy him?" Leo asked, laughing.

"Keep your voice down. And no. I just think it would be nice."

"It totally is for that reason, but you do you."

"Are you not going to help?"

"What's it worth?"

"Nothing. Just cos you're my friend and we have nothing else to do."

"Meh. Where would we even start?"

"By asking mum, like you suggested."

Tim put the note and the photo back into the envelope and stuck it into his drawer. He pulled his phone and text Johann.

He added a kiss to the end of the text, but then deleted it, re-added it, and then deleted it again before sending.

“Come on, let’s go and speak to mum,” Tim said, dragging Leo with him. He reluctantly stood up and followed Tim downstairs. As they got to the front room, his mum was laying on the couch with the television on but she wasn’t watching it. She was horizontal with a white facemask on and a slice of cucumber over each eye. Tim picked up the remote and turned the television off.

“I was watching that,” she said, unsure who she was speaking to.

“Mum, can I ask you something?” Tim said, leaning over her.

“If it’s about the mess you made in your bed then no, it’s fine.”

“Mum shhh, Leo’s here,” he replied embarrassed, before looking at Leo and saying “It was chocolate. Honest.” This only heightened Leo’s curiosity about what might have happened, having had no idea of any mishap. “I want to ask you about something else.”

“Go on,” she said, sounding a little bored.

“Have you stolen a tortoise?”

Katherine Johnson removed a slice of cucumber from one eye and looked sideways towards her son. “No,” she said firmly, before putting the cucumber back and facing the ceiling again.

“Johann has said that you have stolen his tortoise.”

“Why would you believe what he’s telling you? He’s just like his mother I bet.”

“Oh, that’s another thing, I hear you had an argument.”

“No. I saw her as I was driving through town, and she shouted an expletive at me.”

“And you didn’t do anything back?”

“No. I don’t do conflict. I don’t fight in the street, and I don’t steal animals.”

“Well, if it has gone missing, I want to help find it. Leo does too.”

Tim put his hand over Leo’s mouth to stop him denying this. “And you definitely haven’t heard anything from anyone about it?”

“Where would I put a tortoise, Tim? You can’t hide anything in this house. You can’t get peace and quiet either it seems, so if you two wouldn’t mind...” she said, hinting at them to leave with a wave of her right hand.

“I dunno whether you’re lying.”

“When would I have chance to steal a tortoise, Tim?”

"I'unno, maybe when you sent me out of the house to do your stupid jobs for you or maybe you got someone to steal it for you."

"You got the money for those stupid jobs, didn't you?" she added, ignoring the second half of his sentence.

"Yeah, but that's not the point. Did you steal it?"

"No Tim," she said dryly, "I did not steal a tortoise."

Frustrated, Tim left the room with Leo in tow. He jumped onto the kitchen counter and grabbed the jar of biscuits, hoping the sugar in a Custard Cream would help him think.

"Well, there goes that idea then," said Leo, wishing to forget the whole thing. "I believe your mum, sorry. You'd notice a turtle in your house, wouldn't you?"

"It's a tortoise, not a turtle," said Tim snappily, still angry.

"Same thing," said Leo as he took a Jammie Dodger.

"No, it's not. Turtles are, like, wet."

Two biscuits each later, Leo tried calming Tim by stating again that you would definitely be able to spot a tortoise in their house.

"I guess," answered Tim sadly. "I don't know a great deal about looking after them though to be honest. Like, do you just let them loose around a garden?"

"I think so, but they need other things. And look at the size of your garden," he continued, looking out from behind the sink down to the shed. "Your garden is alright, but there's nowhere for it to be kept, unless it's in the shed?"

"There's barely any room in there. She hasn't cleared it out in ages. The shelves are still full of newspapers from the guinea-pig days."

"I guess. It might be enough for a tortoise to walk around, but not enough to store all its stuff too. They need a lot of things apparently," said Leo.

"Do they?"

"Yep. They had them on that programme the other day. The one on BBC about weird pets."

"I didn't see that one. I prefer the ones with snakes and lizards and things."

"Imagine if your mum stole a snake!"

"No. I wouldn't be able to come in the house. What else was on the show?"

"It was boring to be fair. It had this man on it who had two tortoises. Most of his house was taken up by this weird structure in his living room with heat lamps and stuff. It was easy to catch them and put them in the box to take them to the vet though. That's the only benefit. They're so slow."

"Hang on."

"What?"

"Mum was up to something yesterday. With Pat and Pet."

"Tim, stop thinking everyone is guilty."

"No, listen. I saw them stood around a cardboard box in the garden."

"So?"

"What if that was the tortoise?"

"Tim, c'mon," begged Leo.

"No, it could have been. When I went down it had gone, and they even denied there was a box to start with."

"Fine. I give up. I think you're wrong but I'm willing to help."

"Cheers mate. I'll tell Johann."

He pulled out his phone and gave an update.

"Think I have a lead x"

Only after sending it had he realised that he'd left the kiss on the end this time. Johann still hadn't replied to the earlier message, but he didn't care. The first thing he wanted to do was go to Pat and Pet's house.

"Tim?" started Leo as they walked towards the front door.

"Yeh?"

"Why does your mum have salad on her face."

"I dunno. Loads of people do it."

"What does it do?"

"Something about making your skin better I think."

"I might try it then as my eye is still a bit sore from the other day."

"Right."

"Yeh I'll do it tonight. I've got some hummus in the fridge," Leo said happily.

"You can't use any salady thing."

"So, it has to be cucumber?"

"I guess. I mean, things like tomatoes might work, but things like hummus won't. You'd just go all greasy."

"Fair," concluded Leo.

"Fair," said Tim.

TWENTY

The boys had sat in the front garden finalising their next move. Tim had spent a few minutes writing down a plan on the back of an envelope, with Leo chipping in occasionally to pretend he was more eager than he was. Now, however, they were stood outside Pat and Pet's house, ringing the doorbell. They were some of the only people to still have a novelty doorbell, and the boys waited through a verse of a jingly version of God Save The Queen before the door was opened.

"Hi Pet!" said Tim cheerily. "I wondered if you might have a book I could borrow please?"

Pet eyed them both suspiciously. "Hi Tim. Leo. I might do, but it depends on what it is."

Was she on to them already?

"Oh, I am doing a project for school. It's a...." said Tim trailing off.

"Science project!" shouted Leo.

"Yeah, a science project," said Tim, thankful for the help.

"Right. And the topic?" said Pet, her responses seemingly stifled and doubtful at the story.

"It's about the Galapagos Islands. Mutations and species and that kind of thing."

"Oh okay. Yes, I have an Attenborough book you can borrow."

"Does it have tortoises in?" Tim had decided to dig a little deeper earlier than planned.

"Why does it have to have tortoises in?"

"I chose them rather than finches to write about."

"And you're doing this project now, even though you have six weeks off?"

"Yes," said Tim firmly, nodding for extra emphasis. He was starting to sweat at his plan, which was now looking a bit flimsy.

"Wait here," said Pet, who went back inside, closing the door behind her.

Leo told Tim to wait and then disappeared quickly. Tim remained patiently at the front door waiting for the book. He hoped that Pet wouldn't ask for updates about the project as he hadn't thought that far ahead with the scheme. After around five minutes, Pet returned, and handed him a large heavy book. "Good luck with the project," she said, quickly attempting to close the door again.

"Wait!" Tim said, as he put his foot against it to stop him being shut out.

"What is it now?" she said. He didn't like Pet when she was like this. Tim looked around for support but was still alone.

"Have you got a tortoise?" he asked. He was meant to be much more tactful but had panicked.

"No. There isn't a tortoise in the house," she replied and forced the door shut.

Tim walked back onto the road and text Leo asking him where he had gone. His phone beeped loudly, and a picture had been received. It was from Leo. He opened the message and studied the photograph. It was a bit grainy, as if the camera had been on full zoom, but the figure in the middle was unmistakable. Pat could be seen through the gaps in their back fence, and she was crouched down over a cardboard box. He was unsure if it was the same box that had been in Tim's back garden yesterday though as the text on the side was too blurry. Either way, this was what the television detectives would call a breakthrough. He sat on the kerb and waited for Leo to come back. When he arrived, Leo sat next to him.

"I think you might actually be right," Leo said.

"I told you!" Tim replied, almost shouting. "We need to steal it back."

"How?"

"Um, I don't know yet."

"I don't think it will be here for long."

"They're not going to dump it surely?" worried Leo.

"I doubt it. Even those two aren't that mad. The thing is though, as I was watching, Pat picked the box up and carried it out the back gate."

"Did she see you?"

"I don't think so. I hid behind some branches."

"Good, good. Leo, what are you doing tonight?"

"Dinner with the fam. Why?"

"Was gonna see if you wanted to help plan to get it back."

"But we don't know where it's been taken?"

"I know exactly where they would take it. I'll text you in a bit."

Tim was back in his bedroom and brainstorming on a notepad. Leo had returned home for food once he knew his parents would be back from dancing. He had known Pat and Pet long enough that he could second guess what they were going to do in most situations. He took out his pad and wrote OPERATION BARNABY across the top in felt tip, using a different colour for each letter. From this he drew two lines down the page. Each one was connected to a possible location. He circled the first, PET LADY, in red pen as this was the most likely scenario. He had spoken to Pat and Pet previously about pets when he had owned guinea pigs, and he had learnt they knew Pet Lady who lived in the west of town. This friend took in many stray pets, and Tim had been taken to their house on numerous occasions to look at all creatures great and small when he was younger. He hadn't been across there for a long time though but knew that if there was a tortoise to be looked after, this was where it would have gone to. He'd kept Johann fully up to date and had apologised a few times about the havoc that he had caused when sneaking about his house. Johann remained a bit distant and kept providing a countdown with each text. The latest text informed him there was now only twenty hours until the deadline. Tim was annoyed that he had started the countdown when he had been given the envelope and not when he had opened it. He was also a bit disappointed that there was never a kiss at the end of Johann's texts either but that would be a worry for another day.

The other possible location was Pat and Pet's house itself. Although Leo had seen Pat leaving with a box, it may have been a double bluff. They were willing to do more for his mum than they would for him so could be doing anything to throw Tim off the scent. Maybe they wanted to be caught on camera leaving the garden? Pat could have easily spotted Leo through the fence if he hadn't hidden himself properly. Pet Lady was still the most likely location, but he would need Leo so that both could be searched at the same time.

It was nearing 11pm by the time Tim had finished his plans. He'd thought about every single scenario that might happen and jotted down all the key points to then tell Leo in the morning. By the time he had finished he had four sheets of paper. It was all planned right down to the last second, and he had no room for error. Tomorrow looked to be a quiet day, and his paper round was the only thing he had to do. He flicked on the television just in time to catch *Choose That Guy*, even if he had completely lost interest in it. He pulled out his phone and text Lydia.

"Yo Lyds. You awake?"
"Yes. Watching CTG"
"Me too. What you up to tomorrow?"
"Nothing. You?"
"Not much"
"Cool"
"Cool. Wanna hang out?"

"Can do. What's the plan?"
"I wondered if I could borrow your straighteners?"
"Yeah no problem"
"Thanks. Can you teach me how to do my hair?"
"If I must"
"You must"
"LOL fine. What time?"
"3?"
"Yeah. I'll have to leave at 4.30 though for dinner"
"That's enough time ain't it?"
"Easily"
"Thanks x"

He was a bit nervous about having new hair and knew that Marty would laugh at him to start with. It was okay for Marty with his naturally straight hair. He needed to keep Marty on side as he would be instrumental in allowing the Operation Barnaby recovery plan to work out. He assumed that his brother would be in and needed to try and catch him early. Checking over everything one more time, he folded the paper and stored it away. Having some free time tomorrow would also allow him to head back to town again and buy things from his list. With that and his new hair, the summer was really about to start.

FRIDAY

TWENTY ONE

The following morning was bright, and Tim was excited to get the day started. Fridays were always good, but without school they were even better. He was optimistic his plan would work and had sent Leo his instructions. They were to meet at four thirty in the alleyway at the end of Oak Tree Crescent. This would be secluded enough for them not to be seen, but also gave a vantage point from which they could see all the people coming and going from both his house, and that of Pat and Pet. Feeling buoyant, he cycled slowly to Singh Stars and took his free Wispa, deciding that he would eat it before he left for his deliveries.

When Tim had entered the newsagents, Mr Singh was in a cheerful mood. He was whistling as he filled Tim's paperbag. Friday was the day the local paper came out, so he knew that his round would take a few extra minutes today. With no school to go to though, he could take a leisurely approach along his route, hopefully also getting some tips from his customers.

"You seem happy, Mr Singh," Tim said, interrupting the whistling.

"It is the cricket today," he replied.

"I didn't know you played cricket?"

"Oh, I don't. What I mean is that I am going to watch it."

"Where is it?"

"It is at Lord's, in London," Mr Singh replied, "I am excited as I will be meeting my brother there and I haven't seen him for a while."

"Oh cool. Who's playing?"

"It is England against India."

"And you will be supporting India?" Tim assumed. He knew Mr Singh was born in India and still visited regularly.

"Yes, technically I should, however I do not mind if they lose. It is always a good day out."

"What does your brother do?" asked Tim, realising that he knew little about Mr Singh's family, which made him feel a bit guilty.

"He is a barrister in London. He got the brains, and I got the looks," he said laughing. "Do you like cricket, Tim?"

"Um, I play a bit at school, but I am not very good. I get scared that the ball will hit me."

"That's why you have a bat."

"My hand-eye coordination is terrible though," said Tim honestly. "Every sport at school seems to involve a different type of ball that wants to hit me in the head."

"You should come to watch a game with me sometime. I go to a lot of the local matches."

"That'd be fun actually. You should start playing."

"I'm too old for that now," said Mr Singh, slightly sadly.

"You're never too old, Mr Singh. I think you'd be good."

"That's very kind of you to say. Maybe I will one day."

"I'm going to start diving this summer."

"Oh, that's exciting. Have you done it before?"

"Nah, but I like watching it on the telly. They do lessons down the leisure centre now and everything."

"I think that you would be good at that."

"Thanks, I hope so, but I'm scared of deep water."

"Oh," replied Mr Singh.

"And I am afraid of heights," added Tim.

Mr Singh laughed but added "Just make sure you stick at it, and you will be great!"

"Thank you. I'd love to be in the Olympics one day."

"Remember your favourite boss when you win gold, won't you."

"I will," promised Tim. "I worry that I won't be very good though and then I'd want to give up."

"Well, how about this. If you stick to diving, I'll join a cricket team. Deal?"

"Deal!"

This conversation made Tim feel a bit guilty. He knew that Mr Singh was a good friend to have, and knew he should make more time to speak to him about his family and his interests. He would add to his list that he needed to spend more time speaking with Mr Singh over the summer. He was the only person in the town, aside from Leo and Lydia, who had always been kind to him. If he had something that caused him stress, he could mention it to Mr Singh, who would always promise that everything would work out okay.

He left Mr Singh to pack the papers and searched through his phone for cricket teams. To his surprise, a few came up. One of the teams, Viking CC, played each week at The Rec, and Tim realised that it was probably one of the players from their match who had come to his rescue when he had lost Adam in the park.

"All set young man," said Mr Singh, holding up Tim's bag.

"Thanks Mr Singh. I found a team for you. Vikings CC. They play in Greenwood."

"I hope they take beginners," replied Mr Singh.

"I think they do. I saw one of them once and he didn't look as fit as you, so you'll be fine."

He meant it as a compliment and hoped that it had come across that way.

Tim took hold of his heavier-than-normal bag and took it to a bench outside, where he would read the local news before setting off. The Greenwood Gazette was notorious for being awful. The main stories revolved around issues that wouldn't even be of interest at a coffee morning. He mainly read it to see if he knew anyone in the pictures or to find out if there was any gossip from the local court reports. It used to be much larger, however with cuts to the local journalists' roles, over half the paper was now made up of adverts for carpet shops, estate agents and car salesrooms. He reached into his bag and pulled a copy out. Opening his Wispa, he folded the paper open and checked what non-story would be on the front cover this week. It wouldn't take much to beat last weeks' story about a man who found an apple that looked like a pair of buttocks. He had been impressed with the "*Core* blimey" pun in the headline though. Tim took a bite of the chocolate bar and then stopped dead. Right in the middle of the front page was a picture of a tortoise. The headline "WARNING AFTER LOCAL PET THEFT" screamed out of him. Tim pulled out his phone and text Johann.

"You said you wouldn't go to the papers until after the deadline."

Tim was angry that he had been betrayed, feeling much worse as it was Johann who had betrayed him. Inside the story continued, and a picture of Johann was on the second page. He was stood in his garden looking sad and pointing at an empty tortoise enclosure. Tim was conflicted between wanting to go around his house and shout at him and wanting to go round his house and tell him how beautiful he was. At least he could show Leo why he found Johann attractive though. He snapped a picture and sent it to Leo. The paper gave some more details about Johann's family though, and he now knew that Johann had a sister named Hanna, and that they were originally from Southern Sweden. That would explain the accent anyway. Tim's phone beeped as a message from Johann came through.

"The story was mum's work sorry :(. She said it will be worse if you don't get Barnaby back to us. 10 hours"

The deadline was meant to be set as the time they would go to the papers, but now that had already happened, Tim was unsure why Johann was still issuing a countdown with each text. Tim ate the remainder of the Wispa quickly and jumped on his bike. He just wanted the round to be over today now, but as it was Friday, he had to knock on every single door so that he could collect the payments. The betrayal had ruined the round and he trudged up and down paths, his mood at odds with the sunny weather, and he found himself to be less polite than usual. The only saving grace was that he got some tip money that would go into paying for his cool list. With it being the summer, some customers had already left for their holidays so a fair few houses had to be missed. If anyone wasn't in at other houses, he slammed their papers through their letter boxes. His mood was noticed by a few of the customers, and they had told him to cheer up. Tim didn't care though, not today. He wanted to get home and check over his plans once more. He cycled back to Mr Singh and handed over the list of those who had paid, along with the money. Mr Singh was still cheerful and was just about to hand over to a colleague as he prepared to head to London.

Tim threw his bike down onto the front lawn when he got home and stormed upstairs. Before he could get into his room, his mum stopped him on the landing.

"Tim! Can you go one day without embarrassing me?" she said angrily.

"You can talk. You're the one who is in the paper."

"For what?"

"For stealing that bloody tortoise," he said, trying to get past her and into his room.

"That wasn't me. Stop blaming me for it."

"I saw the box. I know you and Pat and Pet have got it," he protested.

"We haven't. Now, listen to me. You've gone and got us into a lot of trouble."

"What have I done now?"

"Come in here and I will show you."

She grabbed Tim's arm and dragged him into her bedroom. She turned on her phone and went to the photo gallery. "Remember those envelopes you delivered for me?"

"Yeah."

"And you know I told you that it was a favour for my friend."

"Yeah." Tim wasn't really interested and sounded bored.

"Well, did you read them?"

"No. I just posted them like you asked. I didn't even look at them, I promise."

"And there lies the problem."

"What's happened?"

"You didn't think to check the addresses?"

"I didn't know there were addresses?"

"I told you there were."

"You didn't?"

"I did. Well, you went and put the envelopes through the wrong doors."

"Is that all?"

"No. That's just the start. I didn't think there was a problem until I got a text late last night. It was from a woman called Sheila. It was her son that was having a party."

She waited for Tim to say something, but he just remained silent, still confused as to the issue at hand.

Continuing, she said "Sheila texted me asking why a make-up artist thought it was appropriate to give her son and his friends eyeliner, eyeshadow and lipstick. I called her up straight away and she told me that she had been in the kitchen preparing the candles on the cake and getting the sausage rolls out of the oven and that kind of thing, whilst the children were outside with the make-up artist. When she came out, they all had eyeliner on."

Tim thought that this smashing down of the gender stereotypes was a great step forward and wanted to tell her that he wanted to do the same, but decided that now might not be the best time.

"I don't see how that's bad mum. Boys can wear make-up too, you know," he said finally.

"I know that, I grew up with older brothers who did all that during the eighties remember."

"So, what's the problem? And why didn't the children say anything?"

"Well, because they are five and didn't know any different. They thought it was great."

"So...it isn't a problem then?"

"Sheila was very angry about it."

"Well, that's her problem."

"And now it's mine. I managed to calm her down, although I had to agree for a seventy-five percent discount, and I know Sarah won't be happy when I tell her."

Tim knew Sarah, and he knew that she would not be happy if her party planning reputation had taken a negative turn. Tim still didn't feel at fault though.

"If Sheila is calm, then that's okay, isn't it? Do you expect me to apologise to Sarah as well or something?"

"No. And Sheila isn't the main problem. It was the other envelope that's done the most damage."

"The engagement people?"

"The engagement people," Katherine confirmed. "I told you how the husband had planned it all, and the theme was to be a surprise didn't I?"

"Yep."

"Well, it was more than a surprise. Look."

Katherine swiped through the photos more and extended an arm out towards him. The fiancé's face filled the screen. Well, he thought it was her anyway, but it was hard to tell when she was covered in facepaint and made to look like Spider-Man.

"Oh," said Tim quietly.

"*Oh* indeed young man. How am I meant to explain to Sarah that instead of looking like a princess, the woman looked like a friendly neighbourhood bride-to-be instead?"

"How did she not notice?"

"Because it was a surprise. She was told to just lie still and listen to the calming music that her fiancé had put on. He had gone into the garden to put the champagne out and left them to it. She apparently thought that all the rubbing on her face was some new beauty technique, and that her blemishes would all be gone before the photoshoot."

"Well, you can't see the blemishes to be fair," reasoned Tim.

"Now is not the time for jokes," snapped his mum. "She almost had a heart attack when she saw it, and thought it was just a big joke that her other half was behind. She was so angry that she threatened to walk out, saying that he had deliberately mocked her."

"Walk out or swing out?"

"I told you, no jokes. I've tried calling her, but she still seems to be quite angry. It's also caused a bit of a reaction to her skin, so she looks like she has fallen asleep in the sun. She's had to take another day off work because of you."

"I didn't know the envelopes were different though."

"That's your own fault."

"Fine, I'm sorry. I'll go to Sarah's and apologise if you like."

"Nope. This is one step too far now. What with ruining the dog, feeding my biscuits to pigeons and now this, you are not leaving my sight."

"None of those were deliberate though," he pleaded.

"It doesn't matter. You're grounded. You can stay with me today and paint the front door."

"That's Marty's job."

"Not anymore. He hasn't made the family look like idiots."

"Says the woman who stole a tortoise and made front page news."

"Just go to your room," she said, guiding him towards the door.

"I'll walk Adam today if you want me to. It's so nice out and I don't want to be trapped in here all day," he added, trying his best to change her mind.

"I'm walking Adam because you can't be trusted to do that either."

"Fine," he said, finally defeated.

Tim was happy to get away from her and slammed the bedroom door before diving onto his bed. His plan to recover Barnaby had now become a bit trickier. He needed to keep his mind focused and pulled the plan out the drawer. The cool list came out with it, and now that he couldn't go shopping, he tossed it aside. He had to get out of the house somehow and needed Marty to help more than ever. He sent a text to his brother to come in but heard a shout from the neighbouring room immediately after, letting him know he was playing bass. He sent another text, telling him it was urgent. Reluctantly, his brother stomped across into Tim's room.

"What," he said grumpily, stood in his boxers and with his hair going in all directions.

"I need your help."

"I'm busy," he said, before turning to walk out.

"You're not. And anyway, not now, but later."

Marty stopped and leant on the door frame.

"What's it worth?"

"Um, I'll repaint the front door," he said, knowing his brother would be glad to not be doing this task whilst unaware that this had been decided already.

"Deal. Now what do you need me to do?"

"I have to leave the house at four thirty, so I will need a distraction."

"Just say you're going to town or something."

"That's the thing. I'm grounded."

"Why?"

"Oh, mum is blaming me for delivering envelopes wrongly."

"You've seen Spider-Man then?" he asked, laughing.

"Yeah, she isn't happy."

"For what it's worth, I thought it was quite funny," said Marty.

"Me too, secretly. Mum didn't think so, and nor did the woman."

"Don't worry about it, they'll come round. Why have you got to leave anyway?"

"I'll show you."

Tim took the photo of Barnaby and read his brother the note. He then showed him the front page of the gazette.

Marty studied both for a couple of minutes.

"Do you think mum did it?" he asked Tim eventually.

"She definitely did. She says she didn't though, but I saw her, Pat and Pet with it yesterday."

"Where is it now?"

"Do you remember that pet lady with all the animals?"

"From Hollybush?"

Hollybush was another estate on the western side of town. It was built just after the war and the houses had large gardens, not too dissimilar to Johann's.

"Yeah, that's the one," confirmed Tim.

"I didn't think she would be still alive? She was like eighty when we used to go round there."

"I know, but she is. I saw her shopping a few weeks back. Anyway, listen. Leo saw Pat carrying out a box, which I think the tortoise was in, from her back garden. If she was going to take it anywhere, it'd be there wouldn't it?"

"Or it could have been a double bluff."

"Yep, that's why Leo is going to check their house too."

Tim was pleased that Marty seemed to be on board with helping find Barnaby.

"You've really thought this through, haven't you," said Marty, silently impressed with his brother's detective skills.

"Exactly. So, what's going to happen is this," Tim said has he pulled across his brainstorming pad, pointing to each element as he discussed it. "At four thirty you're going to make a scene somehow, and I'll slip out and meet Leo outside. We need to make sure Pat and Pet are here because I will bike across to Hollybush and break into the Pet Lady's garden. Once I locate Barnaby..."

"Stupid name for a tortoise." added Marty dryly.

"Better than being a dog called Adam."

"True."

"Anyway, as I was saying, once I locate Barnaby, I'll jump over the fence, pick him up and put him in my rucksack, bike to Johann's, sneak through his fence, put Barnaby in the garden, text him that all has been sorted, bike back home and get back into my room before anyone notices that I've gone."

"You'll have to bike quickly."

"I will."

"I don't think you'll be able to do it."

"The alternative is for you to do it yourself."

"Okay I'll think of a distraction. What will Leo be doing?"

"He will wait around the back of Pat and Pet's, and when they have left, he will go into their garden and see if Barnaby has been brought back there."

"But you think it's at the Pet Lady's house?"

"I think it is. But we have to check both places in case it was all a ploy by Pat."

"Jeez Tim, you're making it sound like the world's biggest crime."

"To Johann it is."

"Can we go back to the start a second. Why is mum involved in all of this?"

"Well, you know that whole thing about a woman stealing her biscuit business?"

"Yeah, she said it was someone called Anna."

"Exactly. Anna is Johann's mum."

"Got it. And mum definitely has it?"

"I'm like eighty percent sure. If she has, then we need to fix it otherwise we will all be in the paper and then other people might go to the paper with other stories."

"Like Spider-Man?"

"Especially Spider-Man. You know how little happens around here. We won't come out of it well."

Marty agreed that it was in the family's best interests if the problem was solved and he couldn't think of a better plan given how little time there was before Johann's deadline (not that this mattered now Barnaby was in the Gazette). Tim asked Marty to check the plans over whilst he went downstairs. His mum was in the kitchen, stood on the counter and wiping down the insides of the cupboards. He asked a few things, but she wasn't feeling very talkative. Tim asked her if Lydia could come over for an hour during the afternoon. Having her do his hair would waste one of the hours that he needed to kill before having to leave the house. Luckily for Tim, his mum agreed to this, saying that Lydia was sensible, so it might do Tim good. Tim knew that Lydia was susceptible to making mistakes as well but didn't argue this point. She reminded him that he needed to do some of the door otherwise he would have to stay in tomorrow and do it as well. He agreed, but really didn't fancy sitting in the sun. Despite this, he was mostly satisfied things were going to plan, so he went back to his room.

"Plans are fine," said Marty as he passed Tim on the landing.

"Cool. So, four thirty, yeah?"

"Yeah."

"Cool."

"I'm heading out to town, but I'll be back I promise."

"Thanks Marty. I owe you."

"Don't worry mate," he replied and gave his brother a long hug. Tim couldn't remember the last time that his brother had showed affection, but it felt good. Some of his friends had older brothers who were horrible to them. They often told stories how they would be blamed by their siblings for everything, and never spent time talking. "Everything will be fine." Marty said into Tim's ear, still embracing him. "If you ever need me, come and find me," he added.

TWENTY TWO

Tim still had two hours to kill until Lydia arrived. He tried putting off painting the door but there was nothing else he could do to delay this any longer. He'd finally read the Olympic magazine from front cover to back and had researched the timings of the new diving classes. The next round of beginner's lessons were due to start a week on Saturday and he desperately wanted to be involved. Hoping that his mum would agree, he had called Greenwood Leisure Centre to reserve two places, presuming that Leo was still keen. The cost was forty pounds for the six-week course, so he counted all the money that he had. He didn't want to choose between buying items off his cool list and diving but hoped that if he was well behaved over the summer, and saved his earnings from Singh Stars, he would be able to do both. As things stood, he could pay the deposit for the course, and this made him feel a little happier. This week had been full of drama, and with six weeks until school he knew that there was plenty of time for more to go wrong.

Being trapped in his room for so long had made Tim agitated. He wanted to write down everything that had happened so that he could better understand it all. His dad would have been able to solve everything if he was here, and Tim resented the fact that he was away so much. He needed the advice of his dad as he always knew what to do. Cameron Johnson could fix everything. Getting hold of him wasn't easy, but he knew that he'd have to send a letter to him soon. Tim took out a new piece of paper and wrote down everything that he wanted to tell him. He didn't even know where his dad currently was. When they had last spoken about a month ago, he was in Bermuda. The time before that it had been Hawaii. He had seen some photos of his travels, and one day Tim wanted to travel the world. There was so much to see outside of Greenwood and Tim wanted to see it all.

Whilst writing, Tim had fallen asleep on his bed, partly due to exhaustion from the heat of another summer day. He was only woken when Lydia had called him to say that she was outside. Annoyed that he had failed to start painting the front door, he stood up quickly, sprayed on some deodorant and went to head downstairs. The way he had slept meant that he had a large red crease down the left side of his face. He looked in the mirror and pressed it with his palm, but it didn't make it change at all. He pulled at his hair, but it also just stayed motionless. All he wanted was a straight style similar to Marty's, pushed across his head at the front to hide his forehead. He didn't even care what his mum would say. She must have gone through all these sporadic fashion changes with Marty anyway.

"Hi Lyds," said Tim as he opened the front door. "I'm painting it later," he said when he saw her pick at the last bits of green gloss that remained on it.

"You good?" she asked as she entered.

"Yep. Looking forward to my makeover!"

"Just to warn you, I'm not very good at doing other peoples' hair. I've only just managed to sort mine properly."

"Yours is good though," said Tim. "You can't make mine any worse, let's just put it that way."

"True," she said. "Where are we doing it?"

"I was going to say my bedroom, but mum would definitely walk in and we aren't talking, so how about the shed?"

"Is there room?"

"There will be when I move the bikes to the side. Plus, it has plugs in there from when dad does his DIY."

"How is he by the way?"

"Fine as far as I know. I've just written a letter to him."

"Did you tell him about the dog?"

"Yeah. And the disco. Most things really."

"Make sure you tell him about the biscuits," she said, still seeing the funny side.

"No need, mum will have that covered in her letter."

"She is writing as well? What have you done?"

"I'll tell you in a minute."

"Why don't you ever phone your dad?"

"He does call occasionally when he can, but because of his work it's not always possible. He likes getting letters as he can keep them as a reminder of home."

"That's sweet," said Lydia.

"He's always been like that. Him and mum even used to do love letters to each other even though mobile phones existed."

"I can't remember the last time I wrote a letter."

"Without dad I think it would have been a couple of years for me at least. I wrote off to a magazine to get some free sunglasses."

The pair walked to the garden. Tim's bike was still on the front lawn so it was perfect for an easy getaway for Operation Barnaby. They moved the remaining two bikes against the back shelves of the shed. Dust hung in the air in front of a solitary lightbulb, the sun weakly coming through the dirty windows. As the pair started clearing a space in the centre of the shed, Tim told Lydia everything. Like Marty, she found the make-up incidents humorous. Tim also had to explain the situation about

Barnaby for the second time that day, but he promised that she still wouldn't have to be involved unless she really wanted to. She confirmed that she didn't. Lydia thought that his mum was telling the truth anyway, so he was glad to keep her out of this one. Before she had arrived, he'd put on his new belt and was pleased when Lydia noticed it. She even said it looked cool. He knew it. He couldn't wait for the full transformation.

"Right, sit down," she said to him once there was enough room. Tim sat on an upturned bucket. She held her straighteners in one hand whilst they reached the optimum temperature. There was no mirror in the shed, so Tim put his entire faith in her to do the right thing. He tensed up as she pulled on the first part of his hair, clamping the straighteners to the right side of his fringe, and moving them along slowly.

"Don't burn me."

"I won't if you just relax and sit still."

"Sorry."

He remained as calm as possible but was sweating immensely from the heat that was being radiated onto him. There was something about the situation that meant the conversation fell into the realms of small talk, exactly like it would be if she was an actual hairdresser with him as a customer. They discussed the weather, the news and finally holidays. Lydia's family always went on really nice holidays, mainly around Brittany in France where they had friends. She told him that she would like to retire there one day. Tim thought that it did sound peaceful over there, but making retirement plans when you weren't even sixteen was a bit extreme. She was due to go away in less than two weeks as a late birthday treat and would be away for a whole fortnight. It would be odd not having her around. More to the point, if she was away, who would straighten his hair? He couldn't let Leo do it. All Leo does is clipper his every other week. He would not have the skills to carry out the task. He decided that he would ask Marty. All in all, it took just over half an hour of pulling, clamping, and combing before Lydia declared that the job was complete. He turned around to her, and she crouched down so that she was at his eye level.

"Not bigging myself up or anything," she said, "but I think I've done a great job. You look a couple of years older like this."

"It doesn't look *too* different, does it?" he questioned.

"Yes. It's very different, but it makes you, I dunno, look older and prettier? Is that too harsh?"

Tim smiled. "Nah that's cool. That's the whole point of anything isn't it? Everyone wants to be prettier."

"I guess. You'll have all the boys after you at school with it like this."

"I hope so," he laughed back. "Also," he continued, "at our age it's all just messing about isn't it. Neither of us have a potential husband at our school yet, do we?"

"Maybe not. Like, I mean, does your brother have a girlfriend yet?"

"Not that I know of, but I doubt he would tell me even if he did. Marty tells me nothing!"

"True. I guess brothers are probably more secretive than sisters, aren't they?"

Tim went to continue but was cut-off.

"Hang on. What did you mean by *not at our school*?" she asked.

"Oh nothing...I was just...I just was saying that you were right."

"I've known you long enough Tim. Who is it?"

"It's no one, honestly," he replied, feeling a little embarrassed, sinking his body lower onto the bucket and sitting on his hands.

"I won't judge you Tim. Tell me who it is."

"Fine. But be nice okay. Follow me."

Tim stood up and led Lydia into the garden. He then grabbed hold of Lydia's hand and dragged her behind him into the house, his pace quicker than normal.

"Where are we going?" she asked him as she struggled to keep up.

"I'm not going to tell you but show you."

"He's in your house?"

"No, no, no. I have a picture of him."

"How?"

"From the paper."

"The paper? Who is it?"

"His name is Johann. He's the one who owns Barnaby."

"Woah, you can't ask him out. Your families hate each other. It'll be like Romeo and Juliet or something."

"They don't hate each other, it's just we both have odd mums, so if you think of it that way, we both have a lot in common."

Lydia followed Tim into his room and was told to sit on the dinosaur bedsheets. Tim rummaged around his drawer for the gazette. He opened it up and passed it to her and waited for a reaction.

"He looks nice," she said. "Is he into you too?"

"I doubt it. I had to run out his house because of the squirrel."

"What squirrel?"

"I can't be bothered to explain now," Tim said honestly, just as he had said to Leo. He moved across to his mirror to check out his new hair. Lydia had done a great job and it was exactly what he had hoped. She was right too; it did make him look a bit older. He ran his fingers through it and was happy to see it flopped back into position so that the fringe fell just above his eyebrows. All he needed was the jacket and the jeans and he could pull off a new look properly.

"Lydia?" he said after a short while admiring himself, "what do you think I'd look like with eyeliner?"

"Eyeliner? You probably won't be allowed it at school, but I have some with me if you'd like to find out."

"Why not. Might as well test it out. Can you put it on for me please?"

"Come here then. Just to warn you though it's only a free sample that I pulled off the cover of one my mums' magazines."

Tim sat crossed legged opposite her and allowed her to start. She opened his right eye using her thumb and forefinger and stuck her tongue out of the corner of her mouth. She always did this when concentrating. Tim had noticed it in their first ever geography lesson together when she was carefully tracing the outlines of European countries.

Each time the tip of the eyeliner came near to his eye, he would back away.

"Look, I can't do it if you keep moving away," she complained

"It's hard cos I keep thinking you're going to touch my eyeball and it makes me squeamish."

"Well, I will get your eye if you keep moving your head. Just sit on your hands and think about something else."

Tim did as he was told. All he could think about was Johann. He concluded that Johann would love the eyeliner so tried his best to remain in one place. He was doing quite well at being frozen, however he was now making an odd humming noise out of nervousness with each stroke. Lydia decided to ignore this as otherwise she would never finish the job.

"You still haven't told me about my birthday thing that you've planned yet," Lydia reminded him. He had forgotten all about how he used this as an excuse, and just told her that she had to keep Tuesday free the following week. She pushed for more details, but as he didn't have any, he just told her to be patient. He'd try and get Leo to help with this in return for him organising the diving.

"Right, okay, one eye is done. What do you think?" she said a few moments later. Tim turned and looked in his mirror again. He wasn't sure. It was so different, and when only half done it made it look as if he had been in a fight. "It will look better when the other one is done so turn around and let me at it. I've only got a few minutes until I have to head home."

Tim checked the clock and it had just gone past 4.20pm. There were only ten minutes before Operation Barnaby was due to start. He hummed louder and louder as his friend started rushing through the application to his left eye.

"Don't slip," he asked, a bit worried.

"Just be quiet and I won't. I'm nearly there now anyway," she replied.

Two more touches later and she sat back. "Done!" she exclaimed. He turned back to the mirror. Tim didn't really know whether he liked it or not. On one hand it was cool, especially with the hair too. On the other hand, he noticed that it made him resemble his mum a little too much, which he didn't want. He was about to ask Lydia's opinion when a loud shout echoed around the house, right on time.

TWENTY THREE

"GET OUT! GET OUT!" bellowed the voice of Marty from the bottom of the stairs. It was four thirty now and Tim quickly jumped from the chair and threw his rucksack on his back and his trainers on his feet. Marty had kept his side of the bargain and was being very convincing. He didn't know what technique he had used to distract everyone yet, but there was a perfect opportunity for Tim to leave the house and he couldn't hang around if the plan was going to work.

"Lydia, quick, grab your stuff," he said, trying to hurry her out with him.

"What's going on?"

"I told you. Marty's giving me an opportunity to get out so I can meet Leo and rescue Barnaby."

"OK I'm coming. Let me just get my stuff,"

Tim waited until Lydia had thrown everything back into her bag, bouncing from one foot to the other impatiently.

"I need to grab my straighteners from the shed," she said in a panic.

"There's no time. Mum will see me. I'll bring them round later, just get out quickly!"

She followed him out the door and he ran down the stairs two at a time. He saw Marty at the other end of the downstairs hallway on the phone and shouted thanks over his shoulder at him.

"Tim!" he shouted after his brother, but Tim couldn't waste any time. Lydia followed at speed just behind him as they flew out the front door and into the garden. Luckily the front door had been wide open. Pat and Pet were running across the road towards them, and Tim stood aside to let them past so that he didn't get bowled over.

"Perfect!" said Tim, as he grabbed his bike from the lawn.

"I have to go but keep me updated won't you," Lydia shouted as he started to pedal away.

"Sure thing!" he replied, and he headed down the road.

As he reached the alleyway, he was glad to see Leo was already in place, leaning against the lamppost that stood towards the middle of the path, his bike half falling into the hedge that ran alongside. Leo waved to Lydia in the distance, and then fell silent as he saw Tim.

"You ready Leo? We might not have long."

"What the hell has happened to you?"

"Oh, it's my new style. Do you like it?"

"It's...different," he said expressionless.

"Good different or bad different?"

"Just *different* different."

Tim made a note to bring this topic up again later, but there was too little time to discuss it now. He hoped it would still look good by the time he had made it back home.

"Right, you know what you have to do yeah?"

"Go around the back of Pat and Pet's, find the tortoise, collect the tortoise, take it to Johann's."

"Exactly. Whilst you're doing that, I'll go to the Pet Lady's house and do the same there."

"And if there isn't a tortoise?"

"Well, it will be at one of them, I think. If not, we will work something else out. Text me when you know, and I'll do the same."

Leo put both thumbs up and then collected his bike, before cycling slowly towards the path that ran behind the houses opposite, waiting in the position that he had been in when he had taken the photo of the box earlier. Tim shouted "text me!" again before he went out of earshot and headed off in the other direction.

The quickest route to Hollybush was through town, over the bridge and up the large hill, turning right before you got to Buttercross Road. If the tortoise was indeed at the Pet Lady's house, at least there wouldn't be far to carry it back to Johann's. All the way into town Tim started begging for his plan to work under his breath. Before the sun set that evening, he could have sorted the situation and got into Johann's good books. He could then sleep easy, safe in the knowledge that the week from hell was over. Everything had to run smoothly, but it wasn't long before the first obstacle appeared. Without wanting to waste time, he had stayed on his bike through the pedestrianised streets where the main shops were. As it was the school holidays, town had remained busier than a normal Friday. It hadn't returned its usual late-afternoon peacefulness as the shops started to close. A police officer had been coming out of the butchers' shop on the corner, and as Tim passed by, his handlebars caught his carrier bag, causing the policeman to drop the bag and for the contents to become wrapped around his wheel before being spilled across the pavement. Tim stopped and helped him pick up a selection of sausages, all of which were now probably ruined. He wanted to get away as quick as possible, but the officer looked at him disapprovingly, giving him a lecture on why it was important to only cycle in designated areas. Tim apologised a few times, said yes in the right places, and when he was finally let go, he had to walk with his bike until he was out of view. He was worried about losing time so attempted to speed walk, but due to his clumsiness the pedal crashed into his shin a couple of times causing pain to bolt through his body. Just before he reached the main road towards the bridge he was stopped again. This time Katie stood in front of him. She always appeared at the most inconvenient times. She twiddled one of the two pigtails that her hair had been put in.

"What's happened with your hair?" she asked sarcastically.

"New style," he replied.

"I don't like it."

"I didn't do it for you."

He needed to get on his way, but Katie kept blocking him.

"Eyeliner doesn't look good on you either," she said.

"Again, not for your benefit."

"I'm just saying. It makes you look like a goth."

"Well, I'm not. I'm a rocker."

"Since when?"

"Ages. Just I don't wear it at school."

"What else are you going to do? Get a tattoo?"

"No, they hurt."

"You're such a wimp."

"Do you have one?"

"No."

"Well then. Now get out my way."

Katie went to hold his handlebars, but he pushed her aside, catching the wheel of the bike on her summer dress. She was angered at the stain that appeared by the hem, so he cycled off before she could try and grab hold of him again. He heard her shout 'freak' as he started to speed away. He could feel blood trickling down his shin by now. As he approached the bridge, two fire engines hurtled past a few feet away with their sirens blazing and lights flashing, giving him a flashback to being stuck in the stream. Trying to remain calm, he put his head down and powered into the west of Greenwood.

He arrived at Hollybush ten minutes later. Sweat was pouring down his forehead, and after he rubbed his face with his hand, he noticed black streaks of eyeliner on his palm. He didn't even want to think about what state he was in. Any passer-by might think he was troubled. As he didn't come to this part of town that often, he needed to remember which house was his target. Cycling up and down might raise suspicion, so he locked his bike against a lamppost and then stalked the street on foot. The trees that lined the road had grown a lot during the years since he and Marty were brought to visit, and he was finding it hard to familiarise himself with the area. He had memories of throwing sticks into the branches of the trees on this street, trying to dislodge conkers with Marty. As he had grown, the trees had grown twice as fast. What was planned as a speedy entrance was now likely to take over much longer, and he was annoyed at not giving extra time for this when planning the rescue. He started off walking down the side with the even numbers. The sun was still high, and this meant that a lot of people were out the front of their houses, mowing their lawns, cleaning their cars or on their knees pulling up weeds. There was an old man clipping a hedge halfway down, and he stopped as Tim approached.

"Can I help you?" the old man asked, before catching full view of Tim and stopping dead.

"Nah I'm fine thank you. Just having a walk."

The old man didn't reply, and instead just kept staring. Tim slowly walked past, and the man's eyes followed him. Tim stopped by a plumber's van and crouched down, craning his neck so that he could see himself in the wing mirror. Eyeliner had spread all down his cheeks by now, and where Tim had rubbed it earlier, it was also forming dark patches on his forehead and temple which made it resemble army camouflage. He spat on his hand and tried cleaning it off, but it only made it worse. He had even more reason now to get the operation done and get back home to safety before anyone realised he was missing. He rubbed at his face with his t-shirt but was stopped when the window of the van was wound down. He hadn't realised that it had been occupied.

"Didn't know there was fancy dress today," came a deep voice from inside, followed by a smoker's cough. Tim muttered sorry, noticing the debris of fast-food boxes and tabloids along the dashboard. In the passenger seat a second, slightly weedy looking man sat there laughing at him. Tim didn't have time to argue or entertain the two men so headed off at pace towards the end of the street. When he reached the junction back on to the main road, he still hadn't found the right address, so turned around and walked down the odd numbers. He passed back by the van, keeping his eyes fixed away from it, but knowing that the two men would be watching him still. He then passed the old man who was still clipping away, and who again watched him as he walked by. Tim hated being watched and picked his pace up. He was becoming frustrated and didn't want to have to do a second lap of the street. He could see his bike not far ahead, and the house numbers continued to increase. He was mentally preparing himself to walk back towards the old man when he spotted something familiar. The houses on the northern side of Hollybush were set back behind walled gardens, with a fake timber-framed appearance on the fronts only. They all looked identical in structure, and only the gardens and ornaments visible on windowsills differentiated them from each other. The second house on his right was where he had to go. The windchimes and dreamcatchers hanging off any overhang in the front garden were the same as they always had been, and the slight clang-clang of the chimes took him back a decade. The garden was similar, however it was now full of odd stone statues of every sort of wildlife imaginable. It was like something from a nightmare. He hated the sound the windchimes had made back then, and from now on he would hate them even more as they soundtracked the horrors below. He hoped that the back garden still wasn't full of chimes as it would make sneaking around much trickier, as with one knock he could alert the owner. It would be like a criminal trying to avoid the lasers as he stalked a museum to get his hands on a valuable diamond.

Tim moved past the house so that he was hidden out of sight of the old man and the plumbers, standing this time behind a Royal Mail van. He watched the target house for a couple of minutes casually. The door was central and the windows on either side were different sizes. He waited until he saw movement, but none came. He would feel guilty about distracting an older person and had seen many things in the news about how distraction techniques were being used to rob the elderly. He didn't want anyone to think he was doing the same, even though he was about to technically steal something from the garden of an elderly lady. The last thing that he needed was to get in trouble with the police again and had to think of a reason to get around the back.

"'scuse me mate," came a voice from behind him. He turned around and a postman had returned to his van, his hands full of packages which he must have just collected from the nearby post office. Tim had started leaning on the van whilst waiting.

"Sorry," he said, moving to one side. The driver looked him up and down, mainly at his face unsurprisingly, before throwing the packages through the back doors and heaving himself into the driver's seat. The van started, and a plume of dark grey smoke sputtered out of the back and over Tim. The noise of the van had provided an opportunity though. The radio had been turned on full blast, and the sound of some guitar band disrupted the peace. Anyone and everyone who was in their gardens stopped and looked across towards the noise. In the window of the house, the old lady appeared to see what the disturbance was. She hadn't changed a bit for ten years. A cat jumped up beside her as she stared out at the van. Now he knew what room she was in, he could sneak down the side path and rescue Barnaby. He just hoped he was there to be rescued. Tim walked past the house so that she didn't become suspicious and hid just around the corner.

Once the street had fallen back to its usual quiet self, he waited for a minute before springing into action.

Having refamiliarised himself with Hollybush a little, he snuck down the path that led around the side of the house. He had a flashback to when he had fallen off a skateboard into the fence down here when young. He still had a scar across one of his left fingertips from the incident. Since that day though the tarmac had been replaced by gravel and this made the chance of being completely silent quite difficult. With each step he could easily go wrong and alert people to him. He kept looking over his shoulder as he crept, hoping that no one was watching him from their windows. He only had a few more steps to make before he could use the large bushy evergreen trees as cover. His heart was beating faster and faster and he had started to sweat again, but finally he reached the back gate. He wasn't tall enough to climb over but was thankful to see that the chain-lock was not secured. The gate itself was solid, and only the small hole for the chain to pass through allowed him to see beyond it. He crouched down and peered through. In his eyeline was a rabbit hutch, with four rabbits in a run on the lawn. Two brown, two white. He shifted his head and tried to see as much as possible with the space available but could not see Barnaby. Going through the gate would be risky and the chances of getting caught were high. He sat patiently again and waited to see if there was any noise. As soon as he had convinced himself that the coast was clear, he slowly turned the handle of the gate. It creaked, and he had to stop when a loud squeak was emitted. He stood still hoping nobody had heard. He turned the handle again and the latch dislodged, allowing him to open the gate just enough for him to be able to poke his head through.

"Oh, hello, you made me jump there," came the voice of the old woman. She was stood in the middle of the garden holding a bunch of dandelions. He had no idea that old people could move so fast and thought it impossible to have been beaten into the garden. Tim didn't know what to say back and just stood there in silence. "Did you come to look at the animals?" she asked, taking a step closer. When she moved she made no sound at all. It was as if she was on wheels. He had no idea how anyone could move so silently. She walked across to him and opened the gate fully. "Come in, come in," she said. Anyone else would have asked why he was stood in her back garden, but he figured that she must have been so used to visits by now that it was odd if people didn't come to see her. When he thought about it, they had always entered through that back gate as children and not through the front door. "Take a seat son," she said, gesturing towards a metal bench. "Now, would you like a drink?" I have orange juice?"

"That would be lovely, thank you," croaked Tim, finally finding his voice again. He waited until she had returned with a small glass of juice, quickly rethinking his plan whilst she was away. She passed him a couple of wet wipes also, whilst she took a third and wiped his brow.

"Thank you," smiled Tim.

"Now, what brought you up here?"

"I came on my bike," he said confidently.

She laughed quietly. "I meant why did you want to visit my animals?"

"I used to come here," said Tim, feeling it was better to be honest for a change. "My mum is called Katherine Johnson, and she lives near Pat and Pet?"

"Oh blimey. I remember Katherine. You can't really be her son, can you? Look at the size of you," she said, still dabbing at his face.

"Yeah. Me and brother used to visit."

"Ah yes. There were two of you. Which one are you?"

"I'm Tim."

"Ah yes. Tim, that's right. There was definitely a Tim. And your brother, don't tell me..." she tailed off as her eyes focussed on the far end of the garden whilst she was deep in thought. "Tim, Tim, Tim," she muttered before finally exclaiming "Martin!" so loudly that it made Tim spill juice on his crotch. "Tim and Martin."

"You're very close. My brother is Marty. Everyone thinks it's short for Martin, but it isn't. Dad named him after some character in an ancient Sci-Fi film."

"Of course. Little Marty. Probably not that little these days, is he?"

"Not anymore. He's seventeen now."

"That's the problem with children. They always grow up."

Tim thought this was a weird thing to say but was aware that time today alone was passing by rapidly. He needed to find Barnaby and it had to be soon.

"You still like the animals then," said Tim, somehow thinking this was the best thing to say. The woman remained silent but gestured widely with her arms at the rabbits, guinea pigs and cats that were in every corner. "I like tortoises myself," he continued, trying to mine for information.

"Oh, I have a tortoise too," she said. "I only got it yesterday. It was found by someone whilst they were walking through town."

"Was it Pat and Pet by any chance?"

"It was yes, how did you know that?"

"Just a hunch."

"I've never had a tortoise before. He's a greedy little thing. I caught it nibbling at my rosebush this morning."

Tim saw an opportunity.

"If you would like it to be taken away, I can do that for you," he said. "I think it belongs to a friend of mine. He's upset that it has gone missing. It was in the local paper today. He thought it had been stolen."

"Stolen? Why would someone steal a tortoise?" she asked. Tim had thought the same many times today, but there was no end to his mum's stupid plans.

"I don't know. But if I could return it my friend would be very happy."

Tim opened his backpack and pulled out a copy of the article in the Greenwood Gazette. She took it and read it before nodding.

"It does look very much like this one," she said. "It would be for the best if it was given back to its owners. As much as I would like to keep it of course. How will you carry it on your bike?"

"I can just put it in my rucksack. He only lives a street or so away."

"You can't keep it in there. I will get you a box and a big bag, and that can sit on your handlebars."

"Okay, thank you. I'll ride slowly I promise."

"I'd rather you pushed it. We don't want you, or the tortoise, having an accident now. Follow me and I'll show you it."

"Barnaby."

"Sorry?"

"It's called Barnaby," Tim said

"What a strange name for an animal."

Tim went inside the house, and it was as if he had stumbled through a time portal. It was *exactly* the same as it always had been. The woman must have spent all her time looking after animals, but without doing anything new for herself. He was pleased that people still visited though as he would hate to think of her as lonely. Once this was all over, he would bring Leo and Lydia up to visit. Marty might want to come also, he thought. The lady told Tim to wait in the kitchen, and he did so as she disappeared briefly. He helped himself to some bitter chocolate biscuits that were on the countertop.

"Don't eat those," she said as she re-entered the kitchen. "They're for dogs."

She was holding Barnaby in her hands, and stretched him forwards towards Tim.

"For you," she said as she placed him on the kitchen table. She opened a cupboard and took out a large hat box, before filling it with some straw and leaves, and then placing him carefully inside. Tim noticed the airholes that had been put in the top, seemingly stabbed in by a pen or something, and noted that she probably has a box to fit all kinds of creature.

"Now, before you go, let's clean you up properly. You're in a right state," she said, as she pulled more wet wipes out. She squeezed a small pea-sized dollop of lotion onto a wipe and started to gently scrub his face. She then started pushing with more force than was necessary, and more force than he thought her capable of, and Tim thought this is how the Spider-Man client must have felt when having her make-up done. Once done she held a mirror up and he looked back to normal. His hair was still cool though at least.

Tim thanked the woman for her help and headed back to his bike. He had forgotten to ask for her name and felt guilty. He would have to ask Pat or Pet when he saw them next, so long as they were back on his side. He looked forward to coming back here later this summer, but under more relaxed circumstances. Once outside, he placed the box on the floor and lifted the lid. Barnaby was quite content inside, oblivious to all the trouble that surrounded him. He was just sat there eating lettuce. Tim closed him back inside and took his rucksack off to text Leo about the successful trip. He stuck his hand into the bottom of the bag, but his phone wasn't there. He panicked and checked all other pockets, but still no luck. He patted himself down and it wasn't with him. He must have left it on the side in his bedroom when all the commotion that Marty had made had started. He would need to deliver Barnaby back to Johann's as quick as possible, and then get back without causing any disturbances. If his absence was noticed by his mum, there was a high chance that he would be grounded for weeks, meaning the diving could be in jeopardy.

He got to his bike and started walking as quick as he could, being careful to keep Barnaby's box straight. He walked down the hill towards Buttercross Road and as he turned into Johann's street, he was thankful to see that it was empty. He didn't want to be questioned by anyone and felt nervous as he returned the stolen goods. He left his bike in the same position as he had on his first visit and set off on foot for the remainder of the journey. He was worried about seeing Johann again, hoping that he hadn't ruined any chances of being his friend. Not only that, but he was also terrified of his mum. He thought that the best approach was to put Barnaby straight into the back garden and then leave undetected. As he came to the front of the house, he was glad to see that the family car was not there. There were no lights coming from inside either, not even from the televisions, and all windows were closed with the curtains inside half-drawn.

"Come on then, let's get you home," he said to Barnaby, hoping that it would offer reassurance for when the tortoise suddenly found itself back in familiar territory. For the second time in the space of an hour he was sneaking down the side path of a house, eager to not be spotted by any neighbours. At least there was no old man around staring at him this time.

Tim reached the back gate and listened for any noise. The only sounds were of the water splashing in the pond, and a few birds tweeting from the bird tables. He hoped that there weren't any squirrels about this time either as he was sure they were out to get him. He slowly turned the handle on the gate and headed inside. The benefit of Anna being a keen gardener meant that there were plenty of shrubs and bushes to hide behind. He could have just let the tortoise go at the gate but wanted to make sure that it was fully back home before he left. He crept along the fence and observed his surroundings. Towards the back corner, on the other side to where he stood, was a mini wooden house, surrounded by an area fenced off with a mini-picket fence. Inside the house there sat plenty of fresh straw, and Tim knew that this was Barnaby's home as it was identical to the place where Johann was pointing to in the newspaper. He lifted the shoebox out of the bag and crossed the garden with long, but silent, steps. After placing it on the floor, Tim opened the lid and lifted out the missing pet, placing it in the middle of the pen. He was surprised but happy when it took off at quite some speed and disappeared into its house. With the task finally completed, he ran out onto the road as quickly as possible, double checking that the gate was fully closed behind him. He had no idea what the time was but knew that it was unlikely that he would get home and back to his room without consequence.

The ride home was much more uneventful than his journey out, and before long he had turned back onto Oak Tree Crescent. He couldn't wait for a shower and a lie down. He would give Leo a call as soon as possible too, but first he had to speak to Johann. Maybe this would be the start of a brilliant new friendship. If everything worked out in the best possible way, it might even lead to Johann liking him back too. Tim freewheeled around the junction and onto the crescent, ready for the adventure to come to an end. All was seemingly going to be as smooth as possible, until he looked up towards his house.

TWENTY FOUR

Outside of the Johnson family home were the two fire engines that had passed Tim on the bridge in the middle of town on his way west. The house looked fine from what he could see, although small batches of wispy smoke could be seen over the roof. The smell of a bonfire hung heavy in his nostrils, and he was concerned for his family. He cycled quickly towards the house and was stopped by a police officer who was guarding a blue and white cordon.

"Sorry, this part is closed off for the moment," said the officer.

"I live here though. Is everyone okay?"

"Everyone is fine. You must be Timothy."

"Tim. Yes, that's me," he replied, reassured that no one had been injured.

"Your family are waiting for you. They know you are safe because your brother said he saw you biking off quickly. They're just a bit concerned that you had gone missing, that's all."

"I was just seeing a friend."

"You should have told them. You have to be careful these days after all."

"Sorry," Tim said, genuinely feeling guilty. "Where are they?" he added.

"They're in that house across the road," came a female voice from his left-hand side. He turned around and for the second time in a week, sub-officer Julia was there.

"Hi, Julia," he said, smiling nervously.

"Hello again," she said, plainly. "I seem to be seeing a lot of you this week aren't I?"

"Yes. Sorry. What happened?"

"There was a bit of a fire. It was lucky that it didn't spread to the house."

"It's not the house?" said Tim, feeling relieved.

"No, but it was the shed. The whole thing has completely burned to the ground. I don't think anything has been saved."

"That's awful. I'm glad everyone is okay though."

"Yes, no one was harmed, and it was lucky that it was spotted early. We arrived in time to dampen all the fences so that it didn't spread that way. With this hot weather it would be just like kindling. Who knows what could have happened if we had arrived a few minutes later."

"I don't want to even think about that," agreed Tim.

"Now, we have just got some last bits to do before we ensure everything is safe. Why don't you head along and see your family? They've been ever so worried about you."

"I will, thank you."

"We do some fire courses down at the station. You should come along. It will be helpful for you to know what to do if you ever have another one. They're free as well."

"I will do thank you."

"You make sure you do. Bring your friends along as well if you like. They're on the last Sunday of each month at 9am. If you ever want to come just head to the reception and say that Julia invited you, and they will tell you where to go."

Tim thanked Julia for her helping him again.

"See you soon!" he said as he headed towards Pat and Pet's.

"Yes, but hopefully not like this next time," she responded.

At least it wasn't his fault this time. Well, technically not his fault. If he hadn't asked Marty to cause a distraction, then the whole thing wouldn't have happened. Similarly, if his mum hadn't stolen Barnaby then he wouldn't have had to ask Marty to cause a distraction. So technically, if anything, it was his mum's fault, he thought, convincing himself. He doubted that she would take the blame though. It baffled Tim to think that this entire chain of events had started because of a disagreement about biscuits. Tim turned to leave, and the police officer pointed across to Pat and Pet's house again. It wasn't really where he had wanted to go, but he needed to see his family. At least they wouldn't know about the tortoise situation. Now that he had returned him safely, it would be clear that Leo would not have done so and therefore had no need to break into their garden. He cycled the short distance to their driveway and rang the doorbell. Pat answered and smiled kindly. "Come in," she said. He dumped his bike on the lawn and followed her into the front room and apologised as soon as he saw his mum.

"I'm just glad you're safe," said Katherine, before adding "you have a lot of explaining to do though."

Pat mumbled that she was going to make more tea and left towards the kitchen. Pet soon followed.

"I spoke to Julia, the fire person," started Tim. "She was the one who helped me in the park the other day when I fell in the stream."

"She must be sick of the sight of you."

"She isn't actually. She invited me to the station and said I could take Leo and Lydia too."

"Whatever for?"

"Just to learn fire safety things."

"Not a bad idea actually," she replied, standing up to look at their house from the front window.

As she stood, Tim turned to Marty. "Is she angry with me?" he asked.

"A little bit yeah. Don't expect to get away with it completely. You'll have to do a lot of chores to even start to get back fully into her good books, especially after everything else."

"At least it was only the shed that burnt down," he said to Marty. "Julia said it was lucky that it wasn't the house too. When I asked for a distraction, I didn't expect you to go to that kind of length with it."

"It wasn't me," said Marty a little too loud.

"But you told me to get out the house?"

"Yes, but only because I could see flames from the kitchen. It was just incredible timing if you want to try and find the positives."

"There's probably not many positives, are there?"

"Not really. A load of negatives though."

"Why didn't you tell me before I ran off?" asked Tim.

"I tried, but I was on the phone to the fire brigade so couldn't catch up with you."

"It's one way of clearing the shed I guess," said Tim, trying to make the situation seem less serious.

"True. Don't you want to know how it started anyway?"

"Do they know already?"

"Yep"

"How?"

"Well, they're not one hundred per cent certain, but they think it's probably to do with the hair straighteners that had been left on."

Tim immediately ruffled his hair, trying to make it less obvious that it had been ironed, even though it wouldn't do much good. He was worried that his mum would blame Lydia for it also, and didn't want her to be made responsible as well.

"Don't worry," said Marty watching his brother messing with his hair, "mum knows it was you."

Tim fell silent. There was nothing that he could do to fix this problem now. It really was the worst start to the summer holidays that anyone had ever had. After a minute of silence, he turned back to his brother.

"Marty, you would have created a distraction for me wouldn't you?"

"Yep, I planned to loosen a pipe under the kitchen sink."

"Thank you."

"It's alright."

Marty was shuffling in his seat, and then reached out and took Tim's hand in his and placed it, still held, on his leg, as if he was trying to speak again. Tim asked him if he was okay.

"I'm fine thanks. It's just, well, can I talk to you later...when we're back home?"

"What about?"

"It will have to wait. I don't want to say it here."

"Cool," replied Tim.

Marty got out his chair and towered over Tim. He leant down and put his arms awkwardly around him. Marty gave him a kiss on the top of his head. "I love you, mate," he said quietly. Tim didn't respond, except to hug him back.

TWENTY FIVE

An hour later, the Johnson's had been informed by Julia that they were free to go back home. Tim headed into the kitchen to survey the damage. Where the shed had once stood was now a pile of ash, with twisted metal from the bikes sticking out at all angles. A few firefighters were still present and were busying themselves retracting their hoses and spreading more sand onto the wreckage. They had put up some tape on metal spikes to cordon off the back right of the garden. He remained quiet as he watched and didn't want to think of the consequences that would come from this. He knew that he was going to be grounded still, but the length of time that this would happen for had yet to be established.

The kitchen smelled of smoke, so he closed the windows to ensure no more entered from the garden. He was glad that there was nothing of too much importance in the shed, but the place where he had started to discover himself earlier this week was now gone.

Feeling low, he went up to his room, locking the door behind him. He was glad to see his mobile phone on his bed, and desperately needed to check in with Johann and Leo. He picked it up and realised the battery had drained. He sat on his bed and reached for his charger, waiting for it to spring back to life. As soon as he laid back to relax, there was a knock at his door and Marty asked if he could come in. Tim shouted that now was not a good time and despite his brother pleading with him, he eventually was left in peace. His summer of reinvention was so far awful, and he buried himself face down in his pillow. Tim only became animated again when the ping of a message coming through broke the silence. Sitting up, he checked the screen and a text from Leo was displayed. Due to a short charging cable, Tim hung half upside-down from his bed and flicked open the chat.

"Tim, where are you?"

The message had been sent a while back and he felt guilty that he might have made his friend worried. Tim hadn't had the chance to check the phone and it might explain the many social media notifications that had come through when power had been partly restored. He didn't want to see anything from the outside world, even online, so he typed a reply asking Leo to come over, explaining that there had been a fire. Leo text back an expletive and said that he would be over as soon as possible. Tim stood up and looked at the garden from his bedroom window. His mum was stood in her slippers below, looking at the area where the shed had once stood. There was no expression on her face. As she turned around, she caught sight of her son looking at her from up above, and to his surprise, she gave a small smile.

Everything that he had planned was now at risk. Even seeing his magazine made him upset, unsure as to whether he would be allowed to go diving after all. He couldn't face six whole weeks of feeling like this and frustration started getting the better of him. He wanted to ask more questions to Leo to see if he ever felt the same as he did right now. Not only was he overcome with guilt about the fire, and about maybe dragging Lydia into it all, but also about his sexuality. He was worried at how things would be different in the future. He was scared that he would be made to feel unwelcome at home and scared at the possible repercussions at school. The people there wouldn't understand what it was like. They would bully him and taunt him. Even though Leo or Lydia wouldn't say a word, he was terrified at someone finding out. What if the people that he liked suddenly disappeared? They could just stop talking to him and not give a reason. His remaining time at Greenwood Secondary could be the hardest that he would have to experience. On top of this, what if his family objected? They were supportive of his ambitions, but this was new territory. He didn't want anything to change but now everything would be different and there was nothing that he could do about it. Everything had started spilling out and nothing could be done to put it back in to this huge great box. He thought that maybe his family would stop speaking to him, or even worse, send him away somewhere so that he could learn to be *normal.* He couldn't understand why he was the one who this had happened to. Maybe the cool list wasn't a good idea after all? He didn't see the point of reinventing himself when it would just lead to questions and trouble. As he laid on his bed, hugging his knees to make himself into a ball, a knock came at the door.

"Go away!" he shouted.

"Hey, it's Leo."

"One sec!"

He stood, and after confirming that Leo was alone, he opened the door just wide enough for him to slip inside, making sure to lock the door again. He didn't want the conversation about the fire with any of the others yet, and especially not in front of his friend.

"Hey Tim," said Leo as he pulled out the chair and sat down. "You okay?" Leo knew that he was upset.

"Yeah, I think so. Why does everything I do go wrong?"

"I don't think that's your fault."

"Well, it feels that way."

"It could have been worse. At least it was only really the bikes that perished."

"Have you seen it?"

"Your mum showed me from the kitchen."

"Is she angry?"

"Not as much as I was expecting her to be. She was probably worse after the pigeons."

"That's something, I guess. I can't see us being allowed to go diving this summer though."

"Leave it with me and I'll see if I can help. I'll say that my mum has offered to take us. Gives you both a chance to have some space that way."

"Cheers. I hope things improve soon. I can't spend the rest of the summer being this much of a disaster."

"Well, it can't get any worse, can it?" Leo said, attempting to sound reassuring, but instead confirming that Tim had properly messed up this time. Tim sat there quietly, and Leo watched him. He took out his phone and sent a text to Johann. He told him that he had done as he asked and that he hoped that they could try and get on now. He didn't want any more hassle between their parents.

"Leo do you..." Tim started before stopping. He looked up and saw Leo looking at him kindly. "Leo, do you ever feel alone?"

"Alone how?" he replied.

"Like, with being bisexual and things?"

"I dunno. I don't think I fully understand anything yet."

"Me neither. I'm just scared that things will change though, even between us."

"Why would that happen?"

"I dunno. I dunno anything," he said as everything caught up with him. Tears started falling down his cheeks. "I'm just confused by everything. Why me? Us? I don't want anything to change but it will, won't it?" Tim said through gentle sobs.

"The river!" said Leo.

This confused Tim more. "The river?"

"It's something my dad says," continued Leo. "Life is like a river. He says it doesn't matter what you do, the river will keep on flowing. Like time, y'know?"

"I think I get you."

"Look Tim, whatever you do, whatever I do, time will keep passing. You can try and put a dam in it, but then, well, then everything may start to flood where you're stood. Dad says, just let the river flow."

"I like your dad," smiled Tim

"Yeah, he's a good one. He's right though. Of course. He is always right. But don't worry about something downstream when you haven't started going downstream yet. The river will flow where it flows. So, whatever happens, I will be in the boat with you."

This made Tim cry a bit more, thankful that he could talk to someone about how he was feeling.

"No one knows yet other than Lydia," said Tim finally. "And she only knows about me."

"Wrong."

Tim looked up at Leo.

"I told her this evening," Leo continued. "I had to. It was sort of eating away at me a bit."

"Ah. Well done. And are you ok?"

"I think I am yeah, thanks mate."

"Was she cool with it? She was okay with me, I think."

"Yeah, she was actually. You still going to tell Marty?"

"Not yet. I still want to at some point, but I don't know how to handle it. What if he hates it?"

"I'm ninety-nine per cent sure he will be fine."

"But there is still that one per cent chance he won't be."

"Tim, your brother is so chilled. He'll have your back."

"I'd hope so."

He wanted to discuss this more with Leo, but the more he thought about it, the more confused he was by his own feelings. Luckily, a text from Johann saved him briefly.

"We need to talk. Meet me at the bridge tomorrow morning at 8"

Even if Tim was grounded, he would still be able to do his paper round and would be happy to see Johann again. He replied with a quick 'Righty-O' and sat back on his bed, throwing a tennis ball against the wall out of frustration.

"I have something that might cheer you up by the way," said Leo, catching the ball mid-flight.

"It has to be good for that."

"Oh, it is. Get yourself ready."

Leo threw the ball back and Tim allowed it to bounce across the floor. He sat up on the bed with his legs out straight. Leo stood and walked across to join him.

"Operation Barnaby worked," Leo said, beaming.

"It did indeed!" said Tim, breaking out into a half smile. "I hope that's the end of that."

"I think it will be," said Leo confidently. "I thought I was going to be caught at one point, but that fire was well timed. Pat and Pet left the house as I got near so I had a good opportunity. Tell you what though, tortoises are heavy. I was glad when I finally released it."

"Hang on, what are you on about?" Tim asked, confused again. "I got the tortoise back."

"You did the plan, fair enough, but I want some of the credit."

"I went to the Pet Lady's house and picked it up from there though," said Tim, panicking.

"Are you sure?" quizzed Leo.

"Definitely. She gave me an orange juice and everything," said Tim, thinking this would be proof.

Leo stared at him.

"Tim, I think we have another problem."

"You think?" he replied sarcastically.

"Well, if you picked up the tortoise and took it back, whose tortoise did I take back?"

"No, no, no, you're just winding me up now," Tim replied, jumping up and pacing the room, desperately hoping Leo was joking.

"I'm not. I collected a tortoise, cycled all the way to Johann's and let it back in through the gate. Look."

Leo pulled out his phone and showed Tim a picture of a tortoise in a box.

"Oh Christ, Leo. Where did you find it?"

"When I was behind the houses opposite, I spotted it in the garden munching on some lettuce or something."

"In Pat and Pet's garden?"

"No, the one next door to them. They must have hidden it there."

"So, I guess we all just steal tortoises for fun now then," said Tim. "We will be in the paper again. Or worse."

"What are we going to do?" asked Leo.

"We have to go over and tell them, and then we will have to get it back for them."

"I can't be bothered to go all the way back up to Buttercross Road."

"Well, we don't have much choice. The one you stole is definitely not Barnaby."

"How was I to know? They all look the same to me. And anyway, how sure are you that yours was Barnaby?"

"About ninety-nine percent," replied Tim.

"Ah," said Leo, "so there's a one percent chance it wasn't?"

Tim made a frustrated *argh* sound and punched his thigh. "Come on, let's go sort this."

Leo reluctantly followed Tim out of the room, and they bumped into Marty on the landing.

"Have you seen social media?" asked Marty.

"No, I haven't had time. Tell mum I will be back in a minute. I'll explain everything when I'm back."

"Look at this first," came the reply, and Marty held his phone so that Tim and Leo could read the status update. It was typed hurriedly, and angrily, all in capital letters.

GREENWOOD PEOPLE. THERE IS A TORTOISE THIEF. SOMEONE TOOK MY DAUGHTERS ONE THIS EVENING. PLEASE KEEP EYES OPEN. IF YOU HAVE PETS MAKE SURE U KEEP THEM INSIDE. PLEASE SHARE XOX

It was accompanied by a picture of the second missing tortoise that week, and Tim was horrified to see there were over fifty comments and thirty shares. As much as Tim hated to admit that his friend was correct, the picture of the new missing tortoise did look the same as Barnaby and he told Leo that he guessed that they do all look identical. Tim quickly told Marty what had happened and started downstairs as his brother read out the comments that had been written underneath the post. Marty was seeing the funny side, but Tim, and now Leo, were not in the mood for jokes.

"Marty, do NOT tell mum. I'll think of an excuse."

As they left through the front door before being caught, Tim text Johann telling him that he now knew why he wanted to meet and asked if he could head there now and collect the not-Barnaby tortoise. In the meantime, they would head across the road and tell the people who had shared it online that it was all a big mistake and that it was somewhere safe. Once Leo had confirmed which house he had taken the tortoise from, he pressed the doorbell firmly. It was answered quickly by a woman in Disney pyjama bottoms and an oversized jumper.

"Can I help?" she asked bluntly.

"We've found your tortoise," said Tim, acting cheerful.

"Are you sure? That's brilliant, I thought I wouldn't see him again. Where did you find it?"

"Well, we haven't found it as such. But we know what happened."

"Who did it?"

Tim moved aside and nudged Leo forward.

"I did, sorry," Leo said quietly. Just as the lady started to shout, Leo continued over her, relaying the whole event at speed, without pausing for breath. The woman became less happy and more angry at them, which they didn't expect. Tim kept saying that it was an accident, however she just kept saying that it was all their fault and that they had upset her daughter. Tim reassured her that it was somewhere safe and being looked after, and that they would have it back as soon as possible.

"You better do," she said angrily and closed the door on them. As they walked back to collect their bikes, Tim got another text from Johann.

"Out now. I will bring it with me in the morning. Don't be late"

Tim wanted to go and tell the lady about the update but was scared that she might have a rolling pin or something in her hand this time. "I might just stay home mate," said Tim, thinking that there was nothing much else that they could do. With Leo agreeing, they went their separate ways.

SATURDAY

TWENTY SIX

On Saturday morning Tim woke up at five thirty, well ahead of his alarm. He planned to be at the bridge with plenty of time to spare to meet Johann on time. His round was always much quieter at the weekend, and he could normally complete it in half of the usual time. His mum still hadn't spoken to him much since the fire, but he hoped things would be put right during the day. Sleepy but determined, he dressed in his favourite dark blue jumper, and smarter-than-usual trousers in order to make a good impression, before heading out as quick as possible. It was lucky that he had been out on his bike when the fire had taken hold so that it didn't go up in smoke also. He didn't fancy walking his paper round at all. As he left his home a couple of dog walkers were opposite and he recognised them as residents from the far end of the crescent. As he passed by, they stopped their conversation and glared at him. This happened as he passed by more people on his way to Singh Stars, and a few of them even muttered under their breath and shook their heads. As he parked his bike, another man came through the shop doors and tutted at him. He had no idea what was happening.

"Morning Mr Singh, enjoy the cricket?" he asked, still trying to figure out what was wrong.

"Very good, thank you," he replied in his standard good mood. Tim was glad that at least one person was still normal around the town.

"Who won?"

"India are winning," he said triumphantly. "It is a close match though. England were two hundred and thirty for nine at one point but managed to hit three hundred by the end of their first innings. I thought it would have been enough, but Kohli did it again."

"Is Kohli good?"

"Oh, he is one of the best. He scored one hundred and twenty before being out LBW."

Tim made a mental note to check up on the rules of cricket more. Even though he had played a little bit at school, he still wasn't sure about half of what Mr Singh was talking about. Even so, he felt at ease having the conversation, and for the first time in a while he was having a chat which didn't start with an apology. As he was waiting for Mr Singh to pack his papers, he pulled out his phone to check social media. He wondered if the post from the neighbour opposite had been deleted. He was horrified at what he saw. Not only was the post still up (over one hundred comments and shares by now), but the neighbour had also posted an update. Below it was a grainy picture of both Tim and Leo, taken from a feed that was attached to the doorbell showing who was calling. The post was again in capitals, along with the poor grammar.

PLS SHARE. THESE TWO BOYS ARE RESPONSIBLE FOR THE TORTOISE THEFTS. KEEP EYES OPEN IF ROUND YOUR AREA. HAVE SENT TO THE POLICE.

Tim nervously checked the comments underneath. Along with all the *'Shared X'* replies were a couple from people who had claimed to have seen him. A few were way wide of the mark, with people in neighbouring towns claiming that they had arrived in a van and had been knocking door to door. Not only was Tim two years too young to drive, but he also hadn't even left Greenwood to be 'spotted' in the other towns where those commenting lived. It was clear that word had got around, and what was a genuine misunderstanding had turned into a full-scale manhunt. His frustration was made worse by the fact that he was only trying to solve the problems caused by other people. A couple of them had even named him as 'Singh's boy' too and he hoped that Mr Singh hadn't seen it. If he had, he was doing a good job at not letting on. Others were saying that he was a Johnson kid. This meant that someone would be on the phone to his mum before long. And the police? Was that necessary? Now he'd have to go to the station and let them know it was all a big mistake.

Tim spent his whole round being cautious, and he noted how his customers were avoiding him. He was just thankful that there were no more leaflets to deliver until Monday as the last thing he'd want to do is knock on everyone's door. Having finished with the papers, he arrived at the bridge at quarter to eight and was surprised, but happy, to see Johann already there. Seeing him again made Tim feel a bit better. Tim tried to hide any frustration about Not-Barnaby, and virtually skipped alongside his bike as he approached.

"Hey, Johann!" he said loudly as he arrived. Johann was dressed in a white shirt and dark trousers, and Tim thought maybe he had also dressed up smartly to meet him.

"Hey," came the response.

"How are you?"

"I have the other tortoise."

"Cool, thank you."

Johann passed Tim a bag, and inside was yet another box.

"And this is definitely not yours?" Tim asked.

"No, he is nothing like Barnaby. Barnaby is at home."

Tim wanted to say that they did all look the same but thought best to leave it. Everything about Johann was perfect. He wanted to ask him a lot of questions just to hear him speak more. Before he had the opportunity to try and befriend him, Johann had stood and climbed back onto his own bike. Tim wasn't sure how to keep the conversation going and took so long that Johann had left before he had decided what he wanted to say. Feeling a bit down, Tim hung the bag from the handlebars and cycled back home. When he got to Oak Tree Crescent, he rang the doorbell of the tortoise owners house and gave a cheery thumbs up to the camera, which was now easy to spot. He wanted to look friendly but decided that it had probably come across as sarcastic. The neighbour opened the door and grabbed the bag without saying anything. He wanted to ensure that there would be no more posts on social media so bent over and shouted hello through the letterbox a few times. The woman didn't come back. He rang the bell again but still she didn't come. Defeated, he returned home.

He was surprised to see a text from Johann on his phone as he climbed the stairs.

"Did you deliver the tortoise?"
"Yes."
"Cool."
"*thumbs up emoji* *tortoise emoji."
"*laughing face emoji*"
"Sorry again about everything."
"It is fine. I promise."
"I'm glad mine isn't the only mad mum!"
"Me too!"

Tim kicked off his shoes and laid flat on his bed, staring at the ceiling. When he was younger, he had glow in the dark stars stuck all around his ceiling. He often used to lay staring up at them when he was feeling off, even at a young age. He found that if you stared directly at one star, others nearby would then disappear from your sight like magic. He must have spent hours staring at this ceiling over the years. Thinking back, he was unsure if it was his own small coping mechanism for stress and anxiety.

Outside there was a gentle cool breeze, and the curtains swayed softly as it poured into the room. He was just drifting into sleep when a PING PING brought him back into reality. Another message from Johann.

"I wondered if I can hang with you?"

Tim stood up and started bouncing up and down. This was it. It was as if the previous whole week of drama and bad luck was finally being balanced back out with this one massive slice of amazingness. He needed to reply. He had to find the middle ground between casual and keen. He'd never been asked to hang out like this by anyone. In fact, no one really chose him to be their work partner in lessons other than Leo or Lydia, and they didn't count really. In the end he settled for super-casual.

"Hey. Yeh, can do. I would like that"
"*Smiley face emoji* Yay. Are you about today?"
"Might be difficult but leave it with me."
"Okay let me know."
"Will do. I'll text you by lunchtime?"
"Sounds good."

Tim didn't quite know what to do with himself. The day suddenly seemed amazing, all the clouds (both actual and metaphorical ones) had gone. He switched to his music app and started playing Glove Puppet out loud, dancing around his room. The rock music could wait for a bit now. He was happy in his pop bubble. As he was dancing, his phone PING PING-ed again from the bed, and he skipped over to it and saw Johann had text again.

"Can I ask you something?"

Again, Tim tried to remain calm. This could be the most defining moment of his entire fifteen years and seven months on the planet. He would remember this moment for ever and tried to remember every single detail so he could recount it to anyone and everyone at his and Johann's wedding reception. It would be held in the grounds of a big country house, and all the guests would bring picnics and champagne, all dressed in their best formalwear. Okay, maybe he was getting a bit ahead of himself now.

"Johann you can ask me anything. Any time. My phone will always be on x."

He was less casual this time and thought to hell with it and added the kiss.

"Cool, thank you. Are you sure?"

"It will be fine. Just ask me x"
"Can you get Lydia to come along if we meet. I want to talk to her about something. x"

"NO JOHANN," Tim thought. "YOU DON'T PUT A KISS AT THE END OF A TEXT FOR THE FIRST TIME EVER WHEN YOU'VE LITERALLY JUST BROKEN MY HEART." Tim didn't even want to respond. He didn't even know how Johann knew Lydia. He must have stalked him online to find out things, like who he knew, what he did and more. He hated that Johann might have stalked him, especially since all Johann's accounts were private when he had stalked him a couple of days ago.

Tim turned the music off and sat sadly on the edge of his bed, his feet dangling just above the floor before typing quickly.

"I'll ask."

He wouldn't ask her. He now didn't even want to see Lydia either, despite her being completely unaware of anything. He switched his phone off out of anger and climbed back into bed, pulling the covers over his head, and letting out a muffled shout into the duvet. He hoped that by shutting off the outside world, no harm could be forthcoming.

After spending twenty minutes recovering from the Johann/Lydia situation, Tim had cooled a bit. The day was another hot one and he didn't want to be stuck indoors all day. He'd need to somehow ask his mum about diving as well. The first lesson was getting closer by the minute, and he thought it would be good to be taken by Flo and give his mum some space as Leo had suggested. He pulled out his list and thought about what he could get in town today. He still couldn't afford much of it, but he would go for a walk around town in the afternoon hopefully with Johann. He put the list safely in the drawer and headed downstairs.

As he got to the foot of the stairs, he noticed the front door was wedged open by a box. He poked his head outside and saw his mum taking boxes off a man with a van. The week had nearly gone full circle, and his hopes that she would take a break from selling junk disappeared immediately. He decided that the best thing to do would be to help without asking, so he pulled on his shoes and started bringing the boxes inside. They were heavy and the first one nearly ended up on the floor. He only just made it to the kitchen table, and the table mats jumped as the box landed with a thud. Around ten trips later, and with aching arms, he jumped onto the side and took a few bourbons from the biscuit tin.

"I've told you not to sit on the side," said his mum as she carried the last box through.

"What's in the boxes this time?"

"A-ha, this time it's something good."

"You thought that the Tamagotchi's were good."

"They were."

"Yeah, about twenty-five years ago."

"They sold, didn't they?"

"Somehow."

His mum moved across to grab a pair of the scissors from the drawer, and slapped his legs and told him again to get off the side. This time he obliged and joined her at the table.

"Sorry about the shed, mum."

"It's okay. It was probably the best thing for it."

"And you're not going to ground me for it?"

"I can't be bothered if honest. It's because of grounding you that it happened," she said, pointing out to the remains through the open back door. "It saves me the job of clearing it out this summer anyway. Where did you go when all that happened?"

Tim knew this was coming, and thought it was best to be honest. He told her all about the Pet Lady, about Johann's house and about Leo stealing the wrong tortoise. She seemed to admit defeat and finally confirmed that they had stolen Barnaby. He was surprised to find that she wasn't even angry and now found it quite funny.

"I didn't think that woman with the animals would still be alive," she said casually.

"I thought the same until a couple of weeks back. Anyway, how did you steal it?"

"I got Anna's address from someone."

"Who?"

"Just someone who bought biscuits from her. I was just going to go and knock on her door and have a row with her, but she wasn't in. I thought she might have been in the garden, so I went round the back and all that was there was that tortoise."

"So, you just picked it up?"

"Yeah. I'm not sure why. When I finally realised that it might have been a stupid idea I was half way home and it was walking around the backseat of the car."

"Why didn't you take it back?"

"I dunno. I spoke to Pat and Pet and they thought it best if we just kept it safe."

"You should have just admitted it," said Tim frustratedly.

"Well, it all worked out fine in the end."

Tim didn't answer.

"What are you up to today, anyway?"

"I'm gonna go and meet Lydia and Leo."

"You still have that door to do remember?"

"I know," replied Tim, having been reminded that it needed painting every time he went through it. "I'll do it this evening."

After a few minutes of watching his mum slide the scissors under the tape of the boxes, he took his phone and text Lydia, Leo and Johann, asking them to be at his for 3pm. He decided not asking Lydia on Johann's behalf wouldn't be fair. Once they all confirmed, he texted Johann again.

"Do you think you could get your mum to come too?"
"Why?"
"If we could get them to meet then it will stop any trouble."
"I don't think she would come."
"If you can think of a reason, I'll get Lydia to come out."

Even though Tim had already had confirmation that she would be there, Johann didn't know this, so he wanted to use it to blackmail him to ensure the meeting between the warring mums took place.

"Okay. 3pm. Where is your house?"
"247 Oak Tree Crescent."

Tim was worried that Johann would realise that the Johnson's were not as wealthy as his own family and then make better, richer friends instead. Looking back up at the table, he watched his mum slice open the remaining boxes. Tim crossed his fingers below the table and whispered a small prayer to himself, hoping for it to be something of use being pulled from their cardboard tombs. It was a slim hope, but even he didn't expect to see how bad it would be. She pulled out a stack of cheap ceramic plates. Each plate was printed with a painting of members of the royal family on. Tim took one in his hands and studied it, before realising they were even worse than he initially had thought.

"Pretty snazzy, eh?" she said.

"We can't sell them."

"You'd be surprised how many people buy this kind of thing. I'll knock up leaflets for you to take on your round on Monday."

"Nope. We definitely can't sell them. Look at them."

"They look good, and the painting of Prince Harry is so accurate."

"I'll give you that, but the problem is that it says Prince Garry."

"Damn."

"How much did you pay for them?"

"Twenty pounds. I thought that was a good deal."

"It would have been if there was a Prince Garry."

"Would you mind helping me take these to the tip?" said Katherine, throwing the scissors down.

Tim smiled. "Gladly."

TWENTY SEVEN

The tip was located about two miles out of Greenwood, so the journey only took fifteen minutes by car. Tim's arms were now in pain after having to carry the boxes of plates to the car, and then from the car to the dumping ground. The tip was one of the few chores that he didn't mind helping with. The main reason for this was that you had to walk up a long ramp that took you above the big metal containers, which allowed you to throw all your waste into the correct bin. He followed his mum, each of them carrying a box, to the top. His mum threw the whole box in, which he thought wasn't much fun. Instead of copying her, he took out each plate individually and threw it as hard as he could to see if he could make the loudest smash possible. It reminded him of being a child and throwing stones into the sea. It was a good way of relieving stress, and he didn't care that it was taking him ages. The sight of Prince Garry being frisbee'd twenty feet before smashing into a thousand pieces was pleasing, each clanging on the sides of the yellow containers. All his pent-up anger came out whilst stood up there.

An hour later they were done and back in the car. Having been parked in the blazing sun for that long, it was like a sauna inside and Tim burned his hand on the metal seatbelt clip when trying to secure himself in. He pulled his phone out of the glovebox and checked his messages. It still wasn't working properly, and randomly kept changing to camera mode. Thinking of Leo, he realised that he had completely forgotten to ask his mum about the diving.

"Next Saturday?" she said when she heard that he had reserved a place on the course.

"Yeah. Leo is coming too."

"How much is it?"

"Forty pounds. I've still got money."

"Have you got enough?"

"Not quite. Would it be okay to borrow some please?"

"How much?"

"Twenty?"

"On one condition."

"What's that?"

"You actually paint the door this evening."

He agreed, but if honest he had become used to the front door without its paint and didn't mind it so much.

"Do you know where your trunks are?" his mum asked.

"I think so. I'll have a look when I get in."

“What about the other stuff?”

“I’ve got goggles. Oh, actually, no I don’t. They were in the shed.”

“Did you want me to drop you in town so you can get some?”

“Cheers. I need to get a new nose clip too.”

“Do they make a difference?” his mum asked genuinely.

“Yeah. It’s much easier. I can’t swim properly without one.”

“You can’t swim properly with one either,” she said, laughing. “What about those earplugs too? You know how often you get ear infections.”

“I can’t wear them as well.”

“Why not?”

“I’ve already got my eyes and nose covered. If I had them too, I might as well stick a cork up my arse and make myself completely airtight.”

“Disgusting,” she said, although she did let out a small chuckle. “Have you written a letter for your dad by the way?”

“Yeah, I wrote one last night actually.”

Tim had done an exercise at school in one of the boring Tutor Time lessons. Some self-titled ‘stress expert’ had talked about how to cope with various problems and they said that writing all your problems down helps you solve them. They said that this was the most recommended self-help method. To Tim, it wasn’t as relaxing as staring at his stars on the ceiling. The expert also said that you then just burn the paper, and everything will be better, which made Tim doubt his medical credentials. Either way, Tim did feel better after writing it all out.

TWENTY EIGHT

DING DONG.

The doorbell chimed loudly from downstairs. Tim remained flat on his bed, waiting for someone else to answer.

DING DONG.

Still laying.

DING DONG. DING DONG.

Tim jumped off his bed and looked out the landing window. Leo and Lydia were in the garden. Leo was pulling a leaf off one of the trees, whilst Lydia was typing on her phone. Tim's phoned pinged as a text came through from Lydia.

"Are you here? We're outside."

Instead of texting back, he walked downstairs and opened the door.

"Sorry," he said, holding the door wide open and allowing them both to come through. Once sat in the kitchen, he poured a glass of squash for them both and they took a seat at the table.

"Where we off to then?" asked Lydia, before taking a sip of orange and swirling it around her mouth.

"I thought we could walk into town, maybe get a coffee or something," said Tim. "Johann will be here shortly."

"Everything cool between you two?" asked Leo.

"Yeah, we're good," said Tim, smiling a bit too widely.

Leo smiled back at Tim, knowingly. "That's good," he said, before adding "What are you guys up to tomorrow?"

"Nothing," they replied in unison.

"Well, I was thinking, there's a thing on at the snooker club in the afternoon. It's a fundraiser of some sorts. There's gonna be a bouncy castle and stuff like that outside for kids, but then there's a meat raffle and also a show by a drag queen and things." Leo explained.

"Drag Queen?" questioned Tim, "In Greenwood? That never happens."

"I know, right!" replied Leo excitedly. She's coming down from London and everything. She is friends with someone who used to go to our school apparently."

"What's her name?" asked Lydia. "Anyone we've seen on Drag Race?"

"Nah, not that I know of. She's called Honey Latté and is meant to be really nice."

"I am totally and utterly up for this, Leo," said Tim.

"Me too," said Lydia.

"It's going to be so much fun. My mum and dad are coming. Do your parents want to come?"

Lydia scrolled through her phone quickly, with a finger in the air.

"Mine won't be able to as they've got something on at the tennis club. I'll be able to come and stay with you though all afternoon if that's okay?" she said finally.

"Yeh, course," replied Tim. "My mum will definitely be there. She never misses an event down there. What time does it start?"

"Four sharp," confirmed Leo.

As soon as he finished speaking, Tim's eyes lit up.

"We can invite Johann!" he said, excitedly.

Before anyone responded, the doorbell rang again. Tim got up and was followed down the hallway by the other two. He pulled the door open and saw Johann and Anna stood there.

"Hi," they both said together.

Leo looked at Lydia.

Lydia looked at Tim.

Tim stared at Johann.

Johann and Anna looked between all three of them.

"Are you going to let them in then?" asked Katherine to clear the awkwardness, appearing from behind and wearing large shades.

The trio of friends moved out the way and Anna walked through and was taken to the kitchen. Johann gave a small fist bump to the others. He was wearing a large backpack.

"So, we go to town?" he asked. They nodded.

"Wait there and we will get our shoes," replied Tim.

Fifteen minutes later they were sat on the corner table of Fred's Diner. They hadn't been here for a while and it was Johann's first time ever. Freddie's, as it was known locally, was all 1950's Americana, with glossy laminated menus and chrome fittings. The tables had plastic blue and white striped tablecloths, stood on top of a large chequerboard floor. 20p sweet machines were in each corner of the place, with a fake Wurlitzer jukebox placed behind the counter. Despite the look, the food was a pretty standard café affair. None of those clichéd big milkshakes and greasy burgers.

The foursome all had a coffee each (three mochas and one cappuccino), and in the middle was a large plate of French fries covered in both ketchup and mayonnaise. It was the first chance they had all had to be together, and they, well, mainly Tim, spent a while asking Johann anything and everything about Sweden, although based on very basic knowledge.

"Do you have IKEA?", "Do you like ABBA?", "Do you eat a lot of fish?", "Does it always snow?", "Are the winters dark?", "Are the summers light?", "Is it cold?", "Is it hot?", "Do you all drive Volvo's?"

Question after question after question. Lydia and Leo barely got a word in. They sat there eating the chips and watching Johann as he was interrogated. Shortly after, and in a rare slice of silence that afternoon, Johann thought for a moment, and then pulled his rucksack onto the table. He pulled his sleeve up and dug his right arm deeper and deeper into the bag. Tim thought it looked like a vet trying to deliver a calf from its mother. After a while, he pulled a small box onto the table and dropped his bag back under his chair.

"Open it," Johann said, nudging the box with the back of his hand towards the middle of them all.

Lydia leant forward and lifted the lid. Inside were four small, sand-coloured pebbles, each with a hole in the centre.

"Pebbles?" asked Leo. "What are they for?"

"I'll show," said Johann, with Tim watching him all the time admiringly.

Johann took the pebbles out and put one in front of each person at the table. He then dropped the box into the metal rubbish bin to his right, before beginning to speak again.

"I will go from the start. I collected these over many years," he said in a voice which gave off passion for the stones. "I have an aunt who lives on Öland. It is in the south. In Sweden. It is an island, very long and thin."

He looked at Tim, Leo and Lydia, waited for them to nod, and then continued.

"I used to go there every summer. I was often there for weeks. This is the first summer in years where I haven't," he said with a small smile which was not matched by the melancholy in his eyes.

“You bought these all the way here from there?” asked Lydia.

Johann nodded. “There are beaches. Stone beaches. I used to collect the stones I found nice. I found one with the hole. Then I only wanted to find ones with holes. Feel them. They are smooth, even the middles.”

They each picked one up and ran their fingers around the edges and surfaces.

“They are really nice,” said Tim. He meant it too. He liked Johann’s enthusiasm for them.

“I want you to keep them,” Johann replied, before digging into his pocket. He pulled out four small, black plastic bands, each with a small silver hook on one end, and a loop on the other. “I think we should be friends, and if I find kind people, I like to give them one of these each as a gift.”

“Thank you, Johann,” said Leo first, before the others thanked him too.

Johann slowly put a band through each pebble, before gently putting one around the neck of each of the group. Tim melted slightly when Johann brushed his hands against his neck. He would cherish this silly little stone forever.

At 5pm, Lydia announced that she had to go. Tim walked through the red doors at the back and into the toilets. When he came out, Leo was the only one there.

“Where are the other two?” Tim asked.

“They’re just outside,” replied Leo, whilst turning out some gobstoppers from one of the machines.

Tim walked behind him and straight out the front door. He couldn’t see them. He walked to the alley that ran the length of the diner, and as he turned the corner, he saw them both there, hiding. His heart sank. He knew that Johann was going to take Lydia away from him, but even worse, she would take Johann away. When they saw him, they both walked back quickly.

“Hey,” said Lydia. Tim said nothing. He leant back on the exposed brickwork and gently tapped his head back onto the wall repeatedly. He wanted to leave. It seemed an age for Leo to appear, but when he did, he was holding a selection of different coloured gobstoppers in an outstretched palm. Lydia and Johann took one each (one blue, one green), but Tim shook his head to refuse.

"Oh, Johann," started Leo, his mouth full, which made his voice sound weird. "Forgot to ask." At this point he spat the gobstopper out so that he could be understood. "There's a thing on at the snooker club tomorrow, in the afternoon. Starts at four. It's a fundraiser. Bouncy castle and a drag queen and things. Wanna come?"

He put the gobstopper back in and wiped his sticky hands on his shorts.

Tim didn't want Johann there now, but he said that he would be there along with his mum, as well as his sister, Hanna.

"After it has finished, I do not have plans," added Johann. "Mum may make us go early as she has a pottery class but I will be free. We can go to a park?"

TWENTY NINE

The walk home from Freddie's had made Tim sweat. He walked into the kitchen to pour a glass of squash.

"Hey mum!" he said, sitting backwards on a chair. "How's Anna? Is that all over now?"

"Yes. Was actually alright. We strangely have a lot in common." Katherine Johnson was opening up more new boxes. Tim didn't ask what was in them this time.

"Selling junk and being odd?"

"Yeah, and having strange kids."

"Well, I'm glad I don't have to get involved anymore. Besides, her son isn't the worst," he said, more hopeful than realistic.

Katherine just continued to cut the boxes open, but before pulling out the contents she put the scissors down.

"Tim. I've got an interview this week," she said quietly.

"Seriously?" he said loudly back.

"Don't sound too surprised."

"Sorry. Where is it?"

"Just at the doctors in town. It's for a receptionist job."

"And if you get it, will you stop with this tat?" he said, gesturing to the boxes.

"I will."

Tim was feeling as if things were all working out, and he sat and watched his mum fiddle with the boxes some more as he drained the last of the drink. Putting the glass in the sink, he headed upstairs to lie down.

Tim must have drifted off accidentally. He woke up confused and hot. He was now under the covers and could feel a weight on his legs. As he started to move, the covers were pulled back and Marty was sat staring at him.

"Hey," his brother said.

"Hey."

"You okay?"

"Yeah fine," Tim replied, sounding really not fine. The sleep had made him feel angrier about Johann and he wasn't feeling very talkative at all.

"You sure?" his brother asked, pushing the point when he noticed Tim's mood showing.

"It's just things," Tim said. "This week has been horrible. It's like everything I touch turns to rubbish."

"Like the opposite of Midas."

"Of what?"

"King Midas. Everything he touched turned to gold. I mean, like, you're the opposite."

"That makes me feel better, thanks," said Tim sarcastically.

"Sorry, I didn't mean to make you feel worse. Here, I have something for you."

"Not now. I'm not in the mood."

"Listen, just sit up a minute and let me talk."

Tim reluctantly pulled himself up into a sitting position and put his t-shirt back on properly after somehow half taking it off as he slept. His forehead felt sweaty and he stood to have a quick glance in the mirror to see what state he was in. Marty remained still until Tim joined him back on the edge of the bed.

"I've got you something," Marty said, as he reached to his side and put a package onto Tim's lap.

"What is it?"

"Open it and you'll find out."

Tim tore back the grey plastic parcel packaging, tossing it to the floor as he pulled out the contents. In his hands was a denim jacket with a Mirror Ball patch on the left-hand sleeve. It was exactly what he had wanted and he couldn't believe that he was holding it.

"Is this from you?" he asked Marty, who just nodded and smiled back. Tim leant over and gave him a hug. "I mean, thank you, I love it. And you bought this for me?"

"Yeah. Well, I mean mum gave me some money for doing the door."

"You only did half of it," said Tim before realising quickly that it would better to just be quiet for a change.

"Yeah, well, I think you deserve it."

"Why? I ruined your one. And I ruined a dog. And the biscuits. And two tortoises. And the shed."

"Good week for you ain't it," he said, laughing.

"Seriously though, why?"

"Look, it has been rubbish for you this week but I don't think any of it is really your fault. It's just that whenever something goes horrifically wrong, you seem to be present."

"I know. I've still got five weeks of holidays to go. Think of what else I might do."

"Well, it will be entertaining at least," smiled Marty. "Life always is with you around."

"Thanks," Tim replied, not sure whether this was a compliment or not.

"Are you going to try it on then?" his brother asked.

Tim got off the bed and went back across to the mirror. He slipped the jacket over his t-shirt and loved it even more than he had when he opened it. As he stared at his own reflection, something dawned on him.

"Hey Marty?"

"What?"

"How did you know I wanted this? I didn't tell you because I thought that you'd think I was stealing your style."

"You'd never look as good as me."

"I already do."

"You're wearing a dinosaur t-shirt Tim, so I win."

Tim looked down at his top.

"Dinosaurs are cool."

"Only like two of them."

"Wrong. And you still haven't answered my question. How did you know I wanted it?"

"Come and sit," said Marty. Tim didn't like it when his brother spoke like this. He always knew there was a catch. Regardless, he came towards the bed to join him. Marty moved closer and held his brothers hand.

"Look," started Marty, "I find this really hard, and I didn't know whether to say anything. I wasn't going to, but it's on my mind and I care about you."

Tim remained silent and allowed him to continue. "Earlier this week, when you asked me to look over the Barnaby plans, I started going through them and saw your list at the back of the pad. I know you spoke to me before about wanting to have some kind of transformation, so when I saw the list, I was curious as to what you were going to buy, and I saw the thing at the bottom."

Tim knew exactly what Marty had seen, and even though he had wanted to tell his brother about being gay, he didn't want him to have found out this way. He shifted away and made himself as small as possible, leaning against the wall. He didn't speak. After a few moments of silence, his brother spoke.

"I want you to know that it's okay. Like, everything is okay. It's actually nice that I was the one that you had wanted to tell and I'm sorry for you not having the chance to tell me when ready. That's why I was unsure whether to mention it or not."

"Is that why you bought me the jacket?" Tim said quietly.

"No, I would have done that anyway. Like you said, you've had a pretty rubbish week haven't you," he replied, laughing to try and cheer Tim up. "Honestly, I would have preferred it if I hadn't seen it written down. Not because I think it's wrong, but more that it feels like I have taken something away from you."

"You don't think I'm weird, do you?"

"Why would I think that? Tim, I'm seventeen and not stupid. I don't care who you like or why. Even if I did have a problem with it, it's not my place to say."

Tim tried to smile at Marty but was unsure to what his own emotions were at this time.

"You might annoy the hell out of me Tim, and you might have set fire to my bike but that doesn't mean I don't care about you. Life is hard. I've been through a load too and I know that there will always be someone who is gonna try and tear you down or try and make you feel worthless but you're not. I wanna be here for you, okay? I won't lie and say everything will be fine because at times it will feel really awful. I'm just saying that if you need me, just let me know. Like, mum might be hit and miss with her moods, but she does care for you too. It's harder too with dad not around but when he's back next he will do literally anything for you, and you know that. What you've told me doesn't change anything."

Tim smiled, genuinely this time. "Thanks mate," he said and squeezed his brothers hand.

"Life can be crap Tim, but it's the same for everyone. Trust me I've felt like you before, thinking I don't fit in, but that's just what happens when you're a teenager. You sometimes just have to let things settle. Please just promise me that you won't change for anyone, never compromise. There may be exciting things coming that you don't know of yet. It's the journey."

"The river," said Tim quietly to himself before wiping both happy and sad tears from his face with his sleeve. "Did you tell mum about it?"

"Nope. I didn't mean to find out, but I did and that can't change, but when you want to tell mum is up to you. Just let me know beforehand and I'll be about, okay?"

"Promise?"

"Promise. She will be totally cool with it by the way."

"I dunno. What if she isn't?"

"She will be, trust me. Dad will be too. And Pat and Pet."

"I'm not telling all of them. Pat and Pet think I'm odd already."

"If anyone would be cool with it, it would be them. You know they ain't just friends, don't you?"

"They're not?"

"Nope. They're married."

Tim was surprised and didn't know what to say, so opted to just remain in silence. Marty shifted and punched his brother lightly on the thigh. "You know what Tim?"

"What?" he mumbled.

"You made this list to make yourself cool, but you are cool."

"Thanks, I am getting there. Just need to get a few more things and then I think it will be ok."

"No. Even without the jacket or the jeans or any of the other things, you're still pretty cool. You end up in stupid situations, but you're still cool."

As weeks go, this one had been full of excitement. Whether that excitement was good or not didn't matter. It was already a summer that he would remember. The rest of the evening was quiet, and Tim had spent much of his time in his room trying to take in everything that Marty had said. He couldn't believe that he didn't know about Pat and Pet and felt guilty about being horrible about them to Leo and Lydia so much. He'd even calmed down a bit about the whole Johann situation and text him back as promised to see if he was free at 7pm. He said to him that he would also try and get Lydia out as well, so long as Leo was about too as he didn't want to have to sit and watch them on his own.

As it turned out, no one was free so had time to waste watching films on TV or planning summer trips somewhere. Although it was unlikely that he would travel around the world, he looked at the world map on his wall imagining what it would be like to visit South America or Eastern Asia. His mum was pottering around the garden, so he planned to go and sit with her for some sandwiches or a drink. Marty had been right. She was a good person, and the lack of punishment from the fire showed that she cared.

Tim got dressed, deciding to not wear the denim jacket just yet. He would save that for a more special occasion. His hair was now fully back to its natural state after a shower, but he already missed it being straight. The opportunity for it to happen again though might have to wait as he didn't think Lydia nor straighteners should be attempted at 247 Oak Tree Crescent again just yet.

Before heading downstairs, he opened his drawer and pulled out his list. Although Marty had said he was cool regardless of what he looked like, he still wanted to get the new clothes. For starters, he desperately needed new shoes. Slowly and surely the list was getting smaller. He took his pen and crossed out all the things that had been done.

~~Denim jacket (or leather?)~~
More skinny jeans
Converse shoes
~~One of those belts with metal studs on~~
~~An ear piercing~~ (would hurt. Probs too young?)
Good headphones (£150!!!!)
Hair gel
Headband?
~~Mirror Ball CD~~
~~Hair straighteners (Ask Lydia)~~
Eye liner (buy waterproof one)
~~Tell Marty I am gay (not yet)~~
Get to know Mr Singh more

The penultimate one felt incredible to strike off.

SUNDAY

THIRTY

The time between Saturday evening and Sunday afternoon was the most peaceful for the whole week. His mum had decided to delay going to the car boot, probably as this week had no doubt taken its toll on her as well. Rather than have to spend his time in the Cash 'n' Carry Car Park, Tim spent Sunday morning out on his bike, cycling around the wooded areas just outside the town. There used to be an old oak tree down the end of a small trail and he and Leo had once built a den there that was lost to the elements many years ago. Once home he had a quick shower before heading to the fundraiser.

Greenwood Snooker Club was a strange place. It was a one-story building set back in a small industrial estate, just off the green, near the town's spired church. The pebble-dashed structure sat next to a small brewery, and opposite a printing firm. The outside car park was usually full, although some of the area was reserved for pub garden games.

Tim, Leo and Lydia arrived separately from their families. A large white and red banner stating 'Honey Latté's Fundraising Night' hung above the main entrance and it flapped gently in the light summer breeze. The door to the club was inside a small entrance hall, and Tim pressed the intercom button to gain entry. A small speaker to his right clicked and buzzed and the sound of the door unlocking became audible. He pushed the door and led the trio inside.

The inside of the club was split into two rooms. Immediately through the door, a bar stood opposite. An older gentleman with wispy combed-back hair and a thin moustache was busying himself pouring pints and handing out crisps. Down the left-hand side of the room sat many red sofas, all having slightly faded to a dirty rose colour since they were originally put in. They sat loosely facing each other. Two televisions were fixed to walls at each end. The left wall was mainly windows, with each one draped by dull bronze curtains.

To the right were fruit machines and the toilets, however an entrance to a second room stood centrally. Through here was the main games room. Tim looked through the dividing window and counted half a dozen snooker and pool tables, with an area for darts in the far-right corner. The whole room was only lit by small lamps which hung above each table, and their yellow bulbs made the room have an old smoky sepia appearance.

Honey Latté's event was due to take place in the main bar. A small stage had been set up in one corner, with three school-type chairs lined up along the rear, as well as some kind of large wooden tombola at the side.

"They're all over there," said Leo, waving towards their families who had all taken a booth closest to the large buffet. The three friends approached and squeezed in, with Marty between them and the others.

"What's the plan?" asked Tim.

"There's a raffle and a stage show," replied his mum as she took a sip of a transparent cocktail with salt around the rim. A sad looking slice of lemon perched cautiously on the side of the glass.

"Buffet?" said Lydia, checking out the big beige banquet sat on the long table over her shoulder.

The three stood and each took a champagne-gold coloured paper plate and napkin, and moved left to right collecting pork pies, crisps, quiche, breadsticks, scotch eggs and sandwiches. For reasons unknown, Tim believed the buffet to be the best form of any meal in the world. He avoided taking any of the egg sandwiches on offer as he didn't want bad breath for the rest of the evening, instead sticking to ham and mayonnaise. They returned to their seats as Marty was coming back from the bar, steadily carrying a circular black plastic tray, with four glasses of coke balanced on top. Each contained a handful of square ice cubes, and a small pink cocktail umbrella. He placed each glass down and shook water droplets from his right hand.

Flo Gardner handed round a book of raffle tickets, with each person taking a strip.

"What can we win?" questioned Lydia.

"Depends on when your ticket is drawn," replied Flo. "It could be a full hamper if you're lucky, but there's also chicken breasts, sausages, burgers and mince."

"Wait," Tim interrupted. "It's actually all meat?"

"Yeh, hence the name meat raffle," replied Katherine. "It's always the same. They do this at the karaoke nights also. Where do you think the meat for our Sunday dinners sometimes come from?"

Sunday lunchtime now made sense to Tim. He never knew what they would be having until it was served, yet it was always some form of meat that had been pulled from a polystyrene tray covered in clingfilm, in a small blue and white carrier bag. Today it had been pork chops. Meat raffles or the mobile butcher at the cash 'n' carry provided the family with everything.

As they all tucked into their food, the lights suddenly dimmed and blue flashing lights span on the stage like a cheap version of those found on a police car. A gentle 'thud thud thud' of a microphone being tested came over the PA system before a voice, a little loud for the size of the room, started.

"Greeeenwoooood Snooker Club, welcome to this fundraising extravaganza. Please clap your hands, stamp your feet, and rattle your jewellery for your host.... Miss Honey Latté!"

The room was around three-quarters full and went wild as Saint Monique's 'Glove Puppet' started up. From the side door, Honey Latté appeared in a spotlight. She was tall and in a tight silver jumpsuit. The wig was blonde and large. Tim thought it looked like his mum's hair did in her wedding photos. Honey Latté did not head straight for the stage, but instead danced and lip synced to the song whilst walking around all the full tables. She caught Tim singing along and approached him, grabbing his hand. Too embarrassed to get up and dance, he sat there as Honey Latté waved his arm about. It was his first time seeing a drag queen and he was loving every second. Five minutes passed and she had finally made it onto the stage at the front of the room.

"Hello, hello, so lovely to see you all," she started, whilst constantly pushing her hair over her shoulders. She walked across the stage and spun the tombola with more strength than expected. "Now, let me see those tickets!" She held her arms wide and looked at the audience. All present waved their dull pink strips of tickets back at her.

The meat raffle went on for what felt like an eternity to the school children present. There must have been a whole farms worth of meat to be won. Katherine Johnson won a pack of Chinese style spareribs, and Flo got some chicken and thyme burgers. Tim looked around and wondered if anyone would be leaving tonight without some form of raw meat under their arm.

A glittery sign stating 'Back in 10 Mins' was placed on stage and Honey Latté left into a small office room to stage left. Tim stood to walk to the toilets, but out of the window he saw Johann walking across the car park, a few metres behind Anna and, presumably, Hanna. Johann was wearing a well-fitting black shirt. The cuffs were undone, and his sleeves pulled halfway up his forearms.

"Back in five," he said to those at his table and dropped out the fire exit door. He power-walked along the side of the venue towards the front of the building to catch them before they entered. He felt bad that he was enjoying the show so much that he hadn't noticed they were yet to arrive. Now he had seen him, his attention had switched completely.

"Johann!" he shouted as he got near the corner, just as his crush had disappeared. He kept walking, but then Johann's head came into view.

"Heya!" said Johann smiling. "I am so glad to see you."

He approached Tim slowly and then pulled him into a hug. Tim never felt more sure about anything in his life. He could easily have stayed like this all night. He had to tell Johann somehow. Tim needed to make Johann realise that it was him that he needed, not Lydia. Johann pulled out from the hug and Tim didn't say anything for far too long, to the point where he was asked if he was okay.

"Um...yeh...sorry...I'm...yeah. You?" he replied, stumbling and flustered.

"I am now. My mum. Her car is terrible. It is broken. We had to walk all the way in and are now late," Johann explained.

"Well, I am happy you are here now. I missed you being here," he half lied.

"Me too. We cannot stay long though. Mum must walk to her pottery class now. Have I missed the show?"

"No, just the raffle."

"Ahhhhh," Johann cooed. "Did you win?"

"Um...yeah, I won ten beef sausages," said Tim, blushing. He could guarantee that they had nothing like a meat raffle in Sweden. He knew this as Johann was looking more confused than ever. Cute, but confused. Feeling confident, he put his hand on Johann's shoulder and went to take him inside.

"Hey," started Johann excitedly. "You are wearing the stone necklace that I got for you"

"Of course I am! I haven't taken it off, Johann!"

Johann looked genuinely touched, and smiled at Tim widely before turning towards the door.

Once they were all back indoors, Leo bounded over and said that more drinks were on the table. Tim dashed into the toilets, and when he returned, Johann was sat between Leo and Lydia. Knowing that Lydia might feel the same way about Johann as he did, he felt a knot in his stomach from jealousy. He sat near, restless and not speaking, and when questioned, brushed it off as having eaten too much coleslaw.

Before long, the lights came back to life on the stage and Honey Latté reappeared. She now had hair that was bright blue, paired with a matching sequined dress and wings. Her face was covered in bright silver glitter, except her eyes which were emerald green. She looked as if she had been beamed in from space. Tim sat with his mouth wide open. Looking around, Johann and Leo were the same. They were transfixed.

Music started up, but Tim wasn't listening properly, instead staring at her every move. He knew it was some old disco song about a bell. His mum had played it around the house when he was younger. That's all he noticed about the sounds. The rest of his mental capacity was taken up watching Honey Latté jump and kick her way across the stage, ending with her doing the splits.

Cheers rang out around the room when she finished. Tim sat and clapped wildly, but as he looked across the table his hands froze in mid-air as he saw Johann with his arm around Leo, whispering into his ear. Leo was smiling and laughing, and Tim felt like his heart was being crushed. "Surely, he wouldn't do this to me, would he?" he thought. The same feelings he felt when he saw Johann and Lydia in the alley next to Freddie's yesterday afternoon. His mouth was dry through anxiety, and it felt worse as he saw Leo pull Johann into a tight hug for what felt like minutes. Tim thought he was going to throw up so stood to head to the bathroom. As he stood, the room cheered him.

"We have our first volunteer," said Honey Latté, as she came and took Tim by the hand, leading him through tables and onto the stage, sitting him down on the end chair on stage right. In his panic at seeing Leo and Johann together, he had missed the request for contestants for the second part of the show. Now he felt sick and was onstage. This wasn't good.

"Okay," she continued over the microphone. "We need two more volunteers for my secret society prize game show. If you want the chance to win, stand up now."

Everyone remained firmly in their seats.

"If you don't volunteer, I'll come and pick you at random," said Honey Latté, getting a bit frustrated. "Remember there are prizes!" she added for encouragement.

How had he ended up here? He could feel the sweat running down his back. He stared out but couldn't take anything in. He was snapped out of his trance when a ballpoint pen and a piece of paper was shoved into his hand. He looked around. To his left now sat a lady that he recognised from his paper round. Mousey and plain but in large leopard-print high heels. At the far end was the barman, who must have been dragged up to make sure enough people were available to start the game. He couldn't remember either of them joining him here.

Honey Latté walked in front of the three contestants. "Now, this is a big one," she said, to which some people smirked. "These three are going to write down their biggest secret. The one that is the most shocking, as judged by you, you beautiful audience, will win two hundred-and-fifty-pounds worth of high street vouchers. That's two five zero."

Tim was quite surprised. He was expecting the prize to only be slightly better than the meat, but winning this would mean that he would be able to buy so many things off his cool list. He looked out towards his friends and family. They were all staring back. He was glad to see Leo standing and not cuddled up to Johann anymore.

"Contestants," she said as the game continued, "you have thirty seconds to write down your name and the most shocking secret about yourself. Your time starts.... NOW!"

A countdown started behind him. He needed something big, gigantic even. He had to have these vouchers. He was panicking. What could he write in front of all these people? He looked out and caught Marty's eye. Marty smiled and gave him two thumbs up. The second hand on Honey Latté's comically large clock ticked by, with each second seeming like an hour. Tick. Tick. Tick. He moved his eyes from Marty and looked across the table at all his friends and family, especially Johann. He swallowed deeply and took the lid off his pen.

My name is Tim, and I think I am in love with a boy called Johann.

Tick. Tick. Tick. Bong.

"Time is up!" shouted the drag queen, who snatched the paper out of each contestant's hand straight away. His face drained of colour immediately. It was too late now. Why didn't he just say that he stole tortoises? He had a hundred things from this week alone that he could've written down. What was he doing? Tim felt horrendously sick and dizzy. He looked around to see if he was close enough to the exit to run away but there was no chance.

"Okay," she said, "each of you in the audience now have two pieces of paper in front of you. If you like the secret, hold up the green card. If you don't like it, hold up the red. It's all very simple. The person with the most green cards from the audience will win the vouchers."

Tim felt like he was in a dream now. It was as if he was watching himself onstage, rather than being perched on the chair himself. Honey Latté started to read the secrets, beginning with the lady in the middle. He hoped he would be next at least.

"Okay, darling, you first," Honey Latté said to the only female contestant. She took her piece of paper and read to the audience. The lady squirmed in the chair as Honey Latté read it out. "My name is Cindy, and I sometimes eat my toenails when I cut them." Honey Latté winced as she read the final word.

Tim looked up as the audience gagged. He saw many returning their quiche to their plates. Slowly, the crowd raised their cards. They were mainly red. Honey Latté did a quick count.

"That's fifteen green cards, and twenty red. That gives you a score of minus five. I guess that's a start." The audience clapped, and then it was the barman's turn. Tim would be last. More time for the nerves to eat him from the inside out.

Honey Latté looked at the paper. "Your writing is terrible. Have you been drinking the stock from behind your bar again?" she asked. Jimbo remained silent. "Okay, let's start shall we darlings?" she said as she held the paper up overdramatically. "My name is Jimbo and I give the snooker club members secret nicknames." Honey Latté raised an overexaggerated eyebrow. "So, Jimbo," she said, with her hand on his shoulder, "are these nicknames kind?"

"Not really," he grumbled.

"Well, I think we need some examples."

The cheers from the crowd showed that they agreed.

"Okay, well...we have Big Boss Pam, Dirty Lil, Grannywhack, The Centurions- "

"Okay, okay, I think we get the idea. Audience, let's see those cards!"

She did the maths again. "That's twenty-one green and fourteen red, giving you a score of seven. You take the lead, well done Jimbo! Now, finally..."

Tim could hear his own heartbeat. It felt as if he was drowning. Honey Latté walked over and opened his secret. She looked at him for a few seconds before turning away towards the crowd.

"My name is Tim..." she said.

Tim was on the verge of fainting, terrified and glued to the chair. He could barely breathe now. Each intake was shallow and quick. Honey Latté paused and then read it out.

"My name is Tim and I want to be a drag queen for one night only!"

The crowd laughed and clapped. Tim looked to his table. Leo's mouth was wide open, but both he and those around him cheered. Lydia was stood on her chair, shouting encouragement. Honey Latté put her arm around Tim and squeezed him gently. "Let's see those cards everyone." The room was a sea of green.

"I don't even need to count, my dear. You are the clear winner. The vouchers are yours!"

The room erupted with applause. Another ten-minute interval was announced, and Tim jumped off stage, ran past his table and back out the fire exit. He shouted to his friends and family to stay inside as he passed them by. In the car park, he found an old wooden bench in the corner away from the Bouncy Castle and screaming children, and sat, trying to get as much air in as possible. The cooler temperature eased his sweaty brow. He held his head in his hands for a minute or two until he heard footsteps approaching. He raised his eyes to see Honey Latté walking towards him. She sat next to him, her earrings clanging like the Pet Lady's wind chimes. She was quiet for a few seconds before giving Tim a long and tight hug.

"You okay, kiddo?" she said.

Tim could smell her perfume from this close. "Um, yes I think so." The drag queen didn't reply but was looking at him kindly. Tim smiled at her and continued. "Thank you. Like, really thank you. How come you knew to lie for me though?"

"Tim, darling, I was watching you. I could see how scared you were. I couldn't say it. I'm sorry, I wanted to protect you, that's all."

"It's fine, I appreciate it. No one would understand, I guess."

"I do," she replied. "I've had that look myself many times before. I've been through this. It was a long time ago, admittedly, but I've been there."

"Does everything work out?" he asked.

"Yes, mostly. Look, you're a young kid. Life is hard, whatever you are."

"I guess."

"It's true, everyone is battling something. I mean, look at me. Twenty years ago, I wasn't Honey Latté. I wasn't confident. I was a terrified young boy called Daniel, growing up on a housing estate in east London being bullied and called every name under the sun by a group of horrible, horrible boys in my year. Honey is my mask, my disguise, my saviour. But, once I drag a wet wipe across my face, I am Daniel again. I will never escape that, but you learn to grow, to love, and to care about yourself. The best people stick around. Life goes on, eh. Just remember, you can't tell what's next until you get there."

"Like floating down a river," Tim said, understanding.

"*Exactly* like floating down a river, yes."

Tim leaned into her shoulder for a minute in silence before she pushed him back up.

She took a slow drink of orange through a long metal straw. "Look Tim, I have to be back on stage in five minutes, but first, tell me about this Johann."

Tim told her absolutely everything.

Back inside, Tim sat back at his table. Relieved, embarrassed, maybe happy. Anna was leaving with Johann and Hanna.

"Text me later for the park," Johann said to Leo as he left, waving goodbye to the others as he walked out the front doors.

"Well done mate," said Leo and Lydia together.

"Thanks," replied Tim, feeling a bit flat in their company.

"Who wants a coke?" asked Lydia, standing to get more drinks. Both boys agreed and she wandered to the bar.

"I saw you with Johann, Leo," he said quietly.

"Yeh, he's really sweet," Leo responded.

"Yeh, you two looked close." Tim felt jealous. Why hadn't Johann asked him to text him for the park and not Leo?

"He will be a good friend," said Leo, sensing some awkwardness.

"You looked more than friends. It was the same with Lydia and him yesterday."

"Tim, listen. It's not like that."

"Yeh it's okay, I am used to it, don't worry."

"No, you don't understand. He isn't interested in me like that!" Leo said.

"So, what you mean is that we are all just friends then, except he likes being secretive with you and Lydia and not me?" questioned Tim.

"Look, I don't know all the facts, when do I ever, but then again, neither of us have managed to figure ourselves out so far this week have we? Anyway, he was telling me about the last six months in Sweden before they moved across here. He said he had a boyfriend named Henrik and that they had to break up because of the move. Lyds also told me cos he told her yesterday before we saw them outside of Freddie's. Basically, he doesn't know exactly *what* he is, but he likes boys like we do. He isn't big on diving yet, but we can get him involved in that too hopefully." Leo was speaking so quickly that it was close to not making sense. "But yeah, yesterday he told Lydia not to tell anyone, but after today, after seeing you wearing his stone, he wanted to let you know as well. Lydia told him about us being confused about things too, and that he should speak to us. Lydia did the right thing I think."

"Yeah, that's cool," shrugged Tim. It was barely anytime since Tim would have been horrified that people were discussing his sexuality to others, but he really didn't mind in these circumstances. Tim sat up in his chair, suddenly engaged, but not saying anything further. He let Leo continue.

"So yeah, wanna know something cool?"

"Go on," said Tim nervously.

"Well, you know you like him, right?"

"You didn't tell him, did you?"

"Course not. Listen. You know you like him, right?"

"Yeh. Like, more than ever."

"Well about that. He told me to tell you that he really likes you too. As in, *likes* likes you."

THIRTY ONE

The weather had continued to get warmer since the fundraiser. It could not have been a more perfect evening. Although bright, there were some large white clouds floating above Greenwood as the day turned into early mid-evening. The sporadic shade that the clouds caused meant that the air seemed cooler. Tim drank a glass of squash and headed out to The Rec to meet the others. He was nervous, yet excited. Was Leo telling the truth when he told him Johann liked him back? He was scared that something may have been lost in translation, especially with how loud the music had become at times in the snooker club. His emotions had resembled a rollercoaster in the two hours he was at the event, but he felt that his mood matched the current weather. Mostly sunny, with a few clouds of uncertainty passing by. He appreciated Honey Latté taking the time to come and speak to him, especially after covering for him during the game. He hoped that she would be back one day.

He had left his vouchers at home, and Marty had agreed to take him shopping over the following weekend after the first diving lesson. This week had brought the two much closer, and his older brother was no longer annoyed by his presence. Tim felt genuinely cared about.

As he walked slowly down the road, kicking a stone along in front of him, he thought back over the past week. The last seven days had felt much longer. The biscuits. The pigeons. The spider. The prom. The eyeliner. Adam and Snowy. The squirrel. The fire. The tortoise(s). Johann. Oh, Johann. Every thought he had looped back to one boy.

"Johann will be there now," Tim thought, as he approached the green iron gates which were attached to stone pillars at the entrance to the park. Mr Cream's ice cream van was sat on the edge of the road. A shambolic queue of six or seven children gathered around the small window of the van. Tim waited in line for the kids to be sorted, and then ordered four orange flavoured lollies. He poured some coins into Mr Cream's hand and headed through the gates. Lydia had text him to say they were halfway up the hill towards the eastern side, near to the rope swing. The rope swing hadn't been attached to the big tree for about two years, but regardless, the name of the area had stuck with him and his friends. They often came up here after school, however, hadn't for a few weeks.

Tim reflected on his life so far and looked towards the future. Although excited about the potential transformation into a *cool kid*, he felt sad about leaving some parts of his life behind. Although Clacton was an annual Johnson holiday, maybe this would be the last time that the family went there together. Next year, Marty would be eighteen and would likely head away with his friends. The problem with life is that you don't know when you are doing something for the last time. At some point in the close future, he wouldn't be in the arcades with his dad, trying to win a keyring. He wouldn't always mess about on the beach and get splashed with sea water by his mum. The family wouldn't be together sharing ice creams on promenades or even sat around the kitchen table at home as one. When was the last time his mum pushed him on a swing? It must be years, but at the time you don't know that a final push would be your last one ever. Like the river, time does go on and there is nothing you can do to stop it. After everything that had happened over the previous seven days, Tim would make sure the remaining summer holiday would be full of everything good, starting with now. Who knows, this might be the last time he and his friends sat under the old rope swing tree.

He could see the others in the distance, gave a wave which they didn't notice, and walked up to meet them. On arrival, he handed the lollies across, and the four sat in a circle chatting about everything and nothing. From up the hill you could get a good view of everyone in the park. There were dog walkers and joggers everywhere, and groups of kids were playing rounders on the cricket pitches.

"You enjoying Greenwood?" Leo asked Johann.

"I think so, yeah. It is less pretty than my town in Sweden, and it is harder to get to the beach, but it's nice. Did I tell you I saw a crow eating sushi earlier? It can be odd here."

Tim laughed at this but was happy that Johann was settling in okay. "Yep. Greenwood is odd," he said, knowing that his own life was probably the oddest.

They continued talking for a while, asking Johann more about life back home in Sweden, learning more about Henrik and all other things that he had left behind. Johann must have gone through a lot of *last times* recently and Tim hoped that this didn't get him down. He wished that one day he could travel to Sweden himself. In an ideal world, Johann would take him. It would beat Clacton, that's for sure.

"Oh, Lyds, Tuesday night. We thought we can all go to Freddie's for your birthday if you fancy it?" said Leo. Tim had forgotten that they had to plan something, but this seemed a suitable arrangement.

"Yeh, sure, I'm glad it's nothing big. Can it just be us four?"

"Sounds good to me," Tim confirmed.

"Yeh, me too," Johann said, smiling.

Once their lollies were gone, they laid side by side. Leo then Lydia then Tim and then Johann.

"That cloud looks like a dinosaur," said Tim, pointing at a cloud which, being fair to him, did actually look like a dinosaur.

"Tim is obsessed with dinosaurs, Johann," said Leo, jokingly.

"Dinosaurs are the best," stated Johann.

Another thing they had in common.

"What's your fave, Johann?" asked Tim.

"Pterodactyl. You?"

"Stegosaurus, I think."

"That cloud over there is a dog," said Leo, changing the subject back whilst pointing up to a large cloud towards the horizon.

"They all just look like clouds to me," said Lydia, ruining the game.

The group of four rested on the cool grass for a few more minutes.

"This is going to be a good summer," said Lydia finally. "When I am back from holiday, we have to do this more."

The others agreed.

They laid there, eyes closed, relaxing and at ease with each other. They didn't need to say anything.

After everything that had gone, all was now still. Tim never wanted to leave this moment. He wanted absolutely everything to remain absolutely the same for absolutely everyone.

Thirty seconds later Tim felt Johann take his hand.

ACKNOWLEDGEMENTS

First and foremost, thank you massively to David Brown, without whom this book would not exist. Not only as someone who has read it at least five times to help edit, but as someone who listened to my ideas and made me believe that this story could actually work, and who wasn't afraid to say when an idea needed changing. Not only that, telling me when I had written parts in my west Oxon accent, or had given people and places the wrong name. Oh, and for providing the tiramisu.

Thank you to Numan Ahmed for the brilliant front cover artwork. Considering all I provided was a sharpie drawing on a paperbag, the final result is wonderful! To Emma and Evie, my Paper Boy guinea pigs, thank you for reading the early version and providing your feedback and the online love. It makes a big difference. To Mum, Dad, Andy, Howi, Rob, Simon and Eddie, thank you for helping keep me sane over the last three years.

Also, massive respect to other LGTBQ+ young adult authors whose works I have enjoyed during the writing process. To Max Deacon, who I always knew always had a story in him (check out Cold Like Ash, his excellent debut), as well as Simon James Green, Alice Oseman, Adam Silvera and anyone else who has ensured LGBTQ+ stories are accessible to the current generation.

Gay's The Word bookshop, thank you for providing such a fantastic range of LGBTQ+ books, and where I have spent more money than planned. You can't visit and *not* buy something there every time. Finally, to Foyle's bookstore (with the best scones inside the M25), Café Nero in Holborn, and Cremma Café in Bournemouth who all provided a space to allow me to write and edit this book.

Finally, thank you to you if you are reading this book. It makes it all worthwhile.

FFLAG

FFLAG is a national voluntary organisation and registered charity who offer support and resources for LGBTQ+ children and for parents.

They offer support to local parent groups and contacts in their efforts to help parents and families understand, accept and support their lesbian, gay, bisexual and transgender members with love and pride.

www.fflag.org.uk/

THE PAPER BOY: ROUND TWO

BEING DELIVERED IN 2023.

Printed in Great Britain
by Amazon

86964004R00111

info- TECHNOLOGY

info- TECHNOLOGY

CHANGING THE WAY WE COMMUNICATE

JACK MEADOWS

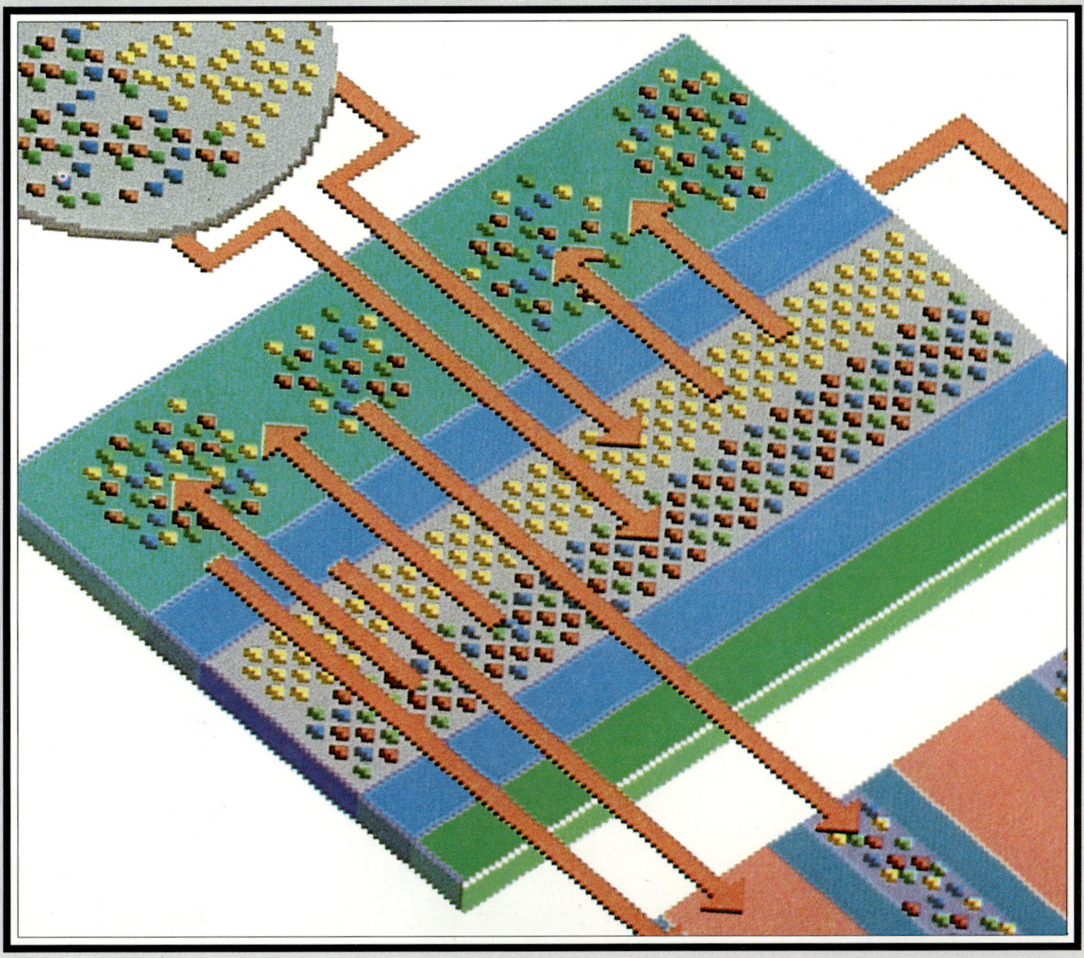

CASSELL

Editor Mike March
Designers Niki Overy,
Frankie MacMillan
Picture Editor Alison Renney
Picture Researcher Mary Fane

Design Consultant John Ridgeway
Project Director Lawrence Clarke

Advisor Steve Connor

Contributor Jack Meadows

Computer graphic illustrations produced by Alex Quero of 4i Collaboration at Imagine

AN EQUINOX BOOK

Planned and produced by:
Equinox (Oxford) Ltd
Musterlin House,
Jordan Hill Road
Oxford OX2 8DP

First published in the UK 1989 by Cassell, Artillery House, Artillery Row, London, SW1P 1RT

Distributed in Australia by
Capricorn Link (Australia) Pty Ltd
PO Box 665, Lane Cove, NSW 2066

British Library Cataloguing in Publication Data Meadows, Jack Infotechnology: changing the way we communicate 1. Communication. Effects of technological innovation I. Title 302.2

ISBN 0 304 31784 5

Cover pictures

Main picture: Hank Morgan/Rainbow

Corner picture: Imagine

Printed in Spain by H. Fournier, S.A.

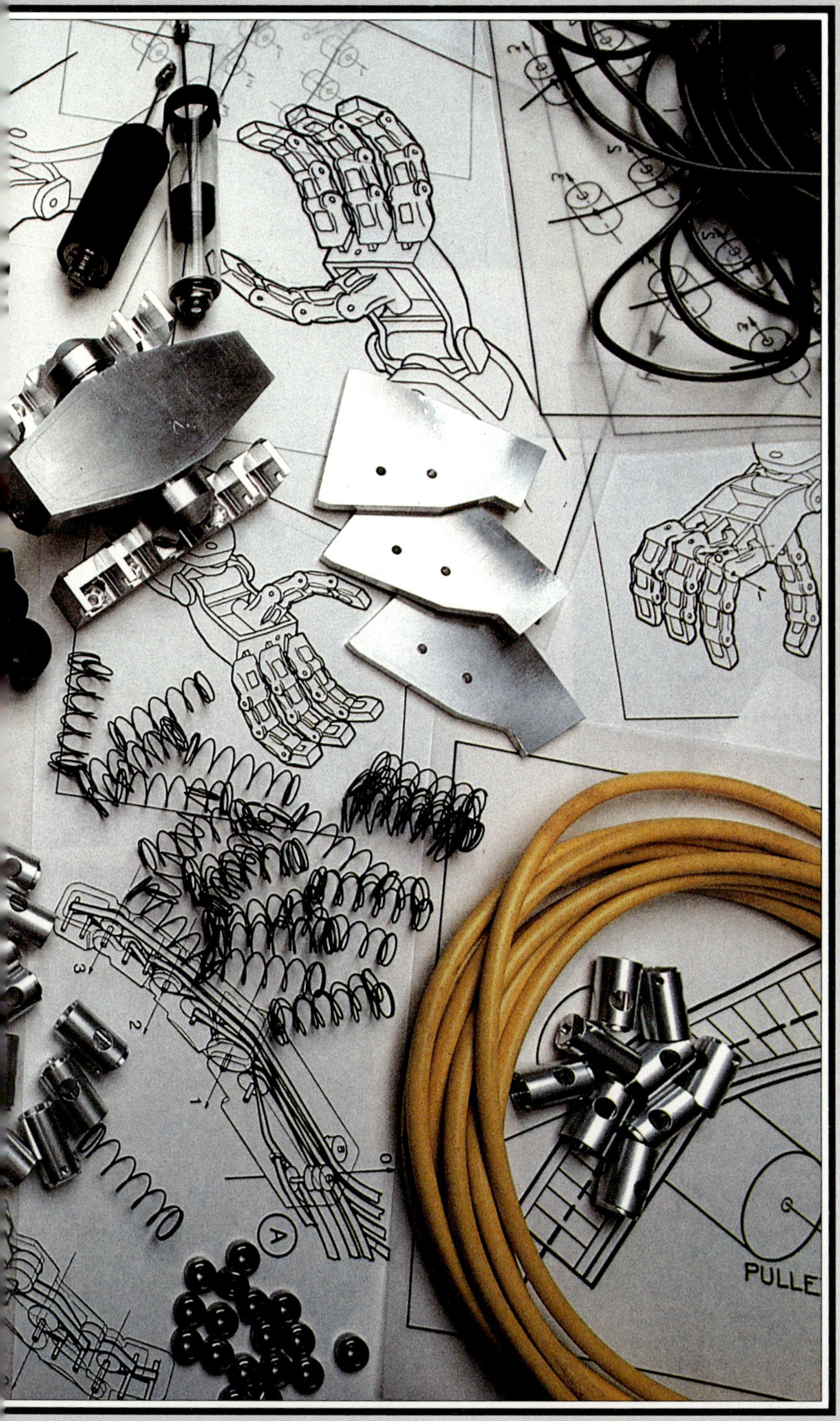

Contents

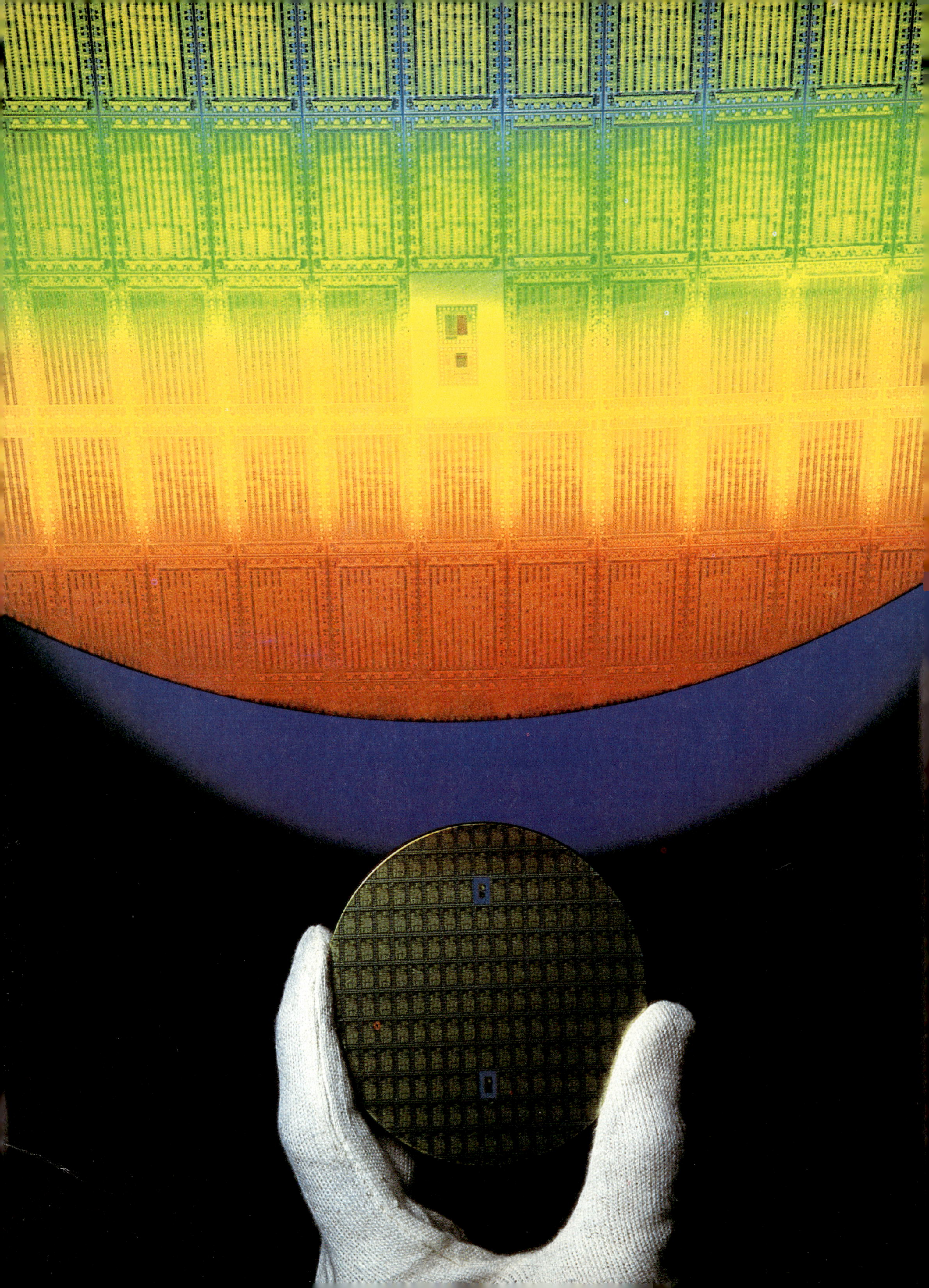

Information and the Senses 1

Information and knowledge...The senses as information receptors...How the eye works...Human and animal vision...Interpreting visual data...Human and animal hearing...Echo sounding...The human brain...The brain and the senses...The brain as information processor...Three kinds of memory

All living things – humans, animals and plants – constantly give out and receive information. Some of that information is accepted and put to use. Some is not. For instance, a scientist might write the formula $E = mc^2$. A recipient sees it and reads it – that is, the message is perceived by the reader's senses and transmitted to the brain. This physical activity, however, is only the first step – that of, in computer jargon, inputting the information. To be properly absorbed, the message must be understood. Does it mean anything to the reader? If so, can it be accepted and stored in the brain as knowledge for future use? $E = mc^2$ is the basic equation for calculating the energy generated by nuclear reactions. If the recipient were foolish enough to start to build a nuclear bomb, that might indicate that the information had been accepted. In information terms, this act would be described as the "output". Information is what we communicate. Knowledge depends on the complicated processing of that information which goes on in our brains. How human beings acquire and process information – in other words, how information is turned into knowledge – is a vital area of current research.

▲ ***Three faces of Albert Einstein (1879–1955), the originator of the equation $E=mc^2$. From the top, each picture conveys less information, making recognition more difficult.***

The senses

How do human beings communicate information to each other? Traditionally, we are supposed to have five senses – that is, five ways of perceiving the world around us – which can act as channels for receiving information. These are sight, sound, smell, taste and touch. Scientists investigating perception say that we really have more senses than these. For example, someone standing on their head with their eyes closed knows that they are upside-down. How? The answer is that the inner part of our ear contains a mechanism – called the semicircular canals – which tells us how we are positioned. If a person riding a bicycle starts falling to the right, which way should they turn the front wheel to avoid toppling over? It usually takes at least one or two seconds to work out the answer. To the cyclist the correct response comes more rapidly. Our balancing mechanism supplies information on position to the brain, and we react at once. Typically, we gather information about most of our activities from more than one sense. When we watch television, for example, we are also usually listening at the same time.

Both sight and hearing are physical senses. In the one, we receive and analyze light waves, in the other, sound waves. Smell and taste are chemical senses, depending on the specific properties of substances. Information passes when chemical substances in some form reach the nose and tongue, and cause a reaction. Physical processes both happen more quickly than chemical, and transmit much more information over longer distances. Hence human beings rely mainly on sight and hearing – the senses that carry the greatest information load.

Sight

The instrument of vision – the eye – is essentially a ball filled with fluid. The transparent front surface – the cornea – is separated by fluid from the lens. This, in turn, is separated from the light-sensitive back surface – the retina – by more fluid. Incoming light bends (is refracted) as it passes through the cornea, and again as it passes through the lens, to form an image of the outside scene on the retina. The lens adjusts the light signal to bring objects at different distances into focus. The importance of the cornea is easily detected when swimming underwater. Because the water has much the same refracting properties as the cornea, it is difficult for us to see underwater without goggles to keep the eyes watertight. Some fish and acquatic mammals overcome this problem by having, for example, a highly curved cornea.

The retina contains many light-sensitive cells which detect the image formed by the cornea and lens. This information is channeled to a central optic nerve, which passes the data received on to the brain. The cells are of two types – rods and cones, so called from their shapes – and there are over a billion in each eye. They are scattered over the surface of the retina except at the point where the optic nerve enters. This creates a blind spot, of which we are usually unaware, but which can easily be demonstrated. As if to compensate, a nearby part of the retina – the fovea – is especially sensitive, for looking at the finest details in an image. Humans with good eyes can see a coin at a hundred meters. Kestrels, who have a similar eye structure, can detect a mouse on the ground while hovering a kilometer above.

Human eyes are so positioned in the head that they allow us to gauge how far away objects are – binocular vision, as it is called. Try holding two matches, one beside the other, at arm's length. How much can one be brought toward you, before you perceive that they are at different distances? For most people, it is not much more than the thickness of the matches – a very fine feeling for relative distance.

Nevertheless, human eyes are not perfect instruments. Most optical devices suffer from some kind of defect – or "aberration" – and the eye is no exception. One defect common to all simple lenses is "spherical" aberration, which results in a blurred image. It occurs when light passing through the center of a lens does not form an image at the same distance as light passing through nearer to the edge. The human cornea and lens manage to correct for much of this, helped by use of the iris – the colored part of the eye. Light enters the eye through the pupil, the hole in the center of the iris. Changing the size of the pupil regulates not only the amount of light, but also its distribution over the lens. If the pupil contracts, light passes mainly through the center of the lens, and the slight blurring due to the outer parts is reduced. So, when we concentrate hard on an object, our eyebrows automatically wrinkle up and the pupils contract.

Many people are shortsighted. A common reason is that the eyeball is too long, so that light from the lens comes to a focus in front of the retina. (Correspondingly, in longsighted people, the light comes to a focus behind the retina.) The defect is usually corrected by adding artificial lenses – spectacles or contact lenses. Spherical aberration can, however, sometimes be used to advantage. A short-sighted person looking at a piece of text that is blurred to them sometimes finds that it looks clearer when read through a pinhole in a piece of cardboard. The reason is that the text can be viewed through the part of the lens that brings it to best focus.

▲ In order to see things our vision breaks down any scene into a series of steps. The picture at the top shows the final version of the scene as it is perceived. It is made up, as the successive frames below show, of three steps. The first picks out the color in the picture. The second identifies information relating to the static parts of the scene. The final component distinguishes the movement and depth that are present. The three steps together provide a unified, three-dimensional image.

► The picture at the bottom of the page represents a cross-section through the human brain. Above it is a diagram showing how visual information is analyzed in the brain. Information from the retinas of the two eyes is channeled to the respective optic nerves. These optic nerves cross as they enter the brain. Information from the left-hand sides of the two retinas goes to the right half of the brain, and vice versa for information from the right hand sides. The data that reach the visual cortex of the brain therefore represent the visual layout and depth of the scene which is being viewed. In the brain, this information is analyzed at different points vertically in the visual cortex and also at different regions horizontally along its surface.

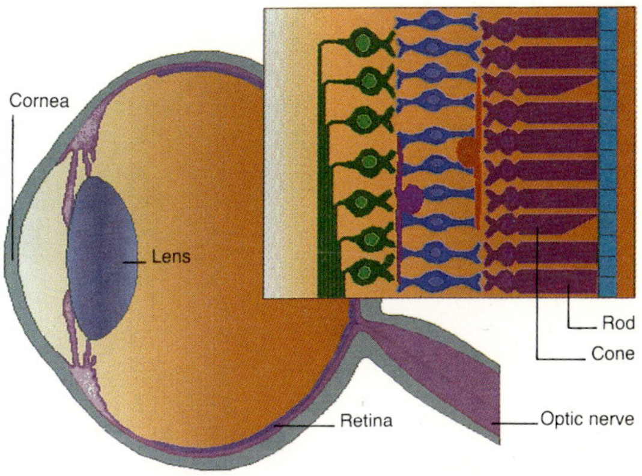

▲ ***The light-sensitive elements of the eye are distributed across its inner surface – the retina. These elements are of two types – the rods and the cones – which react differently to the incoming light. A rod is about 500 times more sensitive to light than a cone, but unlike a cone, it provides no information on the color of the light.***

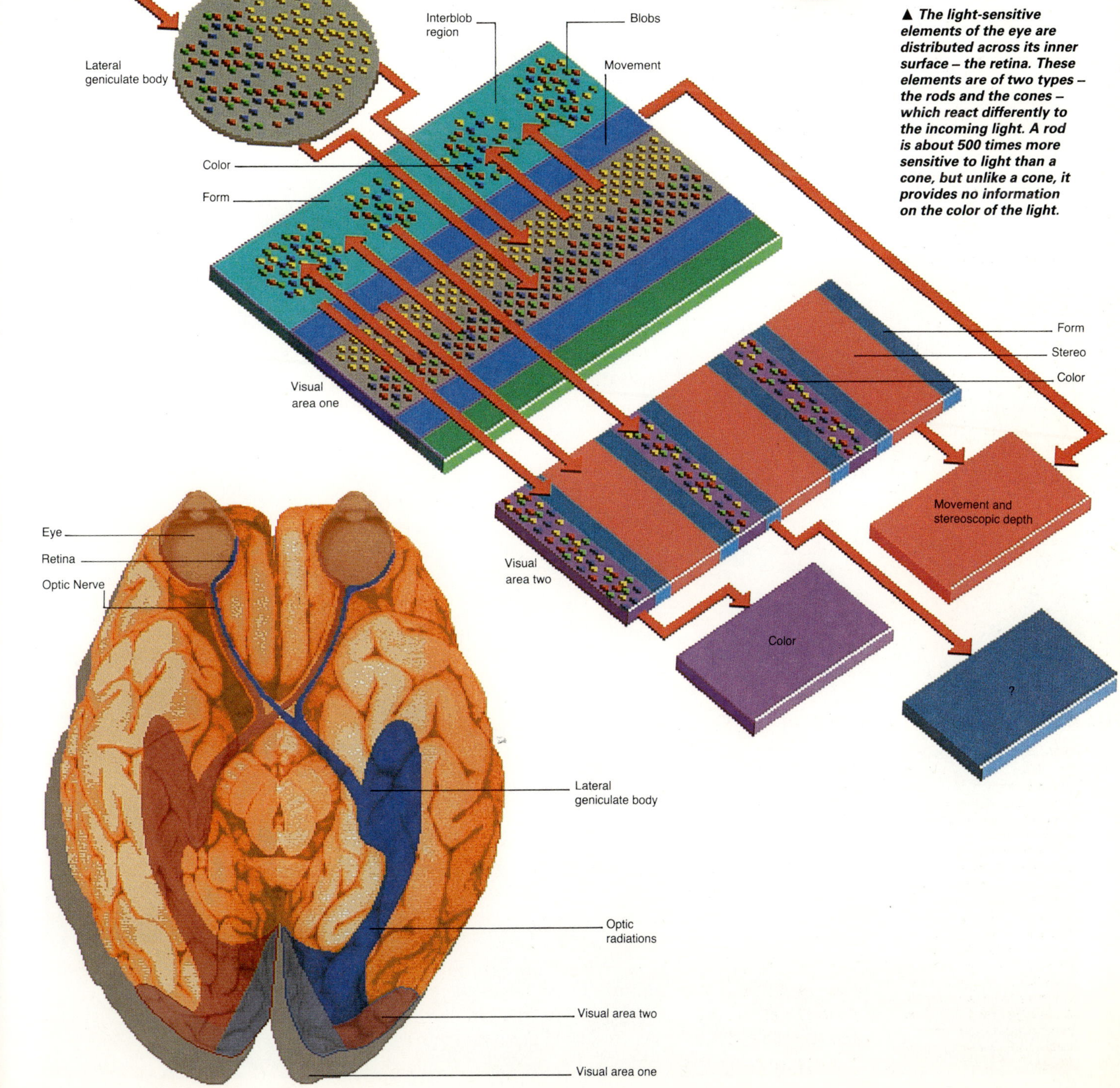

► Two color-blindness tests displayed on a viewer. Typically these consist of pictures that are made up of colored dots. For example, red dots may be put together in an identifiable pattern against a background of green dots. People with normal eyesight who are asked to detect the pattern will be able to. People who suffer from red-green color blindness will not.

▼ Color is often used in nature to repel or to attract. The lurid red mottling of a poison arrow frog warns other animals to steer clear. Dangerous snakes, spiders and plants also frequently display red warning signs (as do traffic signals). In contrast, the red of rosy apples, a baboon's posterior and the traditional attire of Saint Nicholas are all designed in their own way to attract.

▲ The part of the electromagnetic spectrum that is visible to humans. By "light" we usually mean white light from the Sun. White light, in fact, consists of all colors through red, orange, yellow, green, blue, indigo and violet. If sunlight shines through a glass prism, the white light splits into all its component colors. The same spectrum of colors is produced from sunlight by raindrops to form a rainbow.

Another common defect of optical devices is "chromatic" aberration. This can occur in the case of light – such as white light – which consists of several different colors mixed together. If these colors are brought to a focus at different points, a blurred image will result. The human eye deals with this problem by restricting the range of colors we can detect. We usually speak of a visible spectrum of colors from violet to red. Actually, our retina is sensitive to a greater color range than this. Many flowers have markings that are only visible in ultraviolet light, so that they can be seen by bees, but not normally by us. Ultraviolet light is filtered out by the lenses in our eyes. However, patients who have had a lens removed find the retina can detect ultraviolet light.

Color perception is strongly subjective and can vary considerably from person to person. Moreover, to many people the same gray color looks different when it has a spot of red in the middle and when it has a spot of blue. Color blindness, an inherited condition affecting the retina, exists to a greater or lesser extent in one out of twelve men, but in fewer than one in a hundred women. The problem usually lies in distinguishing between red and green, though occasionally blue and yellow are confused. But even among people who are not color blind the perception of color by the same individual can change with time.

Color perception can also change within human groups. Words relating to color did not enter into language all at the same time. For most languages, the first color words were for black and white. Red was added later, followed by yellow or green, and then blue. Judging from their vocabulary, the ancient Greeks distinguished fewer colors than do most modern civilizations. Perhaps this explains their otherwise puzzling description of the Mediterranean as "wine-dark". Human emphasis on black and white as fundamental might explain why black-and-white films were happily accepted by people for many years. Red came next because of its role in nature, either to attract or warn of danger.

Besides being able to detect and distinguish colors, the human eye copes remarkably well with light of different intensities. At one end of the scale, light can be so bright that we have to close our eyelids to protect our eyes from it. In less bright light, the eye has a number of ways of controlling the amount of light it receives. The pupil can expand or contract to allow more or less light to enter the eye. If you were to seat a friend in a darkened room, and after a few minutes switch on a torch and examine the friend's pupils, they would initially look large because the eye has been coping with low light levels, but very quickly the torchlight would cause them to contract to much smaller black spots.

The eye can also defend itself from too much light by a neat balancing act. The retina detects the light falling on it by means of a chemical change. Chemical substances in the rods and cones of the retina react with the light, causing them to lose their pinkish color (in much the same way as colored material is bleached when exposed to sunlight for a long time). Bleaching in the eyes only lasts momentarily. Once the chemical change has been notified to the optic nerve, the chemicals revert to their normal color. If, however, the light level remains high, the bleaching is almost continuous. Dark material absorbs light, but bleached material reflects it. Thus, if most of the retina is already bleached, any extra incoming light will be reflected back out of the eye again. This balancing act automatically limits the effect of bright light on the retina.

► An optical illusion illustrating how the human eye perceives differences of color and differences of lightness and darkness when an object is contrasted with its background. Although the central square appears to vary in shade from picture to picture, actually it is precisely the same shade of gray throughout. In fact, because the larger squares are themselves all superimposed on the uniform white page, the contrast perceived from square to square is even slightly reduced.

Like a camera, the eye can vary the length of time it takes to react to light. This is particularly important for lower levels of light. A camera has a shutter-speed control allowing a short exposure for a bright scene and a long exposure for a darker one. The eye accumulates light to detect faint signals. In bright light the accumulation time may be one-fiftieth of a second, whilst in dark conditions it can increase to half a second. Of course, the time it takes to react to changes increases accordingly. That is why sports where a fast reaction is essential, such as baseball or cricket, are most affected by poor light. At its best, the human eye comes quite close to being a perfect detector of faint light, sensitive to a light source of as few as 10 photons (a photon is the smallest quantity of light that any type of receiver can detect). To reach such a level of sensitivity, the eye has to be completely adapted to the dark. This takes up to half an hour, which explains why astronomers are advised to keep away from any lights for this length of time before they look at faint objects through a telescope.

The light-sensitive cells of the retina, the rods and cones, are not distributed across it in the same way. This is because they have different properties. Cones work better in bright light, whilst rods handle low-light levels more efficiently. The most sensitive part of the retina, the fovea, contains only cones, and therefore works best in bright light. To detect faint objects, an image is formed at some other point on the retina, where rods are present. This is why astronomers recommend detecting faint stars by using "averted vision" – that is, by looking slightly to one side of where the star is expected to be. Cones are the detectors of color in the retina. They fall into three groups, each of which absorbs light of a particular color. Combining the reactions of the three groups makes it possible to detect all the colors of the spectrum. At lowlight levels, colors begin to fade because light is recorded mainly by the rods. Few colors can be seen by moonlight.

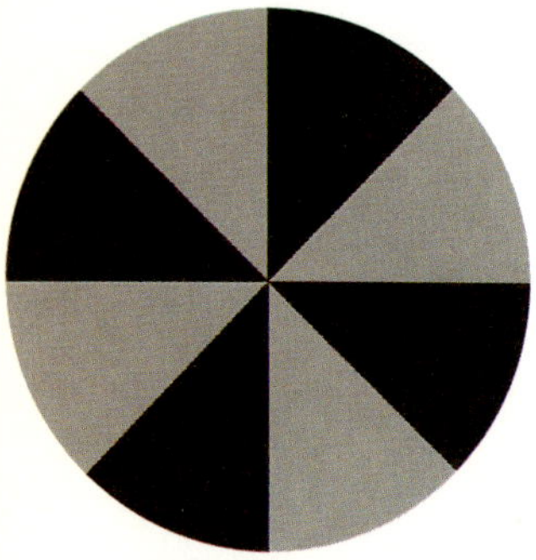

▲ Our eyes have a fundamental tendency to visualize scenes in terms of the contrasts present. Is this a picture of a gray Maltese cross on a black background or is it the other way round? Obviously, it is the same picture in either case, and the amount of light reflected from it remains the same. However, our pupils will change their size according to whether we see a gray or black cross.

► Cover up the picture on the right and then look at the other picture for a few seconds. Did you notice which part of the picture you concentrated on the most? Usually, the eyes jump rapidly from one point of interest to another, returning most often to regions of the picture that exhibit the greatest contrast. This is seen in the picture on the right, where the lines follow the typical pattern of gaze.

► Our eyes are attracted by bright lights. Most people looking at this scene will first be drawn to the sunset and then to the car headlights. The driver of the car will find it difficult to avoid looking at the headlights of traffic coming in the opposite direction, as anyone who has driven at night will know.

Apart from the obvious eye movements we make when scanning a scene, our eyes also continually make small movements which generally pass unnoticed. This perpetual refocusing, it seems, is necessary in order to see objects clearly. Indeed, the eye muscles are exercised all the time because the normal position of the eyeball is not its most relaxed position. When the eye muscles relax, in sleep or in death, the eyes roll upward. Doctors in films flick back the eyelid of badly injured patients to check whether they are still alive. If the eyeball has rolled upward, the patient is probably far gone. In fact, human eyes are designed to work best in the opposite direction – downward. Obviously this is good for monitoring the surface on which we are walking, but it has the unfortunate effect that we are less aware of things above us, such as low-lying roof beams.

When the eyes scan extended objects, their movement follows a few standard patterns. The commonest is a series of rapid jerks, the eye recording what is seen at each point, and then moving on. For example, you are unlikely to be reading this text continuously. Instead, your eye jumps from one word in the text to another further along the line. The whole text is absorbed, in part because the eye can take in a small area round each word, so that eye movements provide something like a series of photographs laid side by side. But there is usually no need to take in the whole text. Readers are continually trying to extract meaning from the text as they absorb it. Because the language in most texts shows a fair degree of redundancy, and because it is possible to guess where the words will lead next, meaning can generally be extracted without reading every word.

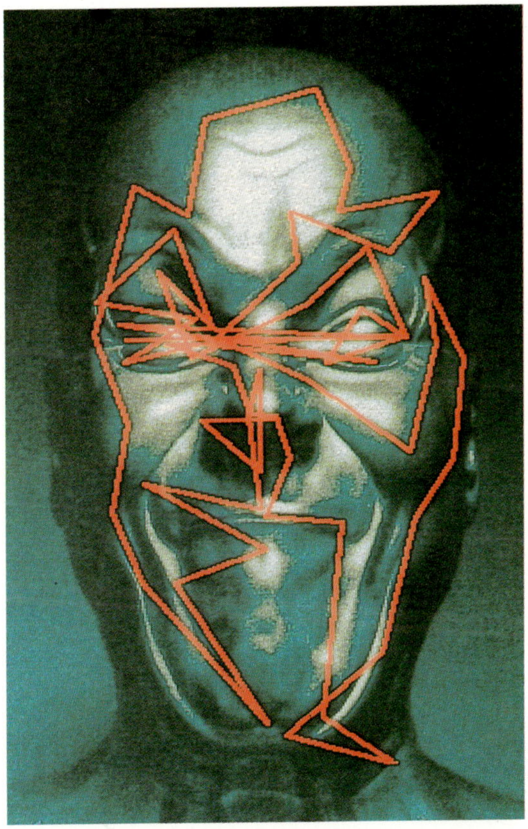

A skilled artist can direct our gaze to any part of the canvas by using biases in the way we see

Glance quickly at the triangle of words below:

Paris
in the
the spring

Many people at first sight overlook the second "the", because they automatically guess what the text is about from the keywords "Paris" and "spring".

Reading is not a purely passive activity. In a very real sense, we re-create the text as we go along. The same is true of pictures. The eyes are drawn to one part of the picture first. Then they jump to other areas, in much the same way as in reading text. Skilful artists can compose their pictures in such a way that our eyes are automatically drawn to the points they wish to emphasize. Interestingly, a mirror image of the picture will not usually produce the same effect. Our eyes are likely to look first at a different part of the picture, and the artist's intention will have been lost.

The human eye can move smoothly and continuously when the occasion demands, as when following something in motion. The eyes of spectators at a tennis match offer a good example. It can also move smoothly in one direction, but via a series of jumps in the opposite direction. Which observing strategy is employed by the eye depends on the circumstances. Sometimes we know what our eyes are doing and sometimes our eye movements are automatic – as in reading text.

How we record the world around us depends on the limitations of our eyes. For example, films work because they rely on the reaction time of the eye and its ability to store an image briefly. They present a series of still photographs rapidly one after the other to give an impression of motion. Television is similar. It also makes use of the limitations of the human eye to provide color. The television screen is covered with tiny groups of three dots, each of a different color – blue, green and red. The eye cannot resolve these dots and so sees them together. By variations in their relative intensities, the three basic colors induce in our eyes all the colors of the rainbow.

Images are not received passively by the eye. The mind is always busy, trying to make sense of the incoming visual data. This is true of both humans and animals, as shown by an experiment carried out with young geese. It so happens that the silhouette of a goose flying in the one direction resembles the silhouette of a hawk flying in the opposite direction. Goslings have good reason to be afraid of hawks. When the silhouette is moved in the "hawk" direction, it evokes a frightened reaction from them, but they are perfectly happy when the silhouette is moved in the "goose" direction. In other words, visual recognition depends not only on the actual appearance of the object, but also on the context in which it is presented.

The role of the mind in ordering visual experience is often best illustrated by the behavior of those deprived of this experience – the blind. For example, blind people often eat all the food on their plate, whereas sighted people often leave some. It seems that visual input to the mind helps decide how much we eat. More generally, the way we conceive the space about us depends strongly on whether we can see it or not. A sighted person thinks of a staircase as a single unit. A blind person thinks of it as a series of separate steps. When blind people regain their sight, they cannot understand the shapes and colors their eyes present to them. It may take years of learning before they can interpret the world in the same terms as normally-sighted people.

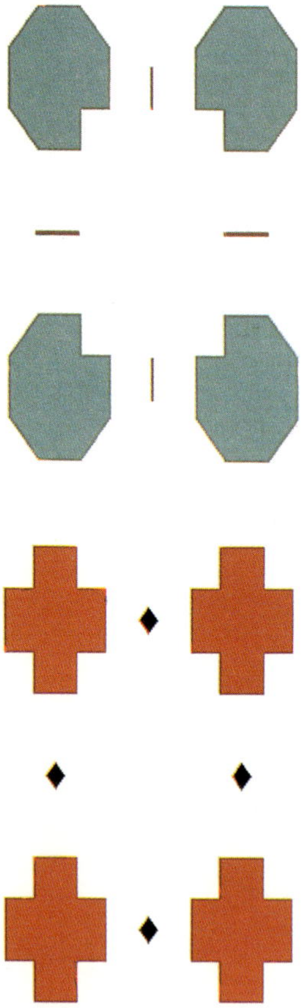

▲ The eye imposes a pattern on what it sees. The upper set of corner figures look like incomplete fragments. The eye reconstructs them to "see" a central rectangle. The lower set look complete with no immediate impression of a rectangle.

► If any color is subtracted from white light, what remains is its complementary color. For example, if red light is subtracted, turquoise is left. Traditionally, artists have represented color differences by a "color wheel", in which complementary colors appear in opposite sectors. Complementary colors also affect reflected light. Thus, if a substance absorbs the yellow component from white light, it will appear indigo in reflected light.

▼ Is this a rabbit or a duck? It depends which way you look at it. Equally, the silhouette of a goose in flight becomes a hawk if perceived as flying in the opposite direction. Goslings became afraid when such a silhouette was moved in the "hawk" direction.

Color in art

Scientific understanding of the properties of light and how the human eye responds to them developed in the 19th century, providing a major stimulus for artists. Particularly influential was the French chemist Eugène Chevreul (1786–1889) who headed research into dyes at the famous Gobelin tapestry works in Paris. In his book The Principles of Harmony and Contrast of Colors and Their Application to the Arts *(1839), Chevreul drew upon his industrial research experience to discuss how juxtaposing different colors affects what the eye sees.*

The first artist to be influenced by this work was Eugène Delacroix (1798–1863) whose later paintings relate the colors of objects to the shadows they cast differently from his earlier works. The interplay between shadow and object was taken much further by the early Impressionists Claude Monet (1840–1926) and Camille Pissarro (1831–1903), both of whom are believed to have had first-hand knowledge of Chevreul's work.

Later scientists too, notably Hermann von Helmholtz (1821–1894) and James Clerk Maxwell (1831–1879), investigated color vision and also left their mark on artists. The greatest exponent of these ideas in painting was the neo-Impressionist Georges Seurat (1859–1891). He set out to establish an entirely new kind of art based on scientific theories of color and contrast.

Starting with black and white to make sure he understood how balance worked, Seurat only later turned to color. In particular, he experimented with "complementary" colors. If you look at a bright red patch and then close your eyes, you will often see very briefly an "after image" of the patch, but it will be green, not red. Green is the complementary color of red. Other colors also have their complements. Complementary colors are important to the artist because they affect the way we see. A color achieves its greatest contrast when placed on a background of its complementary color. Seurat is most famous for his development of the "pointillist" approach to painting. Knowing that small patches of color, viewed from a distance, blur together to form an intermediate color, he reduced his paintings entirely to tiny blue, yellow, red and black dots, applied with small pointed brushes. With just these four colors, he could create any number of shades across the whole canvas simply by varying the frequency with which the colored dots were applied. Seurat's method of exploiting human color vision is the basis of color printing and color television today.

▲ Debbie Thomas performing at the World Ice Skating Championships, Budapest 1988. By concentrating on a distant point, she can keep her head fairly still for much of the time, even though her body is spinning. At intervals, however, she must move her head rapidly, snapping her eyes back, to catch up with her body movements. That way, she does not become dizzy and lose her balance.

Human hearing distinguishes sounds at ground level more easily than sounds from overhead

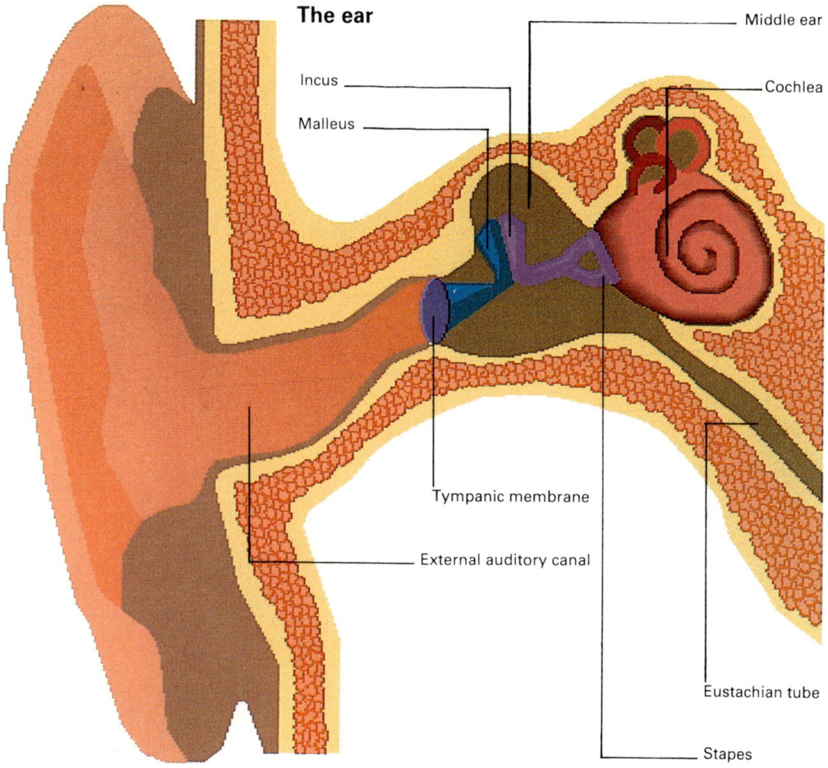

► Sounds are channelled into our heads by the outer ear and focused on the eardrum. The resulting vibrations of the eardrum set in motion a series of three small bones, which make up the "middle ear". They, in turn, transmit the vibrations to the "inner ear", a spiral-shaped tube filled with liquid. There, the motion of the liquid disturbs some 20,000 hairs, which convert the motion into signals that are sent to the brain along the auditory nerve. Different points along the spiral of the inner ear detect sounds of different pitch.

Sound

For the blind, hearing is easily the most important of the senses, and, even for sighted people, it ranks a good second to vision. Like light, sound is transmitted by waves, but, whereas light can cross empty space – we can see the stars – sound needs a medium through which it can pass as vibrations. On Earth, this medium is normally the atmosphere, but sound can pass just as well through liquids, such as the waters of the oceans, or through solids. Human beings can hear sound vibrations which vary in frequency from about 20 oscillations per second (referred to as 20 hertz or 20Hz) up to 20,000. The frequency of oscillation is commonly called the "pitch" of a sound, though the pitch we hear can depend also to some extent on other factors, such as the loudness of the sound.

The three bones of the middle ear regulate the sound intensity admitted to the inner ear, just as the iris regulates the light intensity admitted to the eye. Similarly, having two ears enables us to locate sounds – by detecting small differences in the input to each ear – much as having two eyes gives us vision in depth. The ears are much less sensitive to position, however, than are the eyes. They do fairly well in separating sounds nearby at ground level, which is why most people prefer a stereo sound system to a mono, but are less good with sounds from overhead. Most people have difficulty in locating a high-flying aircraft from the sound of its engines.

Deafness is usually thought of as an inability to hear faint sounds. It can also be an inability to hear sounds of a particular pitch. Typically, it is the higher frequencies that are lost. This disability can often make speech interpretation as difficult as loss of loudness can, because different speech sounds have different frequencies. For example, "d" and "b" are low-pitch sounds (both around 400Hz), whereas "s" and "th" have high pitch (both around 3,000Hz). A sufferer from this defect may, for example, hear the word "sad" as "add".

▲► Dogs, cats and monkeys can all hear to higher frequencies than humans. For example, a whistle in the range 30,000–40,000Hz would attract the attention of an Alsatian, but would be inaudible to us. Human beings can hear sound vibrations that vary from about 20 to 20,000Hz, but are most sensitive to sounds of around 5,000Hz. The note that orchestras tune their instruments to – the A above middle C – has a frequency of 440Hz. Sound intensity, or relative loudness, is measured in bels or decibels (dB). Rock music played through amplifiers in discotheques can approach the hearing pain threshold. People whose work exposes them to noise above this level must wear ear protectors.

◀ ***A section through the human inner ear, pictured by a scanning electron microscope, showing the organ of Corti, which changes sound signals into nerve impulses. It represents part of the liquid-filled spiral magnified nearly 500 times. Some of the inner hairs that line the inner ear are clearly visible. Motions of the liquid corresponding to sounds of different pitch are detected by hairs at different points along the spiral. Thus the nerve impulses that are sent to the brain differ according to the pitch of the sound received.***

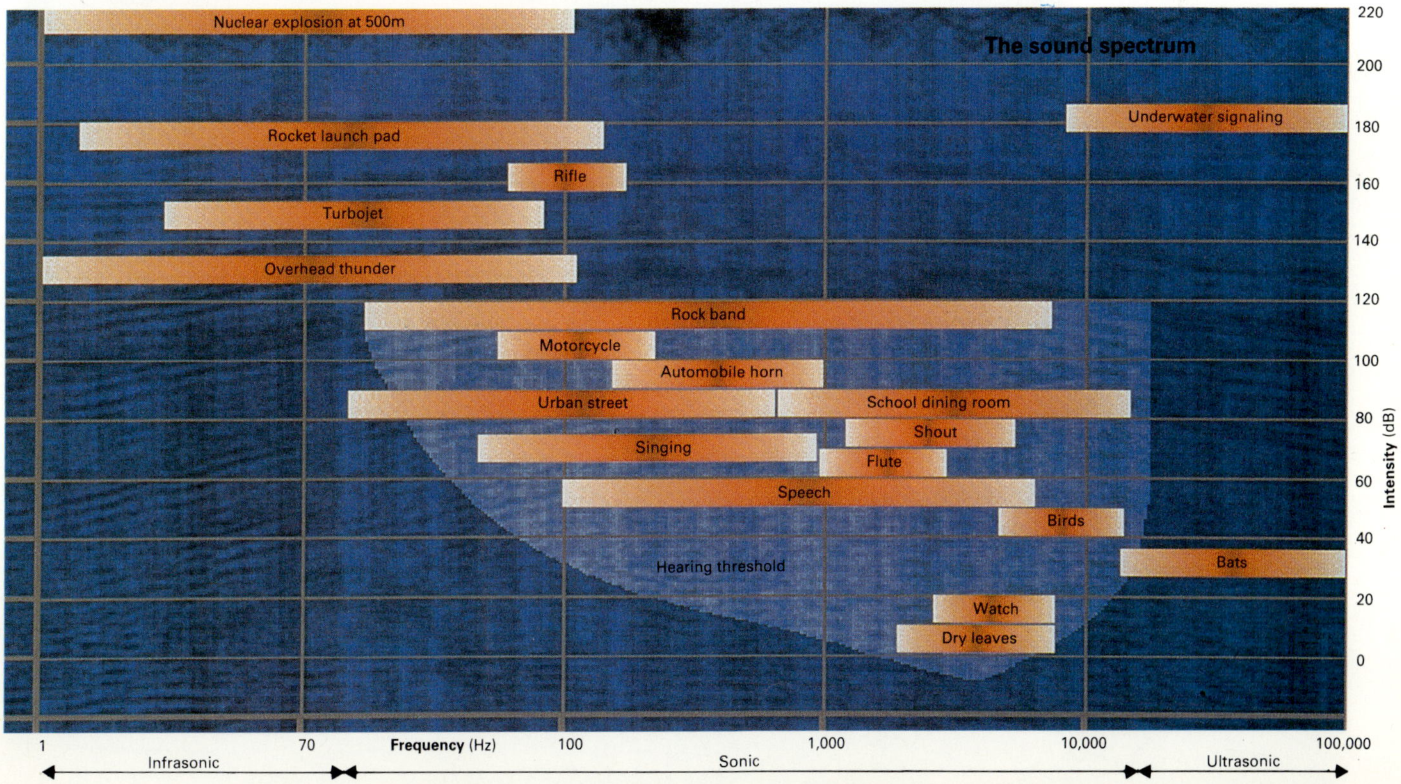

Does our enjoyment of bird song mean that the elements of music go beyond the human race?

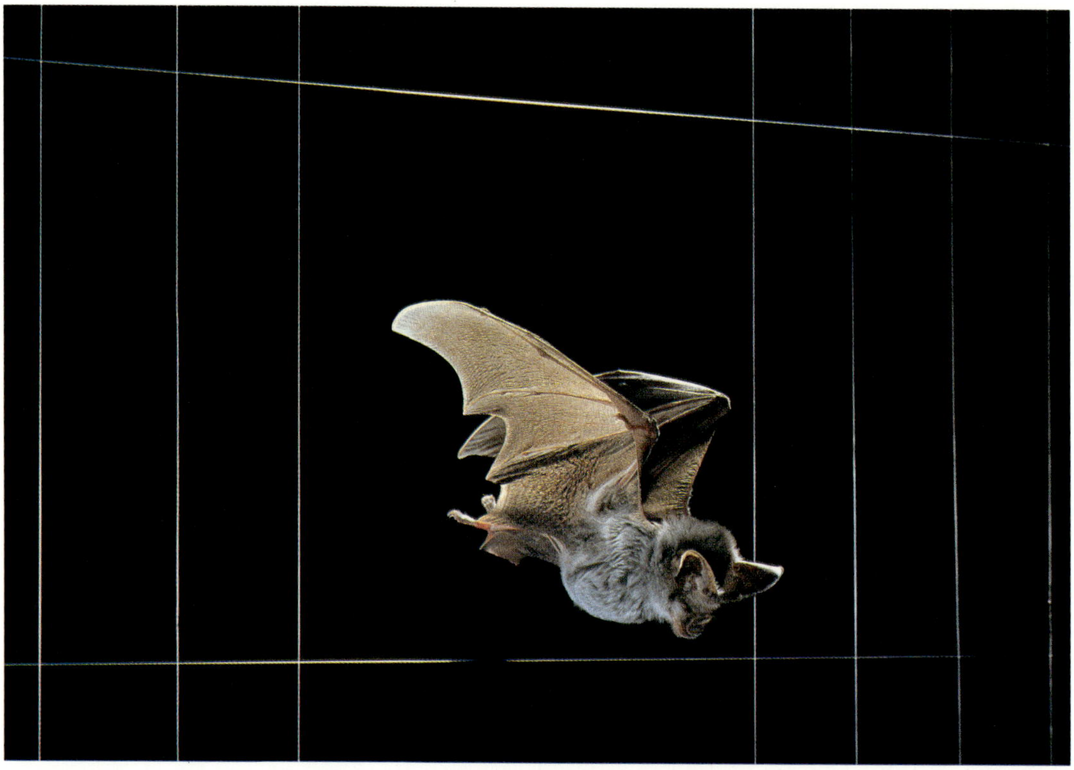

▼ Along with birds and humans, whales also communicate using complex sound patterns. The humpback whale, seen here, has a remarkable song that spans the whole range of human hearing (and probably beyond) and is individual. It can last half an hour, with repeats of intricate variations, as shown in the spectrograph.

Healthy ears are particularly good at disentangling a number of noises coming from different sources. This is sometimes called the "cocktail party problem". When we talk to someone at a party we may have a dozen other groups in our near vicinity all talking loudly. Yet we usually manage to hear what our partner is saying. Unlike some other animals, we cannot use our outer ear to concentrate on sounds from a particular source. Disentangling the sounds is something that mysteriously goes on within our heads. One clue to this procedure follows from the observations that speech is much easier to pin down at cocktail parties than other noises. It seems that, as with the eye, the bits of information that do filter through are pieced together to produce a result that makes sense to us. Many experiments have shown that humans reconstruct speech almost subconsciously in order to extract meaning from it. The following sentence is an example: "They saw that the eel was on the —". If this is read as it stands, with a missing word at the end, listeners will correctly hear the first word as "eel". If the word "table" is inserted for the blank, many will hear the first word as "meal". Inserting the word "shoe" for the blank makes people hear "heel". "Axle" leads to "wheel", and so on.

◀ A bat navigating its way through a set of wires. Bats are the best known, but not the only, animals who find their way around by listening for the echoes of sound waves beamed back by obstacles in their path. The bat emits a stream of high-pitched squeaks and uses the direction and intensity of the returning echoes to map its surroundings. The system is mimicked by sonar (sound navigation ranging) to identify shoals of fish at depth or unexploded mines.

▲ Spectators applauding at a netball match. General applause is commonly a sign of approval. But though we all clap together, we each have our own way of doing it. The rate of clapping and the sound produced vary from person to person. Experiments have shown that about half of us can identify our own clapping when we hear it afterwards on a tape recording.

Usually the more absorbed someone is in listening to a sequence of sounds, the better that person will hear them. Conversely, some background music may pass virtually unheard for long periods. How long noise can go unnoticed depends on the kind of noise. Speech normally arrests our attention. People whispering together can be just as distracting as people talking aloud. Likewise, songs are more difficult to ignore than instrumental music. The notices in libraries asking for silence really do reflect a need of people who are concentrating. Since in most environments silence is difficult to enforce, attempts have been made to introduce some "white noise" into offices. White noise is a mix of meaningless sound covering a wide range of pitch – the sound of wind in the trees, or of surf breaking on a beach. The intention is that the noise will merge into the background, but at the same time will hide distracting noises such as conversation.

Just as an artist can direct our attention to a particular part of a picture by using biases in the way we see, so a composer of music can play on the peculiar properties of our sense of hearing. Some of the biases in our hearing would seem to be universal. Long ago, Pythagoras (c. 572–497 BC) and his followers pointed out that we obtain particular satisfaction from musical notes that stand in a simple arithmetic relationship to each other. For example, a plucked string gives out a specific note. If a string half as long, or a third as long, is plucked, the notes produced seem to be related to the first note, and together produce a pleasant sound. Notes produced by strings of arbitrary length, however, bear no such relationship. Making this connection between notes seems to be a common property of human hearing. Indeed, the fact that we enjoy bird song may mean that the basic elements of music extend beyond the human race.

A very simple form of music is rhythmic noise – such as is produced by tapping a hollow tree trunk, or by clapping. In fact, our reliance on vision as the primary sense often prevents us from realizing how adaptable our hearing can be. Blind people can detect the presence of objects by their echo. Tapping the ground with a white stick produces reflected sound from any obstacle encountered. Most sighted people, when blindfolded, also quickly learn to detect obstacles in this way. The ability to use echoes is apparently common to all of us, but it usually remains latent because we rely so much on our sight.

Blind people can often identify others present by their smell

Smell and taste

As information gatherers, sight and hearing are easily our most important senses. Nevertheless, we still make regular use of smell and taste. For humans smell is a less important and less sensitive source of information than for many other animals. Dogs can be trained to differentiate between a wide range of substances by smell, and they play an important part in drug detection nowadays, sniffing out small amounts of drugs in the presence of other smells. Trained police dogs can also readily distinguish between the smells of human individuals (except, apparently, identical twins). Studies of blind people suggest that the human sense of smell, too, is potentially much greater than is generally realized. There are well-documented cases of blind people who could allot clothes to their owners purely by means of smell. Indeed, Helen Keller, the famous blind-mute, could identify the arrival of a friend even before they spoke by that person's smell. Doctors have detected some types of illnesses by smell. For example, patients with schizophrenia (popularly known as a "split" personality) are known to give off a very distinctive odor.

Odors are, themselves, subject to fashion. It is only quite recently that cleanliness has been elevated to a place next to godliness. Napoleon once sent a message to Josephine saying, "Don't wash yourself. I am coming home." (Yet he often used a bottle of eau-de-cologne a day on himself.) Reaction to some smells may vary with time. Women can detect musky smells better around the time of ovulation. It is generally believed that smells can influence human sexual behavior. The menstrual cycles of women who live together can become synchronized partly through the unconscious mutual influence of their body odors. Yet no one has so far managed to demonstrate that any alleged aphrodisiacal smell justifies the claims that are made for it. In any case, just as peoples' vision or hearing differ, so does their sense of smell. Interestingly, there is no word – analogous to "blind" or "deaf" – to describe someone who has lost the sense of smell.

Taste is usually discussed together with smell because it is impossible to take a substance into the mouth without its odor passing up the back of the throat to the nose. This interaction of taste and smell forms an essential part of wine tasting. The taster always smells the wine before tasting it. Still holding the wine in the mouth, the taster draws in air through the lips, so as to convey some of the vapor up to the nostrils from the back of the mouth. The combined taste and smell is finally described in the impenetrable words beloved of wine connoisseurs, "smoky", "flinty", "woody", and so on.

Although a fairly wide range of tastes can be distinguished – with practice maybe as many as 60 – they all depend on four basic taste senses. These are generally labeled bitter, salt, sour and sweet, and are best detected by different parts of the tongue. The tip of the tongue responds more to sweet tastes, the back to bitter tastes, and the middle part to salt and sour. (This variation is the reason why wine is often swished around the mouth in the process of tasting.) Not all tastes are as expected. Obviously vinegar, an acid, should taste sour, but why should substances containing lead taste sweet? Of course, individuals differ in their taste-detection capabilities, and some people are "taste-blind". Not surprisingly, taste has little application in modern science, though it used to be much more important. As recently as the 1930s, a problem arising in a major industrial chemical process involving the separation of soap and alcohols was finally resolved only after the product had been inadvertently tasted.

▲ Professional wine tasters use a combination of senses – taste, smell and sight – to ascertain the quality of a wine. They can extract a great deal of information from this variety of inputs. Although as we grow older our receptors of taste and smell gradually die off in large numbers, wine tasters can rely on their accumulated experience to compensate for any loss of these senses.

► A human tongue showing how different areas respond to the four basic tastes – bitter, salt, sour and sweet. The tongue of an average adult is about 10cm long and has some 9,000 taste buds on its surface but their number declines in middle age. Relatively few of the taste buds are situated at the center of the tongue. In a child, the taste buds are more uniformly distributed across the surface. The range of tastes that we commonly experience in everyday life are combinations of two or more of the four basic tastes.

► "Scent marking". A male capybara rubs his nose against a bough. Many animals, including humans, have special glands on the surface of their bodies which produce scented secretions. Some animals, such as the capybara, leave this secretion on the ground or on a nearby object. Scent marking acts as a means of communication between individuals.

The tongue

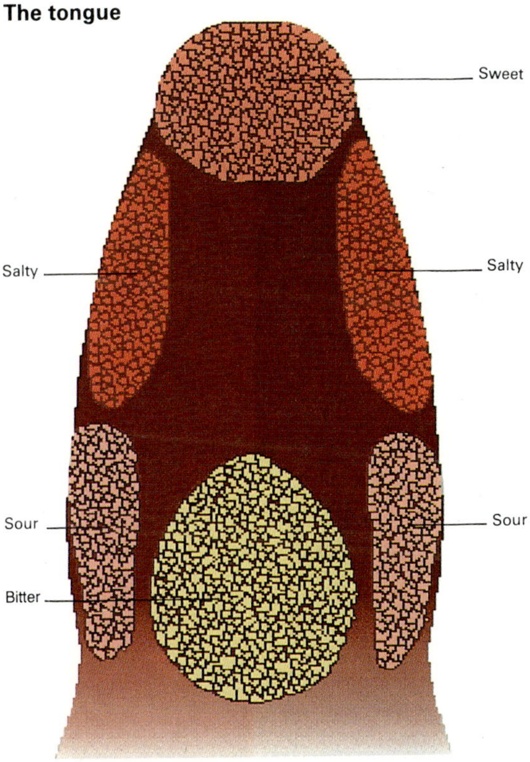

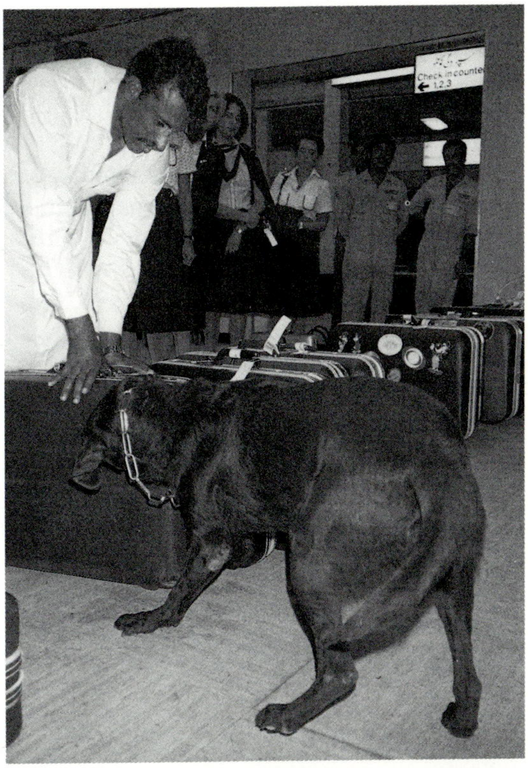

◀ *A labrador, attended by his trainer, sniffs for drugs in the luggage of passengers boarding a flight from Karachi to Europe. Alsatians are also employed as sniffer dogs at Karachi airport, with both dogs and handlers trained in West Germany. Because of their acute sense of smell, dogs can be trained to identify particular smells, whether of a substance or associated with a person, even when disguised by other smells.*

Touch

Tasting involves feeling with the tongue, and so the texture and shape of a substance are detected along with its taste. Most parts of our body can identify properties of this kind because our skin is covered with sensors. Their purpose is to monitor the environment around us. For example, some are sensitive to temperature. The most important sensors, however, are those that can be stimulated by physical contact. Hands are particularly well equipped with sensors of this type, and experiments have shown that sensitivity of touch increases rapidly from the palm to the fingertip. It is easy to show this by measuring how closely two pressure points can approach each other before they are felt as a single point. If two pins are used for this experiment, usually they can be five times further apart on the palm than on the finger and still be felt as a single pressure. In consequence, to explore the world around us we tend to use our highly sensitive fingertips.

For some types of information, touch is the most useful sense of all. The flatness or smoothness of a surface is often better tested by feeling than by looking. Indeed, a good deal of traditional knowledge in crafts such as woodworking is acquired through the sense of touch. Touch is also important in modern technology for inputting data from a computer keyboard. But the most obvious example of its use as a means of acquiring information is in reading Braille. The Frenchman Louis Braille (1809–1852) was blinded by an accident at the age of three. He studied music and became an accomplished organist. The difficulties he experienced in the course of his education led him to produce a new system of writing based on six raised dots in various groupings which could be felt with the fingertips. (He also extended this to provide a musical notation for the blind.) Expert readers of Braille using the fingertips of both hands to speed up the jump from line to line can read at the rate of 200 words a minute.

▼ ***Racing pigeons being released. Pigeons find their way home using the Sun as a guide by day, and the stars by night. They can detect slight changes to atmospheric pressure and probably also sense the direction of the Earth's magnetism, orienting themselves like a compass needle. Humans may have a similar residual ability.***

► ***A blind student working at a computer terminal reads a text he has just printed out in Braille. Using the fingertips of both hands considerably speeds up the reading process. Translating books into Braille has always been costly and time-consuming. Now, however, advances in information technology have permitted all kinds of very specialized information to be made available in Braille which otherwise might have been too expensive to produce.***

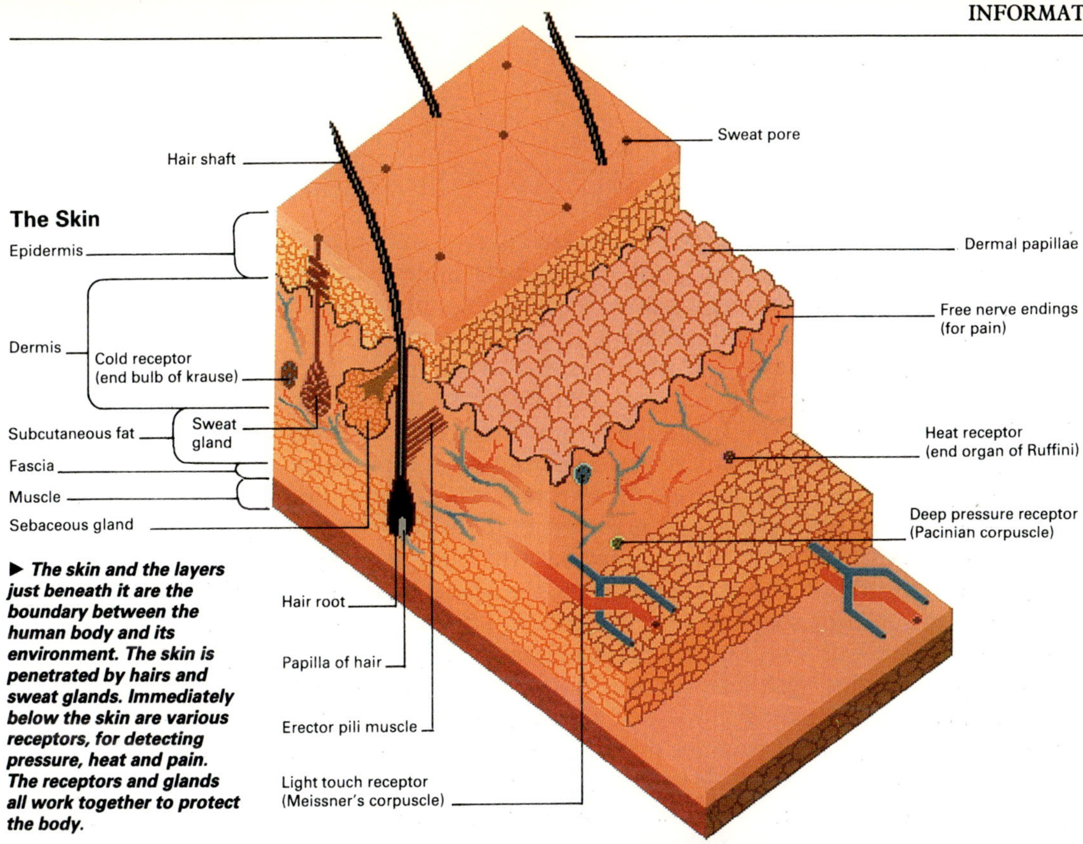

► ***The skin and the layers just beneath it are the boundary between the human body and its environment. The skin is penetrated by hairs and sweat glands. Immediately below the skin are various receptors, for detecting pressure, heat and pain. The receptors and glands all work together to protect the body.***

The brain and information

Human reliance on sight and hearing has had its effect on our brain. A dog's brain has a large area set aside for handling information on smell. Our brain is unique amongst animals for the amount of space it devotes to thinking and communicating. Our senses provide information, but it is the brain that stores and processes it. So far, much more is known about the way the senses work than about the operation of the brain. All vertebrates (animals having a backbone) – fishes reptiles, birds and mammals – have a brain consisting of three parts. From the front of the head, these are the forebrain, the midbrain and the hindbrain. The hindbrain connects to the rest of the body by way of the spinal cord. The brain issues commands which are distributed through a network of nerves connected to the spinal cord. This network is matched by a similar nerve network which feeds messages back to the brain. Suppose, for example, you want to test whether the bath water is at the right temperature. A message goes down the network from the brain saying – put a finger in the water. The temperature sensors flash back the message – too hot; take out your finger and turn on the cold tap. If the water is hot enough to scald your finger, you react immediately, because of a direct reflex connection at the level of the spinal cord. Otherwise, you can take your time in reaching a decision.

The most obvious physical difference between the human brain and those of other animals – apart from its large volume relative to the size of the body – lies in its remarkable development. The human

▼ A view of the human brain seen from the left and slightly from behind. The wrinkled surface of the forebrain and the division between the frontal lobe at the top and the lower temporal lobe are clearly shown. Also visible are the division between the forebrain and the mid- and hindbrains, the cerebellum and part of the brainstem.

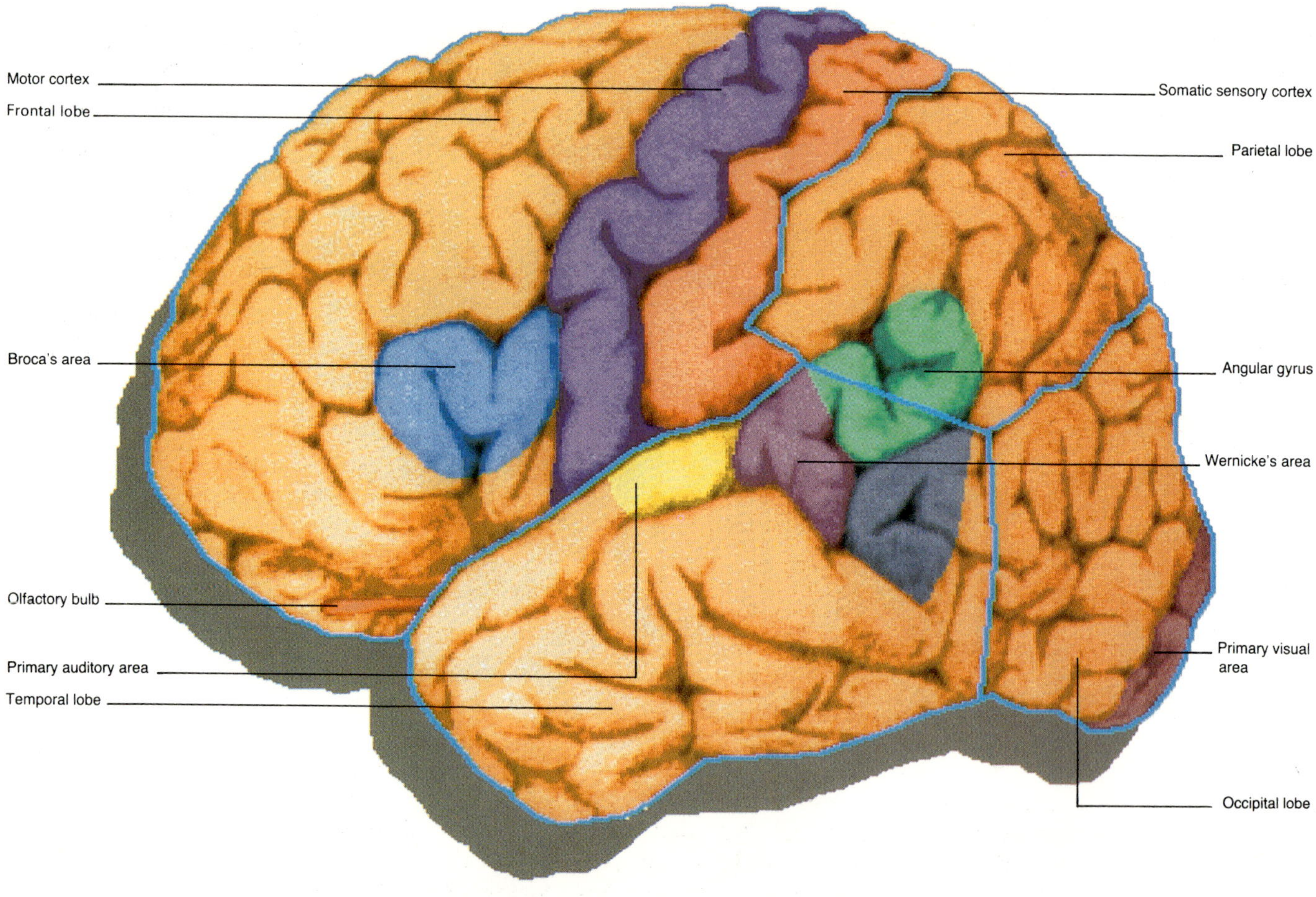

▲ *A captive chimpanzee in Zaire. Chimpanzees are often used as a basis for comparison with human behavior. They are one of the most intelligent animals after humans, and the chimpanzee brain shows a number of similarities with the human brain. However, there are equally significant differences. For example, the brain of the newly-born chimpanzee weighs about as half as much as that of the fully grown adult, whereas the human brain at birth is only a quarter of the weight of the adult brain. In both cases, the anatomy of the mother prevents the baby's head from being any bigger. Thus, the human brain grows and develops much more between infancy and adulthood than does the brain of the chimpanzee. Not surprisingly, these differences affect respective patterns of family life and the abilities of the fully grown adults.*

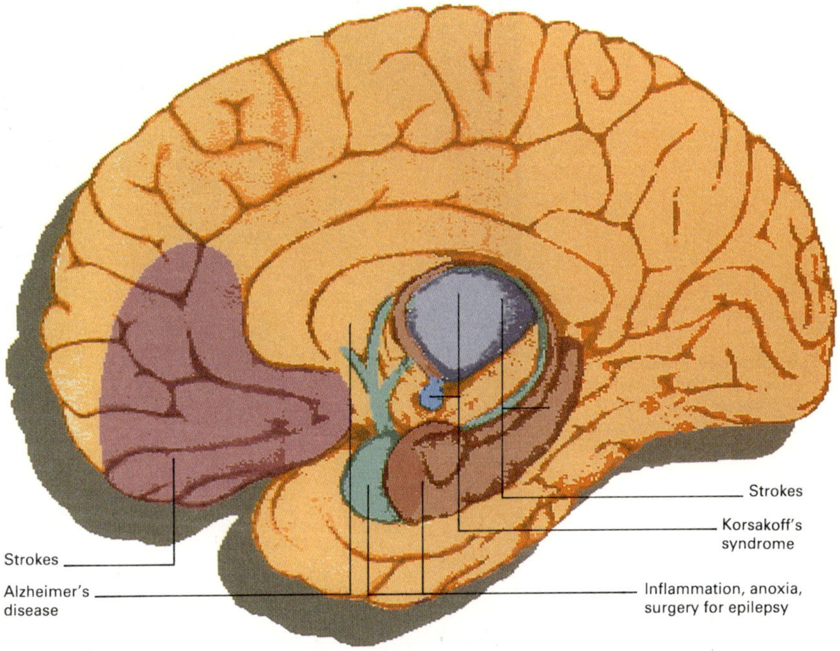

▲ *Cutaway of the human brain showing sites of damage that can cause loss of memory. Since experimenting on living human brains is ruled out information is gathered by studying brain damage caused by accident or disease, or from brain surgery in cases of serious illness. For example, patients with severe epilepsy may have the frontal lobe removed. It is found that this operation always affects their memory.*

forebrain has become much larger than the other two parts. The hindbrain is situated at a point in the head level with the bottom of the ears. It is sometimes called the reptilian brain because it is devoted to the most basic bodily functions, such as breathing, which take up almost the entire brain of a reptile. Attached to it is the cerebellum (little brain) which is mainly involved with such things as posture, but also deals with some kinds of simple memory storage. Above the hindbrain comes a region, sometimes called the mammalian brain, which is devoted to feeding, fighting, fleeing and sexual reproduction. The midbrain in human beings is simply a small upward extension of the hindbrain, but it acts as the link with the forebrain.

When we speak of the "brain", we usually mean the forebrain. In humans the forebrain, or cerebrum, takes up over 90 percent of the entire brain. The skull limits the maximum volume that the human brain can occupy but, by extensive wrinkling of its surface, the brain can greatly increase its area even though the volume remains the same. The surface area is important because most of the activities that we term "thinking" occur in a thin layer, a few millimeters thick, which coats the surface of the forebrain. This layer – the cortex (from the Latin word for the bark of a tree) – consists of nerve cells packed very closely together. The cortex is more popularly known as the gray matter because that is its color when a body is dissected. Likewise, the interior of the forebrain, which consists of nerve fibers interconnecting with the cells in the cortex, is sometimes called the white matter.

The unique expansion of the human forebrain has had an effect on the way family life has evolved. Human babies are born at an earlier stage of their development than other animals. A human child needs to be cared for over a much longer period than does an infant chimpanzee. Thus human organization has arguably been influenced from the outset by the growth of the forebrain.

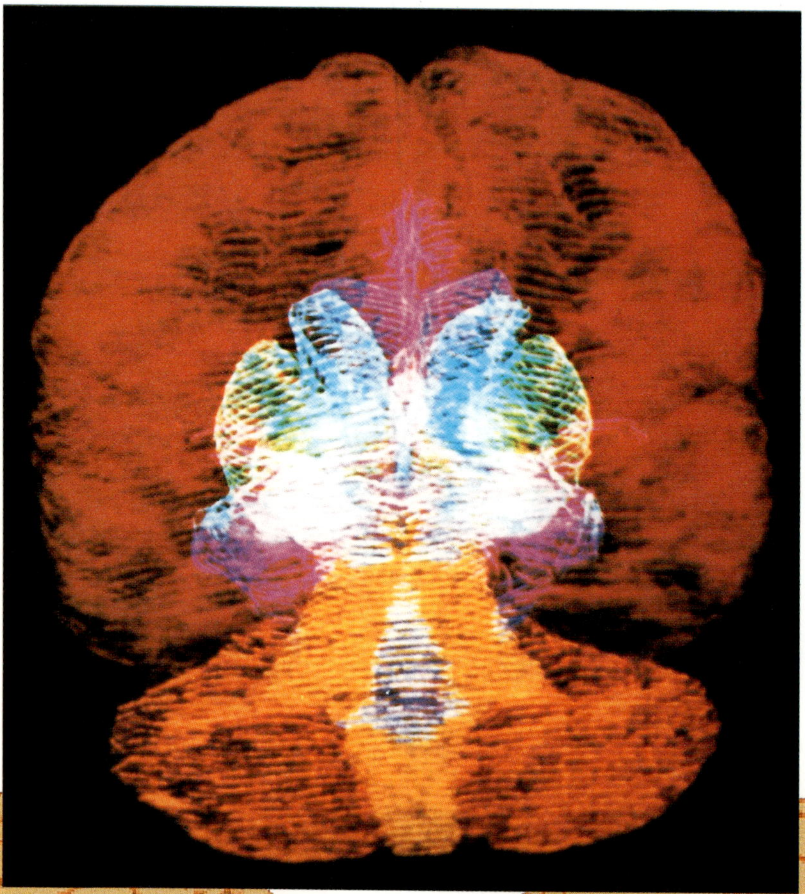

► ***Computer-generated image of an adult human brain seen from behind. The red areas correspond to the hemispheres of the forebrain, which control most of our conscious activities. The blue-white area in the center is the midbrain, which links the forebrain to the hindbrain and cerebellum. The cerebellum, which controls balance and muscular coordination, is shown as the orange region.***

▼ ***The hemispheres of the brain are not symmetrical. The fissure above the temporal lobes slope differently in the left and right hemispheres (upper pictures). The left and right upper surfaces of the temporal lobes also look different (lower pictures).***

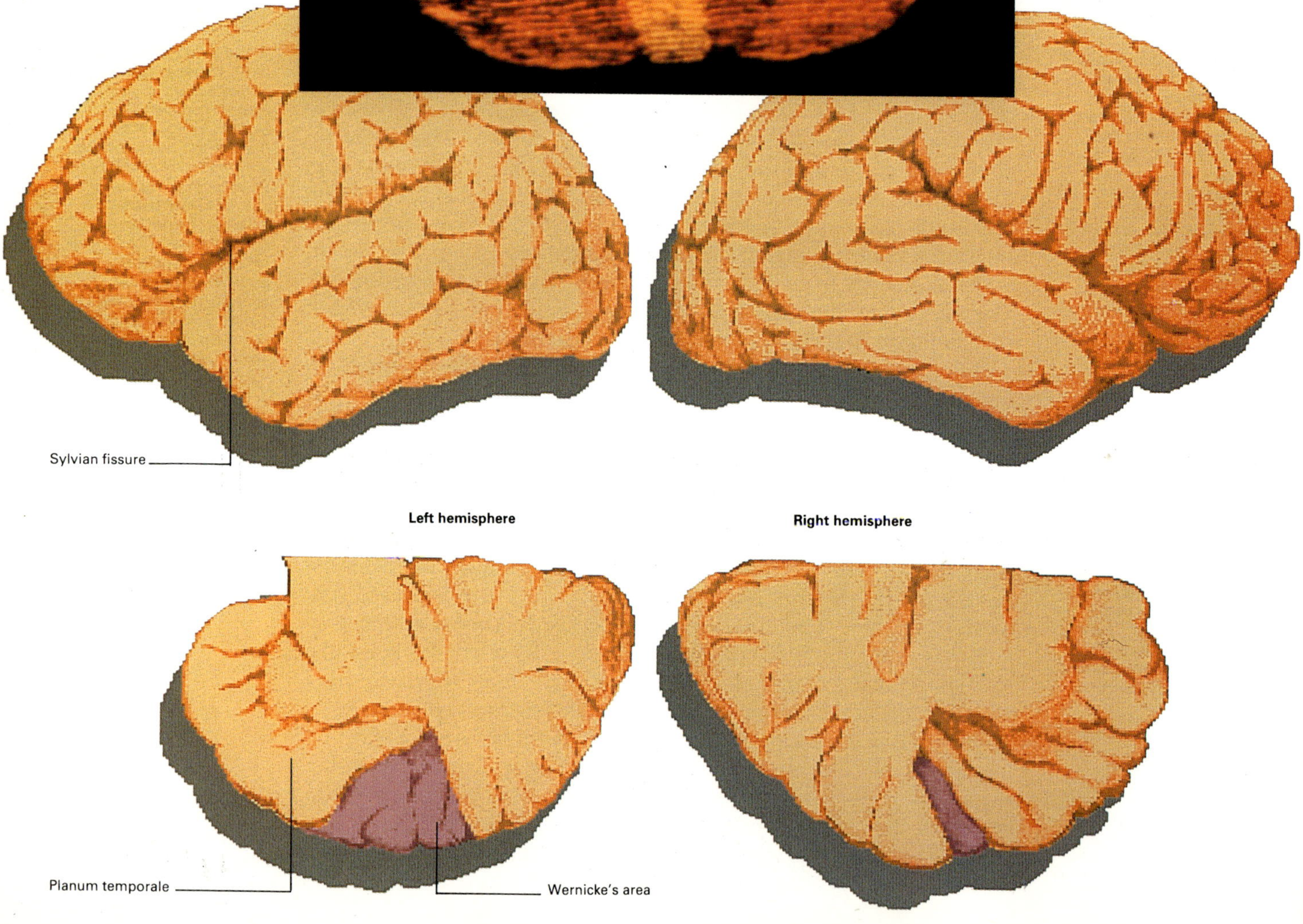

The forebrain is divided into halves, the so-called left and right hemispheres. The left hemisphere controls the right side of the body and the right hemisphere the left side. The hemispheres are connected in the middle by a thick band of nerve fibers. Each hemisphere is itself divided into four lobes. Starting at the front of the brain, the first of these lies immediately behind the forehead, and is called the frontal lobe. It is the largest of the four. Next is the parietal lobe, beneath which is the occipital lobe, and in front of that, and extending under the frontal lobe, is the temporal lobe.

The four lobes have different functions. The frontal lobe is the general coordinator of the brain, utilized in planning, understanding complex ideas and reaching decisions. The parietal lobes, it seems, mark the place where we assemble our general idea of the world around us. In particular, this is the area of the brain concerned with language. The occipital lobe is almost entirely devoted to vision and to analyzing information gathered by the eyes, while the temporal lobes are for hearing, and memorizing information.

The two hemispheres of the brain are not identical, and corresponding lobes in the left and right halves may have rather different functions. However, this left-right distinction is less clear than functional differences between lobes. Broadly, the left hemisphere is more concerned with language and thought processes, whereas the right is devoted more to spatial orientation and applied thinking. This is generally true for right-handed people. It can change for left-handed people, or if one side of the brain suffers damage. Naturally, because of the problems of experimentation with human beings, knowledge about the brain has been gathered largely by studying patients afflicted with brain damage.

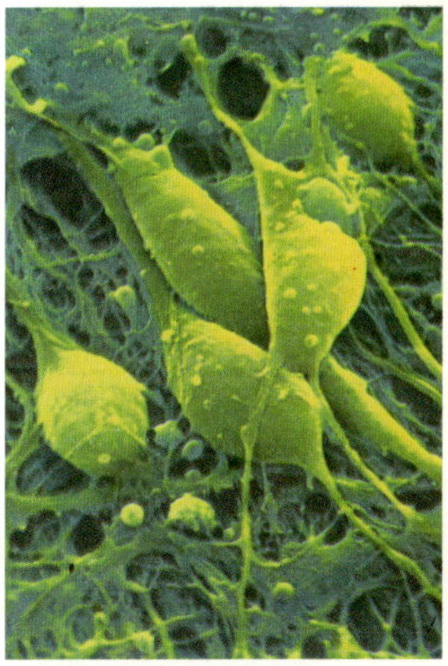

▲ The gray matter of the brain taken with a scanning electron microscope at a magnification of over 150. The number of neurones (nerve cells) that make up the heavily folded gray matter are clearly visible. The large central cell of each nerve appears as a yellow-green bulge. Axons and dendrites, colored blue-green, can also be seen, extending out from these cells.

▼ A patient in whom the connections between left and right brain hemispheres had been severed in an operation was shown the patterns in the central row below, and asked to reconstruct them using first the right and then the left hand. The patients attempts were characteristically different for each hand. This suggests that each brain hemisphere brings into play different skills.

Every day an estimated 100,000 of our brain cells die

The brain and the senses

The senses gather information. The brain processes it. The nerve cells in the body link the two together. The human brain contains some hundred billion nerve cells, each with perhaps a thousand connections to other cells. Thus the capacity of the brain for handling information is truly enormous.

How the senses interact with the brain can be illustrated by considering what happens when we view an object. First the light from the object hits the retina of each eye. The signals from the retina are then brought together in the optic nerve. The left and right optic nerves meet back in the brain where their fibers intertwine so that the signals from both eyes go to both brain hemispheres. The intermingled optic fibers continue to the occipital lobe, where they form some of the white matter, with connections to the gray matter.

The gray matter is divided up in two ways. Along the surface of the occipital lobe, it divides into strips which are dominated alternately by information from the left eye and the right eye. Perpendicular to the surface, the gray matter is divided into half a dozen layers. Each of these helps create an identifiable image of the original object. The retina has broken the image up into a series of dots, which have been mapped onto the brain. The problem is one of assembling these dots into a meaningful picture. Each cell has its own particular role. For example, some cells will react only to dots which reform into lines that are horizontal relative to the viewer. The initial reconstruction of the image is passed forward to another region of the occipital lobe. There it is examined and passed forward again. This process of passing on from one region to another may occur a dozen times or more. Each time, more and more information is extracted from the image, for example, the color of the object and whether it is mobile or stationary. Eventually all the information that has been gathered is passed to the temporal lobe, where it is stored in the memory, and to the frontal lobe, where it is analyzed. Once the object has been identified in this fashion a decision is taken as to what, if any, action should be taken.

The analysis of visual data is especially complicated, which is why the brain devotes so much space to it. Even so, reaction to a visual

1
2
3

▲ Nerves transmit messages by an essentially electrochemical process, rather like a battery. Sodium channels in the nerve membrane open in response to a positive charge (2), admitting sodium ions. They then go into a closed-and-inactive form which cannot open (3). Once the cell's negative charge has been restored they revert to a closed-but-ready-to-open form (1).

▼ Nerve cells of the human brain. Each nerve cell has an axon (up to 1m long), which carries information to other cells. It also has numerous dendrites (each less than 1mm long), which convey information to the nerve. Axons branch at their ends to form "twigs", which connect with the twigs of dendrites of neighboring cells at points called synapses. There, a decision is made whether to pass on a signal to the next nerve cell. In this way, nerve cells in the body or brain link up with others.

image is usually so fast that the whole process is to all appearances automatic. Analysis of data conveyed by our other senses proceeds in much the same way and can be equally rapid. What we hear, for example, is disentangled in the first instance by a region of the temporal lobe and stored there. Information input from the senses must always first be stored, albeit temporarily, before it can be analyzed. Human brains do not regenerate nerve cells in the way that, say, our bones repair themselves during our lifetime. Indeed, cells in the brain can die quite easily. One estimate is that we lose 100,000 every day. But the important thing in thinking is not simply the number of nerve cells in the brain, but how well they are linked to each other. Though the cells die with time, the number of connections – the synapses – can increase. Whether or not they do depends on how much the brain is exercised. It appears that the brain, if used sufficiently, can actually increase in weight. Loss of memory and thinking capability with age is therefore not inevitable. The important question for elderly people is how to avoid the disease of senility.

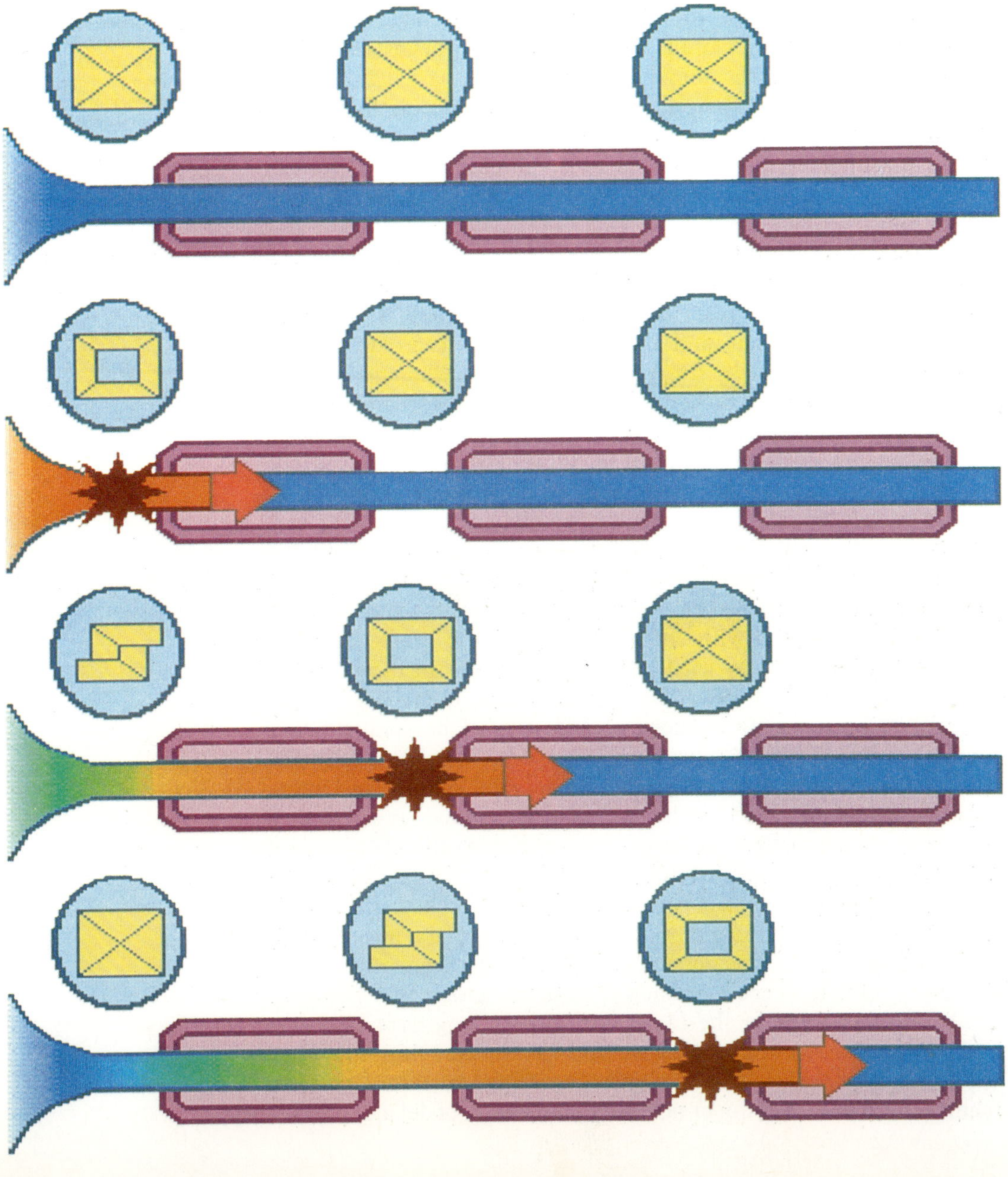

◀ *Diagram of a neuron showing an action potential traveling down its length and the effect it has on the sodium channels. The action potential is brief because after a few milliseconds the automatic closure of the channels prevents more sodium ions coming into the cell. The membrane pumps can then work to restore the negative potential and thus prevent the nerve going into a spasm of firing. When the action potential reaches the neuron terminal, voltaged-gated ion channels open to admit calcium ions, which trigger the release of the neurotransmitter.*

Young children can remember details of pictures for longer than many adults

How memory works

Memory involves three activities – learning new information, storing this information and retrieving it for subsequent use. How these activities develop can be examined in terms of what people remember. For example, it is a common experience that memories disappear, or become distorted, with time. There are two equally plausible, but conflicting explanations, for this. One is that a memory always decays with time unless it is regularly refreshed. The other supposes that a memory is stable in itself, but, as other memories crowd into the brain, so the original memory is weakened and displaced.

◀ *Pairs of objects used to test memory in experiments on monkeys. At first, only one object of each pair is seen by the monkey. The monkey is then shown each object again, but this time paired with a second object which it has not seen before. The monkey's reactions to both the "familiar" and "unfamiliar" objects are monitored in order to relate them to the animal's brain activity.*

There is greater consensus about types of memory. Humans seem to have three basic forms of memory. One is "immediate" memory, sometimes called photographic memory. Most people who are shown a photograph or other picture very briefly can remember its details for about one-tenth of a second. After that, much of it is forgotten. Young children can retain the details in their heads for rather longer, as can many adults with nonliterate cultural backgrounds. It seems that learning to read somehow interferes with the ability to remember graphical features. Short-term memory is the retention of certain types of information for periods of up to a few minutes. For instance, after looking up a telephone number in a directory, we can usually remember the number while dialing it, but many people find that if they have to try the number again an hour later, they have to look it up once more. Short-term memory has only a limited capacity. We can remember one telephone number for a short time, but find it difficult to remember three numbers.

"Long-term" memory has its own peculiarities, for not all individual memories are equally well remembered. The two groups of memories best retained are those relating to specific tasks (such as riding a bicycle or driving a car) and those inspired by fear (such as the memory of being burnt by fire). Memory experts, who amaze us by their recall ability, have developed techniques for transferring information from short-term to long-term memory. Even so, the brain can only retain a small proportion of the information received from the senses, which may be the equivalent, in computing terms, of 10 million bits per second. Over a lifetime of a billion seconds, we receive 10 million billion bits. The brain has a storage capacity of perhaps 100 billion bits – 100,000 times smaller than the total information input.

Laboratory experiments have shown that at least some types of memory are associated with specific regions of the brain. But they have so far failed to show what happens to the cells in these regions when a memory is stored. Two points seem clear. The initial mechanism must be electrochemical and it must be confined to a limited number of cells. Studies carried out on animals, such as snails, which have a much simpler brain and nervous system than ours, suggest that the first effect, when a memory is stored, is a chemical change at the synapses – the links between nerve cells. This is then translated into an electrical effect. The effects are not long-lived, but may be sufficient to explain short-term memory. These results are believed to apply to humans too. Long-term memory must have a different explanation. One possibility is that the storage mechanism in this case results from the formation of proteins. Drugs that affect the synthesis of proteins in the body also disrupt long-term memory. Proteins are large stable molecules and can remain near the place where they were formed for some time, providing a basis for long-term memory. Whether they do, or not, remains a matter of debate.

Language and Information

2

The human voice...Speech...Language learning in children...Meaning and context...Nonverbal communication...Information through unofficial channels... How information diffuses in a community...The function of the media

When humans or animals make contact with others of their species, they need to be able to communicate effectively. Communication has developed in such a way that it best aids the survival of each species. It thus helps animals most in cases where it serves to protect the individual or to protect the species by the production of offspring. All groups of higher animals have some method of communicating, but differs from group to group. Many birds have two important calls – one to show alarm and one to attract a mate. Many follow up their courtship songs by some form of visual communication. A peacock displaying its tail is a spectacular visual aid. As with all birds, however, the peacock's most important communication channel is sound. Sound carries over a fair distance, can be heard even when the sender cannot be seen, and can be varied easily to transmit different kinds of information. In humans, the system of producing sounds is so flexible that we have developed language, providing us with almost endless opportunities for expression.

Sound production

The alarm calls produced by birds are often similar for a whole variety of birds, and most within hearing distance react to them. Their mating songs, however, are each distinct, so that only birds of the same species respond. Interestingly, birds and humans both produce their range of sounds by the same basic mechanism. Air is blown past a vibrating surface, in much the same way as sound is produced in a clarinet. A tube called the trachea stretches up from the lungs to the mouth. In birds, the bottom end of this tube produces the sound: in humans, the upper end – the larynx – does so.

Other mammals follow the human pattern, but differ from humans in the space allotted to sound production. Compared with apes, humans have noticeably larger throats and larynxes. Both of these factors are important for increasing the range of sounds we produce. Apes are physically incapable of talking like humans.

However, a larger sound-production system has its dangers. Food passes down the esophagus, a channel directly behind the trachea. A bigger top end of the trachea makes it more likely that our food will take a wrong turning and choke us. It seems that speech is so important for humans that this greater risk has, in evolutionary terms, proved worthwhile. Interestingly, a new-born baby has a small throat and larynx, like an ape, and so is physically unable to speak as a grown up can.

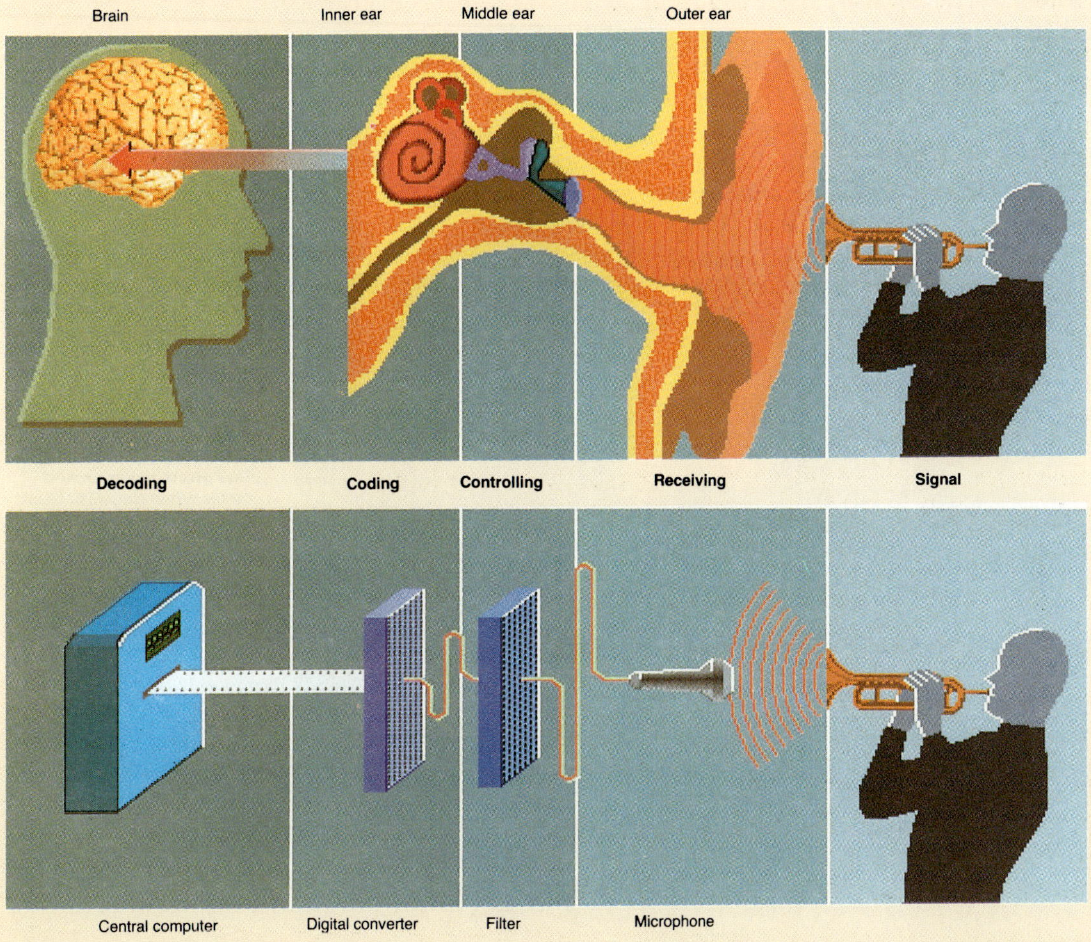

◀ People and computers analyze sounds, including music, in rather similar ways. First, the sound must be collected by the outer ear, or by the microphone. Next, the mechanical motions produced by the sound must be changed into acceptable signals. The middle and inner ears change the motions into electrochemical nerve impulses, while the microphone and converter change them into electrical impulses acceptable to the computer. Finally, the impulses go to the brain, or to the computer, where they are analyzed in detail.

The human voice

When we speak, we continually adjust the tension in the vocal cords. These are contained in the larynx and their vibrations can easily be felt by placing a hand on the voice box (the "Adam's apple" in the throat). When we speak, we continually adjust the tension in the vocal cords. The sounds produced by air passing up from the lungs vary with the tension, but they can also be changed by altering the tube itself. In a similar way, a vibrating reed in a clarinet produces sound but the notes also change by opening and closing holes in the tube. In humans, the throat and mouth are the equivalent of the clarinet tube. Because the length of the tube is constant, we make the necessary adjustments by altering the size and shape of the throat and mouth cavities. For instance, if you clench your teeth while pronouncing the letter "t", you will notice the effect of the tongue moving.

A sound can be defined by its frequency – the number of vibrations per second it contains. A pure sound – for example, from a tuning fork – consists almost entirely of vibrations of a single frequency. On the other hand, the sound of an orchestra contains a very large range of vibrations. The human voice is more like an orchestra than a tuning fork, having a range of vibrations with peaks of intensity at various frequencies. To analyze speech, spectrograms are used. These show the spread of vibrations that occur when different words are pronounced. In particular, spectrograms show immediately that letters cannot be taken in isolation. In pronouncing the word "peep", for instance, the lips are in a quite different position for the first "p" and for the second.

Speech spectrograms also highlight other differences. The sounds of whole words can also change according to the words that come before or after, and often depend on the meaning of the whole sentence. Compare how the word "it" is said in the two sentences "You finished it", and, "You finished it?" These characteristics become obvious if you listen to a foreign language of which you have only a limited knowledge. The sounds of the words you know are modified because they are embedded in an entire speech sequence, making them more difficult to distinguish than when they are spoken individually.

The larynx

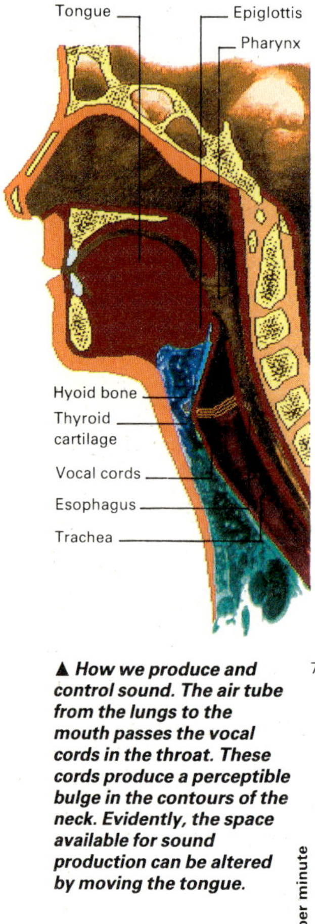

▲ How we produce and control sound. The air tube from the lungs to the mouth passes the vocal cords in the throat. These cords produce a perceptible bulge in the contours of the neck. Evidently, the space available for sound production can be altered by moving the tongue.

► Speech spectrograms illustrating similarities in pronunciation of two phrases with totally different meanings. The upper spectrogram corresponds to "recognize speech", the lower one to "wreck a nice beach". The similarity between the two spectrograms is striking. Only a close examination reveals the differences. The time scale for the phrases runs from left to right. The frequency of the sound runs from bottom to top. The colors represent the sound energy at each frequency. These range from dark blue the least energy, increasing through red, yellow and white, which represents the greatest energy.

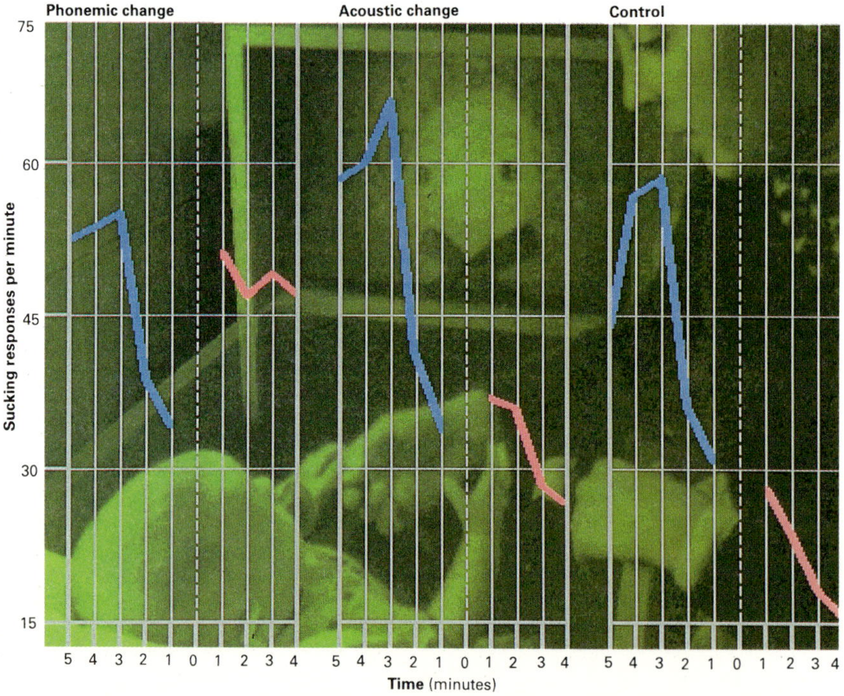

◄ Even young babies can, it seems, distinguish between speech sounds. In an experiment, sucking infants at first sucked more quickly when they heard a consonant repeated, and then more slowly again when they got used to it. One group again sucked faster when they first heard a new consonant (left-hand graph). Two other groups, however, recorded little changes in their sucking rates on hearing the same consonant under changing acoustical conditions (graphs, center and right).

Indeed, a listener may feel that the continuous sound of foreign speech is not split up into words at all. This is not far from the truth. An average English speaker produces about a dozen sounds a second.

If speech is so complex and difficult to disentangle, how did humans manage to acquire language abilities in the first place? Babies can articulate only a limited range of sounds, but they can distinguish many more, apparently from birth. One explanation is that an understanding of how language works is inborn. Indeed, it seems that there are basic similarities between different languages across the world. Gramatically many English sentences follow the order – subject, verb, object. In Japanese the verb comes at the end and in Hebrew it comes first. However, the order subject-object seems to be universal. The position of the verb is apparently less important in fixing the meaning of the sentence in our minds.

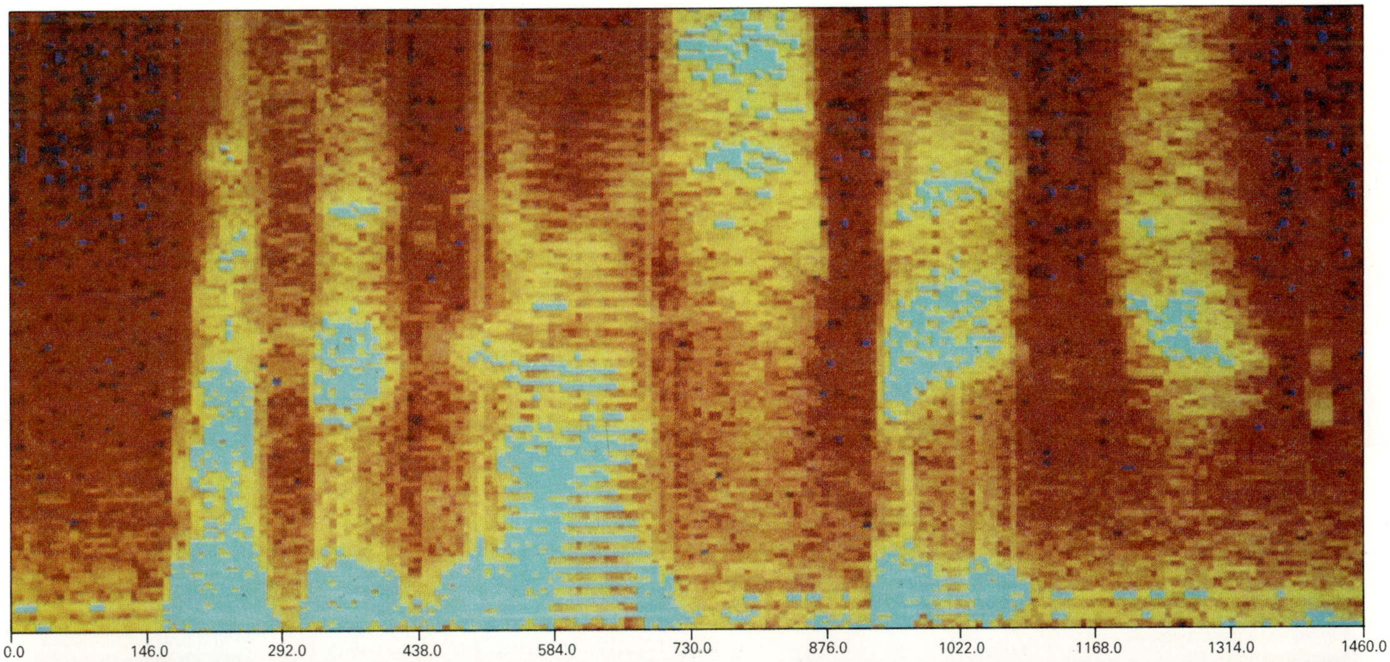

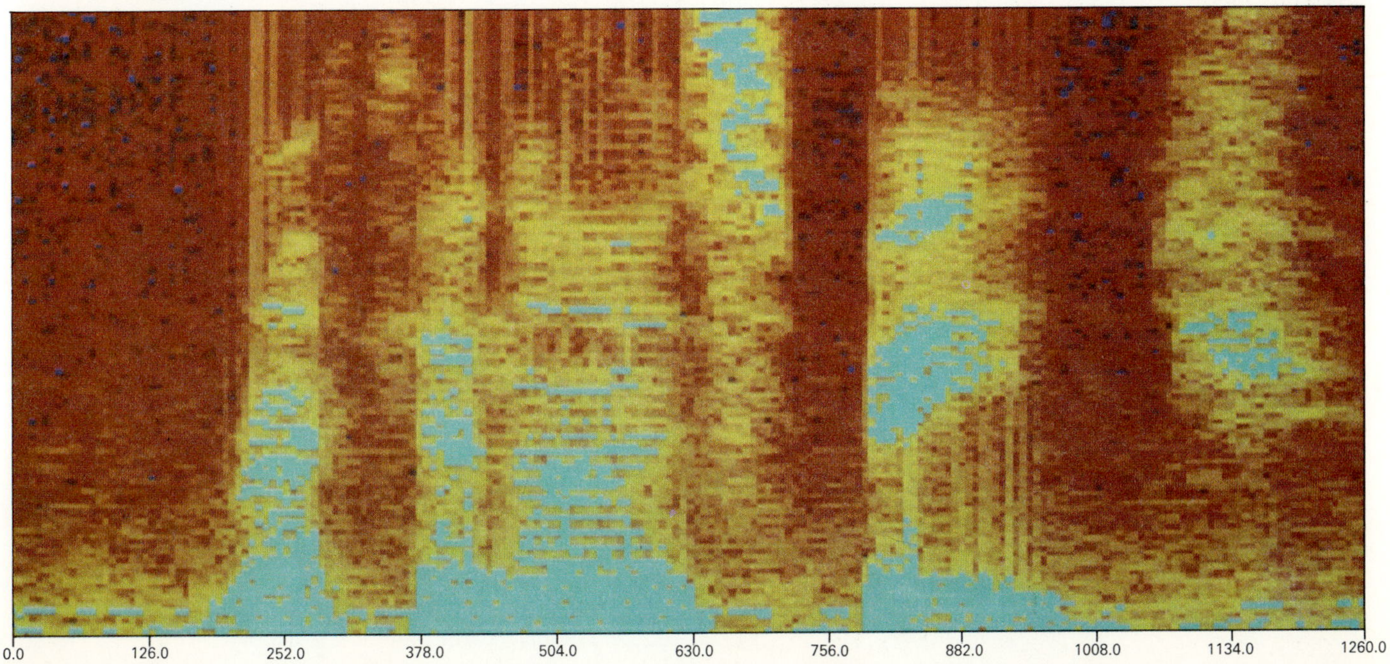

Language learning

The idea that language is innate in human beings is rather surprising. However, it fits the pattern of language development in children reasonably well. Yet even if we do have an inbuilt tendency to use language, obviously there is also a lot for us to learn as we grow up. The dominance of the left hemisphere of the brain for language first becomes evident in children aged between four and five years, and is finally fixed by the age of 10 or 11. During their first decade, children's perception of speech is especially acute. The small linguistic differences that distinguish a native speaker of a language are picked up automatically. However, to speak properly children need feedback. They listen to themselves speaking and compare it with speech from other people. How important feedback can be is shown by the difficulty often experienced by deaf children in trying to reproduce standard speech. Recently, computerized speech spectrograms have been introduced to assist deaf children. A speech therapist pronounces a word which then appears as a colored pattern on the upper half of a computer screen. The child tries to repeat the word, and the pattern corresponding to the sound produced is displayed on the bottom half of the screen. The two patterns can be compared and the word repeated until they match. Effectively, visual feedback is being substituted for aural feedback.

Learning to speak seems to follow a definite sequence, which depends mainly on the age of the child. Attempts to speed up this learning sequence have shown that it is very difficult to produce more than minor improvements. The first step occurs at about six months, when children can utter single syllables, such as "ma" and "da". By the time they are a year old, they have progressed to more than one syllable, and can use words like "mamma" and "dadda" in the correct context. By 18 months, they have a vocabulary of up to 50 words, but use each word separately from the others. At two years old, their vocabulary is increasing rapidly and they can string words together, though their speech is often ungrammatical. A year later, a child may have a vocabulary of up to 1,000 words and is capable of using basic grammar correctly.

The acquisition of language is thus relatively rapid, but the ability to apply and understand it as adults do comes more slowly. The Swiss child psychologist, Jean Piaget (1896–1980), who pioneered studies of language development in children, divided children's learning of language into four periods. The first covers the time from birth to two years old. During this period, while speech skills are developing, the child's interest is almost entirely self-centered. A typical word at this stage might be "more". In the next stage, 2–7 years of age, the child learns that language provides symbols for the things around us. "Mummy" at the beginning of this period denotes a means of satisfying certain of the child's needs. At the end, it is the name of a particular person. About this time children also realize that names are arbitrary – "Mummy" might equally well be called something else. During the period 7–11 years old, the child learns to use language symbols in an abstract way. To many children in this age range logic and mathematics now begin to make sense. However, it is only from 11 into the teens – in the final stage – that children begin to use abstract terms creatively and to understand the problems they raise. Out of a group of boys aged between 9 and 12 who were asked what was wrong with the sentence, "I have three brothers, Paul, Ernest and myself", only a third of them could spot the mistake.

▲ The Swiss psychologist Jean Piaget studied children's biological and logical development. He investigated how language and conceptual thinking arise by looking at how children's mental processes change over time. He concluded that children pass through several stages, essential to their learning and development.

► Special regions of the brain are involved in the use of language. Information passed by means of the spoken word is first received by the auditory area of the brain and then processed in the nearby Wernicke's area. If a spoken reply is needed, the information, after processing, is forwarded to Broca's area. Written information received by the eyes enters the brain in the visual area at the rear, then passes to Wernicke's area for analysis.

► A language class. When children attend school new demands are made on their language skills. Educationalists are increasingly concerned with the way children should best acquire these skills. Although there is some disagreement over method, all methods agree in their emphasis on the need for practice.

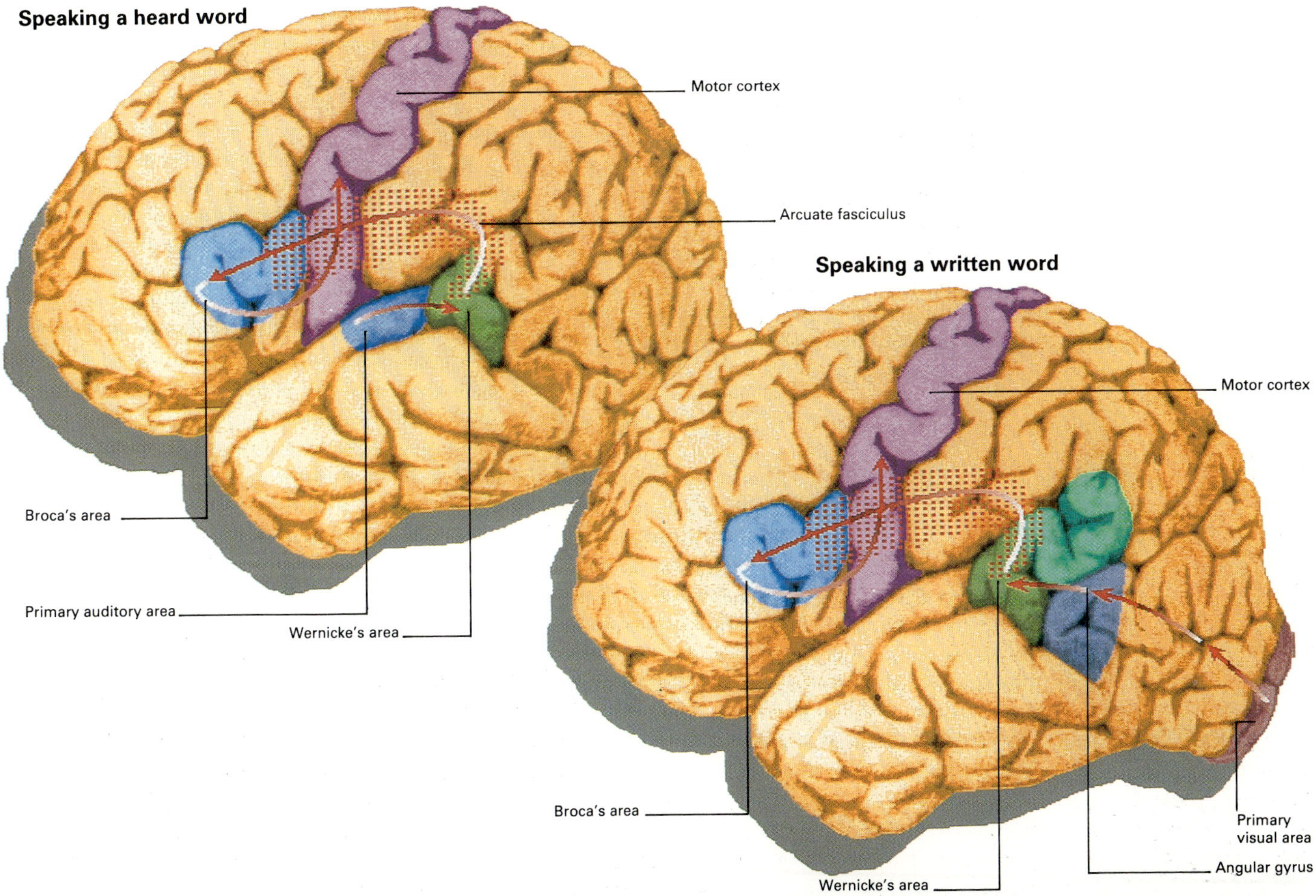
Speaking a heard word
Motor cortex
Arcuate fasciculus
Broca's area
Primary auditory area
Wernicke's area
Speaking a written word
Motor cortex
Broca's area
Wernicke's area
Primary visual area
Angular gyrus

In all cultures, the most used words are also often the shortest

Understanding and using language

Vocabulary grows rapidly at all stages of development. It is estimated that university students can recognize, or guess the meaning of, 100,000 words. Their undergraduate essays are more likely to employ one-tenth of this number, and 5,000 words may suffice for their every-day discussions. In fact, the 50 most used words in English make up 60 per cent of our normal speech. Inevitably, "I" is often the most common word. Even in writing, where most people display a larger vocabulary, the 50 most frequent words account for some 45 percent of the total text (typically "the" is the commonest word). What is true of English is true of other languages. Generally, our spoken vocabulary is smaller than our written vocabulary, which, in turn, is smaller than the vocabulary encountered in reading.

Children learning language find some aspects easier than others. The names of objects – "Daddy", "doll", "dog" – are the easiest to understand. At first, they may apply these to anything with similar properties. A child may, for instance, call a cat a dog because it walks on four legs and looks generally similar. (In fact, many children say "bow-wow" because it is an easier word for them to say.) Sometimes it works the other way. Having learned to call a dachshund a dog, a child may not realize that a St Bernard is also a dog. In this, children reflect the basic problem of classification – the factors involved when we generalize to an abstract concept from a few specific instances. Similarly,

▼ The average information content of a word plotted against the average number of syllables in a word for various languages. English has the most monosyllabic words but the average word in English conveys less meaning than it does in other languages. English generally uses more words than does Japanese, for example, to say the same thing. However, monosyllabic languages are easier to learn, which has helped English to become a world language.

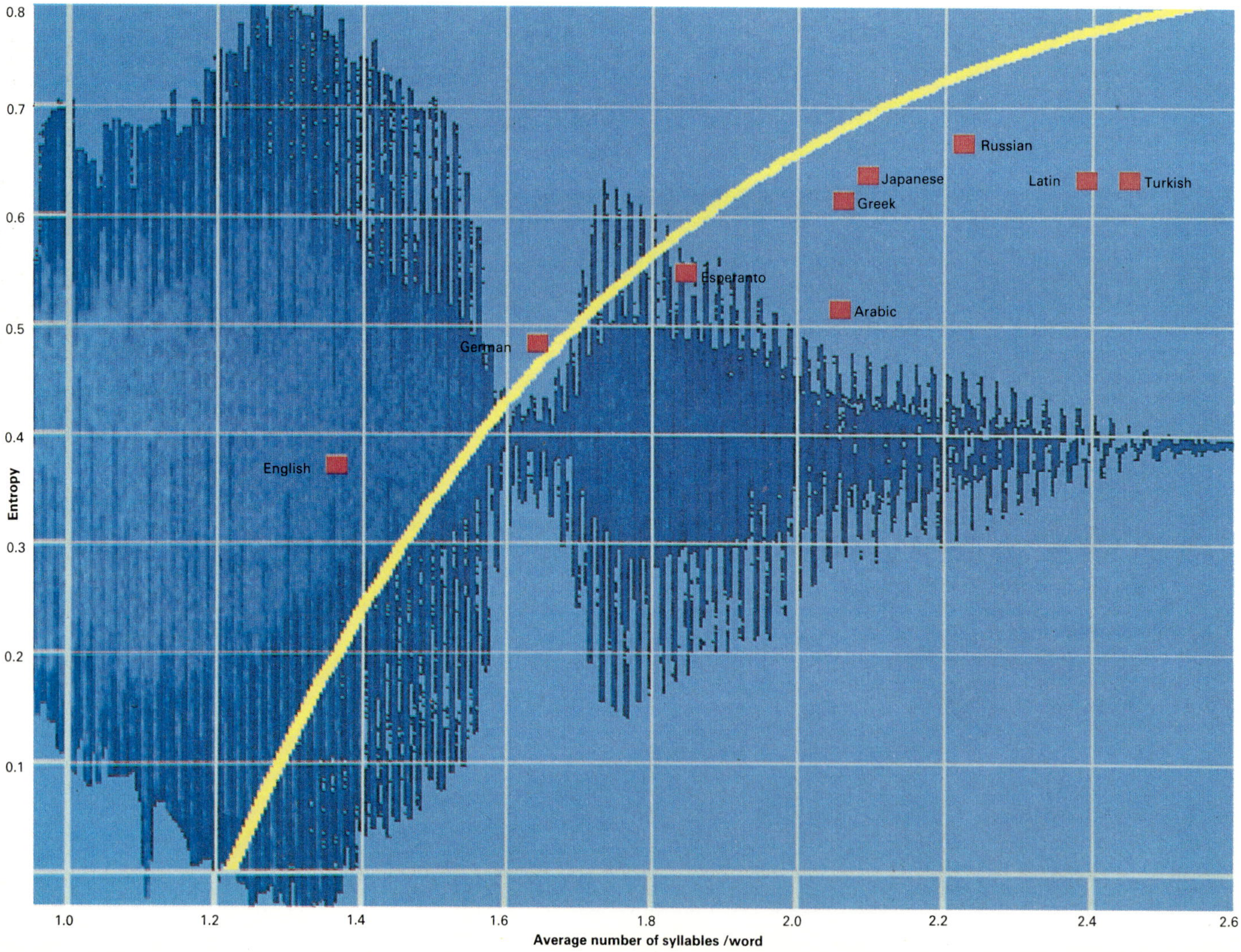

verbs, which children cannot readily identify with an object, are harder for them to grasp. Not surprisingly, verbs – such as "want" – that relate to the child's needs are learned first. Initially, verbs are used in an all-purpose way. The words "all gone" may be applied to food, but can also mean that someone has left the room, or that the child has dropped something on the floor. This is not so different from the way an adult learns a foreign language.

Children often use abbreviated speech – for example, "Pick doll." Parents can usually interpret this as meaning, "My doll has fallen on the floor, please pick it up." If the child says "Mummy eat", a typical response might be, "Yes, Mummy is eating her lunch." In this case, the parent is providing an example of a correct sentence from which the child can learn. Correcting a child's speech also assists the child in working out the rules of language usage. For example, "I throwed the ball" will usually produce the parent's response, "No – I threw the ball." The child has discovered the general rule that things in the past are referred to by adding -ed, but is now being told by the parent that this is not always true. It seems that, in learning rules, children can benefit as much from conversation as from correction. In fact, they can learn from talking to other children, or even to themselves. This is a major reason for children being so fond of asking the question "why?". It is not so much that they need an answer, but rather that the question helps to prolong the conservation.

▼ Parents can play a constructive role in aiding their children's language development. Reading to a child, as well as correcting grammar or syntax when the child makes a mistake, will help to teach and reinforce patterns of correct language usage.

▼ The structure of a sentence can make it seem meaningful even if the individual words are nonsense. A line of Lewis Carroll's (1832–1898) poem about the Jabberwock reads: "the slithy toves did gyre and gimble in the wabe". Nearly all the words are made up, but the form of the sentence is familiar. "Toves" is clearly the subject, suggesting some kind of animal. "Slithy" is an adjective. "Gyre" and "gimble" must be verbs, while "wabe", is obviously a place.

Language in context

To discern the deeper significance of conversation, children need a large amount of experience. The same question may receive a different response depending on who is asking it. If a child sees its parent working at a microcomputer and asks the question "Why?", the answer may be, "I have to add up some numbers." If an adult asks the same question, the response may be, "I am trying a new method of handling my accounts." But to a friend interested in computers, there may be a different answer: "I am trying out the new spreadsheet program we talked about last week." The language used by adults depends on their perception of the listener.

One of the problems in acquiring a language is the complex meaning that even apparently simple words can have. We might say, for example, "John and Mary were married yesterday." We do not usually remind ourselves of the numerous implications built into the word "marry". For example, it may mean they attended a church yesterday. We certainly expect it means that they are now living together. How words surround themselves with a cloud of meanings is common to all languages. In one of the less-common South American languages, the same word is used for hatching eggs, committing suicide and making cakes. In that particular culture, people are buried with their legs drawn up to their chests, so that they look egg-shaped from above – which explains the suicide connotation – and cakes are made in the shape of an egg. Such a concentration of different meanings round a single word may relate to the way our memory works. Since our short-term memory is limited, as much meaning as possible has to be crammed into a small number of words, and the shorter those words are the better. Interestingly, the most used words in all cultures are usually the shortest. Indeed, when something that is initially rare, becomes common, its name is often abbreviated. "Television" has become "TV", airplanes became "planes", and "telephone" was reduced to "phone".

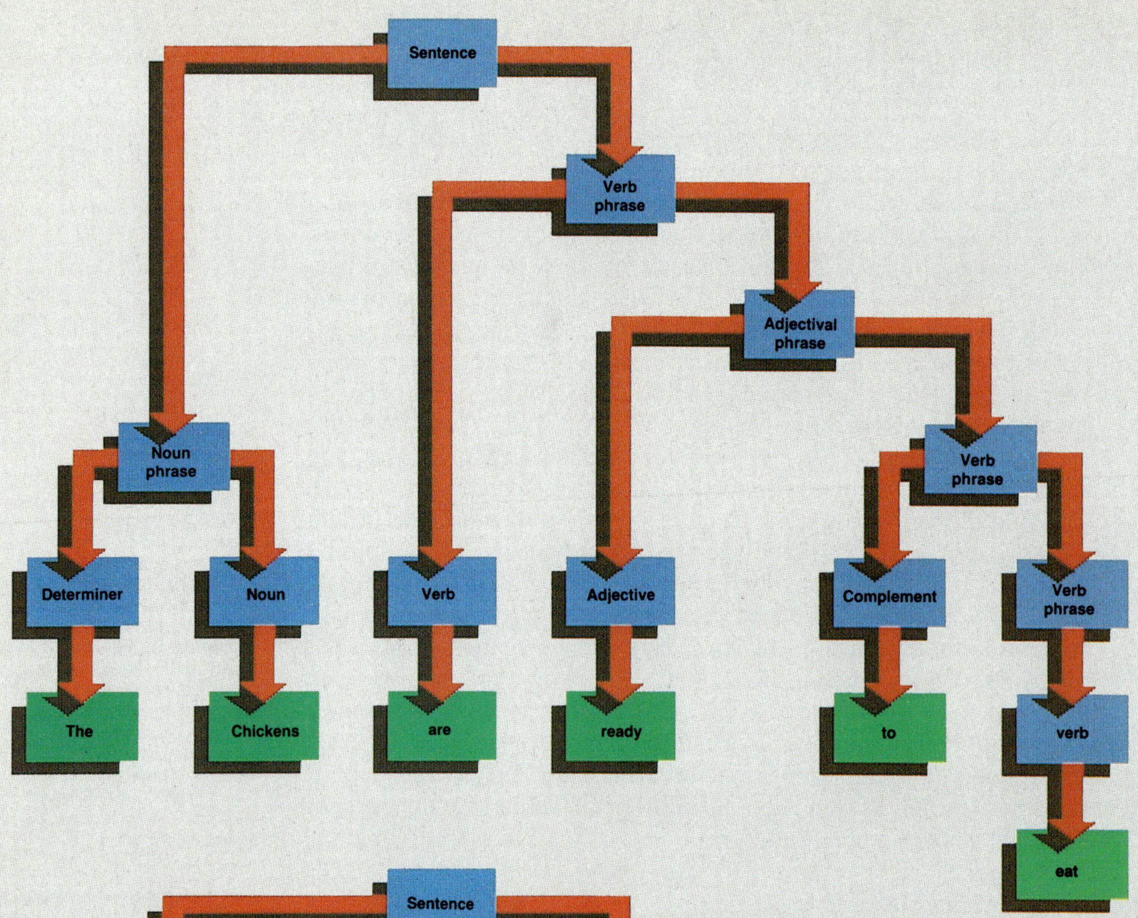
Sentence
Verb phrase
Adjectival phrase
Noun phrase
Verb phrase
Determiner
Noun
Verb
Adjective
Complement
Verb phrase
The
Chickens
are
ready
to
verb
eat

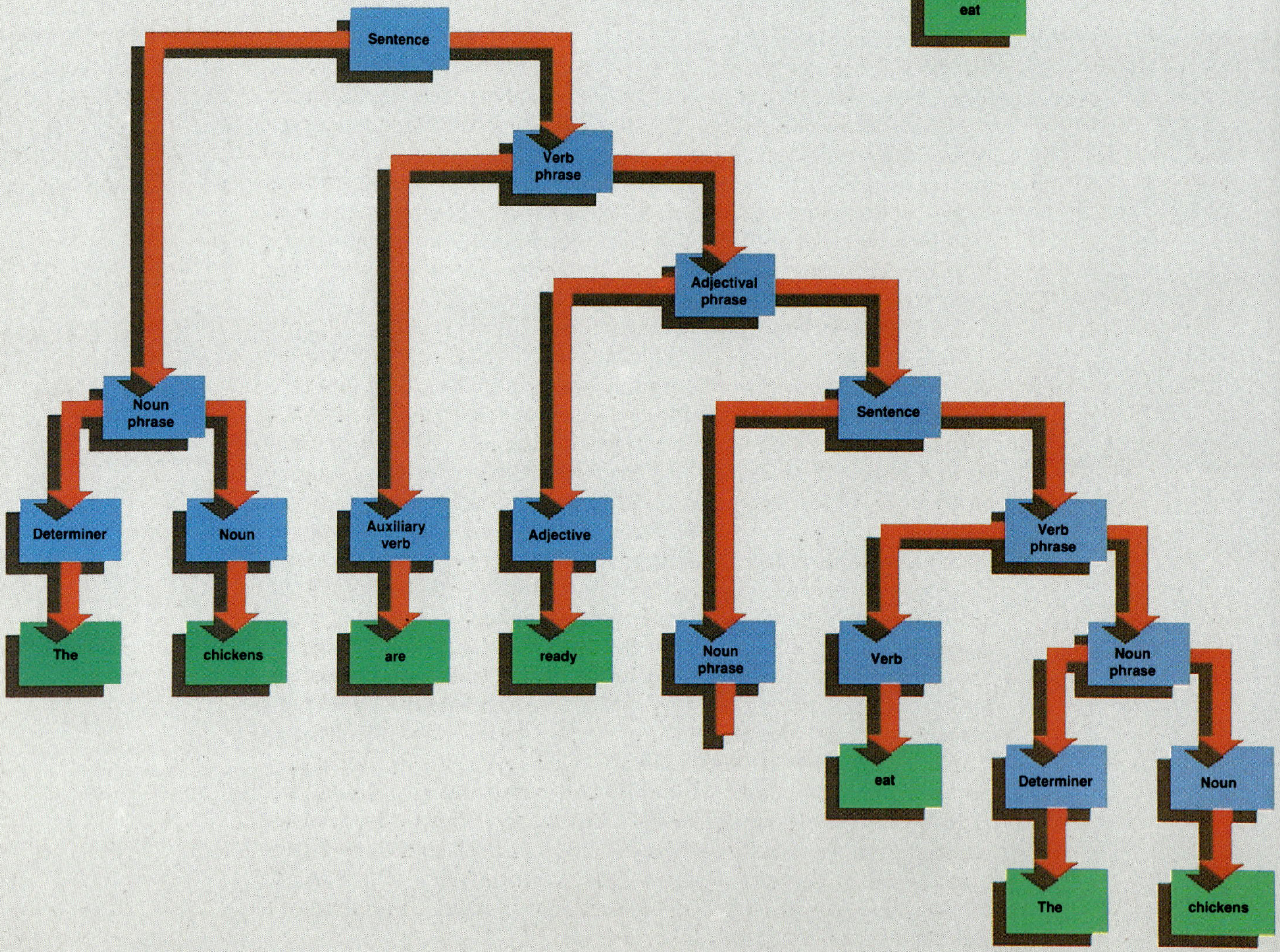
Sentence
Verb phrase
Adjectival phrase
Noun phrase
Sentence
Verb phrase
Determiner
Noun
Auxiliary verb
Adjective
Noun phrase
Verb
Noun phrase
The
chickens
are
ready
eat
Determiner
Noun
The
chickens

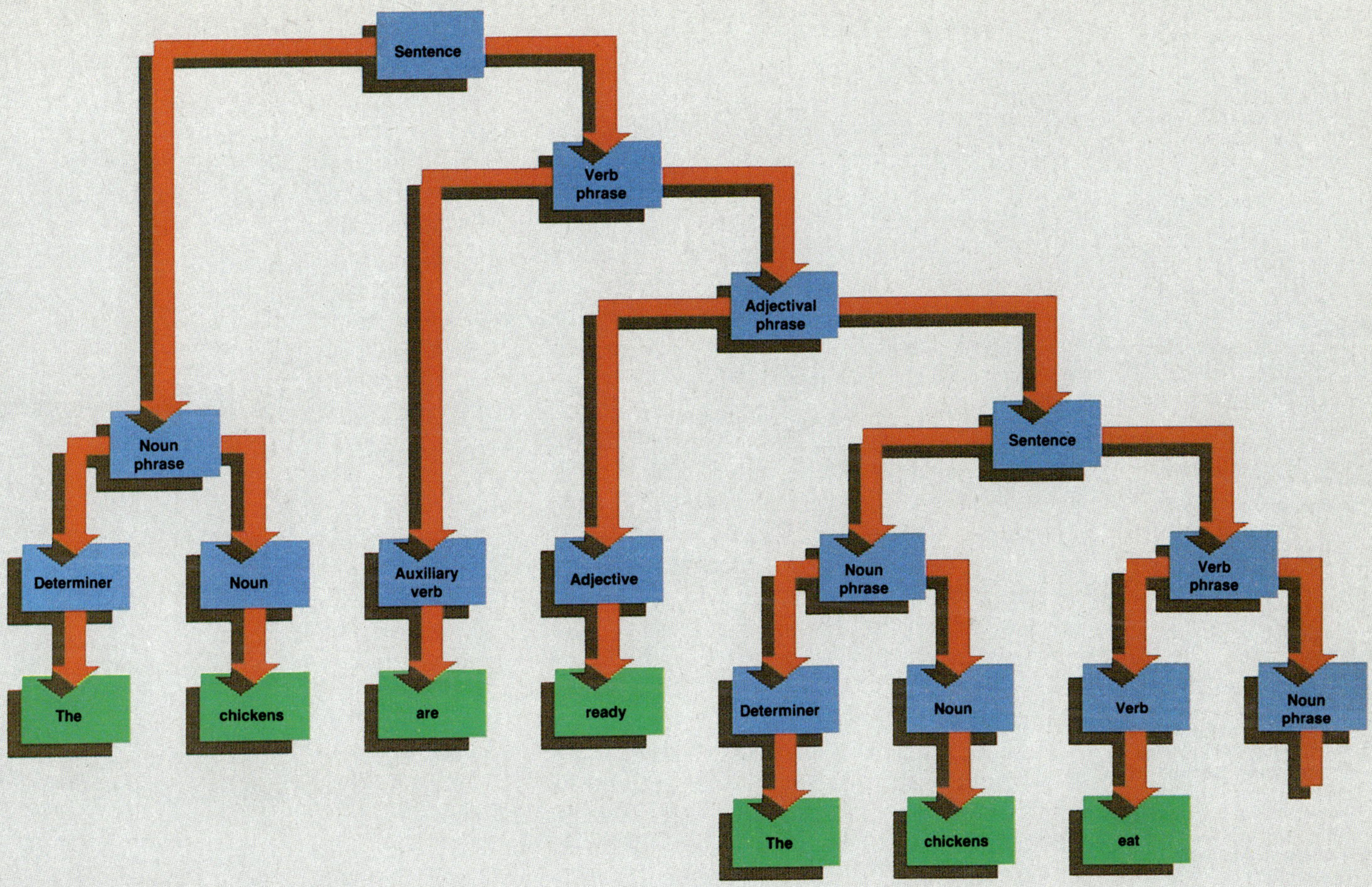

◄▲ The study of sentence structure is an essential part of understanding how languages work. For the purposes of linguistic analysis, the parts of speech commonly mentioned – such as subject, verb and object – are subdivided more finely. This helps in exploring the various problems caused by the ambiguities of language. For example, "The chickens are ready to eat" has more than one meaning. Will the chickens do the eating, or are they the ones who are going to be eaten? In the simplest analysis of the statement (top left) the ambiguity of meaning remains unresolved. The second, deeper analysis (above) corresponds to the meaning that it is the chickens who will eat. The third example applies a similar analysis to the statement when the meaning intended is the passive voice – that it is the chickens who will be eaten.

Human limitations affect the way we process the speech we hear. To interpret information economically, we must constantly try to guess what is coming next. If someone tells us, "John saw the film", the first word we hear is "John", and we immediately try to identify who is meant. If we know of one John who is an acquaintance of ours and of the speaker, then we presume that it is he. Otherwise, we must guess from the context of the conversation, or even ask at the end. ("Oh, you mean *that* John.") While identifying the subject, we hear the word "saw". This might be a saw for wood (or even "sore"). Since, however, it follows a name, we expect the next word to be a verb and so we interpret it to mean vision. After this verb, we expect to hear what was seen. The following word, "the", is an important guide. It tells us that the object is something we already know about. When we hear the next word, "film", we should therefore be able to decide from prior knowledge which film is meant. (If we had heard "a film", we would expect to be told later which film.)

This process of analyzing the meaning of speech as it progresses is essential, because we are relying on our short-term memory. It is aided by the way in which an English sentence unrolls. In a language such as German, where certain parts of the verb can come at the end of the sentence, analysis often has to be delayed until that point is reached. This places a greater strain on the short-term memory. In written communication generally, there is less strain on the short-term memory because it is always possible to read something over again. The printed page thus provides a substitute memory. Correspondingly, longer and more complex sentences can be used in writing than in speaking. Since it is easier to analyze a long statement in English than it is in German, there is greater similarity between written and spoken statements in English, in terms of their length and complexity, than there is in German.

Not only do children need time to learn the uses and structure of language, they must also learn the rules of conversation and etiquette. The simplest of these is not to interrupt someone who is speaking. Oxford undergraduates used to be told to take a breath in the middle of a sentence rather than at the end, when they were debating, in the hope that their opponents would be too well-mannered to interrupt at that point. Similarly, children must learn to interpret the hidden meaning of statements. For instance, when someone asks the question "How are you?", the questioner seldom expects a truthful answer.

Conventions relating to language are so strong that violating them can sometimes produce physical effects in the speaker. Because in many cultures it is wrong to tell a lie, a speaker who lies will often become tenser. The heart beats a little faster, and the body sweats a little more. These changes form the basis for polygraph (lie-detector) tests. But lie-detectors can be fooled, because reactions to telling lies are not constant. We often lie almost automatically to avoid hurting our friends' feelings. Asked the question, "Am I as beautiful as ever?", most people reply, "Yes". Very few add "but it costs more and takes longer nowadays". "White" lies are regarded as acceptable, and therefore produce less stress.

Another problem in learning to acquire and use language is that we have to translate what we think or feel into words that often do no more than approximate what we want to express. Sometimes this is because we cannot remember, or perhaps do not know, the right word but expect others present to understand what is meant and supply the right word. Often there is no way of expressing ourselves easily in words. We may try to suggest our intentions by the use of analogy, as is often done in the Bible: "The kingdom of heaven is like to a grain of mustard seed, which a man took, and sowed in his field." Alternatively, we may assert that one thing actually is another. "The whole Earth is our hospital", the poet T.S. Eliot (1888–1963) once remarked. The use of metaphor is a powerful way of expressing ideas in shorthand and extending the scope of language. The meaning of "cold" as in "He is a very cold person", is so accepted that it figures in our dictionaries as one of the standard uses of the word.

▶ A white-throated capuchin male opens his mouth and bares his teeth to look menacing. Pulling an aggressive face and other facial displays are common over a wide range of animals and usually express corresponding emotions.

▶ A man with a menacing expression on his face in a confrontational situation. The way the eyes are narrowed in a frown and the neck is thrust forward are signs of real hostility. Human facial expressions, however, often reflect more than one basic emotion. Sometimes a man's snarling face may display as much fear as hostility. Wide-open eyes and an upright neck are tell-tale signs. On the other hand, a tightly drawn mouth, though perhaps less dramatic than a growl or a snarl, can harbor real menace.

Nonverbal communication

Though speech is for us the normal channel through which information is exchanged, it is often supplemented by other channels. In the animal world, bees pass on quite complex information without the aid of speech. For many years Karl von Frisch (1886–1983) studied the "dance language" of bees. A bee returning from a foraging expedition communicates its findings, he discovered, by dancing over the honeycomb in its hive. One pattern, Frisch noted, was to dance round a figure-of-eight. The direction of the figure-of-eight on the honeycomb shows the direction of any food source the bee has found. The bee measures the angle at the hive between the direction of the food source and the position of the Sun and communicates this information through the dance. The speed of the dance – both the rate of turning and the rate at which the bee's abdomen waggles – indicates the distance of the food from the hive. At the same time as dancing, the bee produces a buzzing song to show that it has been feeding. As much information is contained in the dance as in a short conversation between two people. Bees also have a good sense of smell, depositing a scent at the entrance to their hive, so that they can recognize it quickly on their return.

Gesturing

In humans as in animals, a significant amount of information is communicated by gestures. Charles Darwin (1809–1882) remarked how gestures and facial expressions found in monkeys are also to be found in human beings. In recent years a good deal of attention has been paid to "body language" – the gestures, often almost unconscious, that we make in conversation. Rubbing your hands together may reflect anticipation of a forthcoming event. When people approach and greet each other they typically raise their eyebrows briefly, a signal that is often reciprocated, albeit unconsciously. It has been claimed that humans, like animals, also have a courtship pattern – smoothing one's hair and clothing, standing with hands on hips, and so on. Some gestures are almost certainly automatic. Most, however, must be learned, since the same gesture often has a different meaning in different cultures. Stroking the chin is an example. In many western countries it implies indecision, but in some Mediterranean cultures it can also mean derision. On the other hand, gestures are often better understood universally than languages. The complex sign language used by deaf-mutes has a long history. Many centuries ago, harem attendants in Constantinople had their tongues cut out to ensure their discretion. It is said that the practice lapsed when they developed a sign language for communication.

◀ As well as using words to communicate, people also use "body language". For instance, hand movements are used to emphasize conversational points. Two people talking together and both sitting cross-legged unconsciously reflect each other's body language.

◀ George Bush being sworn in as Vice-President of the United States. All over the world, from the worshippers of Isis in ancient Egypt to the present-day civilisations , holding the right hand raised with palm open has featured in ceremonies relating to justice and the vestiture of authority. Few gestures have traveled so well through time or across cultural barriers.

Social organization

Communication lies at the heart of organizing human society into groups and communities. The social organization practiced by other animals is far less complex than ours. Large, highly organized groupings are found – among ants, for example – but the interaction between individuals seems to be almost entirely genetically determined with little scope for learning, and little scope for change. Among apes, on the other hand, learning may play an important role, but the groups are small and their organization is fairly simple. Humans combine the ability to learn with a highly complex social structure. This situation can only be maintained by the use of language, which allows us to accumulate, store and pass on a vast range of information from individual to individual, and from generation to generation.

Human societies typically comprise a very large number of interconnected groups. A single individual may have a group of friends at work, belong to a baby-sitting group, play tennis at a club, attend a church, and so on. The way these groups develop depends both on exchange of information within the group and on the input of information from outside. How closely linked even large communities are for the purposes of passing information is easily overlooked. How difficult would it be, for instance, to get a message to anyone else in the country by using personal contact only? Suppose I pull out a name at random – John Smith, say – and look for a personal contact. I finally identify one of my acquaintances who is more likely to know John Smith than I am, someone who is perhaps in the same profession. She may not know John Smith personally, but knows somebody else who might. So the chain of contacts unrolls. How many people will be involved in this chain before I find someone who can introduce me to John Smith? The answer is – rarely more than half a dozen.

Groups have certain advantages over individuals in formulating opinions and reaching decisions. Typically, communication within a group will concentrate on those members holding extreme views until these are modified and a consensus can be reached. Groups can often solve problems more readily than individuals and are better at spotting errors and rejecting wrong ideas.

***►* How easy is it to make contact with someone else in the country whose name has been chosen at random and who is not known to you personally? The answer is, probably easier than you might think. Suppose your acquaintances number around 100, and each of them also knows another 100 people. Then your friends' friends will total 10,000. Their friends will, in turn, number a million. The true figure is probably less because many of your friends' friends are also likely to be part of your own circle of acquaintances. Even so, for communication purposes human society turns out to be surprisingly well integrated.**

***►* Ants are often used as an example of a highly organized animal community. Some of their communal activities are very sophisticated, such as these leaf cutter ants transporting material along a track in Trinidad. Yet most of their activities are genetically determined rather than learned.**

◀ *Why do migrating birds flock together? Possibly, because it helps to conserve their energies and offers some protection against predators. Another suggestion is that it is for communication reasons. Birds in a flock perhaps pool their direction-finding abilities, enabling them to reach a consensus on the direction of a flight, which will be more accurate than if left to the individual.*

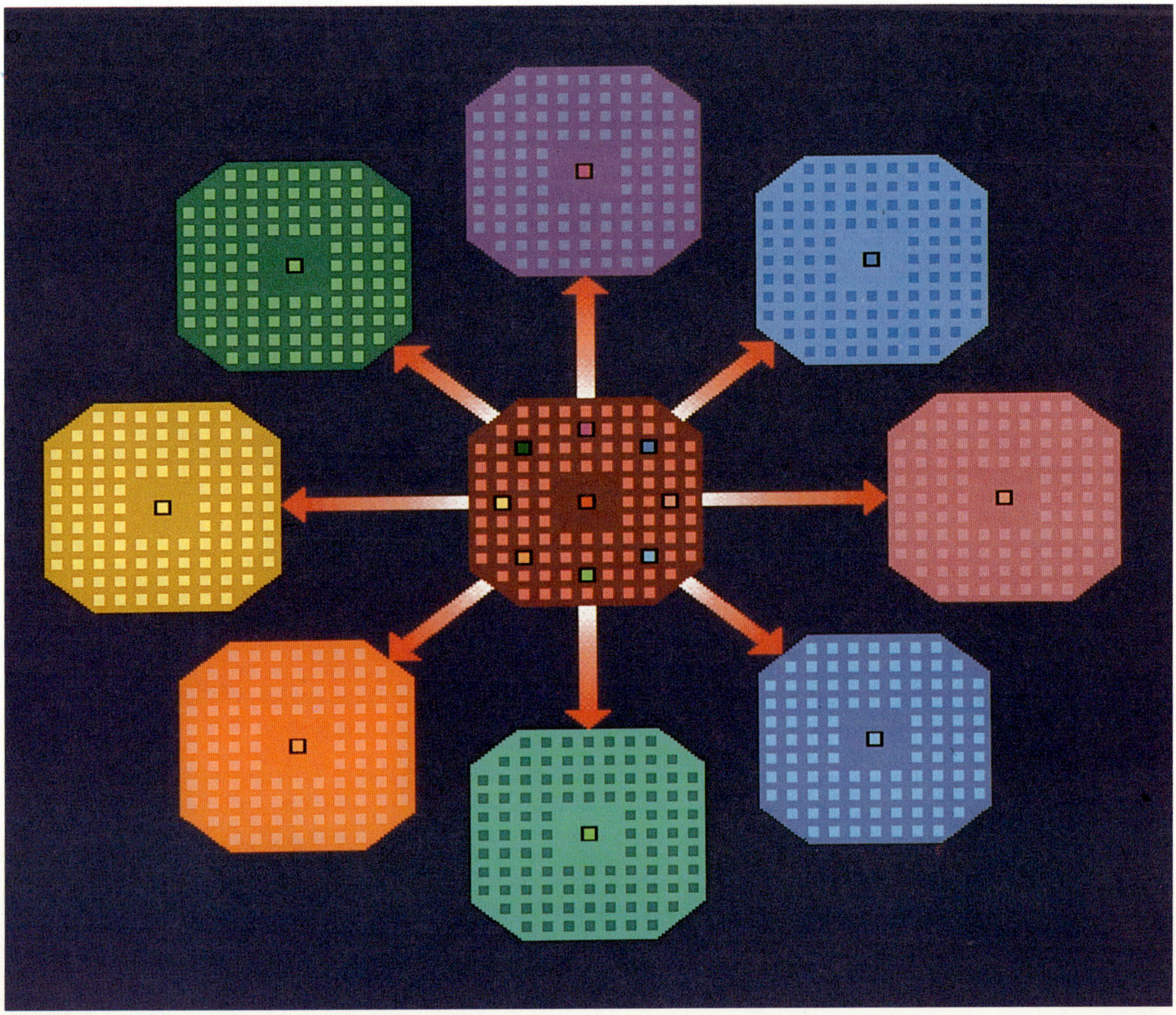

Telephone calls between small towns sometimes outnumber those between large cities

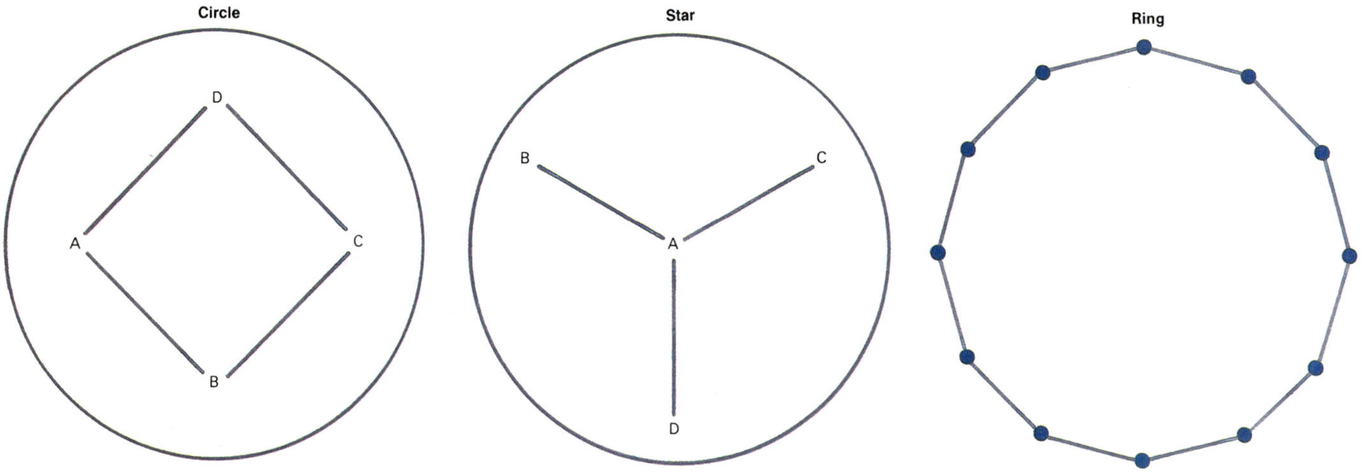

▲ Networks provide a general way of describing communication links. The nodes may equally be people or parts of a computer system. The connections may be personal or electrical. The way the nodes are linked together affects how the information is handled. Thus, in the star system, the node at the center controls the distribution of information to the other nodes. The tree, in which the node at the top contains the information on which the branches depend, is useful in solving decision-making problems.

Networks

The communication links between members of a group, or between different groups, form what is commonly called a network. There are several types of network, with different numbers and different arrangements of communication links (or "nodes"). The form the network takes can affect how information is handled and interpreted. One simple example is when, for instance, information is passed on from one person to another, and then to a third, and so on, by telephone. In this type of network, each individual talks only to the person on either side. The last person contacted finally rings up the originator of the message to confirm that everyone has now received it. If there are four individuals involved – A, B, C and D – the network has a circular form. Bigger networks of this kind are called rings.

Alternatively, all information may pass via a single person in what is known as a star network. Experiments with these two types of network show that the time taken to solve problems is about the same for both, though results from the "circle" contain more mistakes than those from the "star". Members of the two types of network, however, have different perceptions of the information-handling process. Participants in the "circle" automatically assume that there is no specific discussion leader, whereas those in the "star" assume that the person at the center (A in the diagram above) is the leader. One consequence is that people in the circle configuration are happier in their task than those in the star network (with the natural exception of the "leader"). This example supports the general belief that knowledge is power. An influential person is one who has access to, and control of, a wide range of information sources and communication channels. (For these reasons, the first objectives in many political coups have been the radio and television stations.)

Tree networks are often used in decision-making processes, and in the development of expert systems (▶ page 91). The branches represent alternative possibilities. The fully interconnected network links up every node with every other in the system, but has the disadvantage of being unwieldy and possibly wasteful since not all of the cross-linkages may be necessary.

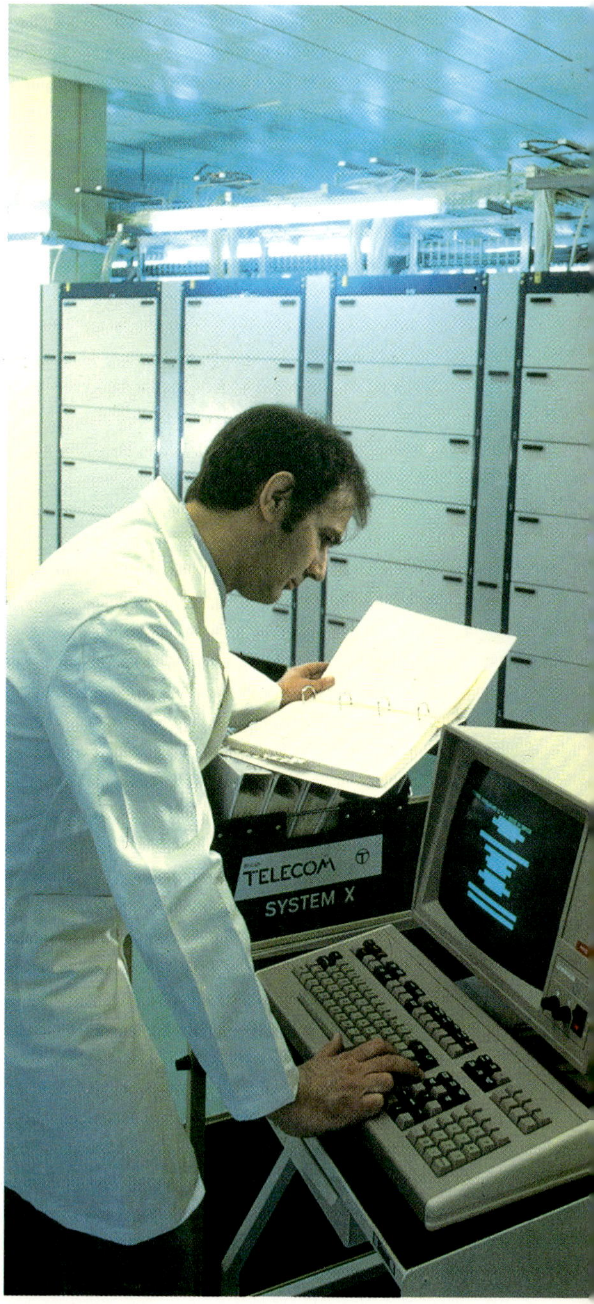

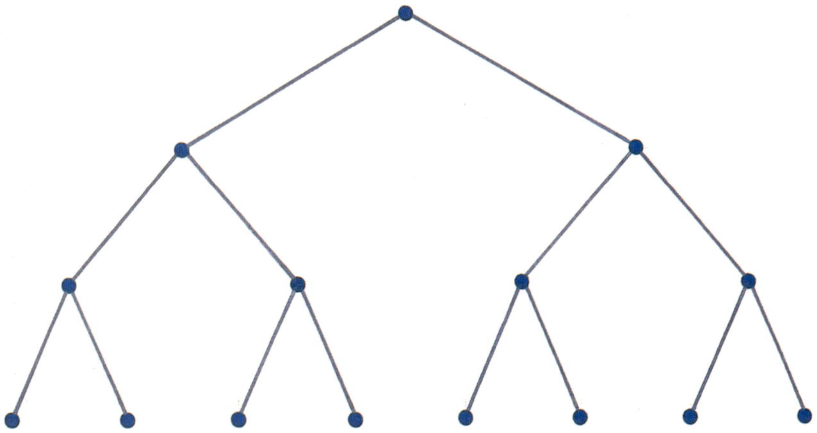

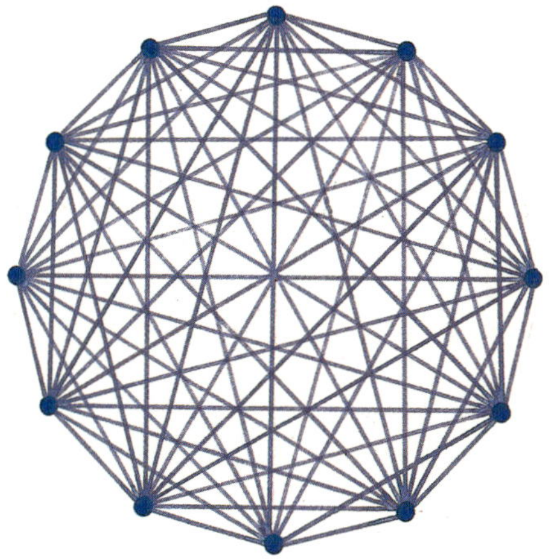

Communication structures

To study small networks, the communication links between the participants (the so-called nodes in the network) can be examined individually, and all exchanges of information monitored. This is obviously impossible for large networks, such as all the telephone subscribers in a city, or country. There, the usual method is to apply statistical techniques to small samples that represent the whole group. Polls surveying political opinions or voting intentions are carried out in this way – which perhaps explains why the result are not always entirely reliable. The main problem is to find a suitably representative sample. For example, an opinion survey conducted by telephone would have to take into account socioeconomic factors such as wealth, size of family and so on. The question of the size of the sample needed for each study would also be important. Some general conclusions about communication in large groups have emerged quite clearly, however. For example, the amount of communication increases with the number of participants and decreases with increasing distance. Usually the number of telephone calls between the inhabitants of two large cities will, hardly surprisingly, be greater than the number between two small towns. If the towns are close together and the cities far apart, however, the reverse may be true.

The industrial firm is a good example of a network that has been extensively studied. In some ways, a firm can be treated as having a life of its own. It has its own goals, which continue to be pursued though individual employees may come and go, and its own organization, which imposes a work structure on its employees. Communication is obviously essential if the goals of the firm are to be realized and its organization maintained. This communication is typically seen as vertical, starting with the managing director at the top and passing through various levels to the manual workers at the bottom. In such a structure, employees report to someone above them and have others below who report to them. Increasingly, firms are realizing that in the interest of efficiency they must consider not only the flow of information down the chain, but also feedback up the chain. Otherwise, plans made at the top may be frustrated by what is happening further down. Moreover, to concentrate solely on the information flow through the formal structure may also be misleading. The boss's secretary may rank fairly low in the official hierarchy, but can still be a major source of information. Firms also need outside information – for example about their competitors. This can arrive at a variety of levels that do not appear in the usual organizational chart.

◀ A typical modern telecommunications control center. As telephone networks become more and more computerized, the speed of working and the efficiency of switching between connections increase. An automated system can also detect faults, so that if one part of the network fails, messages can be rerouted via other parts of the system.

Many organizations employ, sometimes unintentionally, people who have come to be called "gatekeepers". They are recognized as important sources of information by their fellow employees, sometimes because of their formal standing in the firm, but more often for reasons such as their unofficial contacts both inside and outside the firm. The old soldier in the army may hold a low rank, but he often knows more of what is happening in his unit than many of the senior officers. Gatekeepers play an important part in improving the flow of information and directing it to the right quarter. The average firm is so awash with information that some form of channeling is essential. Many executives suffer from information overload – they receive more information each day than they can handle. Most see the problem differently, that they do not have access to all the information that they need. The basic problem is two-fold. Much of the information they receive is only partly relevant to them, while more valuable information is not getting through. In such situations the gatekeeper can play an important mediating role.

► Once the idea of a "gatekeeper" is accepted, it is easy to spot such people in everyday life. For example, studies of communities living on particular streets usually show that a handful of the residents act as a focus for information and advice to the rest. When the same community is moved to a large block of flats, these gatekeepers often lose their powers. This is because vertical communication proves to be more difficult than horizontal communication.

Screening information for its relevance is an important function that occurs at all levels. A small press agency in the USA provides, say, around 280 news items in one day, selected from an input to the agency of about twice that amount. One state press bureau selects between 75 and 80 of these for transmission to local newspapers, who, in turn, chooses about half that number for publication. Readers of these papers scan, on average, 20–25 percent of the printed material. After successive stages of selection, the average reader thus absorbs only about two percent of the news supplied by the press agency, but this probably includes the items of greatest interest to that reader.

► All the information we receive is filtered in some way. Sometimes this results from censorship – limitations, for example, on the release of military data. More often, it is intended to make the information more relevant to the consumer. Thus a public library selects only a proportion of the books published, depending on its readers interests. Readers, in turn, select from the information that they receive. Often, in the case of a newspaper, only a small part of the available information is read, but it is the part that is most relevant to the reader's needs. Of the total amount of information available to a large press agency (100%), only about 2% is absorbed by a reader, after it has been screened, in turn, by a smaller agency (50%), state press bureau (14%) and local paper (7%).

The spread of rumor is further proof of the existence of informal information networks. "I heard it on the grapevine", we say. Contrary to the beliefs of some, rumors often do contain a grain of truth, though frequently distorted. The formal release of information within an institution usually takes some time to arrange. Events are often known about unofficially long before any official statement is made. One reason for this is that rumor is rapidly transmitted by word of mouth, whereas formal statements are generally written and take longer. Once again, the part played by the gatekeeper in providing relevant information quickly and informally on a person-to-person basis is significant.

Might not the gatekeeper function be put on a more formal basis within a firm? This would be difficult mainly because the command structure in most organizations is designed for handling routine information, whereas gatekeepers typically deal in information that is nonroutine. Indeed, for information purposes it is often better for a firm to ignore the formal structure of its organization, and instead to regard information as a system that deserves study in its own right. A "system", in information terms, is a network that can be treated separately from the world about it, which transfers information between "nodes" using various kinds of communication channel. The traditional way of studying an organization is to chart its command structure – who is at the top, who are the middle managers and so on. A systems approach takes the opposite line. Studying the way information actually flows in an organization presents a picture of its communication structure, which is then compared with the supposed hierarchy. This approach, however, also poses problems. The information flows may change as people come and go whereas the hierarchy remains fairly stable for longer.

Daily news items screened (%)
100
50
14
7
2
Herald Tribune

Information diffusion

General patterns of communication in an organization or community are more durable. An example is the way in which new ideas are accepted. Early converts to the new idea tend to be the better-informed members of the community, who read more, have more personal contacts and seek information more actively.

A graph showing the numbers of people who have accepted an innovation plotted against time (when they accepted it) gives an S-shaped curve. The numbers grow slowly at first, and then take off rapidly as the bulk of the particular community becomes interested. Ultimately, the growth rate slows again when most of the community have taken up the innovation and only a few stragglers are left to be converted. An S-shaped curve also represents, for example, the growth in numbers of television sets in the USA and Western Europe. The length of time from the first major purchases of television sets to near-saturation of the market was about ten years. S-shaped curves are common in nature. This is the way a plant grows. At first, a seedling increases its height slowly, then grows rapidly, only to slow down again as it approaches its final height.

The concept of "diffusion" comes from science. New ideas diffuse gradually through a community, rather than sweep through it all at once. If a lump of sugar is dropped to the bottom of a cup of coffee, it does not sweeten all the coffee immediately. First the coffee in contact with the lump becomes sweet, then the sugar gradually dissolves, diffuses outwards and sweetens the whole cup. This analogy can be applied to information. People who are in close contact with information sources are the first to take up innovations. Other members of the community then hear about it, either from the same sources or from early adopters. Gradually most of the community comes to accept the innovation.

Willingness to accept an idea is often affected by organizational, as well as personal, characteristics. A group of executives from one firm were given a report on another firm to read. They were then asked, having read the report, to specify what were the major problems facing the other firm. Almost without exception, the executives saw the main problem as lying in the area of operations that was their own special interest. Sales executives specified sales, production engineers claimed the problem was on the production side, and so on. Most people naturally select and absorb information that is relevant to their own interests.

Any regular reader of a newspaper can try the following test. Which part of the paper do you turn to first? How much of the total text in the newspaper do you actually read? Do you understand all the terms used on the sports pages? The answers to tests of this sort show that any individual reader absorbs only a fraction of the material in the paper. The paper survives by providing a sufficient variety of material to satisfy the requirements of a wide range of readers, each selecting the part that is of interest to them. It is a commonplace in media studies that what people take away from any branch of the media depends on what they bring to it. A political program on television may be watched by both right-wingers and left-wingers. Both will find in it confirmation of their beliefs, and both may complain it is biased toward the opposing side. This subjective response lies behind the continuing debate concerning the possible effects of television violence on viewers. Does it encourage people to be more violent, or provide emotional relief to reduce potential violence?

▼ Just how strongly are children influenced by what they see on television? Certainly, advertisements seem to affect what they want to buy. But does violence on television make children more violent? There is some evidence that it makes them more aware of violence and perhaps shapes their views of society.

► A gathering of molecular biologists in New York State. Traditionally, scientists have publicized information about their work by giving talks. More recently, as the number of scientists and scientific meetings has increased, poster sessions have become a popular way of presenting new scientific advances. Each research group prepares a poster summarizing its work, and a representative is on hand to explain points or answer queries. Poster sessions are a good way of promoting ideas because they allow personal interaction between participants.

► Studies of how innovations are accepted follow a typical course whether the innovation is a new type of seed corn, a new medical drug, or a new scientific idea, such as Einstein's theory of general relativity. First, a small group of people within the respective community take to the new idea immediately. They are followed by a larger group who accept it after further thought and investigation. Their lead then induces the main body of the community to adopt the innovation. Finally, a group of laggards take to the new idea only slowly, while others refuse to accept it at all. This pattern of "diffusion" traces out an S-curve when the numbers of "adopters" are graphed against time.

ANALYSIS OF THE ENV GENE OF A MOLECULARLY CLONED FRIEND-MCF VIRUS
University of Freiburg, West Germany,
Sloan Kettering Cancer Center, New York, N.Y.
DIFFERENCES IN THE ENV GENES OF FRIEND AND MOLONEY MCFV
RESULTS AND DISCUSSION

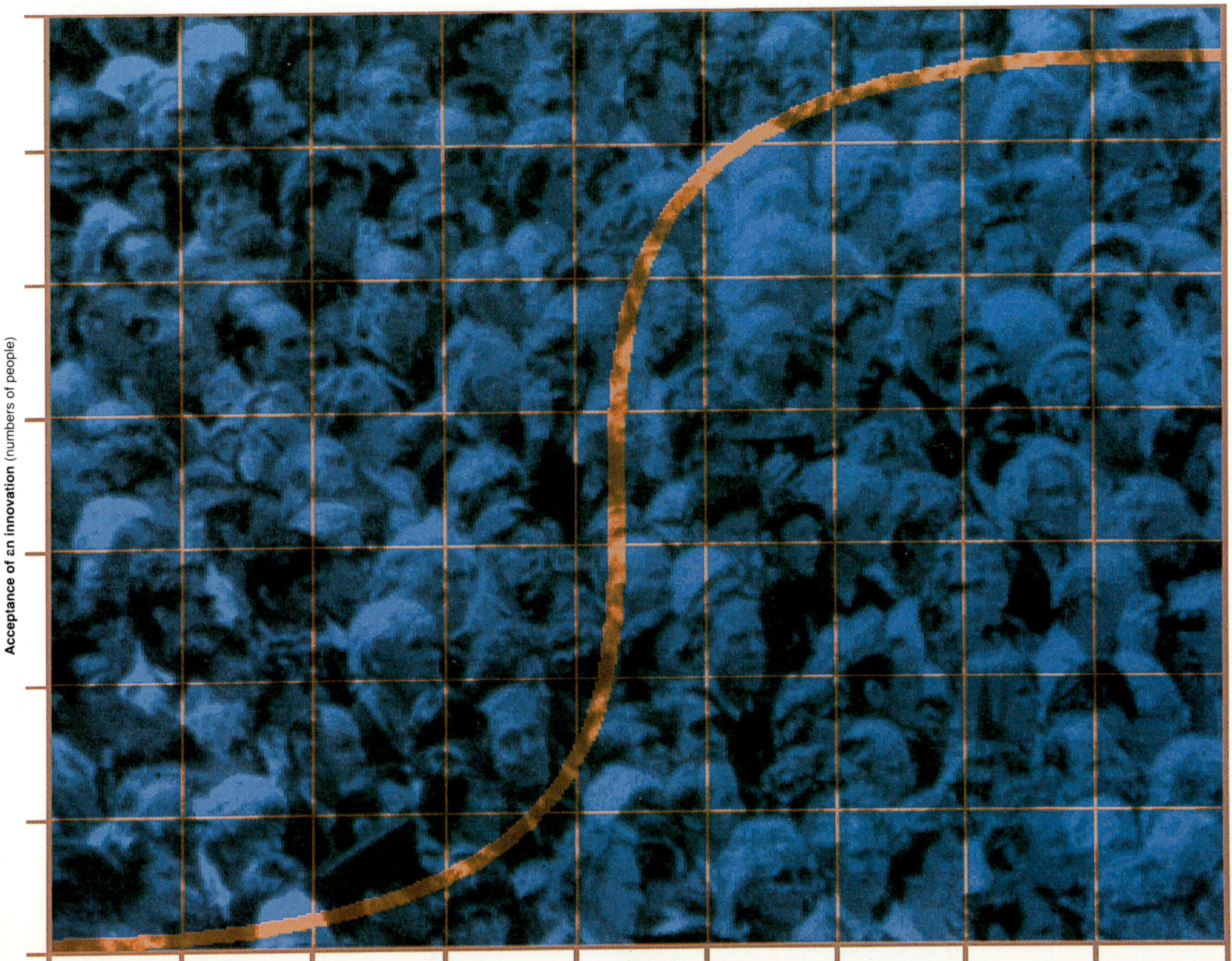
Acceptance of an innovation (numbers of people)
Years

By the age of five, the average American child has watched 5,000 hours of television

The mass media

Within half an hour of President Roosevelt's death in 1945, 90 percent of the students at one American university had heard about it. Only one in seven had heard directly from the radio. The remainder had been informed by word of mouth. A similar study of a Californian town after President Kennedy's assassination showed that 90 percent of the population knew of it within an hour. This time, half heard of it directly from radio or television, and the rest were told. This change in balance is an indication of the growth in the media during the 20 years between Roosevelt's and Kennedy's deaths. Nowadays, a high proportion of people derive their information directly from the media. By the age of five, the average American child will have watched 5,000 hours of television.

The communication channels through which we receive information have increased considerably in the 20th century. But they have complemented rather than superseded each other. People watch television and listen to radio, but still buy newspapers. A high proportion of the best-selling books have some kind of tie-in with other media (the "book of the film"). This is because different media have different characteristics. A book cannot make the visual impact of a television program, nor can television illuminate thoughts and emotions as a book can. Furthermore, information is absorbed better if it is received through more than one channel of communication. Reinforcement by different media can also help offset information overload.

The mass media often feed off each other for material, providing overlapping information. In Western countries, the selection criteria are broadly based on a perception of what the public wants. This leads to its own type of bias. British and American newspapers, for example, generally devote relatively little space to overseas news, because their readers are supposedly not interested. Most of the media include only a small amount of science, though surveys suggest that consumers would like more. The problem is one of feedback. Direct response, such as "letters to the editor", is very limited and sample surveys provide only superficial responses. Thus the media differ from many other types of communication in being essentially one-way.

Because they can reach a mass audience, the media are used extensively for teaching. In developing countries, they play an important part in disseminating ideas about new methods and new products. Even soap operas can be informative, communicating impressions of societies that may be outside the experience of the average viewer. Often such unconscious learning can have greater impact than deliberately planned teaching. This "unconscious" learning is also affected by the environment in which the information is received. A person viewing a television program with other people, and who discusses it with them, is likely to interpret that information differently from a lone viewer.

The major agent of change in information-handling has been the computer. The development and expansion of electronic information-processing is affecting communications throughout the whole of society. Nowadays, leading accountancy firms offer "communications audits", in addition to financial audits. These include an examination of how an organization handles its flow of information.

▼ Media audiences have expanded over the past quarter-century as communications technology has improved. The Live Aid pop concert, held in Wembley, UK in 1985, to raise money for African famine victims, was beamed by satellite simultaneously to audiences around the world.

Computers and Information

3

The binary code...Serial and parallel processing... The computer versus the brain...Digital and analog computers...Magnetic tape and disk...Optical and laser storage...Touch-sensitive screens...Facsimile Transmission...How bar codes work...Computer speech recognition...Computer translation...Speech synthesis...Telecommunications...Fiberoptics... Communications and satellites

Humans have three types of memory – short-term and long-term in the brain and externally stored memory. Stored memory includes everything written down in letters, magazines, or books, as well as sound recordings and the visual images contained in photographs and on videotapes. Computers also have three types of memory. These include a small memory bank for the data being processed, a much larger internal memory for data that have already been processed, or are awaiting processing, and external memory stores that can be consulted as required. Information passes to and from the brain by the senses. Correspondingly, computers have input and output devices called peripherals, for communication with the outside world.

A good deal is known about human senses and the organs, such as those of speech, which are used for communication. Much less is known about human memory processes. The opposite is true of computers. Storage and retrieval of information has always been at the heart of computer design, whereas sophisticated input and output technologies have developed only more recently. In the first chapter human senses are considered first, and memory afterwards. It is more apt in the case of the computer to examine first how a computer works and only then how it acquires and transmits information.

Bits and bytes

In counting and everyday arithmetic we use the decimal system, that is, a system to base 10, employing the ten digits 0 to 9. Thus 365 means 3x100+6x10+5. The binary system is a system to base 2, hence its name. It employs only two digits, 0 and 1, and the value of each digit doubles reading from right to left. Binary digits are often called "bits" for short. Just as in the decimal system you cannot have more than 9 in any column before carrying to the next column, so in binary you cannot have more than 1. For example, the decimal number 2 is represented in binary as 10, that is 1x2+0. The number 5 becomes 101 in binary, and so on.

In computers, binary notation is used to represent information of all types. The commonly used ASCII (American Standard Code for Information Interchange, and pronounced "Askey") assigns a unique binary number to every letter of the alphabet, small or capital, every piece of punctuation and so on. Each number consists of eight bits, known as a "byte". The information in an average 250-page book would correspond to around five million bits.

Illustrations can also be represented by bits and bytes in a computer. A television picture may be built up from some 600 horizontal lines, which the computer subdivides into picture elements or "pixels". If each pixel is either black or white, its information content is one bit. But with more light levels and color, the total information content increases rapidly. Some microcomputer screens have only a "low resolution" of about 600 pixels. They are only adequate for simple diagrams, such as bar charts. A screen with 360,000 pixels has "high resolution".

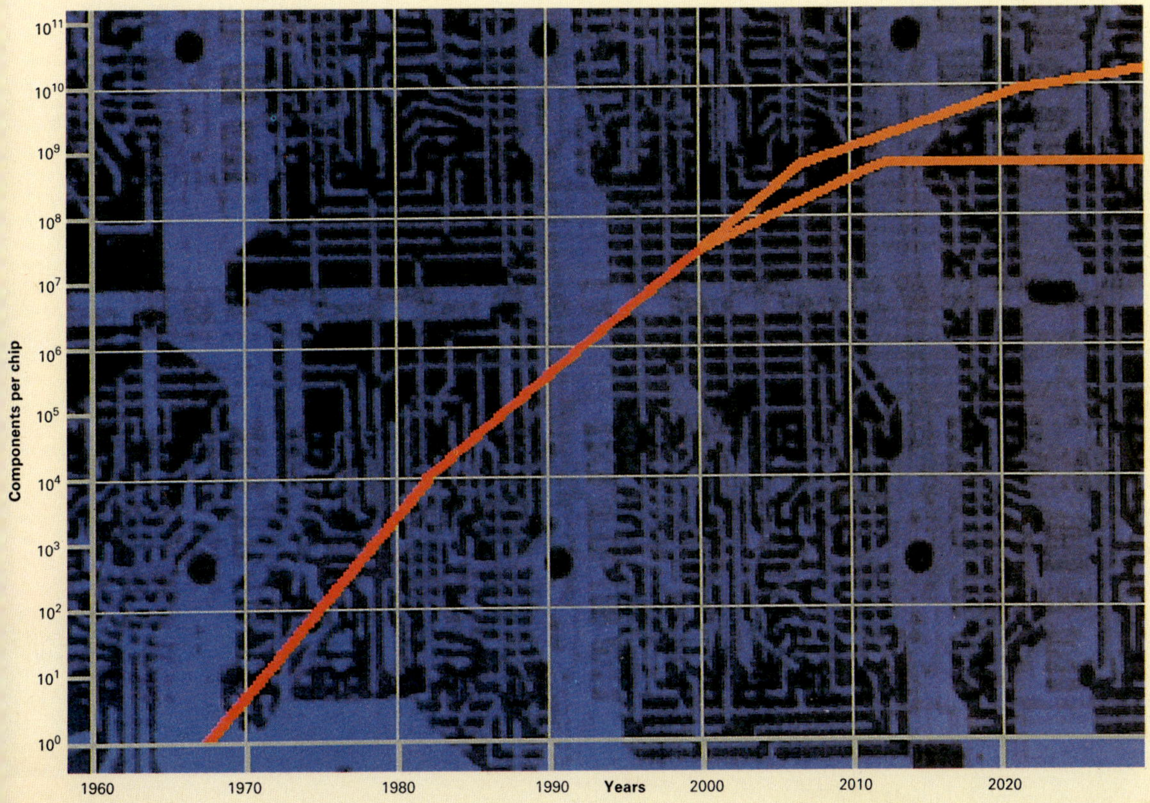

◀ Graph showing how the density of electrical components on a microchip has increased rapidly with time. During the 1960s the number of components that could be built into a chip doubled every year. (The scale on the left increases by a factor of 10 with every step.) In the 1970s the rate of increase slowed a little, but projections show that the one billion-component chip will be achieved by the year 2000. Experts are divided (orange lines) as to how future manufacturing processes will impose limits on the number of components.

The chemical properties of silicon – the basis of the modern computer – are very similar to those of carbon – the basis of the natural world and human life

A computer's make up

The working of a modern computer depends primarily on the properties of a single element—silicon. Compounds of silicon with other elements are familar objects, from everyday substances like glass and concrete to gemstones such as amethyst and opal. The commonest compound of all, formed by silicon and oxygen, makes up all the grains of sand found in deserts and on beaches. The chemical properties of silicon are very similar to those of another element, carbon, which is the basis of the natural world and of human life. Silicon is the basis of the world constructed by humans. Silicon compounds are typically hard solids, whereas carbon compounds are gaseous, liquid, or soft solids. The solid computer with its metal frame contrasts with the flexible human being encased in skin.

Silicon compounds, such as sand, are mostly insulators, that is, they prevent the passage of an electrical current. The element silicon itself is different. It is a semiconductor, and it is this property that makes it important for computers. As the name implies, a semiconductor allows some flow of electricity, but much less than the copper wires found in typical domestic appliances. More importantly, the quantity of electricity transmitted by a piece of silicon can be radically altered by adding small amounts of other elements. Adding a small amount of gallium, for instance, enhances the electrical conductivity considerably. The process of addition is called doping. The "dopant" – in this case gallium – has to be added in very precise quantities. A hundred dopant atoms to every billion atoms of silicon might be a typical ratio for the semiconductor used in computers. The manufacture of materials to this level of precision is difficult to achieve and very costly. Computer components are cheap to buy, however, because they are manufactured and sold in huge quantities.

The great virtue of semiconductors such as silicon is that they can be built to form switches, to permit or restrict the passage of electricity. Semiconductor devices of this type are called "transistors". The transistor is as vital to the operation of the computer, as the synapse is to the brain (◀ page 26). In both cases, information needs to be stored and moved between different parts of the memory. Originally, transistors were made as single units, but by the 1970s whole electrical circuits were being built on a single piece of silicon. This was the birth of the "microchip". Since then, further progress has been made in packing more and more transistors and circuits onto each chip. In the 1950s, a 25mm cube contained ten transistors and their associated circuits. By the 1980s, a similar cube could hold over a million such components. Expressed as information content, a standard microchip of the 1970s might store the equivalent of all the information on a map of a medium-sized American town. In the 1980s, a microchip holds the same level of information for a whole state.

Packing large numbers of transistor circuits onto a single silicon chip is called integration. The microchips of the 1970s were examples of large-scale integration (LSI). The current generation of microchips, with their more numerous circuits, are described as VLSI (very large-scale integration). Over the years, the decrease in size of electronic components has been dramatic. A modern pocket calculator provides as much information as a room full of computer equipment in the 1950s. Not only is it more convenient for the user to work on a much reduced scale, but having the electrical components so close together also speeds up the information flow. Modern computers both handle much more information and do so faster than ever before.

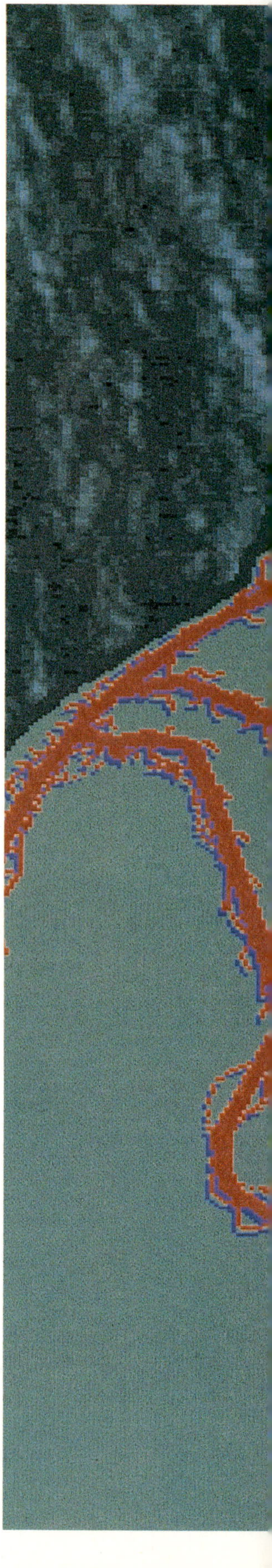

▶ The human brain and the computer are similar in that both accept information from the outside world and then process it. In the human body the main input sources are the three sensors (enclosed in boxes) of sight in the eye, hearing in the ear and touch in the hands. These feed to the brain (central box). The computer (far right) processes information fed to it by an array of sensors. These include a keyboard as well as other input devices such as a "mouse", an electronic pad and pen, a microphone and a video recorder. Computers usually obtain information from only one input device at a time, humans typically gather information simultaneously from all their senses.

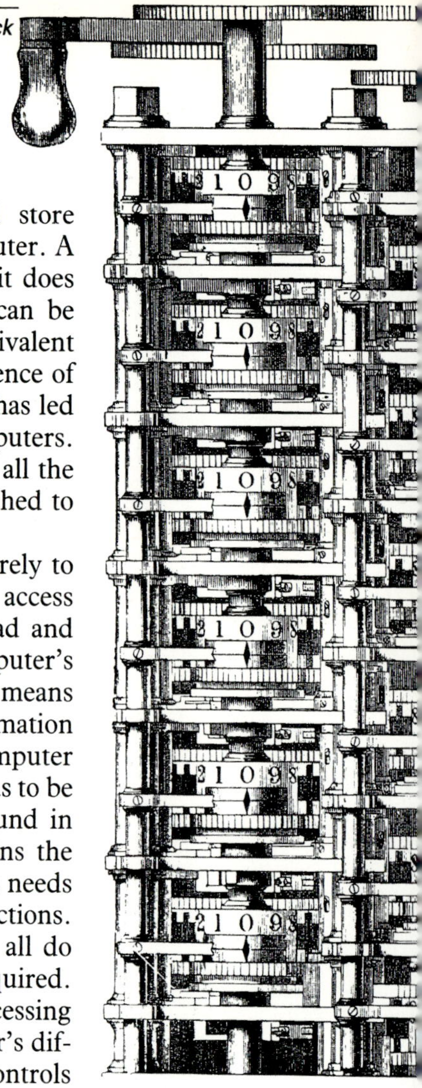

▲ ***Charles Babbage (1801–1871) began work on his "difference engine" in 1823. The part shown was completed 10 years later. Its purpose was to carry out complex calculations automatically, so it is considered a forerunner of the modern computer. It uses mechanical gears – seen as vertical columns – rather than electricity. The machine was abandoned still incomplete in 1842, mainly because Babbage kept modifying the design as it progressed.***

Handling information in the computer

The way transistors use electrical pulses to transmit and store information is fundamental to information handling by a computer. A simple transistor circuit either records an electrical pulse, or it does not. It is in one of two states, either "on" or "off". "On", can be regarded as the equivalent of a 1 in binary notation "off" the equivalent of a 0. Thus any binary number can be represented by a sequence of transistors which are either on or off. The use of binary digits has led to computers that operate in this way being called digital computers. To retrieve the binary digits only requires an electrical scan of all the circuits. To alter them, a new set of electrical pulses is dispatched to the appropriate circuits.

▼ ***The arithmetic and logic unit (ALU) in a computer makes decisions concerning the handling of information. It controls the sequence of steps to be followed when working on a problem. The unit contains large numbers of switches (usually called gates) which decide how information will pass through it. An input of two 1s or two 0s is arranged to close the gate, so that no electricity flows. Conversely, an input of 1 and a 0 together opens the gate and allows a signal to pass.***

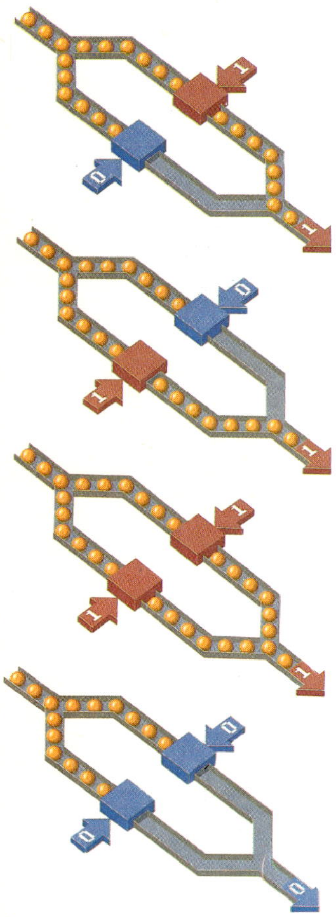

All computers contain a number of microchips devoted entirely to memory. They are called RAM chips. RAM stands for random access memory, but could more meaningfully be interpreted as "read and modify", because this is what is going on all the time in a computer's memory. In computer jargon, "writing" information to a chip means storing the information in its memory. "Reading" the information means finding out what is held in a particular part of a computer memory before changing it as necessary. Memory of this type has to be specified as RAM because another type – ROM – is also found in computers. ROM stands for "read only memory" and contains the information that is necessary for running the computer. It thus needs to be read, but must not be changed or the computer malfunctions.

The rows and rows of circuits contained on memory chips all do much the same job. They store information and release it as required. In contrast, the circuits making up a computer's central processing unit (CPU) must be of more than one type to fulfil the processor's different functions. The CPU is the central part of a computer. It controls communication with the outside world and accesses the various types of memory. It contains the arithmetic and logic unit (ALU). If the RAM and ROM banks are analagous to long-term human memory, then the CPU is the equivalent of short-term memory.

Why does a computer need an ALU, a unit devoted exclusively to arithmetic and logic? The arithmetic function is self-explanatory. The logic part makes deductions based on statements such as, "If it quacks and has webbed feet, then it is a duck". One of the great advances of the 19th century was the realization that statements of this kind and arithmetic statements such as 2+2=4 can be treated in the same way. Not only can they be written in a similar form – for example, quacks + webbed feet=duck – but, more importantly, two items are involved in each. First, there are the data – 1,2,3, quacks, webbed feet, duck. Second, there are the operations that are to be carried out using these data –, +, =, if, then. Clearly, the data can be represented by binary numbers in the computer, but so can the operations. For example, the binary number 11000110 can represent the + operation. It is the job of the CPU's control unit to ensure that this number is understood as a command to add two things together, and not as the equivalent of the decimal number 178. The control unit recognizes the numbers being fed to it as coded instructions to carry out the corresponding operations in a specified sequence. Data are brought out of the memory banks in the form of electrical pulses. As these pulses pass through the control unit, transistor switches send them through the circuits corresponding to the required operation. If the process is one of addition, they combine. If it is one of subtraction, they cancel. The new data, in the form of the modified pulses, are then stored in memory circuits.

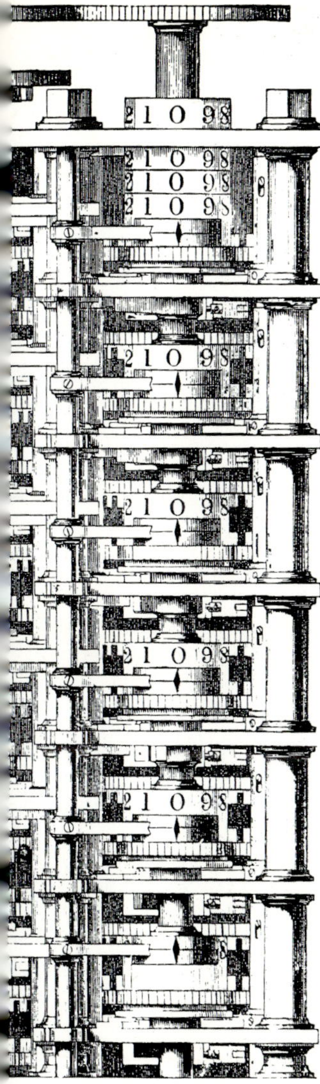

Specifying the sequence of operations to be carried out, and which data are to be used, is central to the whole procedure. The list of instructions that perform these functions is called a computer program. Because computers operate at such high speeds, the program must be held in electronic form in the computer memory before any operations begin. Early computers were called automatic machines for this reason. They did not require new instructions or data to be fed in at each step. One such machine, developed in the USA during the 1950s, was ILLIAC (Illinois Automatic Computer). Acronyms have always been a part of the world of computers, perhaps reflecting their military origin during World War II.

Like the human brain, an electronic computer takes in data, processes and stores them and produces the results when required to do so. The computer and the brain both contain large numbers of switching mechanisms, which allow messages to be diverted through a variety of pathways. A traditional computer, however, unlike the brain, always works in a strict sequence. To ensure that each step forward in the program is carried out to order, all the operations within a computer are controlled by an accurate clock. Every time the clock moves forward, all computer operations move on by one step.

▼ The binary number system works. The numbers we normally use are based on factors of 10. They start with 0 and count up to 9, then start again from 10 and count up to 99, and so on. For computers, it is more convenient to count up in multiples of two. The first numbers are again 0 and 1. But, instead of 2, the next number becomes 10, while 3 is 11. Whereas ordinary counting goes in units, tens, hundreds, thousands, and so on, binary counts in units, twos, fours, eights, and so on.

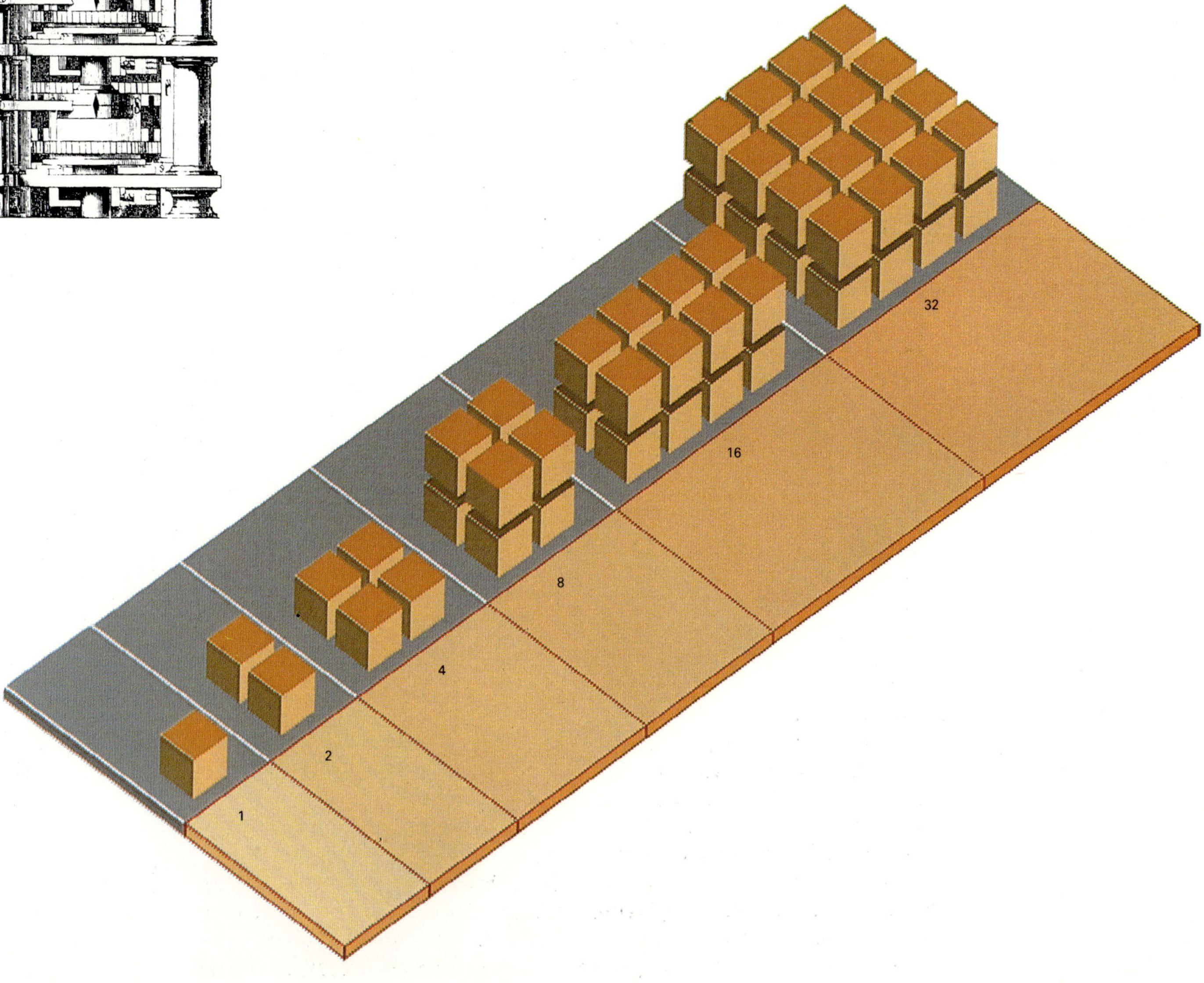

The human brain has no exact equivalent of the computer's clock and can handle several problems simultaneously. Computers sometimes seem to be doing this – for example, when several people are using the same computer at the same time. But what really happens is that the computer goes round each user in turn to find out its next task. This is satisfactory provided that all the users are working interactively with the computer – that is, the computer has to refer back to each of them at intervals for further instructions. A secretary editing a letter, for example, spends an appreciable length of time just looking at the words on the screen. During that time, the computer can be servicing another customer because it works so much faster than human beings. If, however, all the users load in long programs that do not require reference back, the computer can soon become overloaded.

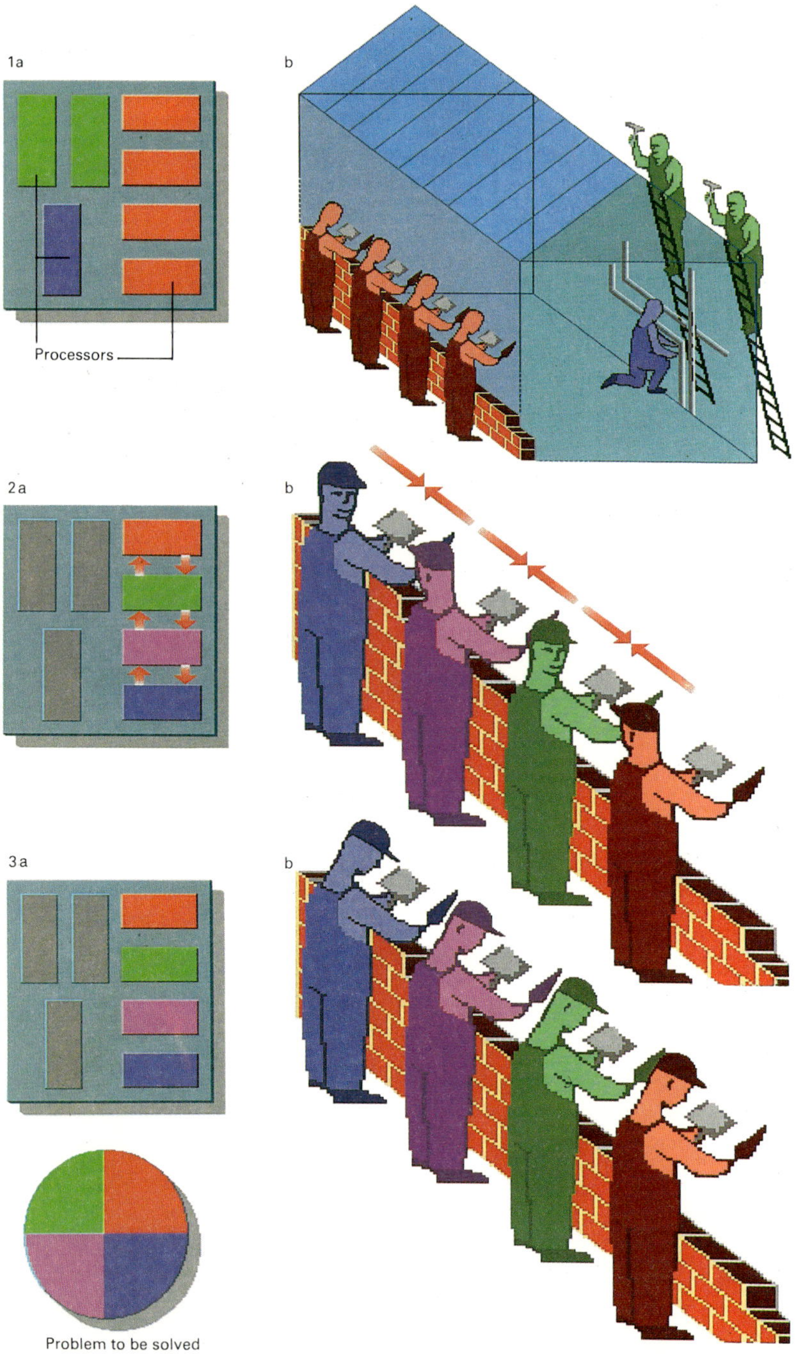

▼ A comparison between the operations of a parallel processor (1a) and a team of construction workers building a house (1b). Each worker represents a single processor. Numbers of workers, and processors, are simultaneously employed on different specialist tasks – bricklaying, plumbing, carpentry etc. Each worker or processor must be able to communicate with the next (2a, b) but each must work in a different place (3a, b) within a defined area.

In contrast to the computer, the human brain can comfortably deal with simultaneous input of information from different sources.

Parallel processing

The brain's method of processing information in parallel, instead of in sequence, is more efficient. Because of this, a new generation of computers is being designed which, like the brain, use parallel processing. They will have several central processing units, but it is expected that they will normally be used to solve different parts of the same problem, rather than work on different problems. This is equivalent to having several computers operating at the same time. The difficulty arises when the different parts of the operation have to be combined. For example, if the computer is designing an airplane, it can work on the wings and the fuselage separately. However, the results have to be compared at frequent intervals because any change in fuselage design obviously affects the wings, and vice versa. This means that the CPUs have to be connected to each other. Cross-relating different bits of information is what the human brain does supremely well. It is not yet clear how well computers can imitate it.

Brains and computers differ in another important respect. The vast majority of computers are digital, operating on discrete units of data only. The brain is equally at home in dealing with a continuously varying input. In the early days, analog computers, which employ a continuously changing flow of electricity, were built alongside digital computers in places such as garages. Gasoline for a car is bought with some unit of currency – cents, pennies, or whatever – and so it is reasonable to use a digital computer to add up the total. The amount of gas purchased, however, can include any fraction of a gallon or liter. This can be measured more accurately by an analog computer.

In practice, the distinction between discrete and continuous is less clear-cut. Any continuous change can be represented as a series of very small jumps. For example, gas pumps do not need to measure to an accuracy of more than a hundredth of a gallon. If this is used as a basic unit, a digital computer can measure gas consumption as well as an analog computer. The same computer can than handle both the gas and the cash, whereas an analog computer is less able to cope with the money. A digital computer can do the same work as an analog computer simply by taking account of the instructions fed to it in a program. To change the task, all that is needed is to change the program. To change an analog computer to cope with another sort of problem would mean rebuilding its circuitry from scratch.

In computer terminology, an analog computer relies on "hardware", whereas the digital computer relies on "software". "Hardware" refers to all the equipment that makes up a computing system. "Software" includes all the programs and data fed into the computer. Similarly, the turntable, loudspeakers and other components of a hi-fi system are its hardware, and the recordings on tape or disks are its software. Sometimes the operational instructions held permanently in a computer, usually on ROM chips, are regarded as in between and called the "firmware".

In the early days of computers, the hardware was more important than the software. Hardware was difficult to operate, whereas the software, which was mainly concerned with adding numbers, was simple. That situation has now changed. Problems with hardware have been considerably reduced while software continues to grow in complexity.

◄ Silicon chips are cut out from a large silicon wafer on which the integrated circuits are all made together. The manufacturing processes include doping (to produce conducting and nonconducting regions on the chip), etching and lithography. The "semi-customized" wafer (here, illuminated and held in a human hand to show color and size) allows users to make final design changes to suit their own specific needs. The wafer has two rows of integrated circuits and two sites for attaching equipment to inspect and alter features on the chip.

By the end of the century computer experts hope that one square inch of storage medium will be able to hold a terabyte (a trillion bytes) of information

Outside memory

A computer needs sufficient memory space both to handle the data fed in and to store its own operating instructions. Memory is usually measured in kilobytes, or K.1K=1,024 bytes (◀ page 49). A small desk-top computer may have a 64K or 128K memory. Some of the latest micros have memories in the 1,024K range, which is equivalent to saying that they have reached the million megabit level. This is still far below the memory capacity of the human brain. Yet humans required aids to their memories, which is why there are such things as books and libraries. Computers with their much more limited memories have an even greater need for external aids. Furthermore in many cases a computer's memory is "volatile". That is, when the computer is switched off, all the memory, except that held on ROM chips, disappears. It is usually necessary, therefore, to store data and programs externally.

The simplest form of external memory is ordinary audio-cassette tape. A similar, but better medium is magnetic tape. This, too, is a flexible tape coated with a magnetic surface. All tape, however, suffers from the disadvantage that each entry on the tape has to be scanned serially (one after another) to find the item required. For this reason, disks have become a much more popular form of storage. While the disk spins rapidly, a detector moves in and out from the center across to the edge, scanning for the required item.

The commonest storage disk for microcomputers is the "floppy", so called because it is made of flexible plastic. Data are stored on a magnetic coating in much the same way as for tape. Floppy disks vary in both size and storage capacity. Some currently available floppies can hold information equivalent to 200 pages of a book. "Hard" disks (which, as their name implies, are not flexible) come in packs and can hold more information, currently the equivalent of five average-length books. Like floppies and tapes, they rely on magnetic recording.

Storage by optical recording is a more recent development, relying in particular on the use of lasers. (Laser stands for "light amplification by stimulated emission of radiation".) When a laser beam is concentrated on a surface, the heat it generates can gouge out a small pit. If a less-intense light beam is later reflected from the surface, the pit can be detected because it scatters light differently from the rest of the surface. This is the basis of the so-called optical disk. Currently such disks can hold up to a gigabyte (a million bytes) of data.

Computer storage capacity has increased dramatically over the past few decades, along with computing power. Today, one square inch of storage medium can hold as much information as was stored on ten square feet only 20 years ago. By the end of the century, it is hoped that one square inch will be able to hold a terabyte (a trillion bytes) of information. Such a massive reduction of scale will make information retrieval that much faster. For all these media, however, long-term stability poses a problem. Properly cared for, books can last for centuries. In contrast, magnetic memory fades with time, and so magnetic media have to be "refreshed" at intervals if they are to retain their information. Optical storage was expected to be much more stable because the surface of the disk is covered with a transparent plastic to protect the pits. However, recent experience suggests that their surfaces may still deteriorate with time. Computers are not yet as well served in this respect by external storage as are human beings by books. But computer storage media are still changing rapidly and the technology is improving all the time.

► All major computer companies are now experimenting with parallel computers. IBM have produced the test-bed computer (far right) to investigate different ways of organizing and extending the parallel computing process. Many of the problems parallel computers are designed to solve concern computer graphics. The advanced computer display (right) is based on a program designed to show a continuing array of cubes each of which can be made to rotate in a variety of ways. Future hardware is being designed to manipulate several thousands of shapes simultaneously.

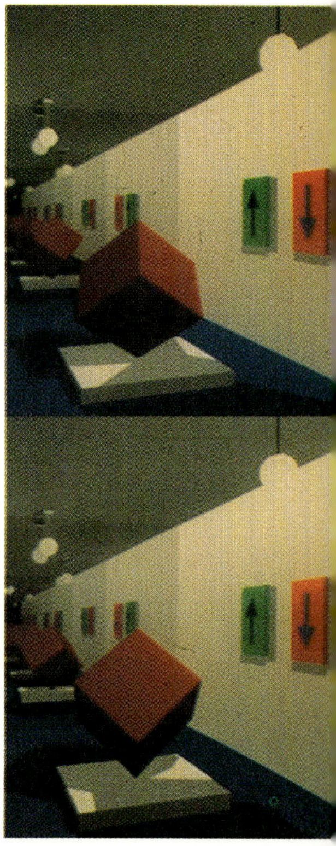

► The storage capacities of different types of disk are compared to a typical 200-page book. Unlike floppy or hard disks, which rely on magnetic recording, the optical disk makes use of laser technology. Light is a far more versatile medium than magnetized spots, enabling an optical disk to store well over 200 times more than a floppy disk.

►► With magnetic storage, the magnetic and non-magnetic parts of the tape (or disk) are used to represent binary 1 and 0. The tape passes below an electromagnet which can be switched on, to magnetize the metal particles on the tape, or off. Reversing the current reverses the direction of magnetization. To read the information on the tape, the electromagnet senses the magnetized spots as the tape passes beneath.

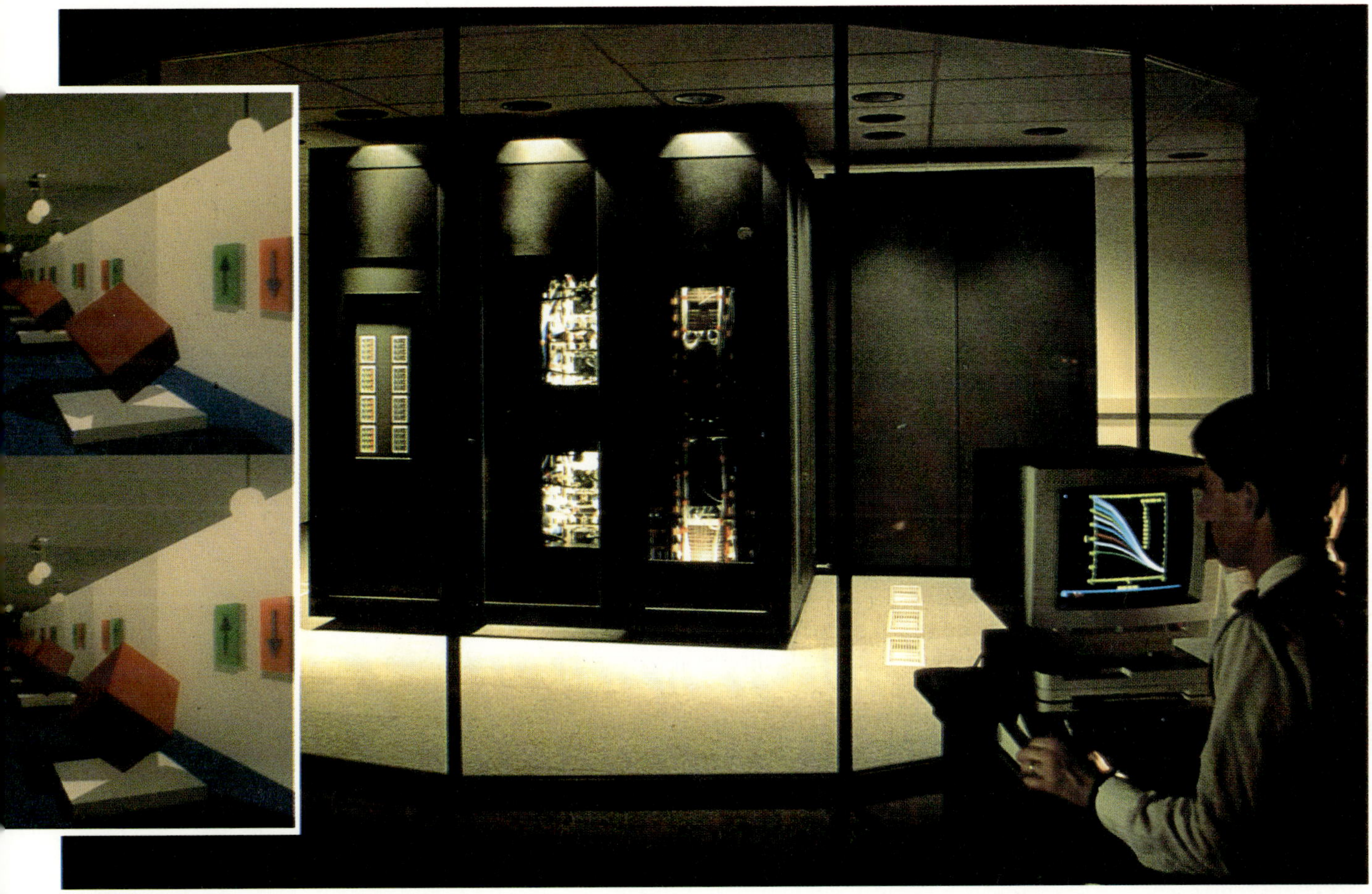

Storage capacities compared

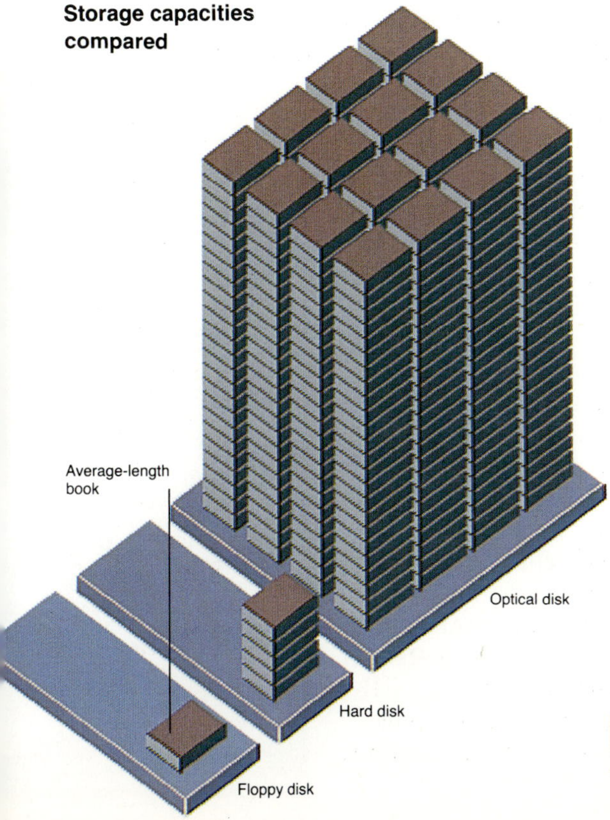

Magnetic data storage

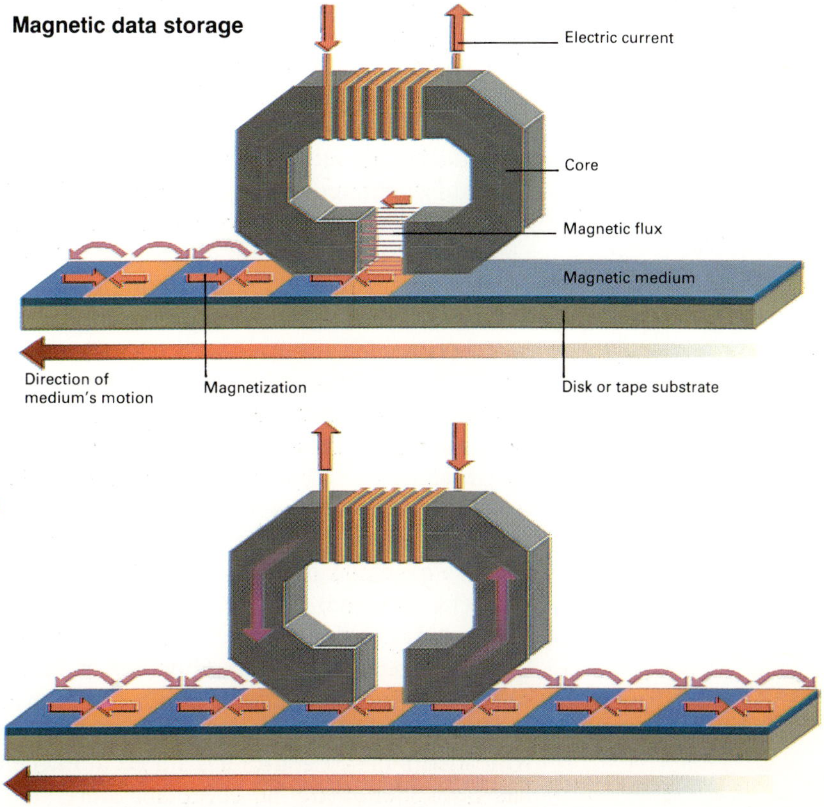

Teaching computers to "see" printed material has proved to be a highly complex process

Information input

As with humans, the input of information to computers depends primarily on vision, speech and touch. Some attempts are also being made to provide computerized versions of smell and taste, including methods to detect small amounts of vapor associated with particular smells. The detector can be linked directly to a computer to analyze the results, and so identify the smell. Still the most widely used input device, however, is the computer keyboard, which follows the layout of a traditional typewriter. A skilled typist can perhaps manage speeds of over 100 words a minute, which is far less than the speed at which a computer handles material. Most keyboard operators are far slower. So there has been a continuing search for ways of bypassing this input bottleneck.

One method is for the computer to do the asking and for the human operator simply to respond. For example, many computer programs provide a "menu" to choose from. All that the user needs to do is to indicate his or her preferred option. In addition, the screen of the computer terminal may be touch-sensitive, recording the user's choices when the appropriate part of the screen is pressed. Some screens are light-sensitive. A light pen (effectively a small torch) pointed at the relevant part of the screen activates the menu. Light pens can be used to draw pictures directly on the screen, which can then be stored in memory. Screen images can also be produced by writing on an electronic pad linked to the computer. In all these cases, the principle is the same. A grid on the surface of the screen is sensitive to pressure or light. When contact is made with the grid, the computer notes the location and stores this information accordingly.

▲ Bar codes on food packages being read. Many goods are now marked with a bar code, which is used to indicate price and other information. Using a special pen, the bars are read directly into a computer for processing.

► A new form of art – painting with computer graphics. The computer makes available a wide range of colors on a screen "palette" (on the right of the display unit). The operator selects a color and directs it to the desired place on the screen, which serves as the canvas. By moving the "mouse" – the small box under his left hand – the operator can change the position of the selected color patch in the display.

An important distinction can be made here. All input can be treated by the computer as pictures with no particular meaning, in much the same way that a non-Chinese speaker sees written Chinese characters. This is what happens in facsimile transmission – "fax", as it is usually called. A light scans the document to be recorded, as in a photocopier, and transmits the information as light and dark regions to another fax machine. But the machine has no *knowledge* of which region corresponds to which letter. The alternative approach is for the computer to recognize each letter or number as it is entered. In this case, the computer can be instructed to alter the text once it has been recorded. The problem lies in developing a machine that can easily recognize a wide variety of characters. In one method, letters printed on a pad are identified by the computer and stored in the appropriate binary form for future use. The commonest input of this type, however, is OCR (optical character recognition), so called because the characters are identified by scanning a light over them.

Teaching computers to "see" printed material has proved to be a highly complex process. Early versions of OCR in the 1950s could only manage recognition of one character per minute. The first useful results were obtained with identification of the simple bar codes now found on many items, including books. Bar codes are read with a wand (a form of light pen which detects reflected light). OCRs today can achieve speeds of up to 120 characters per second, much faster than is possible using a keyboard. The difference is, of course, that for the OCR material must be prepared beforehand, whereas a keyboard can be used for direct input.

OCR works by comparing the shapes of characters in a document with shapes the computer has stored in its memory. Once a character has been identified, the computer stores the corresponding binary

number in its memory and moves on to scan the next character. This works quite well with printed text, as in a book, though the computer may need some training. A new text is presented to the OCR machine and the computer identifies the characters as well as it can. If some are misidentified, further text with these characters is fed to the OCR machine until they are recognized consistently. Handwritten material is much more difficult to recognize because the shapes of the letters can vary so much. The OCR equipment must realize that a character with sloping sides, meeting at the top, and with a bar across the middle is a capital "A", regardless of the angle of slope, or the position of the bar. Hand-printed characters can now be recognized fairly consistently, but joined-up writing still presents major problems. Apart from coping with styles of handwriting, the computer must also decide where one letter ends and the next begins.

Automatic recognition of printed characters is already being put to a variety of uses. A great deal of classical literature is now stored on computer. Using computers scholars can compare texts with an ease and accuracy that had not hitherto been possible. In principle, almost all the material in our libraries could be held on computer, given sufficient storage space. Recognizing printed characters is also the basis for automatic sorting of mail. In the UK, an OCR machine in the sorting office scans the postal code written towards the bottom of each envelope and assigns the letter to the right area destination. Human intervention is still needed, however, when the writing is not easily legible and the code is wrong or missing.

◀ Optical character recognition (OCR), equipment used by the British Post Office. At the top are light sources and a sensor to detect reflected light. Envelopes pass through a light on the conveyor belt at the bottom and the postal codes are read by the sensor. Electronic sorting saves in time and labor.

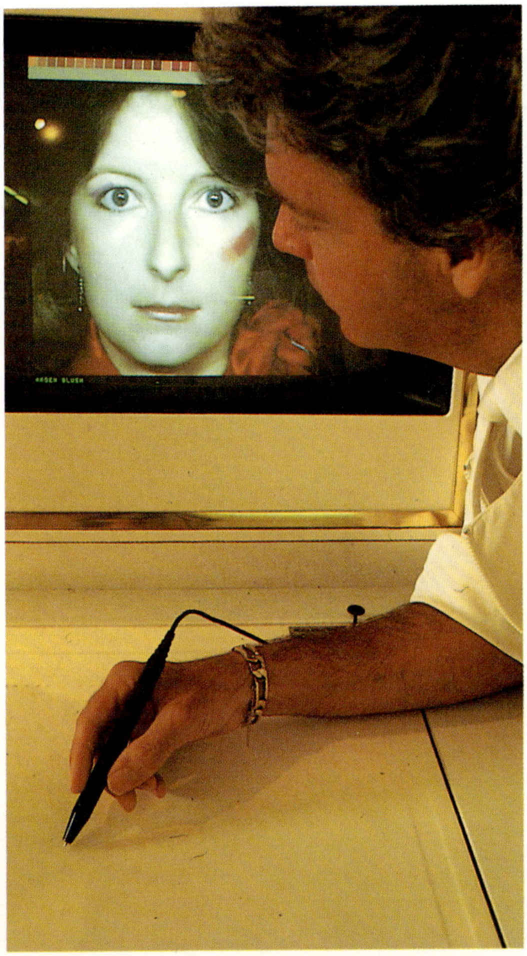

◀ A beautician using computer-aided design (CAD) to try out different combinations of makeup. Using a special pen, the operator traces out the desired design, which goes directly into the computer. The images produced in this way on the screen can then be manipulated to make new patterns. Today CAD is extensively used in all kinds of industries, from automobile engineering to dress design.

Automatic speech recognition and translation

Along with vision, the most important source of information for human beings is speech. Computer recognition of sound progressed slowly until quite recently. The problem was the same as with handwriting. Written characters run into each other and become unrecognizable. So do spoken words. Speech recognition suffers from the problem of dialects, just as handwriting recognition suffers from the problem of styles. Computers can, however, identify simple commands, such as “stop”, “go”, “up” and “down”. Even this has useful applications – for example, in controlling equipment in a factory when the worker’s hands may already be occupied.

Everyday speech uses some 5,000 words, but these are not the same for everybody. Different people have different interests – sports, finance and others. To be generally useful, a speech recognition device would therefore have to be able to identify a vocabulary of well over 5,000 words. One difficulty is the need to distinguish words that sound similar, but have different meanings. How does a machine distinguish between “saw” (referring to vision), “saw” (the tool), “sore” and “soar”, or between “gray day” and “grade A”? We distinguish them, at least partly, by the context in which we hear them. To imitate us, computers must be able to analyze sentence structure. Current speech recognition systems are claimed to understand up to 20,000 words, so long as they are spoken separately and not blurred into each other. The number of errors they make is still quite large, perhaps one in 100 words, which is more than would be acceptable from a secretary taking rapid dictation. The need to speak each word separately

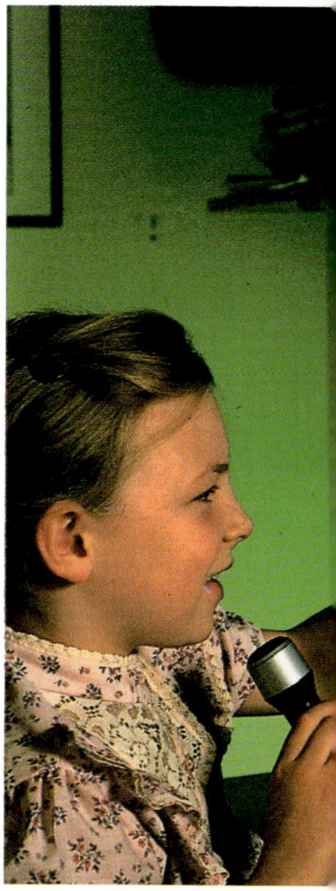

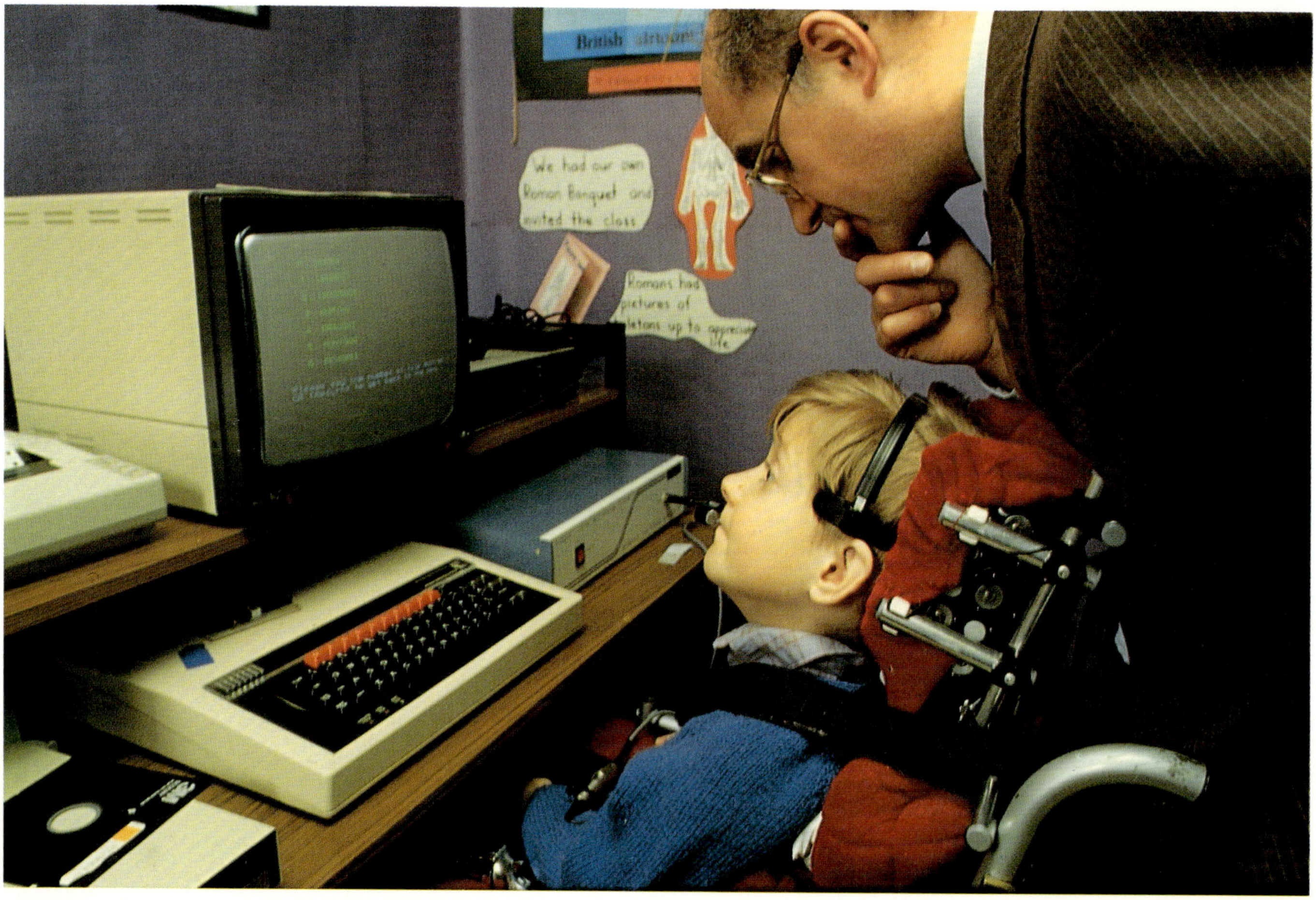

▼ *When he was 18 months old, Nicholas became ill with meningitis which left him permanently paralyzed. Unable to use his hands to write or draw, from the age of four onwards he was encouraged to use a microcomputer. Since he could not handle the keyboard directly, he learned to close a switch with his tongue. Now he can communicate much more easily with the aid of a device for recognizing human speech attached to his microcomputer.*

▲ *Young child using a microphone with a "talk-writer" educational software package to manipulate a computer. Computers are now able to recognize commands quite easily, so long as the words are pronounced clearly and separately. Furthermore, because everyone speaks in a slightly different way, computers can be trained to identify and obey the voice of a particular individual. Voice input is being increasingly used to control a computer in situations where the operator's hands are otherwise occupied, as well as in education and as an aid for the handicapped.*

obviously slows down the rate of input. Teaching computers to recognize sentence structure helps. Short sentences with a standard structure (subject/verb/object) can now be recognized even when spoken in a normal way. Computers can also be trained to use the redundancy of some words in speech to guess at words they fail to hear properly, and to convert shorthand speech into proper sentences. "Go New York a.m." can be stored by the computer as "I am going to New York tomorrow morning". Computer shorthand, like the shorthand used by secretaries, can speed up the input of information.

The same approach can be used in simple forms of spoken translation by computer. Most tourist queries hang on a few key words. For example, in "Could you please tell me where the railway station is?" the key words are "where" and "railway station". The computer can be instructed to look for these key words and fill out the remainder from its memory when giving a translation.

At present, automatic speech recognition poses serious problems, but it offers great rewards if it can be achieved. Humans are accustomed to providing information by speaking, which is our most natural and rapid form of communication. It does not require lengthy training (unlike typing) to become skillful at it. Speech recognition linked to automatic translation from one language to another could have enormous potential for improving international communication and, possibly, furthering understanding between nations.

The translation of language by machine has been an important field of computer studies for the past three decades. Progress has been slow, however, because of the great technical difficulties. All early and much current work has concentrated on written, rather than spoken language. This avoids the problems of speech recognition, and of having to translate from one language to another in real time (while people are speaking).

Written translation can be done at leisure. As in speech recognition, a major problem acknowledged early on was that words could mean different things in different contexts. "Out of sight, out of mind" is once supposed to have emerged from a computer as "Invisible, insane". Now computers are being trained to recognize sense by looking for further information. When the sentence "In 1977, Israel and Egypt buried the hatchet" was first fed into a computer, it took this to mean that a hole was dug in the ground and an axe placed in it. It was then fed the additional information: "Israel and Egypt were involved in a long conflict. In 1977, they signed a peace agreement." Asked to reinterpret the first sentence, the computer replied, "They buried the hatchet equals they terminated the conflict", and stored this new meaning in its memory.

▼ *A computer makes sense of language by analyzing it at several different levels from stored data. Sound waves from speech or written words are studied for their roots and inflection. The computer then embarks on a further sequence of analytical steps: lexical (identifying category of word, such as noun or verb, and features, such as plurals); syntactic (breaking down of the sentence to reveal its underlying grammatical structure); contextual (defining the sentence in time) and semantic (drawing inferences). The computer is now prepared to provide a response to the original sentence.*

Computerized understanding of language

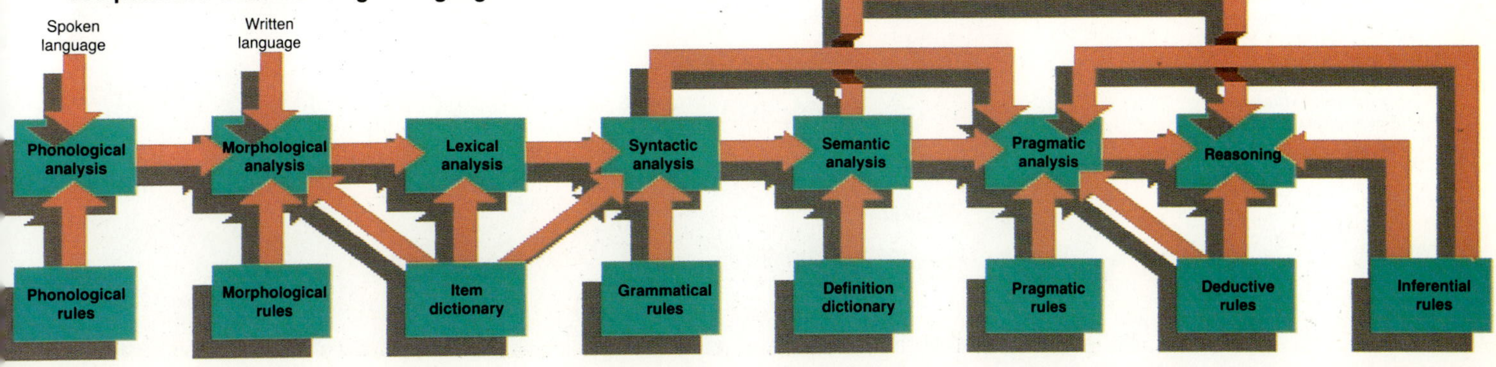

A continuing problem for translation is the ambiguity of language. Taken out of context, how should the following sentence be interpreted? "Avoid flying aeroplanes." Similarly, how can a computer tell that "He eats with his knife" and "He eats with his wife" mean quite different things? For reasons like these, translated output usually needs the attention of a human editor to turn it into acceptable language. However, in a few areas, material written in a straightforward style can be translated into acceptable form by computer alone. The technical manuals produced by the Japanese company Fujitsu are translated automatically from Japanese into English using a system that has already been sold to some 200 other firms.

The great advantage of machine translation, compared with using human translators, is its speed and low running costs. The situation is more complicated when simultaneous translation across several languages is required, as is standard, for example, within the European Economic Community. Computers need an increasing amount of memory for the number of dictionaries they hold. Thus, for two languages, only two dictionaries are needed (English–French and French–English, for example). For three languages, the number rises to six dictionaries, and so on. Work on the development of an intermediate language, into which all texts are first translated, has helped to address the problem. Fujitsu, in their translation work, use an artificial intermediate language called Interlingua, developed by the Italian mathematician Guiseppe Peano (1858–1932) early this century. This is basically a simplified and more logical version of Latin, which is easier for a computer to handle than natural languages. Translating from a language into Interlingua and from Interlingua into the target language involves two stages instead of one, but there is a saving in memory space because fewer dictionaries are needed for multilingual translation. Many experts in the field, however, still prefer direct translation by machine from one language to another because they say that two-stage translation can result in some loss of meaning.

► A trainee air-traffic controller using a MACROSPEAK package to learn radar and other basic skills. The main applications of speech recognition and synthesis have so far been in the industrial and military worlds. However, a variety of applications for computer speech are now being considered in the consumer market, including voice-controlled televisions, ovens and wristwatches. Experts forecast that computerized dictation machines will be available by the end of the century. Computer systems with a good range of vocabulary might perform a large range of office jobs and even replace some staff.

Outputting information

Computer output can express information as either sound or vision. Considerable effort has gone into the synthesis of speech by computer to allow spoken output. Reproducing the sounds of words is much easier for a computer than recognizing those sounds when they are spoken. However, it is less easy to produce continuous speech that sounds natural. Two methods of speech synthesis are currently in use. In the one, words spoken into a microphone by a human speaker are translated into digital form and stored in the computer's memory. (Each word occupies about a kilobit – more than 1,000 bits – of memory.) This is the same procedure as for the digital recording of music. The voice reproduced at the end will have the same accent and intonation as the original voice. The computer can then rearrange the words stored in its memory to form new sentences. By itself, this approach cannot reproduce the subtle intonations of normal speech.

With the second method, which is generally considered better, the computer generates electrical oscillations which are then modified until they resemble the sound waves that are to be imitated. The computer has to be told beforehand, of course, which oscillations are needed to make up the various sounds. Both methods require considerable storage space. (Readers may recall how, in the motion picture *2001*, the computer Hal regressed from ordinary speech to a blurred monotone as its memory banks were removed.)

▼ The steps taken by a computer to reply to a spoken statement. First, the speech input is converted from sound waves into electronic input. The computer analyzes this input in terms of syntax (the grammatical arrangement of the words) and semantics (what the words mean). Next, the computer compares the results with its knowledge of the world. Its memory contains facts, concepts relating to these facts, and procedures that tell it how to use the concepts. Finally, the response generated from these is changed back from computer language to ordinary speech using the vocabulary from grammar in the computer's memory.

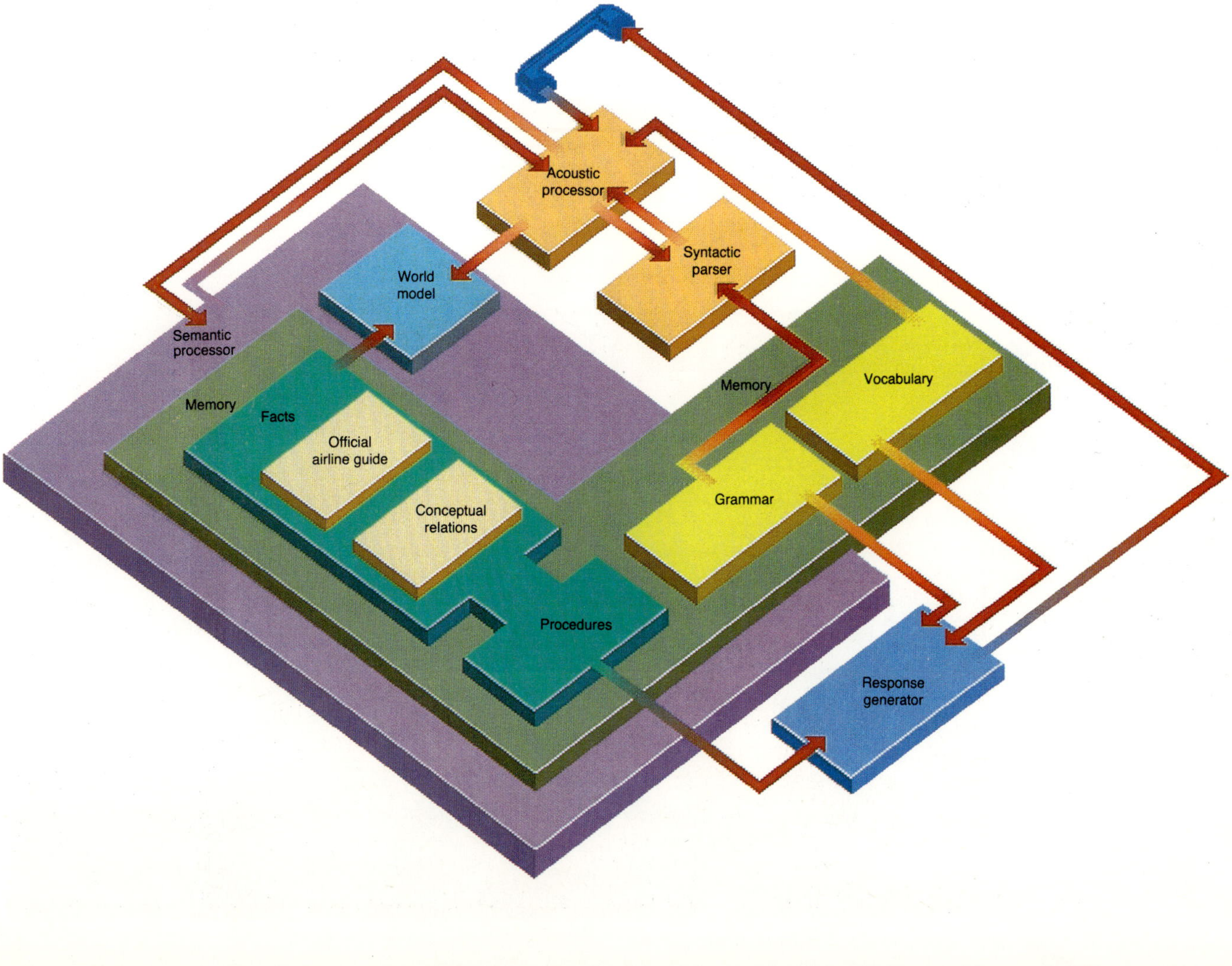

Applications of computer-synthesized speech are already fairly common. Sometimes OCR technology is used to provide the text input. The computer then converts the written words to spoken words and reads the text aloud. This method, in principle, allows blind people to select any book and have it read to them. In practice, suitable equipment is still too expensive for the facility to be generally available. These reading machines can equally well produce material in Braille, an example of computer output that depends on the sense of touch. But the vast majority of information produced by computers is visual, whether appearing on the screen, or as "hard copy" (printed out on paper).

Printers have become more sophisticated in recent years, and the quality of reproduction is much improved. All the early printers, and many current ones, make an impression on the paper by impact – much like an ordinary typewriter. More modern printers use other methods. In laser printers, a very fine beam of light writes on paper that is sensitive to heat (similar to paper in photocopiers). Laser printers can be used to draw pictures, as well as to produce characters, and to a very high level of detail. They are still quite expensive, but their prices are falling all the time. Computer-controlled color printing is also on the increase. Computers can now produce printed material as attractive as any found in a book. Indeed "desktop publishing" systems – software that combines text-editing and page-design facilities – are now available quite cheaply. Many publishers and printers nowadays use computerized editing, typesetting and printing techniques. The traditional world of printed paper and the modern world of computers have become thoroughly integrated.

▼ *The British Civil Airline Authority control room. Computer handling of information has particularly affected the aviation industry. In the latest aircraft, all movement of the pilot's controls involve an onboard computer. Also, now that it is computerized, the "black box" flight recorder, which is retrieved after an accident, can give much more information as to its cause. Control of aircraft from the ground also depends on the latest technology.*

▲ *Each of this group of optical fibers consists of a thin, flexible thread of pure glass. Light can be beamed down the fiber. A light source, such as a laser, can vary the way it produces light so that the light can carry a message from one end of the fiber to the other. A single fiber not only takes up a tiny fraction of the space occupied by the copper cable, it can also carry far more information. Thus optical fibers can be used to transmit pictures, which have a very dense information content, as easily as text or speech.*

Telecommunications links

Unlike human beings, computers are not normally constrained by where their input comes from, or where the output goes to. The source of information may be sitting beside the computer, or it may be on the other side of the world. The connections that allow computers to operate on information at a distance are the telecommunications links, of which the ordinary telephone cable is the commonest. Telephone cables were not designed to carry computer messages, so the computer's digital information must be transformed in some way before it can be transmitted. The simplest method is to change the binary data into sound. If "1" corresponds to a high note and "0" to a low note, then the data can be transmitted as a kind of warble. A machine that converts digital information into a form that is acceptable to the telephone network and reverses the procedure is called a modem (short for modulator demodulator).

The communication channel employed often limits the speed with which information can be passed. For example, space probes sent to investigate another planet send back information using a radio transmitter attached to the probe. Because the distances involved are so great and the radio transmitter is small, the signal received on Earth is weak and the data have to be sent back slowly. The pictures of planets that appear in the newspapers may have been built up over half an hour on Earth from these weak transmissions, using techniques of computer enhancement to improve the image (➧ pages 100, 101). Furthermore, pictures contain a lot of information, and can clog communication channels.

The volume of information a channel can accept is measured by its bandwidth. When water flows through a pipe, the amount that passes is ultimately determined by the cross-sectional area of the pipe. This area is the equivalent of bandwidth in communication. If the pipe is narrow, and the volume of water trying to pass is large, there will be a backup of water. Similarly, if there is a lot of digital information to communicate, and the communication channel has a narrow bandwidth, it will take the information a long time to get through. Ordinary telephone cables have a moderate bandwidth, which is not all used up by voice communication, and therefore much computer traffic still goes via the telephone network. For maximum efficiency, however, the cables should be used for computer communication only – dedicated lines, as they are called. But as the amount of information generated by computers is increasing rapidly, so there is a greater need for channels that can carry more data than telephone cables.

One way forward is to provide a new cable network with much greater bandwidth. This need has led in the past few years to the development of the fiberoptic cable. This consists of numerous, very fine glass fibers which carry messages in the form of light pulses from lasers. Fiberoptic cables have a much higher bandwidth than traditional copper cables, and they suffer less from loss in transmission, so that messages go further more easily. Installation of fiberoptic cable is growing rapidly. In 1980 some 6,000km were installed worldwide. By 1986, the network had expanded to well over 60,000km. Most of the cable is on land, but submarine fiberoptic cables have also been laid. A new transatlantic cable will carry nearly 50,000 telephone calls simultaneously. Fiberoptic cables can also transmit several television programs at once. The cable of the future will be multipurpose, simultaneously carrying voice transmission, computer data and television pictures.

▲ *A machine laying telephone cables in shallow waters. Telephone cables have been laid across the floors of oceans since the middle of the last century. With the introduction of optical fibers, however, far fewer cables have been needed to carry as many telephone conversations. The method of laying cables has also developed since the 19th century. Then, heavy cables were lowered from the decks of ships and were often liable to break in the process.*

The communication channel with the widest bandwidth is, of course, the space around us. Any number of messages can readily travel through the atmosphere, or out into space beyond the Earth. So space is the natural and obvious channel for transmitting television programs. However, things are not so straightforward. Television transmissions, in common with other electromagnetic signals travel in straight lines, whereas the Earth is round. This means that, beamed from Earth, television signals cannot be received beyond the horizon.

Most communications satellites are put into "geostationary" orbit, meaning that their orbit is synchronized with the Earth's so that they remain perched over the same spot on the Earth's surface, and are always visible to the same television transmitters. To achieve this, the orbiting satellite must be positioned at nearly 36,000km directly above the Earth's equator. At this height, transmission of signals beyond the horizon becomes easy. A transmitter sends its message up to the satellite, which beams it back to ground stations invisible to the original transmitter. Signals from satellites are quite weak, but receivers are becoming more sensitive. By the 1990s, the saucer-shaped receiver dishes should be small enough to be set up easily by individuals. Not only television programs, but many types of digital information can then be beamed directly to the home.

Information technology (IT) is the interaction of computers and telecommunications. How does it compare with our natural means of communication? Clearly, the computer wins out in dealing with large quantities of data. It can add numbers, scan pages of type and produce ordered lists much faster than we can. IT can send information across the world at the speed of light. As against this, computer memory is both smaller and much less complex than ours. Human input and output of information may be slower than a computer's, but it is also more versatile and subtle. In particular, human speech conveys more meaning than is contained in the words themselves. In short, computer capabilities complement those of human beings. With properly designed IT systems, and computers and people working alongside each other, much will be achieved in the future.

◀ Communications satellites can be put into "geostationary" orbit in two ways. They can be sent up directly in the nose cone of a rocket, or they can be released from a spacecraft. Here the Arabsat Communications Satellite, intended especially for the Gulf states, is being ejected from the cargo bay of the US Space Shuttle. (The Space Shuttle is lying on its side with the Earth below.) The satellite is not being launched at the right height for communications purposes, so it has its own rocket (on the left hand side) to raise it into a higher orbit. Contact is maintained with ground stations on Earth.

Handling Information

4

Information and memory...The information explosion...Classification systems...Hierarchical and alphabetical ordering...Cross-referencing...Roget's thesaurus concept...Information retrieval: human and computers compared...Computer databases... Online communication...Developments in indexing ...Citation indexes...Electronic messages... Office automation

Although human memory has a greater capacity than is normally allowed for nowadays, without some form of external memory the information passed on from generation to generation would be strictly limited. For many years all the older religions transmitted their beliefs by oral tradition, before they were finally written down. Yet because of this they were limited by the amount of information people could remember, and by the time people took to memorize things and their ability to forget. In principle, there is no limit to the storage capacity of external memory such as books and journals. Information can be stored by successive generations, each inheriting more than the last. In earlier times the volume of information preserved was constrained by natural disasters, which ensured that an appreciable fraction of written material was lost. Since the invention of printing, however, it has become increasingly likely that at least one copy of any book will survive, and its information content preserved. But, for such a vast accumulation of information to be useful there must be some means of sorting it and identifying what it contains.

The information explosion

The volume of information worldwide has grown enormously since World War II. In science and technology, some 12–15 million articles were published from the time journals first appeared in the 17th century up to 1960. During the 1960s, as many articles were published as during the previous three centuries, with production running at between one and two million a year. How has this information explosion happened? In fact, it had been simmering below the surface for some time.

There is a story of a man in times past who was offered a reward by a king. The man took a chessboard and said he would accept one grain of wheat on the first square, two on the second, four on the third, eight on the fourth, and so on until all the 64 squares had been covered. The king happily accepted, not realizing that all the wheat in the kingdom would have been used up well before the final square of the chessboard was reached. So it is with the growth of published literature. The amount has been doubling quietly every decade or two for several centuries. But it is only in this century that the store has become so massive that it commands attention.

As the size of information warehouse increases, so do the problems of access to it. Botanists need old, as well as new literature when they try to identify plants. Lawyers need to consult reports of old cases, as well as recent ones, in reaching their conclusions. To be of continuing value, this growing mass of literature must be organized in a way that still allows items to be identified and extracted. What can be done to ensure that information retrieval operates as efficiently in the future as it has done in the past?

▲ The parable of the king and the ears of wheat on a chessboard illustrates the pattern of growth of information. The man whom the king wished to reward asked simply for one ear of wheat on the first square, two on the second, four on the third, and so on until the 64th and final square. The king agreed, not realizing that, by the end, the number of ears of wheat would run into billions of billions – far more than his kingdom could possibly provide. Such growth by multiplication is also common in nature.

The idea of alphabetical ordering probably came about with the invention of printing

Classification

From earliest times, human beings have tried to impose some mental order on the world around them. The process is called classification, and usually requires two steps. The first consists in finding sets of characteristics that can serve to separate objects into groups. The second is to link these groups into some kind of order. An obvious example is the way we classify animals. Dachshunds, beagles, spaniels and many other varieties makeup the group labeled "dogs". Dogs, cats, cows, horses and other groups are then linked together in a category of "mammals", to distinguish them from other categories such as fish or birds. Classification of this sort is seen as natural, because it is supposed to reflect the way the animal kingdom has evolved with time. Many classifications are more arbitrary. A group labeled "soldiers" might contain generals, brigadiers, colonels, captains and so on. They are put in this order because those earlier in the list can command those later in the list. This kind of listing is referred to as a hierarchical organization.

All early attempts to classify knowledge assumed that it could be put in an order of importance. For many centuries, from the Middle Ages onwards, education in Europe was dominated by what were called the seven liberal arts. Three of these were taught first. This "trivium" cons sisted of grammar, rhetoric and logic. They were regarded as the more elementary parts of knowledge (hence the word "trivial"). The higher level "quadrivium" (four subjects) followed only when the first three had been mastered. It included arithmetic, geometry, music and astronomy. They were arranged in this order because music was thought to be applied arithmetic, whilst astronomy was applied geometry. During the medieval period and perhaps beyond, the hierarchically arranged seven liberal arts were supposed to cover all important secular knowledge. Our word "encyclopedia" derives from Greek words used at this time meaning "general education".

Many classification systems have some underlying hierarchy. The different branches of science are often written in the order – mathematics, physics, chemistry, biology, psychology. Implicit here is that the hierarchy of knowledge runs from the most mathematical and quantitative subjects to the least. Such classifications can facilitate retrieval. Knowing which topics fall under which headings and how these are ordered can lead the searcher as far as the desired subject area. But to find the final specific item of interest usually requires a further step.

If a chemist has an information file on metals, how should it be arranged to enable him or her to retrieve information quickly? Almost certainly, the answer is in alphabetical order. At least the chemist would then know that silver came after iron in the file, but before tin. This habit of relying on alphabetical ordering to form an information index is relatively recent. It seems to have been stimulated by the introduction of printing into Europe in the 15th century. Faced with their series of boxes for type, each containing a different letter, printers began to think in terms of sorting words alphabetically. This gave rise, in the 16th century, to the idea of alphabetical dictionaries. The language of contemporary scholars was Latin, but the various national languages were becoming increasingly important. As an aid to translation to and from Latin, dictionaries began to appear and in some the words were listed in alphabetical sequence. During the 17th century, alphabetical indexes began to be used in other contexts. Nowadays, it seems natural to put things in alphabetical order.

◀ *A teacher with his students, from a 16th-century manuscript. The teacher addresses the class from his chair (a term still used to describe academic office). Books were becoming more common, and the written word a growing source of information.*

◀ *A group of animals classified as dogs, though they are of recognizably different breeds. Dogs, cats and others are further classified as "mammals", to distinguish them from, for example, fish or birds. Classification of animals is seen as natural because it relates to how they are supposed to have evolved in nature.*

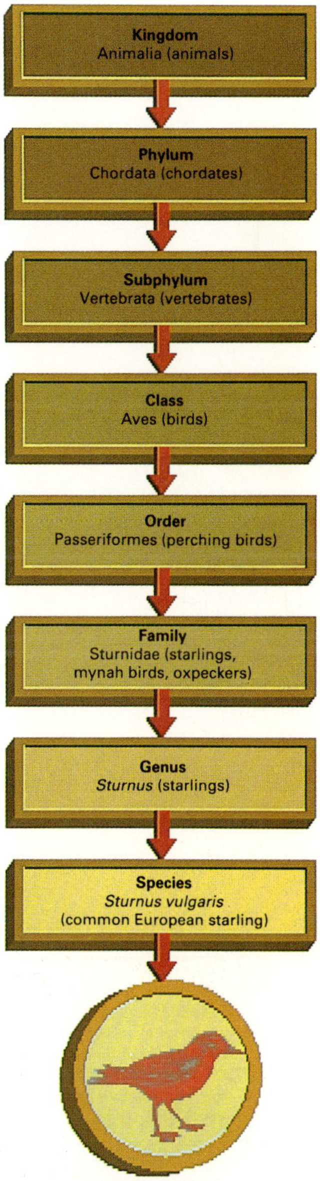

▲ *Biological classification, taxonomy introduced by the Swedish scientist Linnaeus (1707–1778). He gave plants and animals two Latin names, one to indicate the general group (the "genus") and the other the particular branch (the "species").*

Originally, classification by theme and listing by alphabet were seen as alternative ways of retrieving information. They are now used as complementary methods. Classification is mainly concerned with placing items of information in the correct pigeon hole (correct, that is, from the viewpoint of the particular classification used). Indexing provides a label for the item of information. For instance, books may be classified in terms of their subject matter, but indexed by their authors' names. So much information is available that it makes sense to do a rough search by classification order, then apply fine tuning by alphabetical sequence. This is how most libraries work. In a public library, often there will be separate sections labeled, for instance, "Crime", "Sciencefiction", "Westerns" and so on. In each of these sections the books are arranged in alphabetical order by author's surname.

The library will have a book catalog which readers can consult. It will certainly contain an alphabetical index, and also possibly a subject index. It is only when you start to use these that some of the problems of information retrieval become apparent. For example, under "mercury" does the entry in the catalog refer to the chemical element, the Roman god or the planet – all of which have the same name? How much detail is needed in an index? The average non-chemist may be satisfied by an entry which says simply "chemistry", but a chemist will require much finer subdivisions. Suppose you want to obtain information about stealing. What should you look up in an index – "theft", "burglary", or "robbery"? All languages – and English, in particular – have several words relating to a single concept.

▲ *Peter Roget was the Secretary of the Royal Society in London for more than 20 years, and thus was close to intellectual developments of the 19th century. He saw his work of classifying words as being similar to a botanist's task of classifying plants.*

► *The US Library of Congress building, Washington, DC. The need for central libraries to collect all the material published in a country was fully understood by the 19th century. By then, too much was being published for ordinary libraries to maintain comprehensive collections. The US Library of Congress began in 1800. During the 1840s it became the depository for US government publications and for all books published in the USA. The volume of material grew so rapidly that a new building, shown here, was opened in 1897. The Library of Congress continues to provide a service for Senators and representatives.*

All these problems have a solution. Ambiguous words can be defined. For example, "mercury (metal)" is unambiguous. If you choose to find out about stealing by looking up "robbery", and this turns out to be a wrong choice, a properly constructed index will give a cross-reference. Suppose the information you are looking for is to be found under "theft". Then under the entry for "robbery", it will say, "See theft". Since robbery and theft are not identical, the entry for robbery may give some information and then add, "See also theft". Using such devices, an index can try to bypass the uncertainties of language.

A further aid to retrieval is the thesaurus, which attempts to define the meanings of words. For example, the word "computer" might be given a general definition together with an indication that it includes such subdivisions as mainframes, minicomputers and microcomputers. The thesaurus will also indicate uses of alternative words, as in the example of robbery/theft. This function corresponds to the commonest understanding of the purpose of a thesaurus, to list together words having similar meanings. Originally, the thesaurus (literally a "treasure-house") was more ambitious.

In 1852, Peter Roget (1779–1869) published his *Thesaurus of English Words and Phrases*. His intention was to classify all knowledge in a way that would be universally acceptable and would aid intellectual progress throughout the world. He distinguished between dictionaries, where words were put in alphabetical order, and his own thesaurus which grouped words together according to the ideas they expressed. Roget's hopes for a universal system of classifying knowledge have not been fulfilled. His thesaurus, suitably updated, is still in print, but is mainly used by writers and crossword-puzzle addicts. The thesaurus concept, however, remains a valuable aid to information retrieval.

Information retrieval

How do the methods of retrieving information that were developed for human use compare with those of the computer? Think about how we consult the bound volumes of a large encyclopedia. The volumes sit in alphabetical order on a shelf (A–ANA, ANA–ATH, ATH–BOI, and so on). Suppose information on "hair" is needed. H is about a third of the way through the alphabet, so we automatically scan the volumes at about that point along the shelf. Having found the appropriate H volume (GOU–HIP, say) we open it about the middle. "Hair" must come near the beginning of the H list, and we would expect the G words to end and the H words to start near the middle of GOU–HIP. What we are doing is using our knowledge of words to guess whereabouts in spatial terms a piece of information might be found. A computer does not usually operate in this way. It is designed to search things in sequence. Asked to find an item under "hair", it will scan through all the entries under A, then all the entries under B, and so on until it reaches H. If the information required next is about "hats", a human reader automatically stretches out a hand for the same volume. The computer, however, cannot match this subtlety and wastes time by starting back at A again. But even if computers are less flexible than humans in retrieving information, they easily make up for this by their speed of scanning. Such speed is vital given the ever-increasing volume of information.

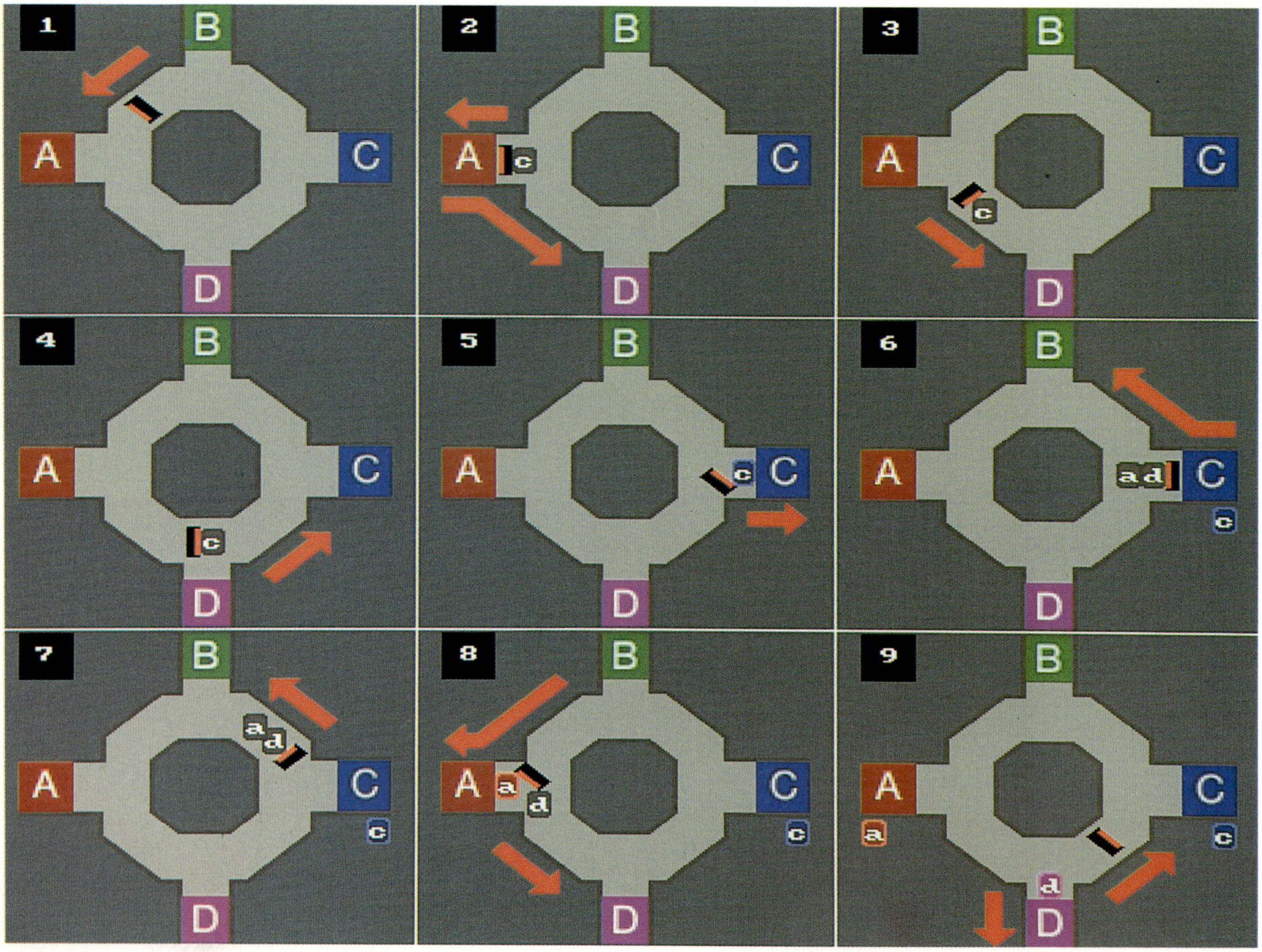

▲ *A magnetic tape library. For many years magnetic tape has been the standard medium for communicating with computers. The tape is made of plastic coated with a magnetic oxide, and is normally about 1cm across. It comes in reels about 27cms wide, each of which contains some 73m of tape. Tapes are stored in drums in a computer library.*

Even if computers cannot match human ingenuity in retrieving information, they can easily adapt to many of the classification, cataloging and indexing systems developed in a pre-electronic age. Several classification systems use numerical indicators. For instance, the whole of scientific knowledge might be labeled 5. Chemistry might then be distinguished from other sciences by adding the number 4, so any chemical information would be assigned the number 54. Different branches of chemistry may be identified by adding further numbers. Organic chemistry, for example, could be indicated by adding 7, giving it a classification number 547. More numbers can be added to reach as fine a division of knowledge as desired. Obviously, this classification system does not use numbers in the usual way – an item classified as 55 comes after one classified as 547. Computers are well suited to handling such sequences of numbers.

The use of computers for classification has a further advantage. Classification schemes have often been used for the purpose of cataloging books and placing them on shelves. Anyone wishing to find a book on organic chemistry, for instance, will look under 547, and all books dealing with this subject will be grouped together under the same heading. Thus a reader who goes to the shelf for a particular title will see other related books clustered round it. Many library users find that browsing through material nearby can provide a valuable lead to new information. This is why libraries try, whenever possible, to have their shelves open to access by readers. Problems can arise, however, with books that deal with more than one topic. For example, a book on biotechnology is likely to refer both to biology and technology, which appear in different parts of most classification schemes. If there is only one copy of the book should it be placed under biology or technology? With information held in a computer this problem does not arise. Biotechnology information can be classified under both headings and the same information retrieved, whether the biology number or the technology number is entered. In fact, computers are used in this way to retrieve genetic information directly.

◄ *Token ring in a computer network. It is used to ensure that the electronic messages passing round such a network do not get confused. To send a message, any computer attached to the network waits until an electronic "token" passes by, then captures it and attaches it to the message the sender (A) wishes to dispatch. Both are then put back into circulation together. The token automatically diverts the message off at the appropriate station (C).*

◄ *IBM's GF11 parallel processor, intended for use on scientific problems that require very lengthy calculations. In parallel processing, the computer carries out more than one operation at the same time (rather than one after another, as in most computer processing). This not only speeds up the rate at which information can be handled, it is also much closer to how the human brain operates.*

▲ ***George Boole was born in England, but spent much of his working life in Ireland. He developed a mathematical logic, which is often called Boolean algebra to distinguish it from algebra that deals only with mathematical relationships. Boolean algebra is used in computing because it is especially suited to binary arithmetic.***

The logic of retrieval

Computers are also very good at classifying information by means of identifying key words in titles or text. Usually the computer is instructed to look for words that occur in the text with moderate frequency. Very common words, such as "a", "about" and "across", seldom help in classifying material. Equally, very rare words, which may only appear once or twice, seldom indicate the content. The moderately frequent words, however, often do provide a key to the content. If a text contains a number of references to "Reagan" and to "President", it is fairly clear what it is about. Key words can be sorted by a computer and printed out in alphabetical order for the user's convenience. Alternatively, the words can be compared with an existing classification scheme for the purposes of cross-referencing.

◄ A modern computer room. Computers have become much smaller and housing them has become easier. For example, good air conditioning and temperature control are less important now than in the past. The future may see computer storage move from magnetic tape to yet more compact media.

Traditionally, documents have been cataloged for retrieval by assigning to them a range of descriptive terms. A book on the history of land-warfare might be labeled WARFARE, HISTORY, ARMY, whilst one on warfare in the air would be WARFARE, HISTORY, AIR FORCE. Such descriptive terms will appear quite often in the text and could easily be extracted by a computer to provide its own descriptions for each document. In fact, key words chosen by a computer can be more accurate than those chosen by humans. A computer can, for instance, identify minor themes in a text which might escape the attention of a casual reader. This gives a greater depth – and a greater complexity – to some computer searches. Equally, the computer can often correlate different bits of information better than humans can. For this reason the stock control in many firms is now highly automated with lists of items, names and addresses of suppliers, prices and so on stored on computer. Each of these lists may need to be changed separately, as happens when prices increase but everything else stays the same. The lists must be searchable in any order, to provide information such as which range of parts is available from which supplier. Searching and modifying information in any sequence is something the computer does well.

◄ A warehouse with its stockpile of spare parts at Landrover, UK, motor-vehicle manufacturer. Keeping a record of the components on a computer allows both rapid retrieval and immediate updating of stock lists. Garage owners, too, have to maintain stock lists covering a wide range of spares. Lists must include a variety of information – the names of the components, how many are available, how much they cost, and so on. Much of this information is held on computer, since it is changing all the time and must always be up to date.

Retrieval of information is, in part, an exercise in logic, to which the computer is ideally suited. The basis of computer logic derives from the work of the English mathematician George Boole (1815–1864), who explored the links between logic and mathematics. He postulated that three types of condition are required for logical thinking. For example, suppose a woman goes to a tennis club looking for a male opponent who is free to play. We can say that the condition for a suitable opponent is "male AND free". But she may not mind what sex her opponent is. In that case, the condition to be fulfilled is "male OR female AND free". But perhaps she is young and wants to play against someone of her own age. This imposes another condition, since she wants an opponent who is "male OR female NOT old AND free". The terms "OR", "NOT" and "AND" are the means by which logical requirements can be expressed. Any instructions for dealing with information in computers can be expressed using only these three terms. In particular, they can be used for the purposes of information retrieval. Suppose, for example, that information is required on marine vertebrates. These might be either fish or mammals. We may be interested only in items dealing with fish and mammals together, not separately. These requirements can be formulated as "fish AND mammals NOT fish OR mammals". When computers use these terms (which may seem a little odd to us) they are said to be carrying out a "Boolean search".

Databases

Any compilation of data stored on a computer is called a database. Many early databases were "bibliographic" databases concerned with keeping track of literature. Stores of numerical data are sometimes separated out and called databanks. The word "database" now covers a variety of options, including full-text databases (containing the complete texts of articles or books) and graphics databases (containing primarily pictures). Some databases refer the reader elsewhere for further information, whereas others hold the required information themselves. A bibliographic database is an example of a referral database, listing books or journals for the reader to consult. In contrast, a chemical database holds information concerning the properties of chemical substances and their uses.

Databases are expensive to establish. Many of the early ones in the 1950s and 1960s were set up using military funding and concentrated on science and technology. Today the range of topics covered by databases is far wider, including everything from financial information to humanities subjects, and they receive commercial and academic funding, as well as military. The vast majority of the earlier databases were constructed in the United States, but now an increasing number are being developed in Japan and Western Europe. Databases concerned with science and technology are the biggest and most expensive. One of the world's main biological databases, BIOSIS in the USA, now holds a total of nearly five million records of research publications and cannot be searched satisfactorily without the aid of a computer. Biotechnology is an example of a rapidly expanding area,

▼ Sophisticated information handling by computer at mission control during a Space Shuttle flight. The equipment and activities aboard the Shuttle are constantly being monitored and recorded, as controllers follow the Shuttle in its orbit around the Earth. All this information forms a vast database. Other databases supply essential background information during the flight.

with more and more research papers going onto databases. The most profitable databases carry financial and commercial information. Using the computer facility they can be updated very quickly, which can be vitally important for information such as stockmarket quotations. Some databases have immediate economic value – patents covering new inventions, for example. Others are important for professional activities – medical information for doctors and legal cases for lawyers. Many newspapers and magazines are also now available in electronic form.

Graphics databases are more complex. Pictures take up large amounts of computer memory and there is no standard way of retrieving the information. Some years ago, a film was made of two politicians walking together through Trafalgar Square in London, and the film stored under their names. Later, a producer of a natural history program discovered by accident that the film contained in the background a rare breed of pigeon. How could the person who cataloged the film have guessed that it should have an entry under "pigeon"? The problem is similar to that of key words in text retrieval. Human searchers may capture only some of the key words associated with a text. Computers can search the text in greater depth, but have no equivalent facility for automating picture searching.

This question of retrieval has become especially acute for remote-sensing pictures. The first satellite to obtain pictures of the Earth from space was launched in 1960. Since then, many satellites have remotely sensed the earth and its atmosphere. Satellite weather pictures are well known from television. Equally common are satellites to examine land and sea resources. Millions of electronic images are now stored, and must be capable of rapid retrieval. These may be cataloged by the satellite's target location on Earth at the time, but users often want something else. The oil industry, for example, looks for geological structures that might indicate the presence of oil deposits. Can a computer be taught to recognize such features automatically? To some extent, this is already happening. The computer is shown examples of known geological structures and then searches for corresponding features in other pictures. The process is similar to optical character recognition, but with the added problem that geological features are much more variable in appearance than text characters.

◀ A radio dish in Sweden built to receive data beamed from the LANDSAT satellites. Several of the satellites launched over the past quarter-century have been designed to examine the properties of the Earth. Space-based data have been obtained on matters ranging from geological structures of interest to the oil industry to the spread of plant diseases affecting farmer's crops. Many of these observations have been carried out by the LANDSAT series of satellites.

◀ A mistake made by an air-traffic controller, through an error of judgement or incorrect information received, could so easily result in tragedy. With more and more aircraft taking to skies, air-traffic control systems are becoming increasingly sophisticated and dependent on the latest computerized technology.

Online communication

Much database work is now done "online", which means that the human searcher has direct access to the computer database. Essentially, an online database is any collection of data that can be accessed using computers and a telephone, or other, link. Normally, several users will be able to search the database simultaneously. Online searching of a large database can be very rapid.

A ten-minute online search for a bibliographic database can often produce better results than several hours of manual searching. The information retrieved is sent by the host computer – the computer holding the database – to the searcher, usually down a dedicated (special) line. It flashes onto the recipient's screen, so that its relevance can be assessed. Relevant information can be printed out locally, or loaded onto a floppy or hard disk. This is known as downloading. Several thousand databases are now available online, and finding the right one for a particular purpose is not always easy. A further complication arises because the people who provide databases and those who transmit them to searchers are not usually the same. The transmission is done by entrepreneurs – "hosts" – who pay fees to run databases on their own computers. Hosts may run several different databases, whilst providers may hire out their database to several different hosts. The world's largest host is the American company Lockheed, which offers access to well over a hundred databases. Using telephone cable links, these databases can be searched online from all over the world. International access is generally more expensive than local access, but the ease of having such a wide range of data available from a single connection can often make it worthwhile.

Often different procedures are required to access the different hosts and databases. This has led to difficulties for the user and to the emergence of specialists in this activity. They are often called information "intermediaries" (though generally this term covers people who handle information from other sources besides computers). Defining precisely what information is required is an inherent problem in information retrieval. Either the information retrieved will contain some irrelevant items or if the definition of requirements is too precise, almost invariably some of the information needed will be lost. A fine balance must be struck between these extremes of too wide or too narrow a definition of needs.

► Control room the of the Chase Manhattan Bank, New York. Banks are one of the major users of databases, handling all their customer accounts on computers. Databases are also being accessed more by customers. Banking requires further computer links with databases containing financial information, and with those of other banks.

Bibliographic databases

*These refer users to printed documents. Armed with that information the reader can then consult the local library. A public library, however, will not contain all the books or journals referred to by a large database. Most countries therefore have a national center from which documents may be ordered. Orders can be placed by traditional methods, such as letter or telephone, and often electronically from the same terminal used for the database searches. Most orders are fulfilled through the mail, and often in the case of shorter items photocopies are sent rather than the originals (copyright laws permitting). A shorter item needed urgently can be sent directly by facsimile transmission (**◀ page 58**).*

If the information sought from a library is scattered at random across the whole of its collection, a quick response for specific items will be difficult. Fortunately, information usage typically needs concentrate on only a small part of the collection. For instance, many scientists have little interest in research that is more than a few years old. In the world of finance information that is even only a few weeks old is often out of date. Subjects like history are, of course, the exception.

Historians will often need to have access to older documents. Most libraries and electronic databases relegate older material to reserve stores, keeping only newer material available for rapid access. In fulfilling a request for information, it is usually possible to define a "core" collection of sources which contain most of the information required. In physics, for instance, a fairly small number of journals carry the majority of the articles requested by physicists. A local library will therefore confine itself to acquiring the core journals, and rely on the national center to supply items requested from more obscure journals. Thus libraries run on the opposite principle to databases, which try to hold as comprehensive a coverage of material as possible. But even then, total coverage is virtually impossible. Items relevant to, for example, a physicist may not be confined to physics journals. Physics articles also appear in engineering, mathematics and chemistry journals. An important advance in chromatography went unnoticed by chemists for some years because the findings were published in a Russian botanical journal.

◀ Rear view of the Cyber 205 supercomputer, which can carry out millions of operations every second. Supercomputers are the fastest and largest computers available today. They are built to compress the greatest computer power into the smallest possible space. Their wiring is extremely complex and there is a problem as to how to dispose of all the heat generated.

New types of index

The switch from printed records to computerized databases has led to the development of new types of index to aid retrieval. The KWIC (Key Word in Context) index makes use of the computer's ability to sort words into alphabetical order quickly. The computer records all the key words in the titles of articles stored in its memory. For example, in the case of an article entitled "A study of influenza in Switzerland", the computer would eliminate "A", "of" and "in" immediately as being of no use for retrieval purposes. "Study", too, would probably be ignored because it is too general. This leaves "influenza" and "Switzerland" as key words. All the titles in the computer's store are analyzed in this way. The computer lists the key words in alphabetical order, in the context of the whole title. In the example, under "S" would appear "A study of influenza in SWITZERLAND", and under "I", "A study of INFLUENZA in Switzerland". Anyone searching for articles on a particular topic can look up the appropriate key words in the KWIC index and decide from the surrounding title whether the article is relevant to their purposes or not.

▼ *Dr Peter Adams, deputy editor of the leading US scientific journal* Physical Review*, displays copies of the journal as it appeared in 1931. Despite the impact of electronic databases on the access to scientific information, the journal is as popular today as ever.*

The KWIC index, like many retrieval methods, supposes that the title of an article will of itself be informative. One result of the current explosion of knowledge is that most writers nowadays are aware of this need. In earlier centuries, vague titles, such as "Some speculations concerning the nature of different sorts of heat", were common. Scanning this for key words only yields "heat", and this is so general as to be of little use for retrieval purposes. In science and technology, where the growth of publication has been especially intense, titles of current articles are usually highly informative. In some of the more specialized areas such as crystallography, there is even agreement about which information should appear in a title. Titles are often less informative in humanities subjects, where the expansion of knowledge has been less dramatic. Some subjects – history, for example – have a tradition of double titles. "The way forward: a study of the Reform Act of 1832" is quite typical. Obviously, for retrieval purposes the first part of this title is useless but "Reform Act" and "1832" are informative, and both can be used as key words. In other humanities subjects, such as philosophy and history of art, titles seldom indicate properly the contents of the articles.

► Which research articles are cited the most? Are some articles usually cited together? When the references at the end of research articles are fed into a computer, it is possible to answer questions of this sort. The results are displayed on a citation map indicating, for example, connections between the biomedical and physical sciences. The larger the circle, the more that subject is cited. The distances between circles reflect the intellectual links between the subjects.

It is not only titles that provide material for retrieval. Many articles end with a list of references to other articles mentioned in the text. The list is often arranged in alphabetical order by author, and contains enough information for the reader to be able to trace the original source. For example, a reference might be listed as: Smith, J., *Jnl. of Improb. Res.,* **14**, 22-38 (1988). People working in the field will immediately understand this to mean that an article by J. Smith appears on pages 22 to 38 in volume 14 of the Journal of Improbable Research, which was published in 1988. An author who refers to this article is said to have "cited" J. Smith. Citation indexes, which list the references attached to a series of articles, can therefore be another useful source of information. The Institute for Scientific Information (ISI) in the United States regularly publishes citation indexes covering the major research journals of the world. What can be done for individuals can also be done for countries. A study of how the research in one country is cited by other countries can indicate that country's standing in the scientific world. To compile citation indexes involves a massive exercise in sorting carried out by computers.

Citation indexes

These help researchers to evaluate information published in their fields. The references cited in an article are necessarily to literature that antedates that article. Some of the older references are therefore likely to be less useful to researchers and can be ignored. Working backwards, a researcher can consult a citation index to find out whether an article has been referred to in later articles. If so, they probably cover the same topic, and should be of interest to the researcher. Using a citation index in this way can help to track down more recent, and more relevant literature in the field of the researcher's particular interest.

It is assumed that a reference to another article implies a similarity of subject content. Is this true? Why do writers refer to other people's work? The most obvious reason is that the author is building on work reported in another article. Alternatively, the work reported may be wrong and needs to be corrected. In either case, a researcher in the field will be interested in the new article. Some articles, however, are cited not because they are immediately relevant but out of respect to senior members of the discipline. Furthermore, citation indexes can be biased. Different authors writing on very similar topics may cite quite different sets of articles. There are usually several available on any given topic, so the choice of any one may be quite arbitrary. References by American and Soviet scientists researching in the same fields are nationally biased. Soviet articles only occasionally mention American work, whilst American references to Soviet research are even rarer. Each group selects from relevant articles in its own literature.

Citation indexes can serve the wider purpose of compiling lists of all the articles that have been cited most frequently. Very likely, these would contain the main results in each research field and their authors would be the respective field leaders. By tracing the most-cited articles over a period of years, it should then be possible to draw up a history of how research has developed. At the same time, it may be possible to measure researchers' contributions to their chosen fields by the number of times their works are cited. Obviously, this conclusion would have to be treated with great caution. It may be that an article is referred to so many times because the work it reports is wrong. Equally, an outstanding article may be mentioned very seldom because it is in a field where there are few researchers. These objections notwithstanding, analyses by ISI have shown that there is a link between heavy citation of articles and the award of Nobel prizes to authors.

Another kind of citation index covers research topics, rather than authors. A computer analysis of such references should reveal the emergence of new groupings, and help to chart research progress in new subjects such as biotechnology.

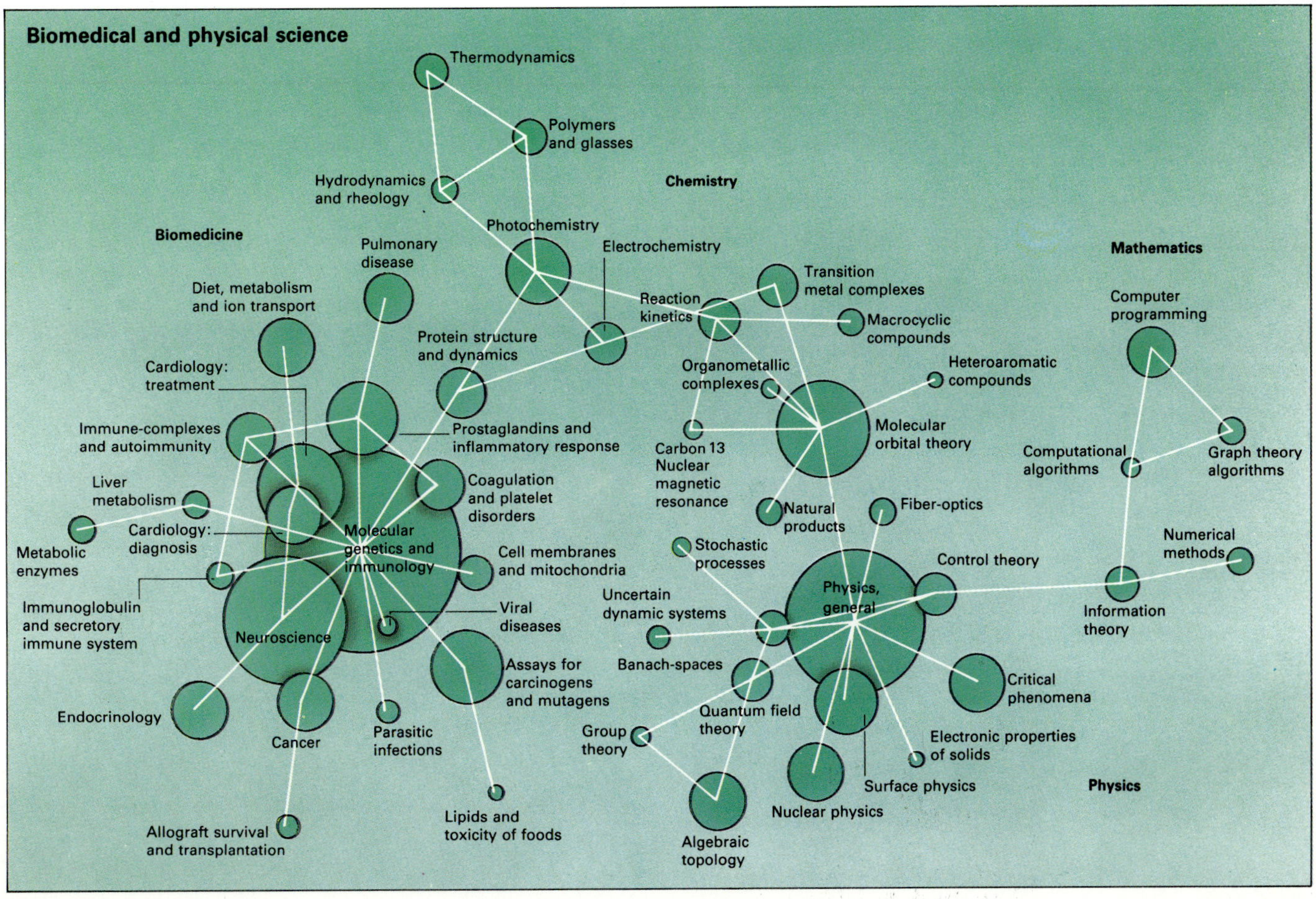

Electronic notices

Specialist indexes are of interest to relatively small numbers of people. But new developments in retrieval are also affecting the general public. With the widespread availability of microcomputers and networks, an increasing amount of information is being distributed in electronic form. Bulletin boards have proved especially popular. These are the electronic equivalent of the board in the window of a village shop, where anybody can pin up notices and messages. Most items found under the classified section of a local newspaper – from messages to friends to the sale of houses – can be put on a bulletin board from a home computer. Contributors to a bulletin board are not in direct contact with each other. The sequence is sender, bulletin board, recipient.

Using microcomputers and public networks, direct communication between the sender and recipient of messages is also possible. This is known as electronic messaging. If the message is intended for a wide audience, a bulletin board is more appropriate. If it is addressed to a few people, messaging is better. Access to electronic messages can be restricted by the use of a password (in much the same way that the owner of a bank card has to enter a private number before using a cash dispenser). If the recipient is not at home, the message is stored and can be read later. The system has advantages over the telephone in that messages of any length and complexity can be sent, and both sender and recipient have a printed record of the exchange.

Other electronic links are increasingly being used to search databases that are of interest to the public. Some libraries now have their entire stock of books recorded on computer. A reader dialing the computer from home can find out whether the library holds a particular book, and if so whether it is currently in stock or out on loan, and can ask for it to be reserved. This system is proving especially helpful to people who are housebound. A few public libraries, mainly in the United States, have put a much wider range of information online for their customers, including all kinds of local news, and council minutes. Reactions have so far been positive, but for the system to be truly effective a greater public awareness of information technology (IT) is needed.

***►** One of the areas in which automation will help international commerce is in the handling of foreign scripts. In Arabic, for example, the appearance of letters can change according to which letters are adjacent. Composing words in such scripts is complicated. The computer starts at the top with the individual letters that make up the Arabic word "al-islam", then combines some of the letters as required, and adds distinguishing marks. Having finally formed the word, it then has to transpose it (because Arabic is read from right to left).*

***►** The most successful public system for electronic messages was set up as a government initiative in France. To encourage the use of electronic databases and networks, the French decided to phase out printed telephone directories and replace them by an online directory. Free terminals have been distributed to telephone subscribers and the Teletel system, shown here, is now in operation. As a result, bulletin boards and electronic messages have become so popular that these activities are now supported by specialist magazines.*

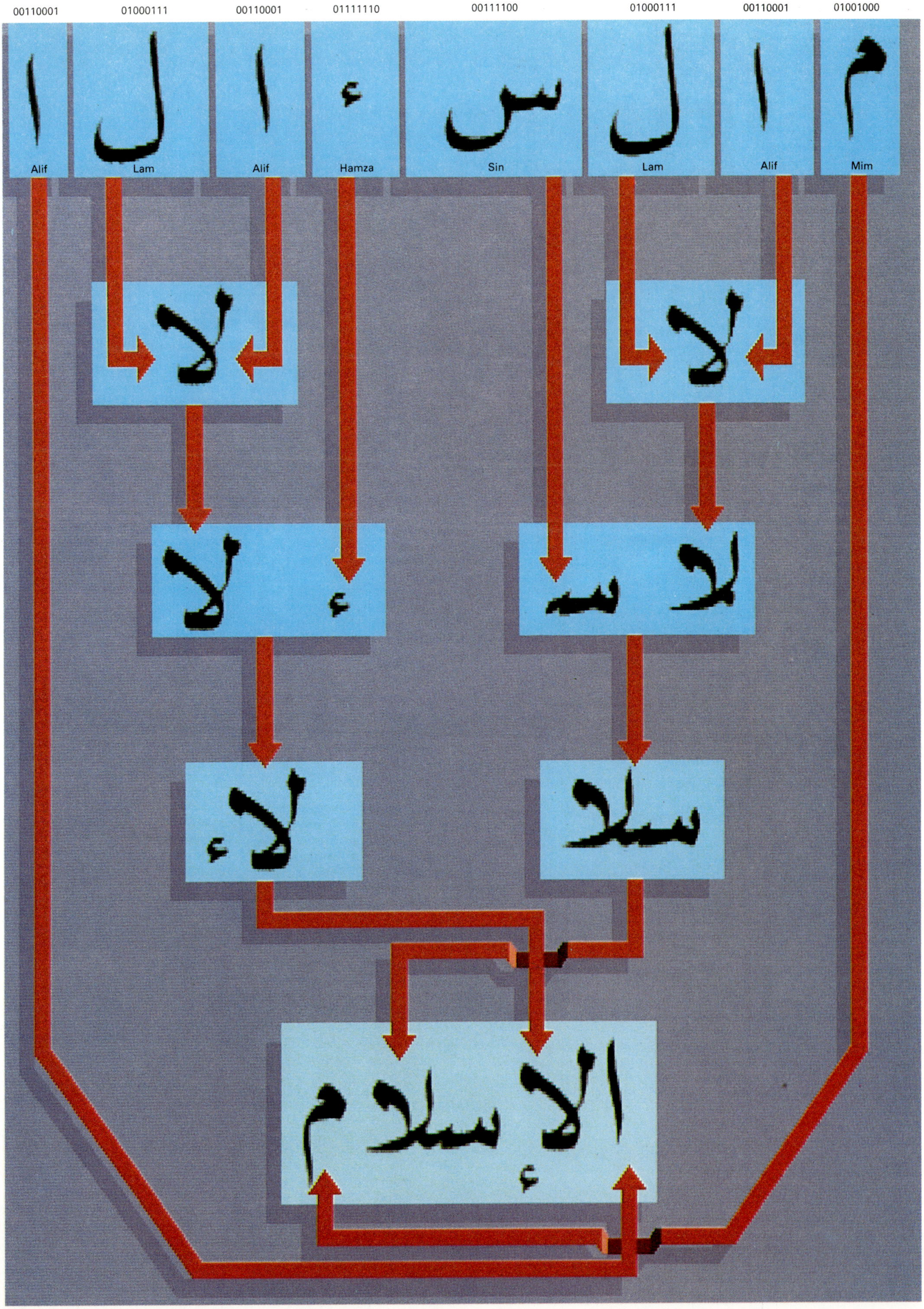
00110001
01000111
00110001
01111110
00111100
01000111
00110001
01001000
ا
ل
ا
ء
س
ل
ا
م
Alif
Lam
Alif
Hamza
Sin
Lam
Alif
Mim
الإسلام

From one point of view office automation is seen as a labor-saving device, from another as creating unemployment

► ***Journalists at computer terminals in the offices of the* Washington Post. *The editors receive and scan the stories on-screen, make any changes and decide on the page layout. This information is then fed direct to the computer-operated printing machinery to begin production.***

Computers have been used in offices for a long time. Originally, it was just the big companies, who used large mainframes, primarily for number-crunching calculations of wages and stock. In the 1960s the minicomputer made its appearance. It could carry out many of the functions of the old mainframes, but was smaller and cheaper. This meant that it could be used by smaller companies. Whereas mainframes needed computer specialists to run them, minicomputers were more accessible to non-experts, especially after the introduction of word-processing software. Finally, the arrival of the microcomputer at the end of the 1970s led to the present position, where the desktop computer has become a commonplace in offices.

Office automation is often seen as a labor-saving device or, put another way, as creating unemployment. At the level of routine operations there may be some redundancy of labor. If the correspondence to be typed consists mainly of standard letters to customers or suppliers, so that only a few items – name and address, date, amount of bill – are different on each letter, word processing can certainly save on typing effort. At more advanced levels, however, the main effect of automation is to increase productivity, rather than to save on labor. Automation has made new types of business activities possible. Banks, in particular, now offer a much greater range of advice and services to their customers than in the past.

During the 1980s, most computers were sold to businesses. Economic problems have caused some cutbacks in recent years but the need to compete necessitates investment in new technology. To newspaper proprietors, for example, the benefits of introducing IT are considerable. Newspapers must gather and distribute information as quickly as possible. With IT, reporters can type stories directly into small portable computers, using modems to send their copy down the telephone line to their paper. Electronic handling reduces the need for labor by eliminating repeated typing and checking of the copy. Speed and productivity are thus both increased.

At the offices of the New York *Wall Street Journal* automation was introduced mainly to expand circulation. Because the USA is so large, distributing newspapers by traditional means had always been an expensive and complicated business. The *Wall Street Journal* set up a number of regional printing centers across the country to produce newspapers from electronically distributed copy. Largely as a result of these changes, circulation rose from 1.4 million in 1975 to 2 million in 1985. Items for publication are now exchanged in a similar way between the *Wall Street Journal*'s US, European and Asian offices.

Japanese newspapers have tried to follow the same path, but automation has been affected by the complexity of Japanese script. Stories are handwritten by reporters and transmitted electronically to the newspaper office by fax. The typesetting of the material by conventional means precedes the printing stage. American and Japanese newspaper owners, among others, have realized that information held electronically has a further advantage. It can be sold directly, as well as in hard copy form as printed newspapers. Consequently, many newspapers and news services have moved into the database business in recent years. The penalties of lagging behind are well illustrated by the experiences of some British national newspapers. The entrenched positions of management and trade unions have made the painless introduction of new technology impossible to achieve. When it has come, it has not been without job losses and bitterness and recrimination on both sides.

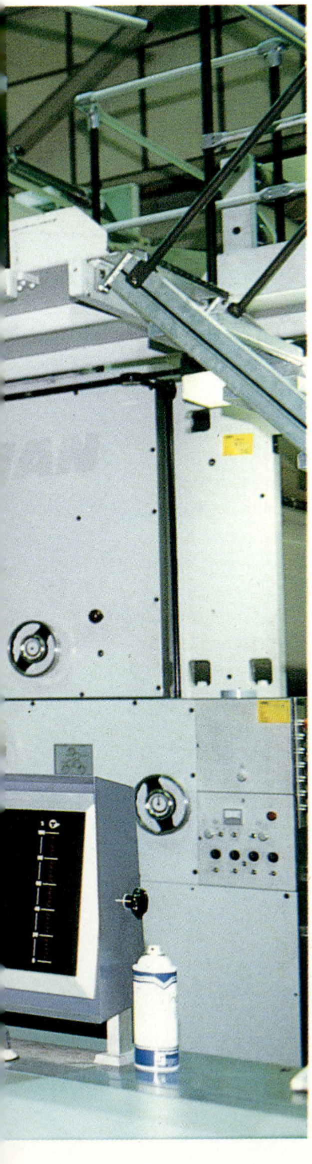

◀ The newspaper* Today, *launched in the mid-1980s was one of the first in the UK to use new-technology production and printing methods. It was also the first daily to appear partly in color. When newspaper proprietors attempted to introduce computerized systems in some of the established national dailies on London's Fleet Street, the craft unions who controlled the printing workers opposed it, fearing deskilling and loss of jobs. The technology was eventually accepted, but not without damage to both sides.

Information technology still has problems of compatibility between computer systems as well as between computers and humans

Technical and human problems

The rapid expansion of the use of computers for business raises two questions. The first concerns software. In the early days of computers, software was sold along with the hardware. Making the hardware work was the main problem. The software was left to professionals who ran the computers. By the early 1970s, software was sold separately, but the demand for software snowballed after the introduction of the microcomputer. Today software limitations are often more important than hardware limitations. Business requirements are better served than most, but there are still gaps in the software.

The second question concerns compatibility and relates to the first. Software that can run on one computer may not run on another. Incompatibility occurs at several levels. Different computers use binary numbers in the machine to mean different things. How they store information and communicate with printers and other peripherals also varies. It is possible to design software to solve these difficulties, but it would be simpler if all computers conformed to a single standard. In practice, the influence of IBM, the world's largest computer company, has led to much of its hardware being accepted as the unofficial standard. Many computers nowadays are IBM-compatible – that is, they will accept much the same software as an IBM machine.

Compatibility also concerns how computers can be linked together. In an office, information held on a computer often has to be transferred from person to person. Hence, creating an automated office implies setting up a local network. This raises new problems of standards. How do the various computer terminals know that a particular piece of information is intended for them? Questions of this sort are said to be matters of "protocol". For a network to function properly, a whole series of protocols must be obeyed.

Many of the other problems experienced with IT are human problems. The interaction between humans and machines can affect the human component in a variety of ways. Some are purely physical. Most work with computer terminals is done sitting down. Although the design of terminals has improved, a survey carried out in the UK in 1985 found that over half of all full-time computer operators suffered some discomfort in their backs or shoulders. More importantly, over two-thirds of those asked had experienced eye strain after long periods at the computer screen. Much work at a computer terminal necessitates looking from paperwork to illuminated screen and back again. Differences in lighting and position of the two can also contribute to eye strain.

Temperature can also be a problem. Computers generate a surprising amount of heat as office staff may discover to their discomfort. Offices designed for cold typewriters are often expected to function with the same amount of ventilation when warm microcomputers are substituted. One common fear – of receiving damaging radiation from computer screens – is less well-founded. The only kind of radiation produced by computers are weak radio waves. These are produced by the pulses of electricity that represent bits of information in the computer (◆ page 49). In fact, one method of modern industrial espionage is to site a sensitive radio receiver close to a rival's computer center. With any luck, the computer transactions will be detected.

Many computer users are more upset by a degree of inconvenience they may suffer than by physical discomfort. One sensitive factor is response time. Users are often impatient if computers take more than a second or two to respond. Furthermore, they expect a dialog with a computer to be conducted in a language they can readily follow. Computer manuals are often at fault because they are poorly written and do not explain things properly. Consequently, inexperienced users often make mistakes. Even the "help" instructions that the user can call up are not always easy to understand. It is for these reasons that there has been so much discussion in recent years of the need to improve the "user-friendliness" of computers. Users expect above all that computers will be tolerant of their errors, and will not go haywire if they press the wrong key. Only computers on board satellites are specially designed to keep going whatever happens to them. They have many interconnecting pathways between input and output points, so that if one pathway becomes blocked, the message can automatically pass down another. Thus, even if they experience hardware and software failures, the hard-won information will get through.

▼ *Computer power is measured by how many instructions the computer can carry out per second. This is plotted from bottom to top in the diagram, and the date from left to right. Big mainframe computers have always been the most powerful, but they are gradually being overhauled by the minicomputers. However, minicomputers, themselves, are currently being overlapped by microcomputers.*

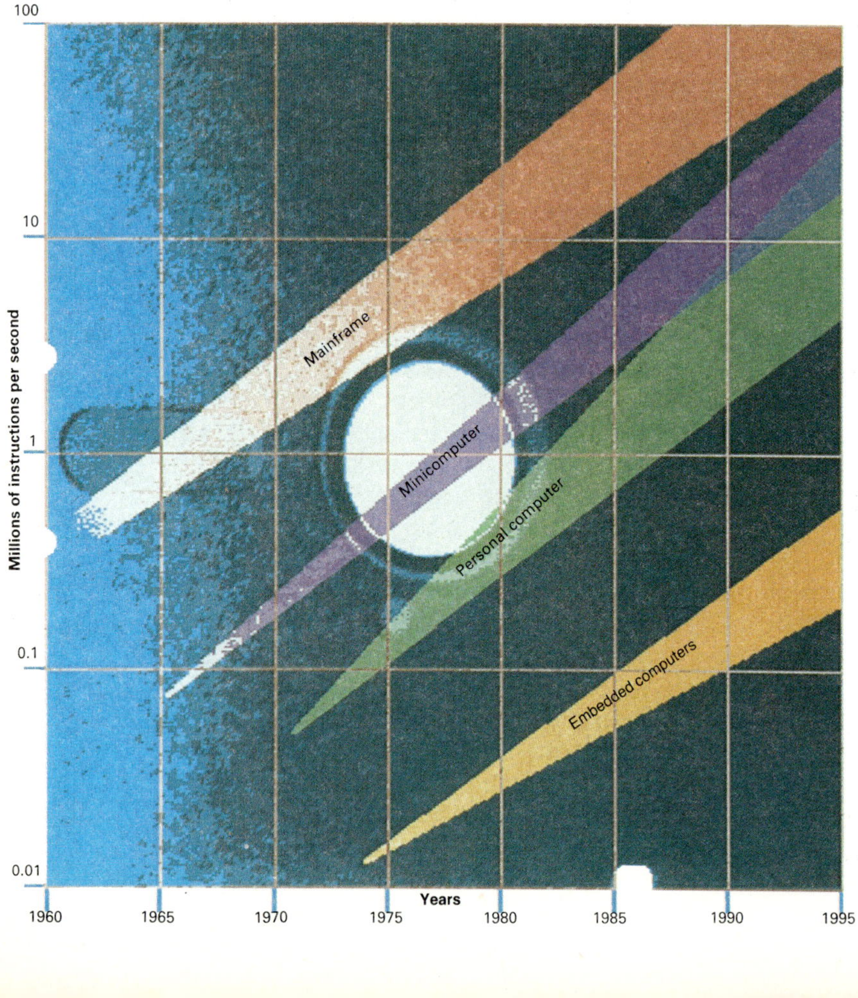

Artificial Intelligence

The "Turing machine"...Human and machine intelligence...Intelligence and problem solving... Computer chess programs...Learning by experience ...Induction by machine...Expert systems... Computer-composed stories and music...Robot devices...Humans and robots compared...How robots are controlled...Robot vision...Computer graphics...Computers and consciousness

◄▼ Alan Turing worked on the first practical programmed computer during World War II. He used the computer in intelligence work to break German military codes. He developed the idea of a "Turing machine" (below) to demonstrate how a computer program might operate step by step, using a tape containing data that can be read and changed by a "head". He asked whether such a machine could in any sense be called "intelligent". Turing committed suicide at the age of 42.

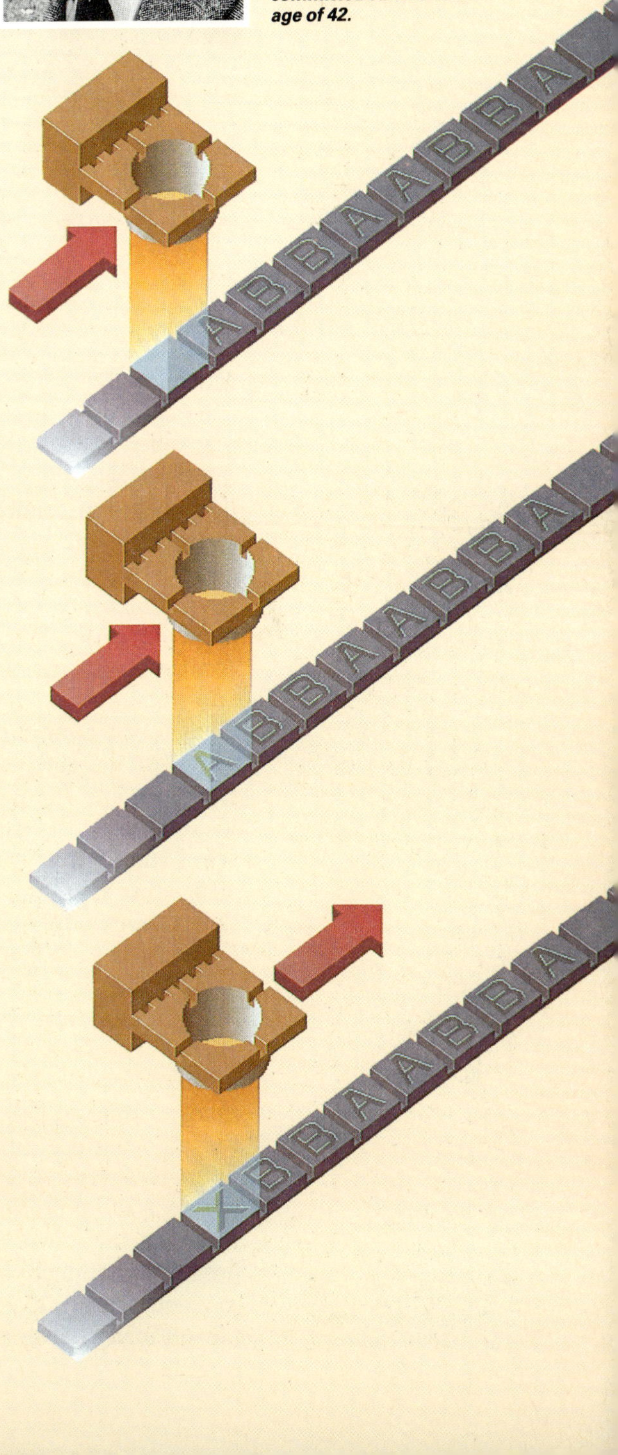

The traditional computer makes no allowances for human fallibility. A misplaced space or semicolon when giving a command will usually cause the computer to stop. At best, an error message will flash onto the screen. For many years, computer operators have had a motto – "GIGO" – which stands for "Garbage in, garbage out". In other words, unless the data fed into the computer are properly ordered, the output will be garbled. Human beings can take garbled messages and generally make sense of them. Computers cannot. The question whether computers can become "intelligent" has been argued from their earliest days. The British mathematician Alan Turing (1912–1954) was one of the first computer experts. He imagined a time when it would be possible to produce a really complex computer. He asked how such a computer, now called a "Turing machine", might be tested to discover whether or not it was intelligent. The answer, he thought, was to seal the computer away in a room and allow people to communicate with it at a distance. They could ask any question they liked, and the computer should reply. If, after interacting in this way for however long, they still could not decide whether there was a computer or a human being in the room, then the machine deserved to be called intelligent.

The "Turing test" relates to the thorny question of how intelligence is defined and measured for human beings. Medical practitioners in the 19th century strongly believed that intelligence was linked to brain size – the bigger the brain, the more intelligent the person. It was not until early in this century that the Frenchman Alfred Binet (1857–1911) concluded that hardly any such correlation existed. He turned instead to psychological testing. In 1904, he was asked to help identify backward schoolchildren who might need special education. He put together a series of tests involving various kinds of reasoning, on the basis of which he could assign each child a score. His methods were later used to construct a numerical score which represented the apparent mental age of the child, as derived from the tests, divided by its real age. For example, a child aged 10 with a mental age of 12 would have a score of 12/10 = 1.2. To avoid decimals, this score was multiplied by 100, and the result called the child's "Intelligence Quotient", or "IQ". So, in this case the child has an IQ of 120.

The question is, What does IQ actually measure? The tests are meant to be objective, but objectivity is very hard to achieve. For example, people have to be told how to carry out the test. But recent immigrants may not understand the language well enough to follow the instructions. Things that seem obvious in one culture may not be so in another. Even within a single culture, IQ is not a number that remains fixed with time. Education can improve IQ scores appreciably, which conflicts with the feeling of some people that intelligence is innate. Given these uncertainties about human intelligence, methods of estimating machine intelligence are naturally nonexistent.

The standard of play of chess programs is improving rapidly, but they still cannot match the playing strength of the top professionals

Inverted tree structure

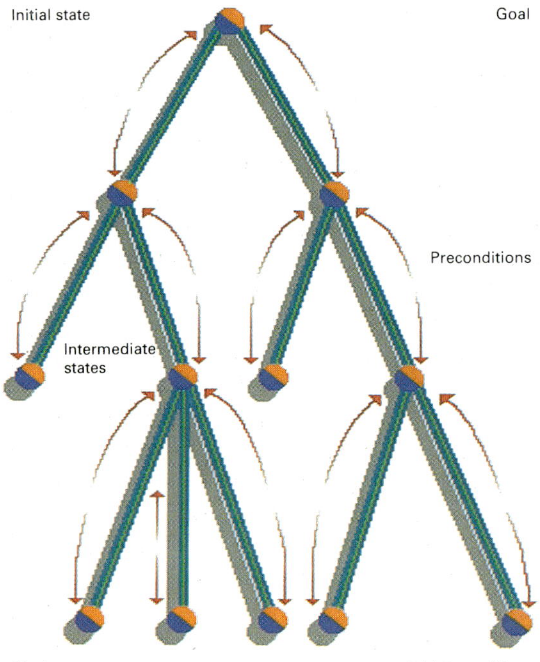

► ***How decisions are made can often be represented by an "inverted tree". The starting point is the node at the top. From there, one line of decision leads to the node on the left, the other to the node on the right. Further decisions lead to further branching. Supposing the initial point is a position in a chess game, then the next level corresponds to two possible alternative moves. The set of nodes immediately below are the opponent's possible replies to each of the two alternative moves, and so on. Using this approach, a computer can plan several moves ahead.***

▲ ***The world chess champion, Gari Kasparov (USSR). Top chess players still perform better than computers. Although both can calculate moves ahead, the best players also formulate strategies in a way that present-day computers find hard to imitate. Chess, because it is based on a clearly defined set of rules, provides a good system for human-computer competition.***

Most intelligence tests are really concerned with problem solving. This accords with the way the word "intelligence" is often used. The greatest scientists are those who have best explored the problems of the physical universe. The study of artificial intelligence (AI) – the intelligence of computers – is thus an attempt to create machines that can handle and solve all types of problem. Considering how long it takes a human child to learn to solve the problems posed by its environment, this is a very ambitious aim for the much more limited computer. Attempts at developing AI have been most successful when confined to specific areas of knowledge, such as games.

Chess – the computer challenge

Many of the early computer experts, including Alan Turing, were chess players. From the beginning, attempts were made to teach chess to computers. In principle, this should be straightforward. Chess has a set of rules which govern how the different pieces move. It also has a clear objective – to checkmate the opponent's king. The basic aim of the computer therefore, is to find the best way of doing this. The difficulty lies in the number of routes that can be followed to reach this end. A chess player may have 30 or more different moves that can be made at each turn. To decide how best to proceed, a player must plan ahead. Thinking two moves ahead might mean examining over a thousand possible combinations. Looking three moves ahead might involve some 40,000 distinct possibilities. Even a large computer can see only a limited number of moves ahead (currently about four moves by each player). A chess game may easily last for 30 or more moves by each player, so clearly no computer can play the game purely by brute force calculation of all the possibilities. Obviously this problem is greater for human players, who cannot calculate as many possibilities as a computer. Yet good players can often employ strategies that only pay off many moves ahead. How do they do it?

Much of the time they are operating by "heuristic" methods, which effectively means they use a rule-of-thumb approach based on their previous experience. For example, some pieces are more valuable in playing the game than others. A player would not normally exchange a queen for a knight, because a queen is more powerful and so is worth more than a knight. Often, pieces are more effective at controlling the run of play if directed at the middle of the board, rather than at the edge. Numerical values can be assigned to each piece and its position to reflect these perceived differences. To progress further, the computer must learn from experience, as humans do. It must note when its opponents make moves that are different from its own predictions, and modify its "heuristics" accordingly.

With this approach, some chess-laying programs can now take on all but the best human players. But they still have their limitations. The main one is a lack of strategic planning in the human sense. A good player will plan ahead by seeing general patterns in the distribution of the pieces, which suggest, for example, that an attack on the king's side may pay off in the long term. Computers, as yet, cannot do this. They have problems in distinguishing between weak players and strong players who make unorthodox moves. It is still possible to confuse chess-playing programs by making moves that have no immediately obvious benefit. But computers may be developing skills of their own. Some end-game positions have been won by computers in a way that has baffled human chess analysts.

▼ ***The "tree" as used in a game of chess. The computer (here, playing Black) selects the best move on the principle of maximizing its score, as it follows through a possible line of play. It assumes that the opponent will try to do the same. The chess pieces are all given numerical values, and values are assigned to threats to each of them. The computer scores each position that might arise from its own point of view. It counts, for example, a threat to one of White's pieces as a plus score, and a threat to one of its own as a minus in order to calculate the net score. In this case Black plays move 1 and assumes White will respond with move 7.***

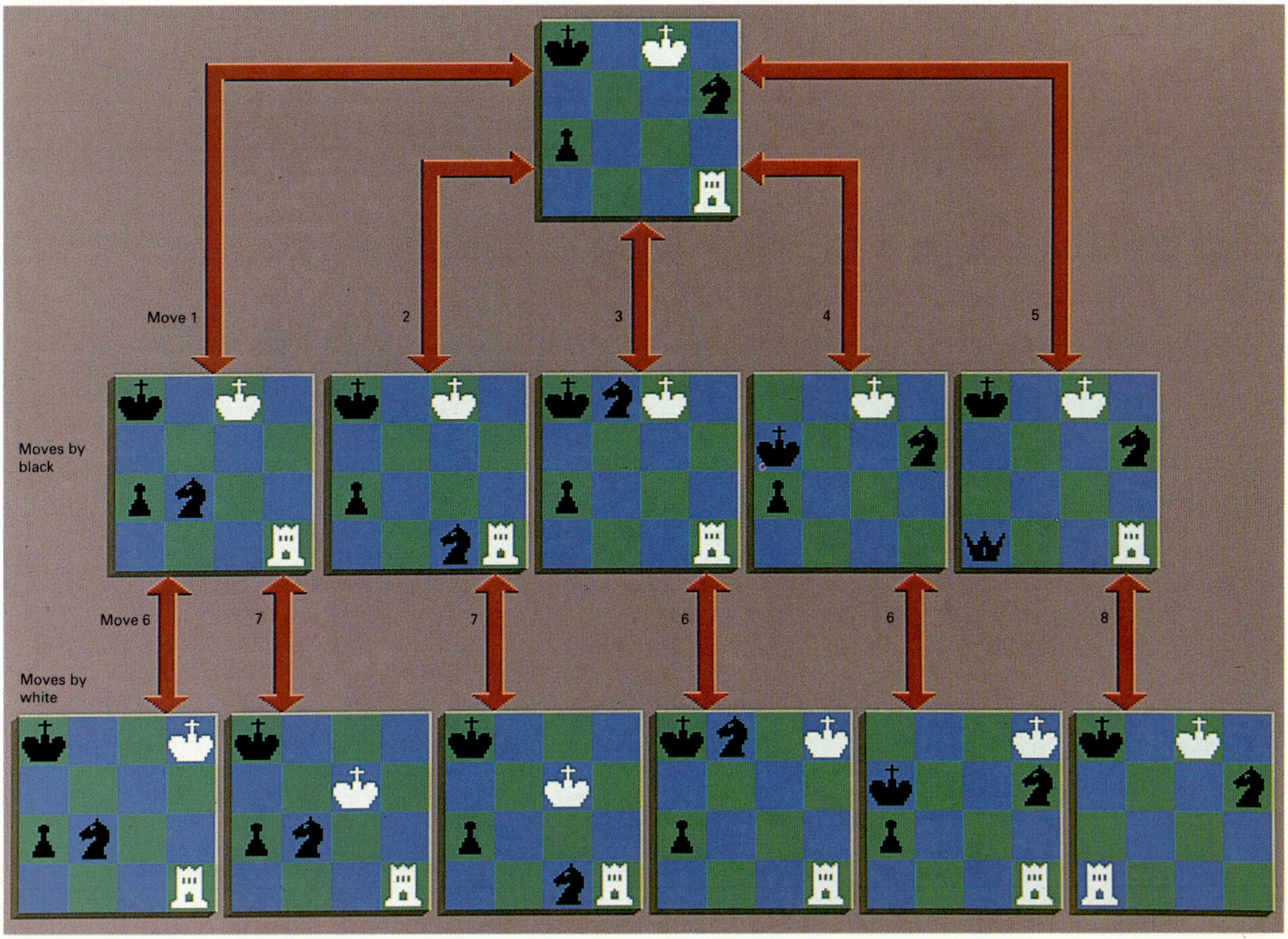

▲ **An expert system at a weather center can assist forecasts by providing a consensus of expert opinion and assessing probabilities. Weather centers employ some of the most powerful computers in the world, but human judgment still comes into the final decisions.**

Induction by machine

Most expert systems depend on "knowledge engineers" analyzing the knowledge of human experts. An alternative, more difficult, approach is to feed a series of case studies and their solutions to the expert system and allow the machine to work out the general principles involved. The process of going from the specific to the general – called induction – is notoriously uncertain. Philosophers have argued over statements of the form: "All the swans I have seen are white". Does it follow by induction that "All swans are white"? If so, a black bird cannot be a swan. Initially the argument seemed valid – until black swans were found in Australia.

Surprisingly, perhaps, attempts to generate expert systems from a limited number of case studies have proved quite encouraging. An expert system built by a computer on the basis of several hundred cases of plant disease in the American Mid-West did an appreciably better job of identifying new instances of disease than one based directly on the input of knowledge from human experts. Certainly, an inductive approach is a better reflection of how experts go about their work – by recalling parallel cases from their past experience. Its drawback is that the expert system has more difficulty in explaining how its conclusions are reached. This may be a nuisance in the diagnosis of plant diseases, but it could be critical if the expert system is interpreting military data. Before launching a major military offensive, it is as well to know why.

Not all types of expertise are suitable for expert systems as they are currently constructed. The subject matter must be restricted to a single well-defined field. For example, expert systems can answer gardening queries, but only if they do not require access to more general knowledge in other areas such as science or history. In contrast, a human expert will often be able to bring in knowledge of other subjects where relevant.

A more basic problem is that expert systems only handle statements that are known to be either true or false. Real life is seldom so clear-cut. In the game of soccer, if one player commits a foul on another, the referee may, according to the rules, stop the game and award a free kick to the team of the player who has been fouled. An expert system would act by the rules. However, a referee can let play continue if he thinks that the fouled player's team would be disadvantaged by calling a stoppage. This kind of judgment is much more difficult to incorporate into an expert system. A present-generation computer is, in any case, limited in the amount of analysis it can handle, and its response time to queries is slow if too many rules are involved.

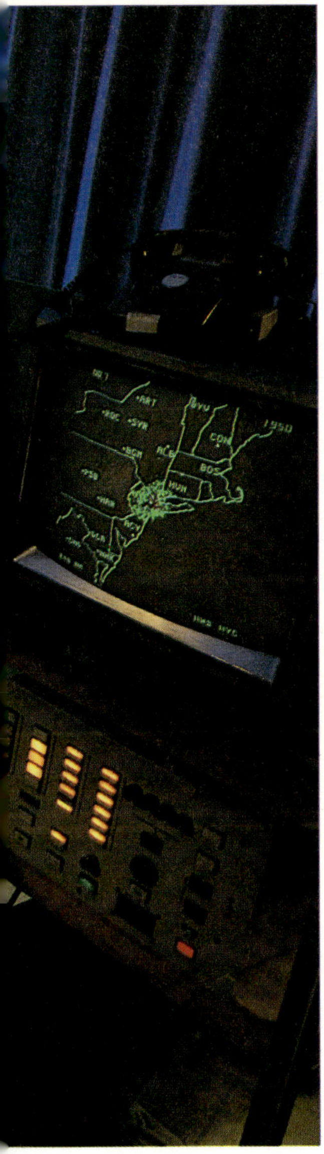

Expert systems

The successes and failures of chess-playing computers are a more general reflection of experience with problem-solving programs. "Expert systems" are so called because they are designed to solve problems in a particular area of expertise, and typically acquire much of their knowledge of how to operate from human experts. An expert system consists of two parts, knowledge of the topic – the "knowledge base" – and rules on how this knowledge is to be interpreted and applied – the "inference mechanism". The knowledge base is simply a database containing a large number of facts. The inference mechanism contains heuristics fed in by human experts, which indicate how the facts should be interpreted, along with logical statements as to how the heuristics should be combined with each other. An example of knowledge that can be handled by an expert system is the analysis of chemical substances. Such knowledge begins with a series of facts about chemical substances, continues with information on methods that can be applied to test for their presence, and ends with a schedule of the order in which the tests should be used. The inference mechanism takes this knowledge, instructs a chemist on which tests to make to look for any given substance and interprets the results.

Expert knowledge is more often concerned with probability than with certainty. A weather forecaster who claims with 100 percent certainty that it will rain tomorrow is hardly to be believed. Most will explain why it is probable (say a 90 percent chance) that it will rain tomorrow. Likewise, expert systems are constructed so that they can tell users how they arrived at their conclusions. This is vital, because human experts achieve their results by balancing all the relevant factors against each other. Different balances lead to different conclusions, and to different forecasts even among human experts. If, as sometimes happens, the experts who have supplied knowledge to the system reached their conclusions intuitively, being able to describe how the results are obtained is particularly important. And it is by no means easy to extract information in a systematic form from experts.

The specialists who do this job are called knowledge engineers. Not only must they obtain information from experts, they must also ensure that the computer presents the results in a way that can be understood by nonexpert users. Unlike a lot of computer activities, expert systems are always designed to be reasonably "user-friendly". Once the information has been acquired, it is tested by knowledge engineers for accuracy and completeness. They then design the inference mechanism. This last stage is becoming much easier, as standard mechanisms – called shells – are now available which can be used to organize a special software range of knowledge bases.

A variety of expert systems are now in use, either routinely or experimentally. One that is in use in medicine is called MYCIN. It takes the results of blood tests (listing such items as numbers of red or white cells), examines them to see whether any abnormality is present, and if so, suggests a diagnosis. When its conclusions were evaluated by a panel of human experts, their own recommendations agreed with about three-quarters of the treatments suggested by MYCIN. PROSPECTOR, another expert system that has been in use for some time, aids mineral exploitation by assessing data fed in from geological surveys. Both MYCIN and PROSPECTOR were developed in the USA. Expert systems are now also being developed in other countries including the UK. In London, an expert system called PLEXUS will help public librarians to answer queries about gardening.

▲ A general practitioner consulting a patient's medical record on a microcomputer. The record will include the usual personal details – plus information such as dates of visits, diagnoses of illness, use of drug therapy and so on. From this information, the microcomputer can be instructed to print out a prescription or appointment letter for the patient, as required.

Artificial intelligence has had some success in creating musical compositions and detective stories, both of which follow fairly well-defined rules

AI applications

Expert systems form only one part of the study of artificial intelligence. They developed rapidly during the 1970s because progress on more general problems of machine intelligence was rather slow. Even so, some general studies have provided interesting insights, especially into the interactions of humans with machines.

A simple early program called ELIZA aimed to imitate a visit to a psychiatrist. A computer analyzed the things a patient said and used the results to encourage further input. The patient talked to the computer via a keyboard and screen. If the patient said "I am feeling unhappy", the computer used the statement to formulate a question, "Why are you feeling unhappy?" Since most people go to the psychiatrist to talk about themselves, the system could sustain a fairly prolonged discussion in this way. The surprising result was that, despite the artificial nature of the "conversation", some patients preferred to deal with a computer rather than with a real psychiatrist. Another program, called DOCTOR, was designed to ask about health complaints. Again, a number of users prefer the computer to human practitioners, not least because they can talk to it for as long as they like. These programs are concerned more with stimulating conversation than with a detailed analysis of language.

Language analysis is an important concern of artificial intelligence, as it is of human intelligence. At the most basic level, it has been explored by a program called PARRY (short for "paranoid"). This was designed to respond like a mental patient suffering from a persecution complex. In this case, the computer was supposed to have fears about the Mafia. The program examined all statements fed to it to see whether any of the words might be related to the Mafia in some way. For example, a statement such as "The exchange rate of the dollar is falling" might receive the response "Yes, they are behind it". Any statement which did not trigger off an immediate response was met by one of a range of stock answers, such as "I am afraid". Though simple, the program reflects a number of the characteristics found in paranoidal humans.

▲ *The American composer, M.Smith, enters a musical score into a microcomputer, using "note processing" software that can handle musical notation (as word processing software handles text). His composition is displayed on the screen. After making any desired changes he will print out the final version in musical notation.*

Whether a computer can respond "intelligently" to linguistic input depends on its ability to place words properly in context. The belief that humans organize their vocabulary into a series of separate "scripts" has provided the psychological framework for a lot of work in this field. The ambiguous words in a language appear in more than one script. The word "drive", for example, obviously appears in a script containing words relating to cars. It also figures in another script relating to golf. The mind sorts out the sense in which the word "drive" is being used by reference to the script concerned. If the word "drive" appears with "road", the appropriate script is "cars". If the associated word is "fairway", the script is "golf". This idea of scripts provides computers with a way of organizing their response to queries. Their knowledge base can be constructed as a series of different scripts. PARRY is the simplest example of such an approach. It is based on a single script labeled "the Mafia".

The use of the word "script" suggests the idea of writing stories. Trying to make a computer write a story has indeed been one of the ways of studying artificial intelligence. Computer writing works best either when the storyline is fairly chaotic, with free associations between words (as in some avant-garde 20th-century literature), or when it is very clearly defined, as in the traditional detective story. There, the setting is usually something like a country house in winter,

◀ *The German band Kraftwerk using computer-controlled synthesizers to play computer-composed music. Much musical composition obeys quite well defined rules governing harmony, key changes and so on, which a properly programmed computer can execute. The computer can apply the rules to help to compose new music.*

cut off by snow from the outside world. The characters are equally typical and distinctive – the retired colonel, the elderly spinster, the butler. The plot is also clear-cut – one character is murdered and another tries to find out who was responsible. Because of these standard ingredients detective fiction has proved a useful area for experiments in story writing by computers.

A very different form of creativity – musical composition – also obeys fairly well-defined rules that can be followed by a computer. Musical rules concern individual notes, combinations of notes and the formation of sequences. Which notes harmonize with which others, and what alterations are necessary when the key changes, are equivalent to the ground rules of sentence construction. Equally important is how the computer puts all these elements together to create an acceptable composition. Music in earlier centuries was often composed according to quite strict rules. A particular theme might appear at the beginning and then be pursued through a series of variations constructed according to certain conventions. Analysis of musical style was popular long before computers appeared. They have made possible a more detailed analysis, the results of which have been incorporated in programs. These attempt to compose works along the lines of the various styles analyzed. As with stories, computers cope most happily with styles that are well defined or with relatively chaotic "modern" music. Recordings of computer-composed music have been available for some time, and programs for musical composition are increasingly common. A typical program might take a melodic line and put in the orchestration. Computers are now so flexible musically that a number of contemporary composers are using them as an aid to producing new works.

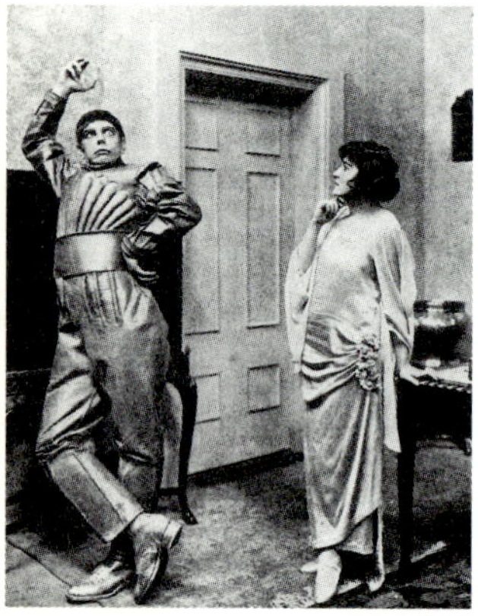

▲ *A scene from the play R.U.R., which made an impact during its first run in London in 1923. The original robot was, according to the author, "a man-made machine of flesh and blood, but lacking a soul".*

Blocks world

As all these examples show, work in artificial intelligence has concentrated on limited areas of activity. One way of avoiding the problem of overlapping scripts that occurs with all real-life activities, is to create an imaginary world specifically for the computer, such as SHRDLU. (The name comes from the first column of keys on a printer's typesetting machine.) SHRDLU consists of a series of different colored blocks and pyramids. These can be moved about and taken in and out of a box by using a robot arm. Though the box, robot arm and pieces are all imaginary, they can be represented by pictures on a computer screen. This simple model is used to explore ways in which computers can obey orders intelligently.

Within its limited world, SHRDLU operates quite efficiently. If, then, an imaginary robot can be controlled in this way, why cannot a real robot? The word "robot" derives from the Czech word *robota* meaning "work". In 1920 the Czech playwright, Karel Capek (1890–1938), published a play entitled "R.U.R", which stands for "Rossum's Universal Robots". These robots were machines designed to look like and behave like human beings. That is the picture most people still have of robots, but few of today's robots look anything like humans. Rather, they are mechanical devices that carry out unpleasant or boring jobs, such as on an assembly line in a car factory. Picking up bolts and screwing them into a piece of metal is very boring. Spraying cars with paint can produce unpleasant conditions. Both activities are now automated – a word which first came into use to describe the manufacture of Ford cars in the 1950s. Earlier types of automation were so far from the human image that they were not even seen as relating to robots. Long ago, the newspaper industry worked out methods of printing, folding and bundling piles of papers without human intervention, but nobody called these methods "robotic". More lifelike were the remote-controlled pincers used for handling dangerous substances. But these, too, were not regarded as robots, because they were manipulated by human beings, not automatically.

▲ *Three states of the "blocks world" run by the program SHRDLU. Despite the apparent simplicity, the computer must handle a range of conceptually different questions. For example, it must distinguish between pieces by their color, shape and size. It must also remember what pieces it has already shifted. If told to move a piece, it must be able to question any ambiguities in the command. Finally, it must have some understanding of space and time to carry out its activities properly.*

◀ *The American astronaut Joseph Allen, a member of the Space Shuttle crew, trying to retrieve an orbiting communications satellite. He is standing on the end of the shuttle's robot arm. Recovering the satellite was a task that combined human intelligence with the precision and power of a robot. During this 8-day mission in 1984 two defective communications satellites were retrieved for repair and two new ones were launched into orbit from the shuttle.*

Robotics

Though the idea of humanoid machines is old, it is only recently that major advances have been made in "robotics". For a robot to operate with any degree of flexibility, it must be computer-controlled. The first stage, however, was to develop the mechanics. For a robot arm to move objects about as easily as a human arm, it must be able to move in all directions – up and down, side to side and in and out. The human arm achieves the first two movements mainly by flexing at the shoulder, and the third by bending at the elbow. Movement of the arm controls the position of the hand, and the wrist makes the fine adjustments necessary for touching or grasping. The final actions are carried out by the fingers and thumb. The entire sequence involves a complicated series of motions and mental commands. What we do automatically, a robot must be instructed to do.

Taking hold of an object involves more than just putting the fingers in the right position. When we reach for the object our arm slows down before making contact with it, and the hand comes to a gentle stop. Two sets of muscles are working in opposition, one moving the arm forward and the other holding it back. An automatic balancing act between these two ensures that arms, wrists and fingers speed up and slow down smoothly. The final grasping of the object also has its subtleties. How we do it depends not only on the shape and size of the object, but on less obvious factors, such as the expected fragility. We pick up an egg according to one set of expectations, a heavy weight according to another. These expectations are modified by feedback. Something that looks heavy may turn out to be hollow. Information on how much power is required by the muscles is fed back to the brain so that the appropriate response can be made as the object is moved around. A robot similarly needs feedback. How does it "know" which position its arm is in, and what is it doing? One way is to measure very

▼ A robot hand holding an egg between "thumb" and "finger". To do this successfully, the robot must sense both the weight and the fragility of the egg. Sensors transmit information about the egg to the computer controlling the robot hand. The plans and materials needed for building a robot arm (below right) fall into three groups – the mechanical parts, the sensors and the computer connections.

◀ ***A highly sophisticated robot arm in operation at Oak Ridge Nuclear Laboratory in the United States. Robots can be usefully employed in work that humans would find unpleasant, dangerous or too physically demanding. Robots can move larger loads than humans can. In the nuclear industry, robot arms handle radioactive materials remotely. Routine operations are controlled by computers, but special work requires direct human intervention.***

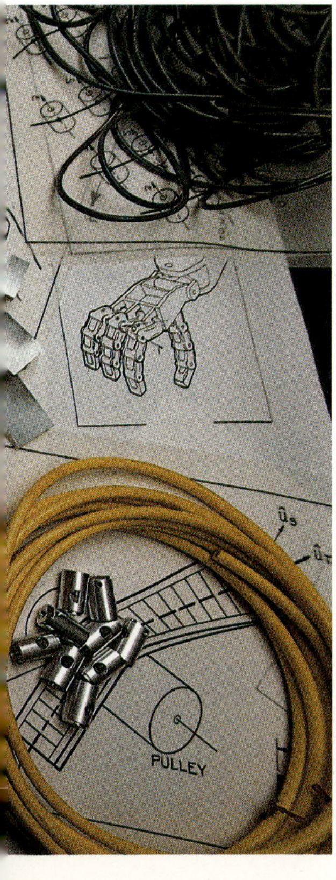

precisely the number of turns made by the robot arm's driving motors and to calculate its position from that. Another is to sense how far away the robot "hand" is from the object to be grasped. This can be done by electrical sensing, which depends on the fact that the electrical properties of two bodies are affected by the distance between them. Many robots make extensive use of electrical sensors to provide feedback and so control their own movements.

Robot arms look a little like human arms, but a closer examination shows that most of them work on different principles. The ball and socket joint found in human shoulders is not easily applied to machines. Robots have other types of "joint", which confer other advantages. For example, a robot "wrist" can rotate through a full circle, whereas a human wrist is restricted to half as much movement. A robot hand consists of two fingers and a thumb which can pick up any object (but cannot manipulate it). Why bother, then, with more fingers? In any case, fingers are not always the best solution. Sheets of glass, for instance, can be shifted more easily by having suction cups at the end of arms. The most obvious differences from humans are found in mobile robots. Two legs are the least popular engineering solution. Most robots have wheels. For traversing rough and difficult terrain, either four or six legs provide a much more stable base than two legs.

A robot can be taught about its surroundings, or how to act within them, or – most ambitiously – it can have its own form of "vision"

Robot control

Basically, there are three ways in which a robot can be instructed by a computer to carry out its work. One way is to calculate beforehand precisely where everything is located and to feed this information to the robot. This is comparable to telling someone who is blind where all the furniture in a room is situated before that person enters. A second way is to teach the robot how it must act. A human controller takes the robot through the sequence of activities that it is required to follow, while the computer driving the robot memorizes positions, movements and other necessary information. This approach pays off when the operations are rather complicated. Planning the moves in the computer beforehand, however, has the advantage that changes in the sequence can be made more easily. (With a learned process, it may be necessary to start at the beginning again.) Furthermore, there is the added advantage that the computer can be asked to look for optimum methods of working – which need not be the same as for humans. The third way of using robots – the most interesting and most ambitious – requires the robot to "see" where objects are and to work out for itself how best to handle them.

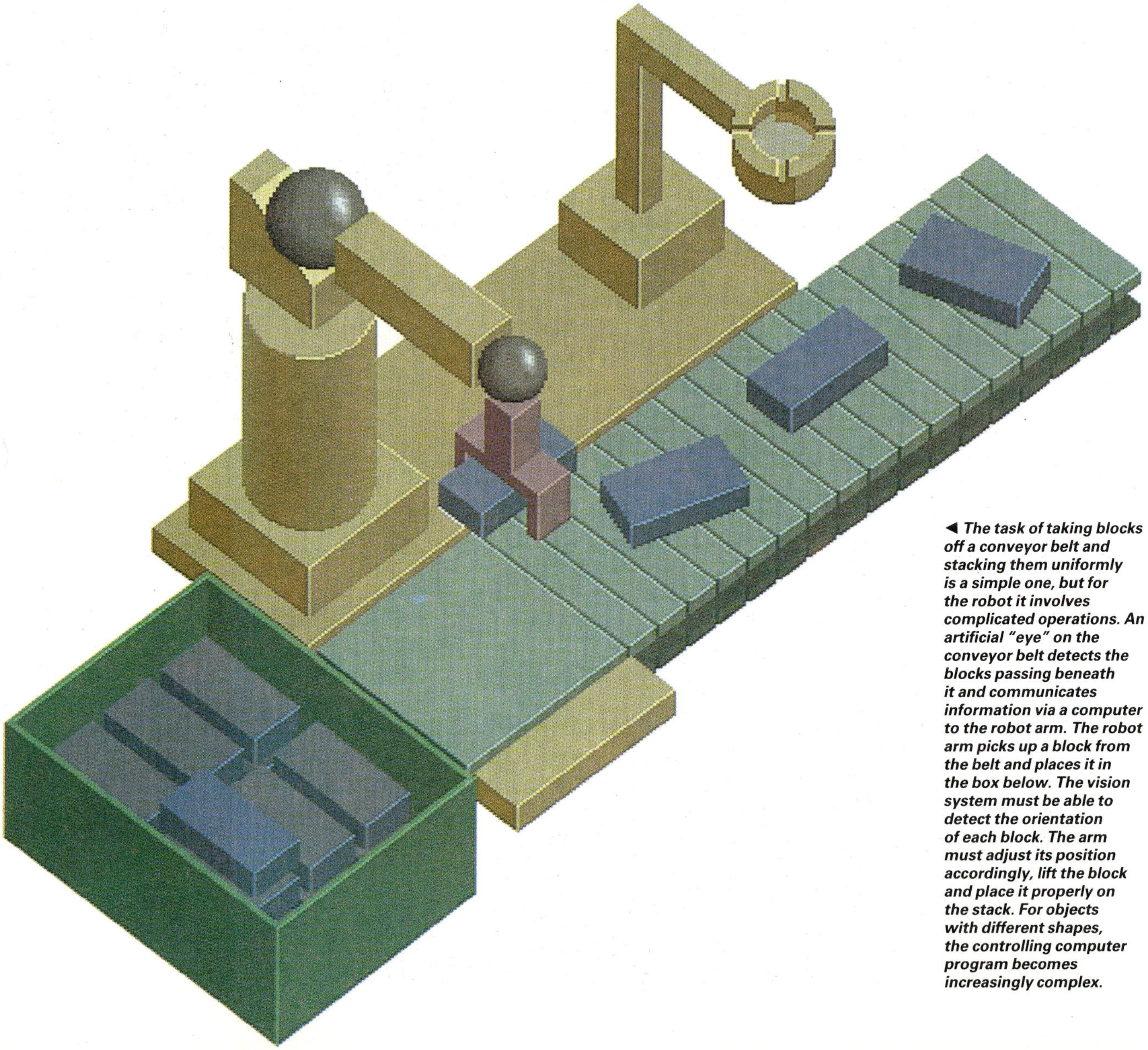

◀ *The task of taking blocks off a conveyor belt and stacking them uniformly is a simple one, but for the robot it involves complicated operations. An artificial "eye" on the conveyor belt detects the blocks passing beneath it and communicates information via a computer to the robot arm. The robot arm picks up a block from the belt and places it in the box below. The vision system must be able to detect the orientation of each block. The arm must adjust its position accordingly, lift the block and place it properly on the stack. For objects with different shapes, the controlling computer program becomes increasingly complex.*

◄▲ A helmeted worker monitoring a robot welding a car chassis. Car manufacture involves actions that are repeated many times, but must always be done precisely. People are easily bored by such work, but it is ideally suited to robots. The human controller guides the robot through the necessary moves which are memorized by the computer.

A computer can take an image that is meaningless to the human eye and turn it into a recognizable picture

How a robot sees

Most robot vision employs some kind of television camera. The camera takes a picture of the scene and passes it on in digitized form to a computer. How does the computer recognize what is happening, so that it can instruct the robot to take appropriate action? The simplest case is when the computer is only required to recognize that something has changed, for example, checking for defects while an automatically controlled loom is weaving cloth. A computer can be programmed relatively easily to spot this kind of change. The situation is more complex when the machine has to deal with different views of an object, and identify it in different positions. For example, to pick up the blocks from a conveyor belt and stack them correctly (◀ page 98), the robot must be able to identify the orientation of each block. One solution is to tell the computer the real shape of the object and instruct it how to calculate the orientation by comparing the real shape with the shape seen by the computer. This will not work so well, however, if several different objects are being handled.

The sophisticated approach to robot vision is to imitate the way human vision works. Humans depend on the ability to identify the edges and corners of objects and how they are oriented in space. A cube viewed from anywhere, except from straight in front of a face, has seven corners visible. In addition, its sides can be grouped into pairs because they run parallel to each other. A cube can be distinguished from (say) a wedge, which has fewer corners and fewer pairs of parallel sides. This approach can be extended to more complex shapes by breaking them up into simpler elements. For example, a table can be represented by four vertical pillars with a horizontal slab on top.

▼ Computer enhancement on trial. A fuzzy video picture of an alleged robber (bottom) was processed by the police computer to bring out more facial details (below). In this case the improved image was still too poor for positive identification.

▼ A computer linked to a television camera can record a scene in its memory. The pattern of dark and light produced by this woman's face has been stored. If the woman sits before the camera again, the computer can sift through the patterns in its memory and try to identify her. Normally her face will be recorded in several different positions to ensure that the computer can make this match.

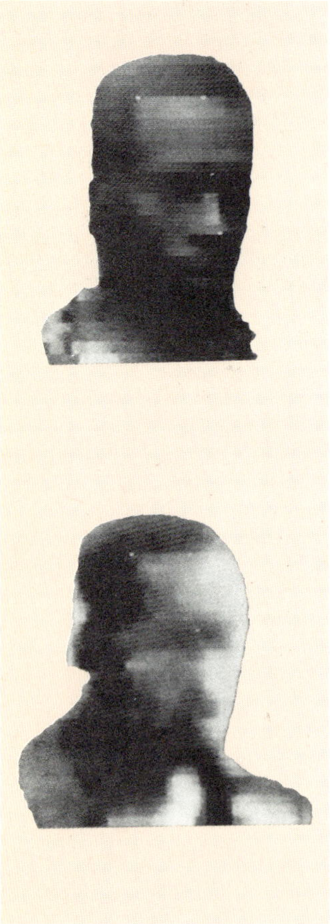

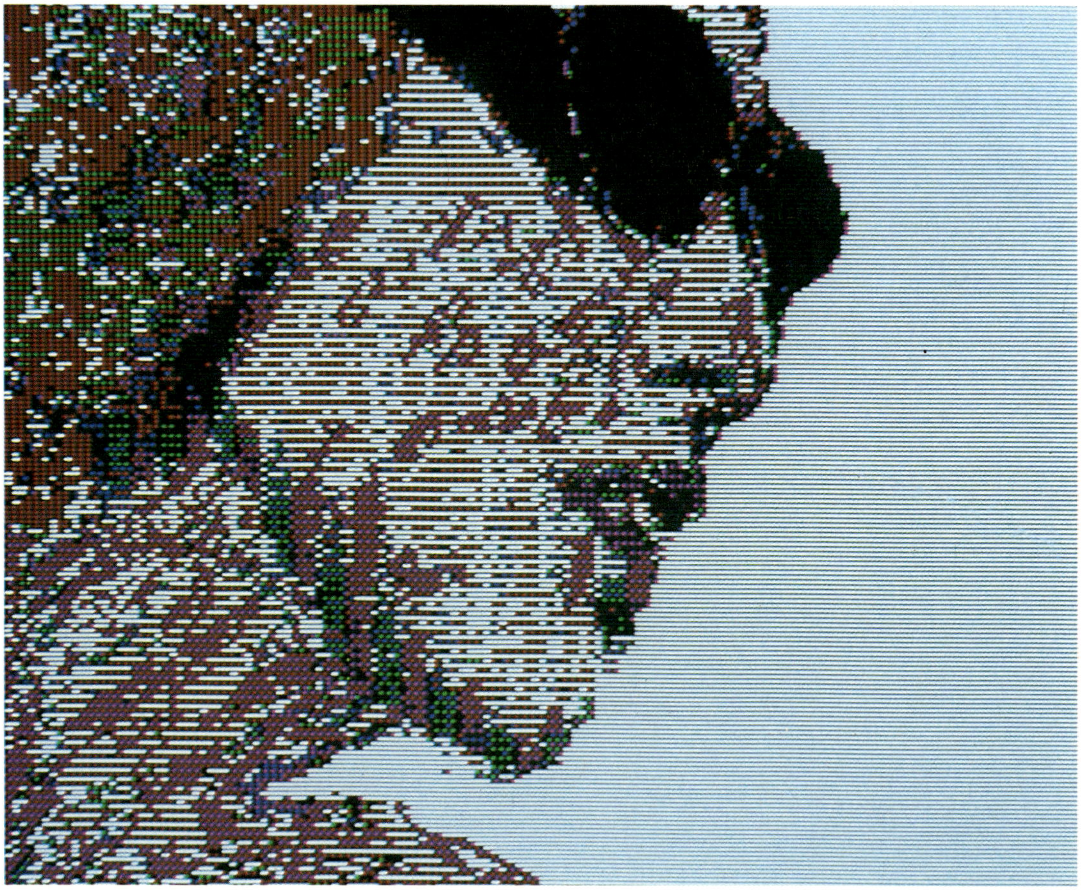

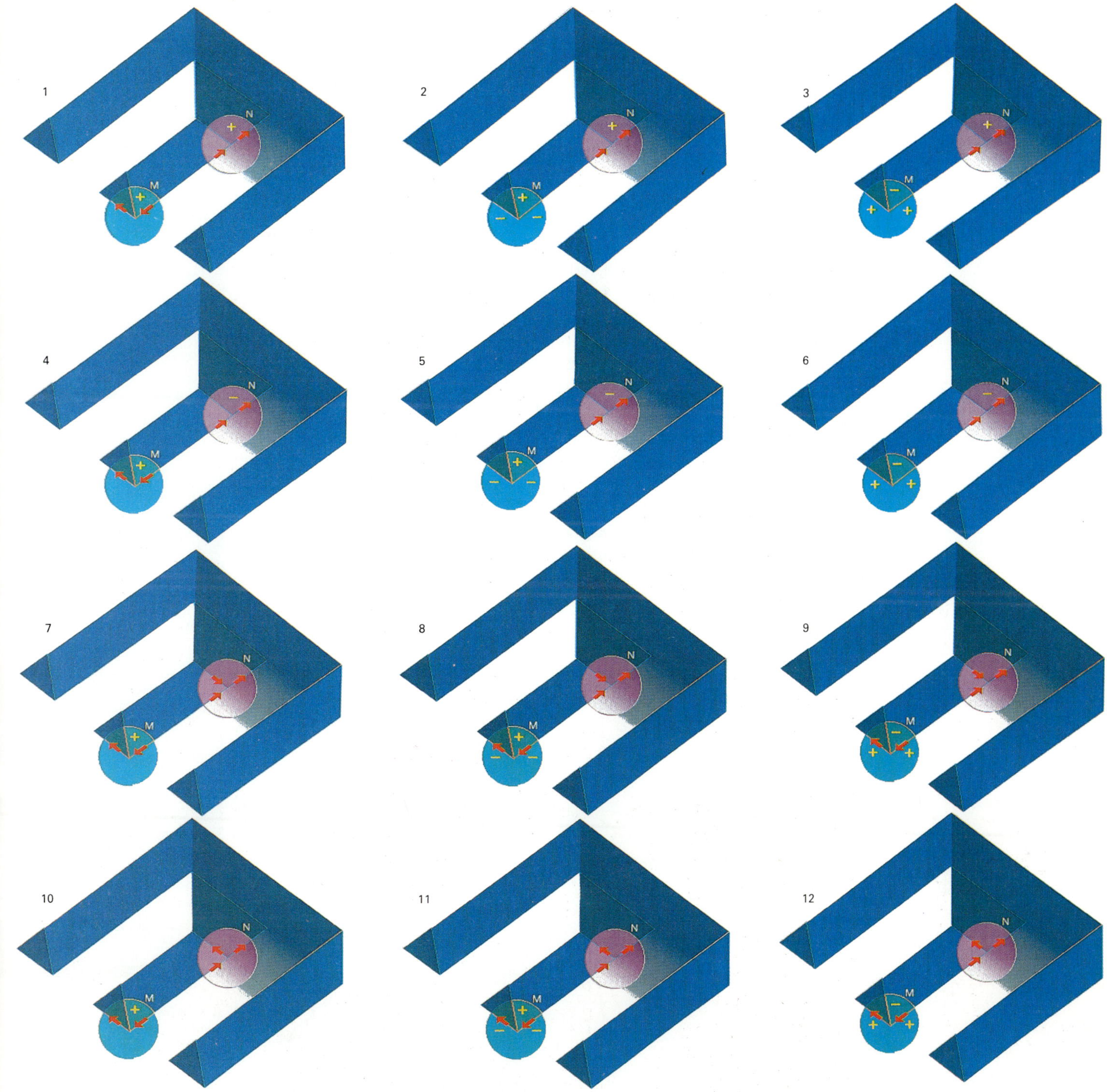

Such an approach to vision entails quite lengthy calculations by the computer. Simply teaching the machine to "see" can be quicker. The image is split up into pixels (◆ page 49), each of which is registered by one memory unit in the computer. The data from each pixel are collected and processed simultaneously. The memory cells all compare their information to look for an identifiable pattern.

Part of the difficulty with computer recognition is that TV images always contain some "noise" – that is, random bits of light and dark mixed in with the actual picture. Averaging over groups of pixels, instead of treating each one individually, can help ensure that such noise does not ruin the identification. Playing with computer images in this way has led to an interest in cleaning up and changing the contrast of images. A computer can take an image which is almost meaningless to the human eye and turn it into a recognizable picture.

▲ Computer identification of shapes typically depends on examining which corners and edges can be seen. For a solid object, these factors are related to the perspective from which it is seen. The spurious object sometimes called a devil's pitchfork looks three-dimensional at first sight, but could not possibly exist. The computer establishes this by identifying inconsistencies in the intersections of the sides.

Computer graphics

Some of the earliest significant computer graphics (images produced by computers) belonged to games-playing programs. Simple simulations of activities such as tennis and squash were superseded in the late 1970s by Space Invaders, which raised the standard of computer graphics to a new level of sophistication. Problems arose, however, over the vast amounts of computer storage space needed for graphics and the limited resolution of most computer screens. The storage problem is now being overcome by the use of optical disks, which have a high storage capacity. Higher-resolution screens are also becoming common for graphics-handling computers.

Basically, there are two ways of producing computer graphics. In the first, called raster graphics, each pixel is filled out individually. The program specifies how light or dark and what color a pixel should be. In the second method, called vector graphics, the computer draws pictures by combining lines of various lengths and orientations. Many shapes, such as the outline of a vase or flask, are simple enough to be described by mathematical equations, which requires far less computer memory than storing information about large numbers of pixels or lines. In recent years this idea has been developed to allow the

▲ A "wire-drawn" computer model of the experimental American aircraft Grumman X-25. The model can be rotated on the screen to study the design from any angle. The design was produced to investigate the possibility of forward-swept wings. The tailplane is placed just in front of the wings.

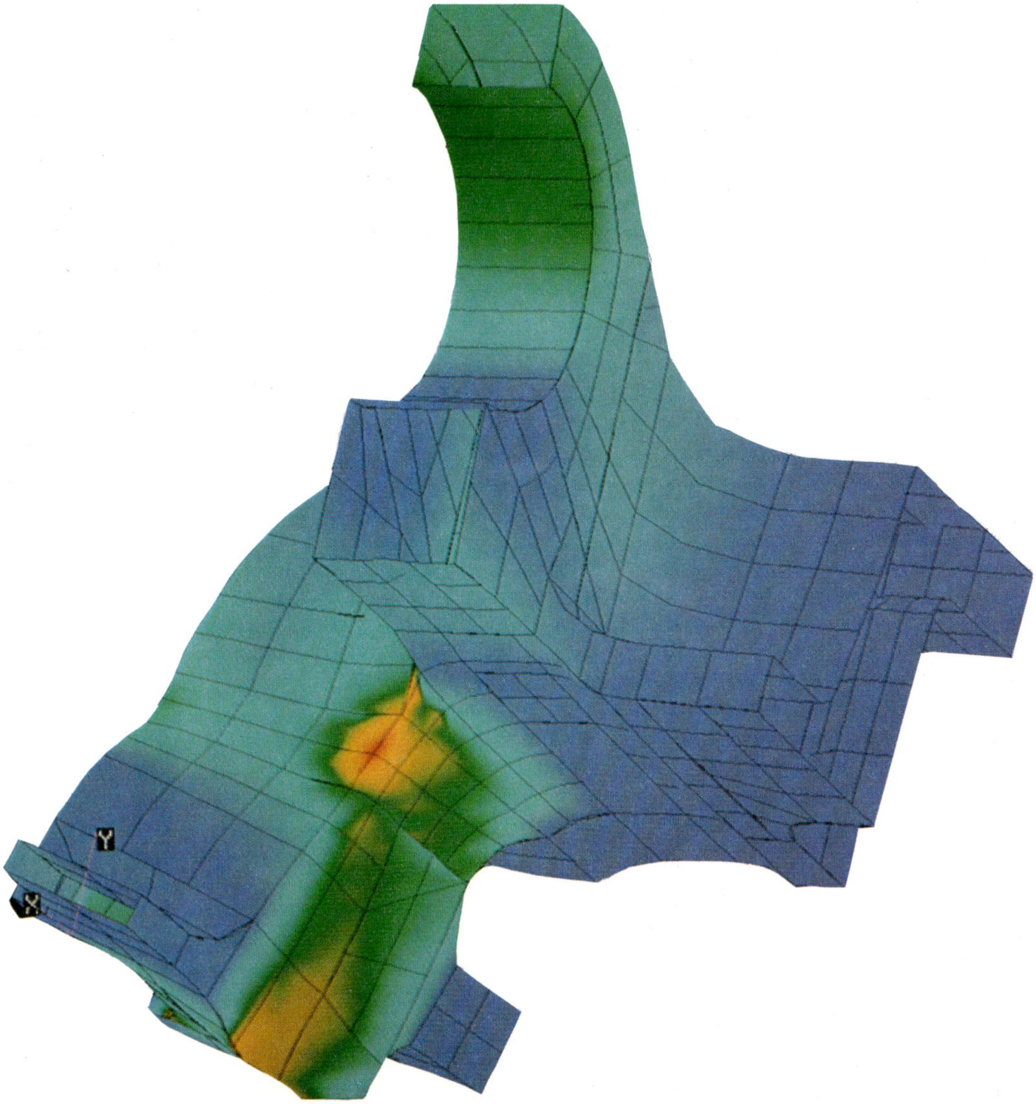

◀ A computer model of the carriage for a wing flap for an airplane, showing its deformation under high stress. Computers calculate pressures and tensions in different parts of an aircraft in different flying conditions. The designer can then ensure that each component is as light as possible, yet strong enough for its purpose. The computer results are used to guide laboratory tests.

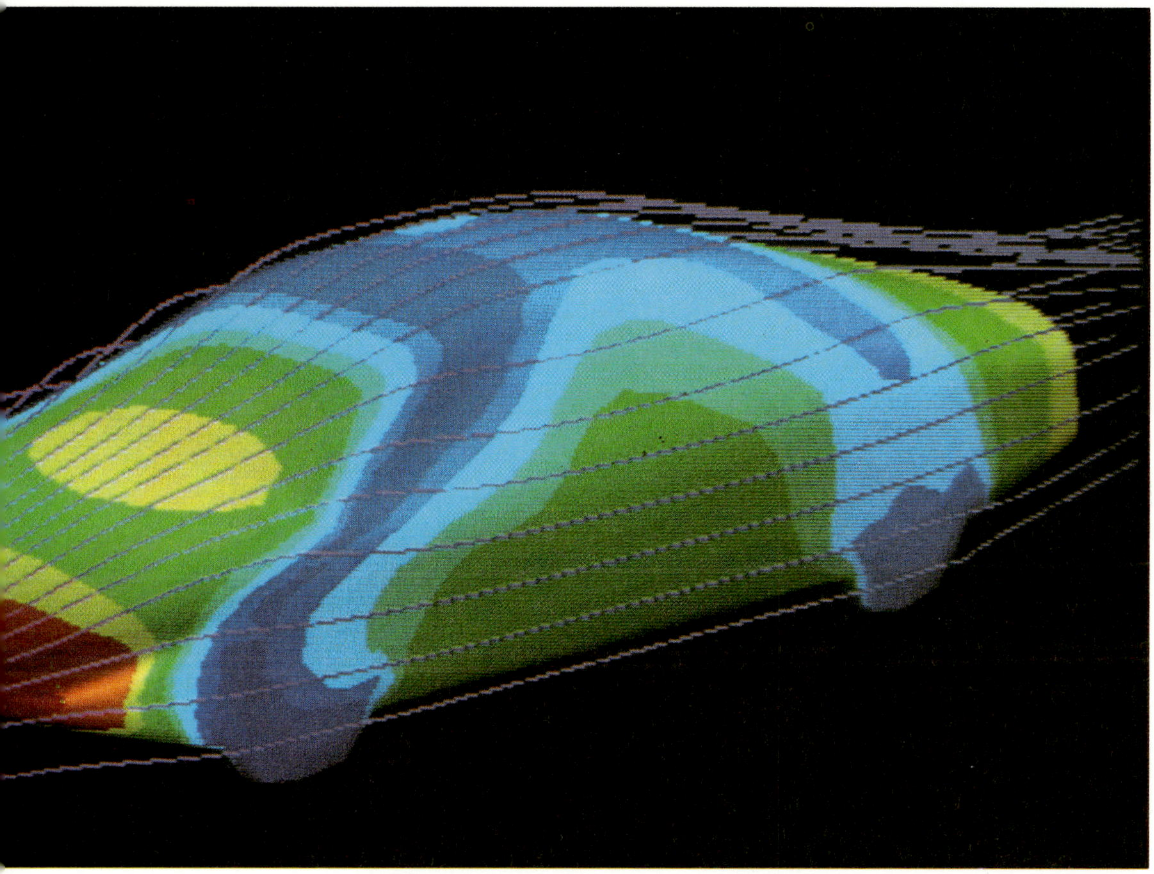

◄▲ Computer-aided design (CAD) can be applied to almost any type of design problem. Above, a shoe designer is working on a new style of shoe. Once the layout has been decided, cutting and sewing instructions are worked out and a sample shoe made. On the left is a computer model of a new design of car, produced on a Cray supercomputer. The model is being used to study the air flow around the proposed car body. The colors relate to the air flow at each point. The calculations and their display are so complex and require so much computing power and memory that only a supercomputer can handle the job.

mathematical representation of a range of natural objects, from craggy mountains to fluffy clouds, so that they can be reproduced by a computer. The mathematics – "fractal geometry" – is concerned with shapes that look the same whatever magnification is used. For example, a coastline can be seen from the air to have bays and headlands. If these are examined from closer to, each bay and headland can be seen to have its own smaller indentations, which, in detail, have still smaller indentations, and so on.

Computer graphics have many applications and are particularly important in engineering, where computer-aided design (CAD) is growing rapidly. Computers are used to design everything from clothes to the Space Shuttle. One approach is to bring together a variety of shapes and to test different combinations of them. For example, the outline of a tie can be filled with a succession of modified patterns until the most attractive one appears. Much computer design, however, starts out from scratch, with the construction of a theoretical model of the object to be designed. In the aircraft industry, airplanes used to be designed on the drawing board. Real models of the final design were built and tested out in a wind tunnel. Now much of this work has been transferred to a computer. The design calculations are carried out on the computer which then presents a picture of how the airplane will finally look. The two-dimensional image on the screen can be rotated by the computer so that the airplane can be viewed from any angle. The computer can also work out how any selected shape will react to a flow of air. The results can be graphically demonstrated so that the computer screen becomes the equivalent of the window in a wind tunnel. This method is much cheaper than using real models and wind tunnels, though the predictions must be tested in practice.

Computer simulation

Simulation techniques with computer graphics are now often used in industry and commerce. Commercial airlines, for example, as well as the armed forces, now employ flight simulators for the training of pilots. These are mock-ups of aircraft flight decks, mounted on hydraulic pistons. The cabin windows are filled with a display scene showing airport buildings, the runway, the surrounding countryside, clouds and other scenery that the pilot is likely to encounter during a flight. The cabin tilts in a realistic way as the pilot moves the controls. The computer, which is linked to these controls, changes the external scenery to mimic the appropriate motion of the airplane. One clear advantage is that the trainee pilot learns to handle the controls in an environment quite similar to the real thing, but with no danger from crashes save that of bruised pride.

To provide a realistic picture of the airplane's environment, the computer uses both perspective and shading. The most accurate way of calculating shadows is by tracing lines from the source of light to all the objects in the scene. For stationary objects this is feasible, but for a moving aircraft, where the scenery outside is changing rapidly, simpler and faster methods have to be used. Shadows are only one effect of lighting. Textured surfaces change their appearance in different ways as the light source moves. Brick and painted wood each looks different according to the angle of the light. Glass and water do not produce the same kinds of reflection. All these effects need to be taken into account if the simulation by computer is to be convincing.

▼ A trainee pilot of the Swiss Air Force (inset), sitting in a mock-up of an aircraft cockpit. All the controls are identical to those in a real aircraft. When the pilot moves the controls, the computer moves the simulated cockpit in a way that would correspond to real movement in flight. All the time, he looks out at a computer-generated scene that simulates the pilot's view from the cockpit. Here, an aircraft ahead is banking as it approaches the landing strip below.

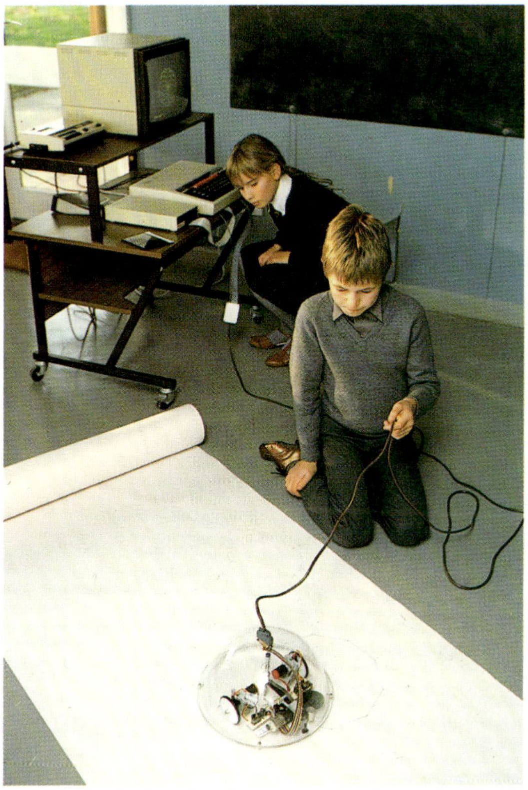

▲ *Computers are playing an increasing role in the classroom. In particular, the turtle, an AI development, has proved a valuable teaching aid. Turtle graphics on a computer screen can be moved around to create and explore different shapes. The mechanical turtle is a robot, that moves under computer control.*

▲ *Using a computer to help match colors and create patterns. Computer "painting" software allows artists to draw shapes on the screen and experiment with different colors. Now that software and color monitors have fallen in price, painting programs are becoming more popular. Professional artists have been using computers for a number of years, and the results are often seen in exhibitions. Similar graphics software is also used in commercial art and design studios.*

Computer teaching

The use of computer graphics is also increasing in schools. A "turtle" is a shape on the computer screen – a triangle, say – that can form the basis for other shapes drawn on the screen. Using a specially developed programming language, the turtle can be moved in any direction by typing in instructions at the keyboard. The turtle's track is recorded on the screen, producing the outline of a figure. Children find geometry much easier to understand when they play about with these turtles. They can, for example, construct figures with a variety of sides and angles to see what shapes result. The word "turtle" also refers to small robots on wheels that can run around the floor in any direction. They are also used for teaching. Both types of turtle represent applications of artificial intelligence. In fact, LOGO, the special programming language developed for computer turtles, derives from a language used in artificial intelligence.

One reason turtle graphics are valuable in teaching is because they allow the child to be creative. Indeed, images produced from computer graphics now feature as works of art in public exhibitions. Computer "painting" programs are available which allow the operator to work very much as an artist works in a studio. The user is offered various ways of producing the texture of an image – paint, chalk and so on. Then the computer provides a palette of different colors. If a shade is not quite right, the computer can mix colors until the desired shade is obtained. This can then be deposited on different parts of the screen in the same way as paint is deposited on canvas. But the computer offers possibilities that traditional painting cannot. For example, a series of rapid variations on a single image can produce animated pictures. Thus, a dancer can be shown in a sequence of positions, or in continuous movement. Nowadays many kinds of film – not only animated cartoons – make use of the techniques of computer graphics.

Perhaps the acid test for artificial intelligence will be whether it can take some account of emotions in exploring ways of applying computers

Can a computer be creative?
In 1976 it was announced that one of the most famous problems in mathematics – usually called the "four-color conjecture" – had finally been solved. The conjecture proposes that to color any map in such a way that each country is clearly distinguished from its neighbors can be done using only four colors. In other words, no two countries sharing a common boundary will be the same color. (They can be the same color if they only meet at a point.) The conjecture was first put forward in the mid-19th century but was found to be extraordinarily difficult to prove. The final proof in 1976 employed a computer which sorted through and analyzed thousands of possibilities to show that none could disobey the conjecture. True, the computer had to be told what needed to be examined, but so too did the mathematicians all of whom had earlier failed to solve the puzzle. Proving a mathematical theorem is normally counted as evidence of human creativity. So, has the computer been creative?

Applying Turing's test (◀ page 87) in this case suggests that, yes, perhaps it has. But is Turing's test sufficient as a reflection of human thinking? Imagine a woman sitting in an office. She knows no Chinese, but is given a set of rules which tell her how to sort Chinese characters into different groups according to their shape. A stream of Chinese characters is presented to her. She sorts them, and the final sequences are taken out of the room again. The characters may, for example, represent people's names and the rules may be to group them into families. Someone sitting outside the room would surely think that the woman knew Chinese. Yet most people would see an important distinction between this person who applied arbitrary rules and another who actually spoke Chinese. The one "understands" the language, whereas the other does not. Similarly, it is sometimes claimed that humans understand what they are doing, whereas computers do not.

The meaning of "understanding" is difficult to define. Perhaps it implies that humans have a conscious awareness of what they are doing. But how do we know that a computer does not have some kind of awareness, too? The problem of whether it is possible to discover what is going on in the mind was at the root of the behaviorist school of psychology: Since what takes place inside the head cannot be directly observed or measured, behaviorists say, the only human aspect worth observing is external behavior. This approach has obvious similarities with Turing's test, and behaviorists have encountered similar objections. The main one concerns how humans relate to the external world. We may have the word "house" stored in our minds, but this refers to something external to ourselves. This fact governs our actions. Humans do not make a clear distinction between what is in the mind and what is outside it. "House" is, moreover, part of a whole web of words – such as "home" – which trigger a range of emotions and recollections. Words are not merely a set of symbols that can be manipulated to produce a stereotyped set of reactions. They have many associations and, often, emotional overtones.

Special areas of the human brain are devoted to the emotions, and they evidently play an important part in generating and controlling our behavior. Can artificial intelligence take some account of emotion in exploring ways of applying computers? One suggestion is that a human being can be thought of as a system that is subject to a whole range of pressures, and to deal with those pressures, the human has to maintain a balance between its internal processes and external actions. Part of the balancing acts requires the emotions to be brought into play. But computers, too, may be subject to pressures. Imagine a really complex robot with a wide range of sensors to monitor the external environment and its own internal operations. If the robot is to work efficiently, the competing signals from all these sensors have to be evaluated and balanced by the controlling computer. Such a complex balance will only finally be achieved, it has been argued, if the computer has "emotion circuits" built into it which can release the pressures and guide the system.

▶ The connection machine, a new type of computer designed to mimic some of the ways in which the human brain operates. The 1.5m cube uses parallel processing to imitate the cross-linkages that occur between different groups of nerve cells in the brain. More than 65,000 processors can carry out several billion instructions every second. Parallel processing not only speeds up the rate of data handling – the connection machine is one of the fastest computers ever built – it also allows the computer to learn from experience.

Information and Society

6

The "biological" computer – how feasible?... Computers and productivity at the workplace...The "paperless office"...Computer workstations... Automated banking and finance...The "smart" cash card...Shopping and banking from a home terminal ...Home working – telecommuting...Automation and unemployment?..."Computer literacy"... Computer crime...The "Big Brother" syndrome

What part will computers play in the world of the future? Will they become more like us, taking over our jobs and possibly our lives? In principle, complex organic (carbon-based) molecules could store other information besides genetic information. Computer designers might explore the feasibility of molecular, rather than silicon-based computers. But what practical advantages would this have? Information retrieval would be much slower than with present electronic methods.

The complicated mix of physical and chemical processes used by the brain for handling information might possibly be duplicated in the laboratory, but the results would hardly improve on present computers. Rather than slavishly copy the physical systems of the brain, a better course would seem to be to copy the way the human brain is used. This is the reasoning that has led to the development of the parallel computer (◀ pages 54–5).

Even imitation of how the brain processes information can be carried too far. Some of the special properties of computers, such as their rapid handling of long strings of numbers, precisely depend on computers being different from humans. Can computers be programmed to reproduce themselves? It is often asked. The answer is – probably yes. But again, the value of such an activity is not obvious. Human intervention, especially when something goes wrong or some change is needed, is surely a more flexible and efficient way of producing new computers. In short, computers and humans work best when they work together and make the biggest contribution to those activities that they each do best.

The "Biochip"

Comparisons between the capabilities of humans and computers prompted the idea that computers might one day consist of biological components.

The adult human being, scientists reasoned, is a complex machine, capable of sophisticated information processing operations associated with sight and thought and touch and movement. But it was not always so. Every human being starts off as a single cell, a combination of a sperm and an egg. This cell must contain all the instructions needed to produce a highly coordinated machine which can absorb, process and retain massive amounts of information over a period of many years. Might it not be possible, they asked, to manipulate DNA (the blueprint of life) so as to produce a biological material – a "biochip" – that would "grow" into an information-processing device? The DNA program would contain instructions for the production of the biological components that would perform high-level data processing.

The "biochip" concept also seemed to offer further possibilities of miniaturization, with components measuring no more than a billionth of a meter. The molecules which made up the circuit elements would be assembled into three-dimensional arrays, and each component would be tailored to a specific purpose. Scientists already knew how to reprogram microscopic living organisms to produce new materials. Given time, they believed, they could surely produce molecules that could be used as components in the biochip.

They had also discovered that protein molecules "self-assemble" – they form regular arrays and three-dimensional shapes both inside organisms and in test tubes. All that remained was to design proteins that would form arrangements of different components, like the elements of an electronic circuit. Indeed, many biological molecules were known to transport electrons around the cell. Others, like chlorophyll, could be "flipped" from one state to another by electrons or by light, and so act like switches.

Unfortunately, the switching and electron transport performed by biological molecules take about one ten thousandth of a second, compared with a speed of around one millionth of a billionth of a second on a silicon chip. Moreover, biological components wear out more easily than solid-state electronic devices, and would lead to more computer errors. Biological systems do have repair and error correction mechanisms, but to program them into the "biochip" would make it far too complex. Scientists are now considering the use of biological molecules, not as the active components of the circuitry, but as a framework for organizing other molecular components (which still have to be developed).

◀ With today's technology, an entire computer can be contained on a single silicon chip. This one was developed by IBM and measures only 10mm square.

Office automation is now often seen as the only way of increasing productivity without increasing costs

Office automation

Office workers are currently the section of the workforce most affected by computers. A few centuries ago, most people worked in agriculture. During the 19th century, the countries of Europe and the West (today's so-called developed countries) experienced industrial revolutions which transferred the majority of the workforce from the fields to the factories. During the latter half of the present century, administrative and service activities have grown so much that they have overtaken manufacturing industry as the major employer. As a result, more than half of American labor is now employed in some kind of office. Whereas agriculture is concerned with food, and manufacturing industry with consumer products, services and administration – and offices in general – are concerned with information. Nowadays people often refer to the "information society".

Agricultural societies functioned at a fairly simple level of organization. Manufacturing societies required greater organizational complexity. Information societies are a step up again. The organization of contemporary society has been complicated by the vast increase in world population over the past century. Modern society is so complex with so much information being passed, that office work inevitably begets more office work.

The need for automating office activities and streamlining procedures was already apparent during the latter part of the 19th century. By 1900, a modern office was equipped with typewriters, dictating machines, telegraphs and telephones. This century has since seen the introduction of telex, duplicating machines (followed by photocopiers after World War II) and adding machines. All these were designed to improve the handling of information, both written and spoken. As office work became increasingly important, so its organization changed. Nineteenth-century offices were typically small, and each member of staff undertook a variety of tasks. The larger offices of the 20th century have been organized along the mass-production lines that were first introduced in factories, with each office worker concentrating on one particular set of tasks. However, the amount of information each employee can handle has grown only slowly. Office work has become labor-intensive with a high proportion of costs going on staff salaries. Office automation is now seen as the only way of increasing productivity whilst keeping down costs. According to one estimate, industrial productivity rose by over 80 percent during the 1970s, whereas office productivity rose by less than 5 percent.

Computer manufacturers have not been slow to respond. Having earlier developed computers to handle business accounts, they tried to extend automation to cover all aspects of office paperwork, which would in future, they hoped, be handled electronically. The vision of the "paperless office", however, has not been realized. The use of computers and printers has increased paper consumption rather than reduced it, and indeed has led to a rapid growth in worldwide paper production. Moreover, productivity has not increased as much as expected. True, labor costs have been cut in areas of routine office work, and in some cases typing staff have been reduced by as much as two-thirds. But in secretarial and managerial work the time saved has usually gone into other aspects of the job, such as better filing of information or more contact with other staff. How to judge this development depends on the meaning and measure of "productivity" when, unlike in agriculture or industry, there is often no specific end product as such.

Local-area network

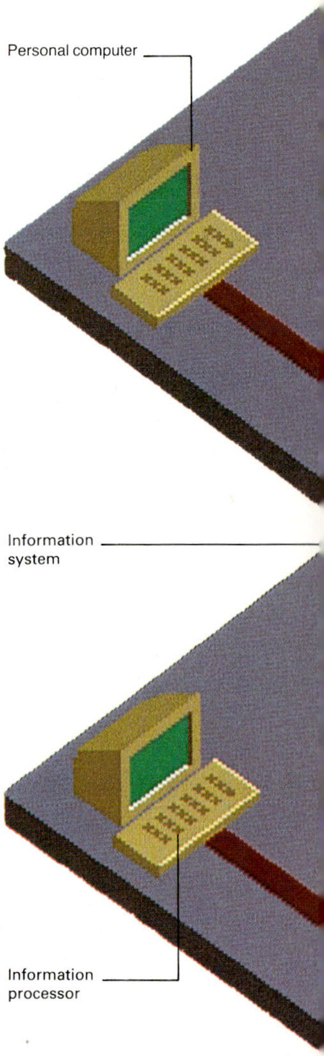

►A local area network (LAN) allows all the computer equipment in a building, to be interconnected, so that each component can interact with any other. Two floors of this building have all the machines linked by a cable system called Ethernet (developed by the Xerox Corporation). This allows, for example, the scanner on the upper floor to input material to the word processor below. There, the material is modified and dispatched, in turn, to the laser printer upstairs, where the information is finally committed to paper. In this way, the LAN ensures efficient use of all the equipment in the network.

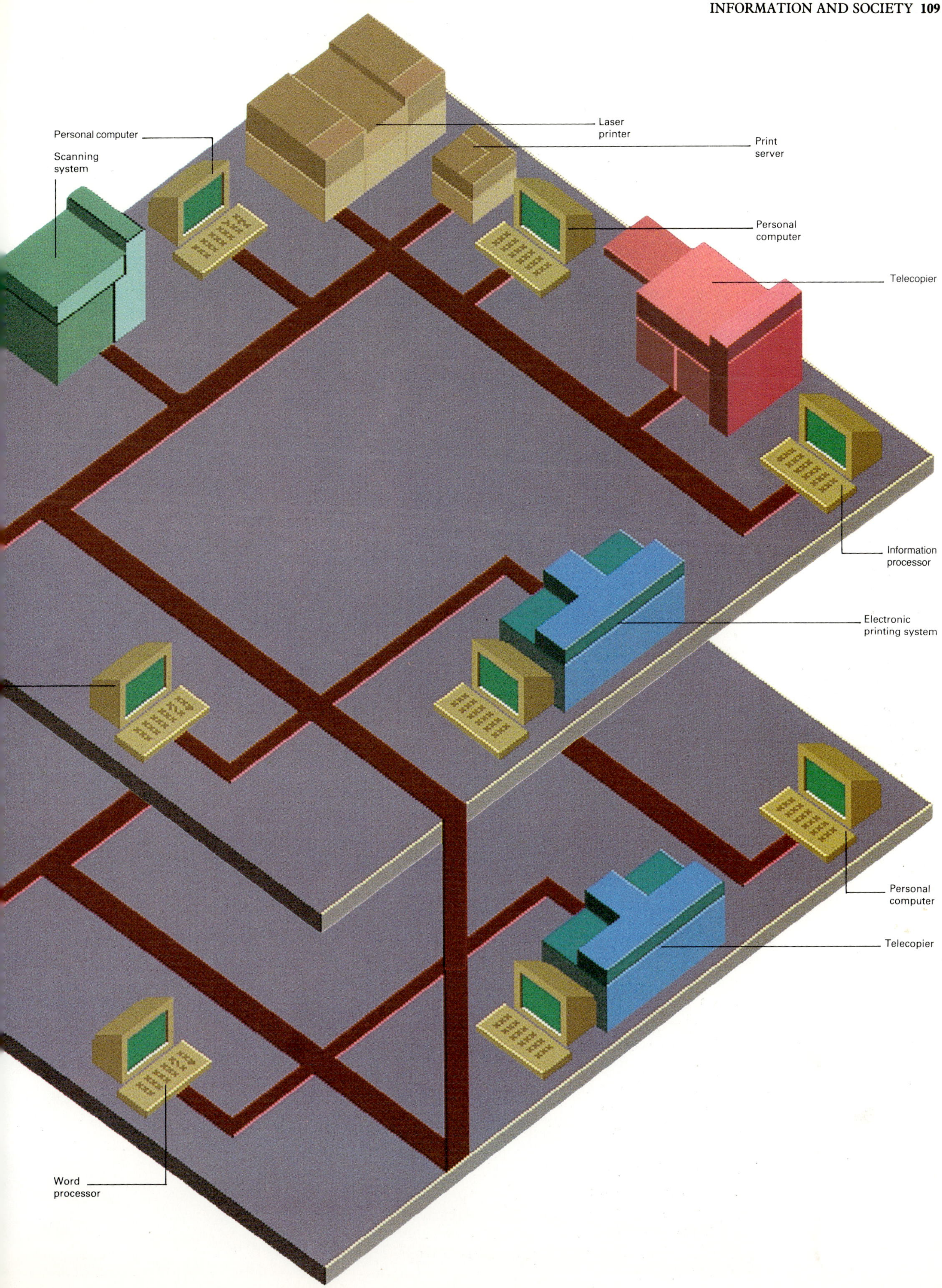
Personal computer
Scanning system
Laser printer
Print server
Personal computer
Telecopier
Information processor
Electronic printing system
Personal computer
Telecopier
Word processor

One factor working against satisfactory automation of the office is certainly psychological. Few senior managers have a detailed knowledge of what computers can do. Yet they are often responsible for deciding whether to purchase computing equipment. They may have difficulty evaluating the technical evidence, and feel threatened by the exposure of their ignorance. At the same time, the computing experts in the firm may feel threatened because the trend towards extending the use of computers may affect their own jobs and career prospects. At another level, there is a physical problem. Few offices have been designed for automated information handling. Many are not capable of providing all the cabling required. In addition, the office layout may need to change. One effect of automation is that some office work is reverting to the 19th-century pattern whereby individuals work by themselves on a wider range of jobs. The factory production-line model is becoming less appropriate.

In the automated office the same computer terminal might handle word processing, numerical calculations, transmission of messages and storage and retrieval of information. Individual members of staff using such a multipurpose terminal – called a workstation – can carry out a wide range of activities without moving from their desks. The convergence of two technologies – computers and telecommunications – has made such new developments possible. In practice, however,

▶ Over the past two decades the appearance of the modern office has changed dramatically. The mechanical typewriter has disappeared, largely replaced by the electronic keyboard and monitor screen. Paper is still the main form of output, but much office information is now stored on floppy or hard disks.

▶ Nurses at computer workstations in a modern hospital. A workstation is essentially a computer terminal which allows a wide range of information-handling activities to take place at the same time. For example, hospital nurses may need simultaneously to consult patients' records, obtain information about vacant hospital beds and send off messages to wards, and so on.

both technologies have created problems for office organization. Workstations must be easy to use, and must be able to communicate via a wide range of networks (◀ page 43). Both these requirements can pose problems of compatibility. A computer that is included in a network and expected to communicate with other computers must not, for example, have physical connections to the electrical system that differ from those of the other computers. Nor must it transmit information at twice the rate at which another computer can receive it. Similar difficulties arise between networks as between computers in networks. Do the two networks to be connected have similar configurations? One might, for example, have a ring configuration, where each terminal receives every message and the users must decide which messages are intended for them. The other might have a star configuration, where the messages go to a central mainframe computer and are directed from there to the appropriate terminal. Current international discussions aimed at standardizing communication between computers have distinguished seven different layers of communication, including those mentioned. The object is to promote methods – called protocols – that will allow any computer and network to combine with any other. The entire system of protocols being examined is called Open Systems Interconnection (OSI). Its investigations offer some hope that the links between computers will develop in an orderly fashion.

▲ ***More attention is now being devoted to the development of voice-detection systems, such as the voice-activated telephone. After analyzing voice patterns in detail, the computer identifies the voice and can react to specific words or particular voices. A telephone can be programmed, for example, to respond to one person only. At present, voice detection systems can only identify a restricted range of spoken words, such as telephone numbers.***

Against the background of these problems, the need for office automation has become more acute as further aspects of office work are affected by technological change. For example, new possibilities have been opened up by telephones with memory that can retain lists of telephone numbers alongside a diary, automatically call numbers at the required time, and redial at intervals if the number is engaged. Some telephones can even be activated by voice. Perhaps more significantly, the telephone network is becoming increasingly adept at carrying other types of communication signal. The new teletex system, whose ultimate purpose is to link up word processors via the public telephone network, overlaps the new telephone system, in that both use computers for the purposes of nonoral communication. In other areas, "intelligent" photocopiers have made their appearance. These store the copied text in digital form, so that their output can be presented in a variety of ways – it is not confined to a straight replica of the original. The perennial worry is that all these changes will go on independently of each other and in a piecemeal way, resulting in a highly computerized office, but with poor internal and external communication. Poorly integrated equipment would bring the ideal of the "office of the future" no closer to realization.

The offices that are most affected by automation are those in firms whose main business involves information handling. In contrast, offices in industry exist mainly to handle the paperwork created as a by-product of work in a factory. Banking is an example of an information-handling business. In some ways, banknotes are like books. They are pieces of paper that convey information. For a banknote, the important words are: "I promise to pay the bearer" or some equivalent. (In fact, the original promise, which implied that the note could be exchanged for an equivalent amount of gold, is unlikely to be fulfilled today.) Banknotes are, however, only one form of "information" in banking. Cheques, cash cards and credit cards are equally important today, and are evidence of the growing role of automated banking.

The most spectacular effects of automation in the financial world are seen in the operation of the stockmarkets

▲ Cash dispensers became a common feature of many high-street banks in the 1970s. Officially called "automatic teller machines", they are intended to cover a range of banking activities including checking an account or transferring funds, as well as cash withdrawal. The number of options available to the customer is still increasing, as is cooperation between different banks.

Automated finance

Banks were among the first to use computers in the 1950s. Originally this was just for internal accounting, but the possibility of applications oriented to the customer was discussed from quite early on. Customer usage took off rather slowly, however, mainly because of the difficulty of using computers, the initial resistance by customers and a lack of agreement between the leading banks. Meantime, bank paperwork was becoming increasingly automated. A system for clearing cheques between different banks had always been a necessity. If a customer pays a cheque drawn on Bank X into an account in Bank Y, the two banks must communicate to ensure that one account is credited and the other debited. An international clearing system was established in 1977 for the whole of Europe and now handles up to a million messages a day. This rate of data handling is far greater than could be achieved using manual labor.

Banks are now irreversibly committed to further automation if they are to maintain and expand their present levels of services. Experiments are under way to allow a wide range of customer queries to be handled. Users will type in their questions and will listen to an appropriate reply selected from a set of prerecorded messages. As with some expert systems, customers often prefer to interact with an automated, rather than a human, teller. It is not unusual to see customers lining up outside a bank when there are very few inside. Public acceptance of automation clearly suits the banks, because it is the customer who does the work, rather than the bank staff. Such savings of time and labor increase productivity.

The most spectacular effects of automation are seen in another part of the financial world – the stockmarket. At the same time, the number of financial databases available online from a computer has risen rapidly. By the early 1990s it is estimated that the market for financial information in electronic form will reach US $4 billion a year. Those firms that were already handling financial information have had a head start. Reuters and Dow Jones, both well known long before the advent of computers, now lead the market in the provision of financial and business information.

► The highly automated Hong Kong stock exchange. In recent years, variable exchange rates, growth in international trading and legal changes relating to stockbroking have increased the need for rapid reactions to stockmarket fluctuations.

7640
3661

►► The use of computers for shopping is moving ahead rapidly. Here, the customer selects his purchases and the shop assistant keys the bar codes for the items into the computer at the checkout. Payment is made through a computer link to the customer's bank. Meanwhile, the shop computer passes information concerning the customer's purchases on to assistants in the store, who bag the items ready for collection by the customer at the exit. Also possible is "teleshopping" – shopping from a distance. Computer links between the customer's home the bank and the shops enable the customer to buy goods without even leaving the house. Booking tickets for a holiday or at a theater, for example, are also possible by this method.

▲ A driver from a Japanese catering service consults a computerized route-planner to find the quickest way to get to her next customer. These useful electronic devices store maps which drivers can call up on the screen to assist them if they are lost. In the future, they will probably become standard equipment in cars. Coupled with a voice synthesizer, a route planner could tell a driver which turnings to take to reach a destination in unfamiliar territory.

Electronic shopping

The system of credit cards dates from the 1950s, before computers had taken a real hold of finance. But their use has increased with the expansion of automation. These plastic cards have become an integral part of the information world largely through the development of the "smart card".

A customer arrives at the checkout in a shop and inserts the card into a socket in the service till. The sum of the goods purchased is automatically deducted from the value of the card. For this to happen, information on the cost of the goods must also be in electronic form. The electronic bar codes that are currently in use first appeared on shop goods in the USA during the early 1970s. The bars on the label identify to the computer the price of the object, its weight, the manufacturer's name and so on. The assistant at the checkout usually passes each item, with bar code downwards, over a laser scanner which converts the code into electronically readable data. This system speeds payments, and can increase the productivity of a supermarket appreciably. Moreover, price changes can be implemented immediately by passing the information to the central computer, and stock records can be continuously updated.

More revolutionary proposals envisage people banking and shopping from home ("teleshopping"), using terminals that link with the bank or shop's central computer. Bank customers, for example, will be able to examine the state of their accounts, authorize the payment of bills and ask for financial advice by keying in appropriate questions to the bank's computer. All this is technically feasible, but do people really want it?

This is a "chicken and egg" question. Clearly customers will not use a home-based system unless it is cheap, easy to use and provides a wide range of options. At the same time, retailers who are expected to put money into a teleshopping venture in its early, risky stages will expect preferential treatment from teleshopping customers. Home-based systems usually require an external stimulus to start them off, such as the introduction of Teletel in France in 1981 (◀ page 83). With encouragement from the French government, private businesses soon

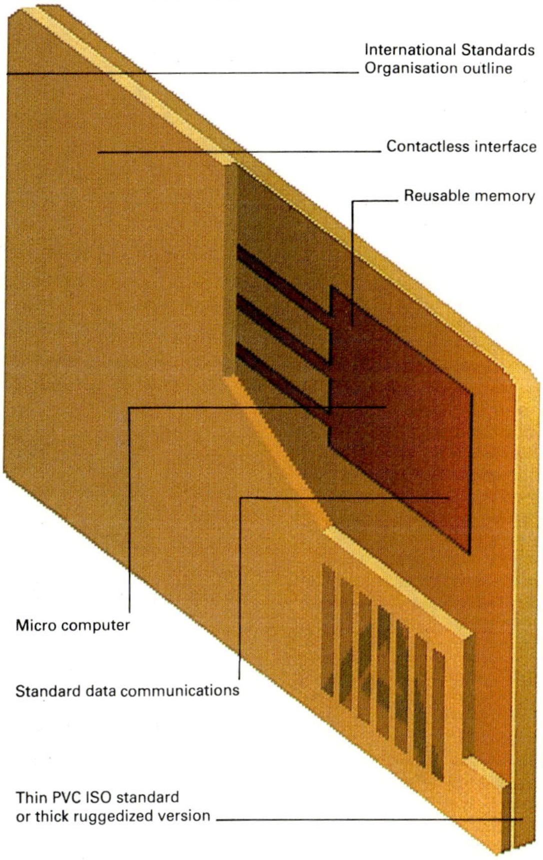

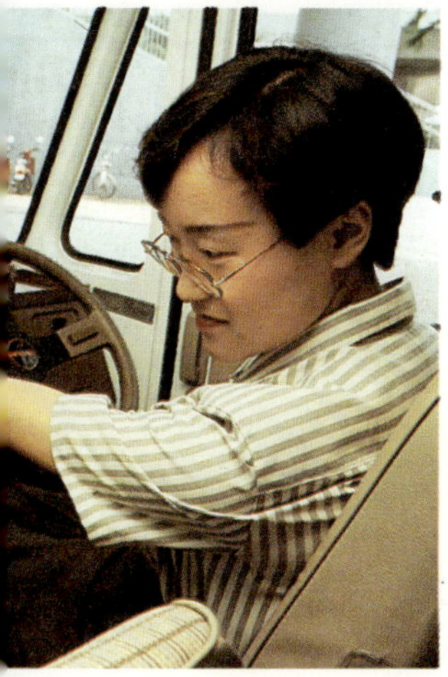

saw the value of having online access to millions of telephone subscribers. The Teletel network now provides a remarkable range of services, as well as experimenting with the use of smart cards to pay for purchases. (Wine bought direct from favourite châteaux has proved especially popular.)

At first sight, it may seem that teleshopping is best suited to firms selling expensive, durable goods where the customer may need some advice before purchase. At present, such advice is more often provided by interactive video on the shop premises than through a remote network. IBM, for example, developed an advanced system which both aimed to teach dealers about IBM products and provided sales talk to customers who came into the shop. The second aim was unsuccessful, purely because casual purchasers made up only a very small proportion of IBM customers. However, similar systems are being used advantageously by car dealers to allow customers to compare details on prices and performance of vehicles and to answer customers' questions. Often, the machine will switch itself on automatically when it senses a customer nearby. Some sales programs have almost become educational devices. For example, the "Floor Fashion Advisor" will take an interested customer through all the necessary steps in buying a carpet. These include everything from selecting a pattern to working out carpet requirements for rooms of different shapes and sizes. Complex programs of this kind that involve two-way communication with the customer work well on the sales floor, but are difficult to transfer online to a shopper at home because of the large amounts of information that make up the computer graphics. Teleshopping is likely to concentrate on goods, such as wine, where most purchasers already regard themselves as experts.

▲ The "smart card" was invented in France in the 1970s. It contains a complete computer system built into a standard-sized credit card and can have a wide range of uses. These might include drawing a pension (the card would be recharged with each new payment), "electronic" shopping, securing authorized access to other computer systems and storing the owner's medical history.

Automation and job location

To use a computer there is no need to sit alongside it. Employees currently assemble in some central place of work, often making long and costly journeys to get there. Furthermore, this workplace is frequently in an expensive area with high overheads. Telecommunication links mean that both the computer and its operators can be anywhere. It is estimated that over 10 percent of the workforce in the USA now works at least part of the time at home and a growing proportion of these are "telecommuters" – people working from home computers.

Some telecommuters find working in isolation difficult, however. Moreover, home working is generally lower paid than working in an office and there is little job security. It has been argued that telecommuting would benefit the nation as a whole. With fewer people traveling to work, less transportation would be needed, leading to savings on the costs of imported oil, building and road repairs. On the other hand, telecommuting on an international scale could mean a net loss of jobs from a country where labor costs were high to another where they were low.

► Computers have become increasingly portable. Small versions can now be used in trains or on aircraft. The back of a car can provide the same facilities as an office by means of a computer link home base. Data can be sent by the car computer to the base computer, using the telephone lines, and return messages can be received in the same way. No longer need business be interrupted by travel.

► Automation in factories is now common, but few workplaces are as automated as the Macintosh computer factory in California. There, people are employed mainly to monitor progress, rather than take part directly in the manufacturing process. Computers are well suited to automated production of other computers. The tiny integrated circuits that lie at the heart of modern computers cannot be made by human craftsmen. Checking to ensure the finished article works properly is also best left to computers themselves.

Because of these problems many shopkeepers question whether being involved in teleshopping is worthwhile. Supporters point to the potential savings it offers. It does not matter very much where the shop is located. The edge of a town will do just as well as a prime site in the center. Moreover, fewer staff may be required, because customers themselves are doing more of the work. Both these issues – the effects on geographical spread and employment – are at the center of current debates concerning the impact of information technology on the whole of society.

Computers and unemployment

Employment is a particularly contentious issue. The job losses of the 1980s have occurred at a time of financial cutback, making it difficult to determine how many are due to economic stringency and how many to the effects of automation. Much of manufacturing industry has been automated, and though reductions in staff may have been attributable to economic problems originally, their numbers are not being increased even when the economy improves.

In the Pittsburgh area of the United States, the number of jobs in the steel industry has fallen from 90,000 at the end of the 1970s to 40,000 today. In the UK it is reckoned that jobs in mechanical engineering and textiles fell by 20 percent between 1980 and 1982, and most of the losses have not been replaced since. Automation at large iron foundries has reduced the work force in some cases by as much as 90 percent. How many staff can one robot displace? Obviously, it depends both on the nature of the robot and of the job. Estimates vary, from one robot equals one member of staff to one robot equals six or more staff members. Certainly, in manufacturing robots win hands down over humans in terms of productivity.

On the one hand, jobs are being lost, but, on the other, the robots installed in factories have to be built and maintained by someone. Even so, most experts believe that the new jobs created in this way will number no more than a half of those lost. Moreover, they will not involve the same type of work, and people displaced from one job will often not be employed in the new positions created. At the same time, many of the traditional skills will be come redundant. In the printing industry, for example, the compositors who used to set up the pages for printing before World War II were highly skilled craftsmen. The automated text-handling systems now available can be used satisfactorily by people with much less skill and training. Even if deskilling does not imply job losses, it can mean some loss of earnings and job satisfaction for those whose jobs are deskilled.

The jobs that so far have been least affected by automation are those at the bottom of the work hierarchy – caretakers, for example – and those at the top, such as managing directors. In between, automation has impacted on white-collar employment and on skilled and unskilled manual jobs. However, the biggest change in office employment has yet to come – when voice input of information becomes possible. Currently, executives need a range of ancillary staff to handle their information problems. Once these managers can communicate directly with computers, the need for such assistance will be considerably reduced. Of course, managerial staff themselves are not immune from the effect of computerization on employment. The growing use of computer monitoring and expert systems, for example, to decide on the purchase and sale of stocks and shares, is already encroaching on their territory.

▼ People are increasingly using computer links to work from home. Working at home has helped to retain the skills of women who might otherwise have dropped out of the labor market when they stopped work to start a family. It has also aided the recruitment of disabled employees, who often find it easier to work from home. Home working has benefited employers, too, by increasing productivity.

Computer training and education

Computers have become more user friendly, but that does not reduce the need for training to handle them efficiently. The drive to make more people "computer literate" now begins at school. Early computer training in the 1950s concentrated on researchers, but by the 1960s the computer terminal had made its appearance in the school classroom. The large mainframe computers then available, however, were too complex and costly for such experiments to spread widely. The breakthrough in school teaching had to wait till the introduction of the microcomputer some ten years later. The earliest national effort occurred in the UK, where the government launched a "Micros for schools" campaign in 1981. Education in most developed countries now relies on schools having the use of a computer. Computers have proved to be good tools for remedial teaching, and have helped overcome the mental block that some children have for subjects such as mathematics. However, teachers have not always understood how to make the most of the modern computer. Moreover, computers have tended to be used largely for scientific subjects, which, in the less enlightened schools, can sometimes result in boys monopolizing machines at the expense of girl students.

These are some of the considerations in the current debate on how computers are best used for teaching. People draw a distinction between "training" and "education". Training is limited in intent. Its concern is to help the learner carry out a specific task (for example, detect a fault in a car engine). Education is more concerned with drawing out and developing a student's abilities and with encouraging independent thought. Computers are particularly useful as training aids, not least for teaching how to work with computers. For instance, programming skills can be taught by a computer which monitors the programs as they are written, drawing the learner's attention to mistakes and to badly written sections. Such training activities are usually straightforward, but they raise interesting questions. Do learners gain different things from computers and from human teachers? It has been found, for example, that students tend to accept commands more readily from computers than from humans.

How much computers can help with education, as opposed to just training, is a more controversial question. Most educational programs are designed to improve problem-solving skills. Some rely, in part, on procedures that have been learnt from computer games. The pupil may, for instance, have to traverse a familiar sort of maze, but planning each escape will involve the application of different types of mental skill. Simulation programs, which model some activity in the real world, are also common. For example, an anthropology package developed in the USA looks at the relationship between marriage practices and land inheritance amongst some Asian tribes. Students are encouraged to try out different sorts of marriage laws – perhaps, changing from one wife per man to several wives per man – and to trace its effects on land ownership patterns after several generations. Computer aids have been shown to stimulate students' thinking, but they have remained largely supplementary to the education provided by human teachers.

One problem in using computers in the classroom is that they do not always fit in well with traditional curricula. The skills that they teach cut across the usual subject divisions. Perhaps, more fundamentally, they challenge the values we ascribe to certain kinds of knowledge and even our definition of intelligence. Traditionally, memory has formed

▼ Children can use computers from an early age. Computer skills have been taught successfully in primary schools in many countries. Whereas older children tend to associate such skills with complex mathematics, younger children more often accept the computer as a general-purpose instrument. Some children who are not outstanding academically turn out to be competent computer operators.

▲► For some children computers are now commonplace. Computer camps in the United States have become a part of the usual round of children's summer activities. There, they are taught about everything from programming to repairing computers. The camps help to engender enthusiasm and extend computer skills gained at home and in school. Some children become really hooked on computers and have to be weaned off. Significantly, some of the best computer hackers are children.

significant part of intelligence. As reliance on computers grows, the importance of this memory element may be reduced and replaced by a greater emphasis on the aspects of intelligence concerned with analyzing and evaluating information. Such a trend would particularly affect teachers who were trained before the microcomputer entered the classroom. Many countries have recognized this and expect to provide continuing retraining in computer skills for their teachers.

Teachers are, of course, only one of the groups that will need to have their skills brought up to date in this way. Such retraining is often, consciously or unconsciously, feared by the recipients. Partly this is fear of the unknown, partly it is the fear of exposing one's ignorance, especially to junior staff who are more computer-literate. Many people are concerned for their own job satisfaction and job security in an increasingly automated world. It is not easy to dispel these worries, but people can gain some reassurance through appropriate training. Nor is it just older employees who will be affected by change. Technological change is set to continue at a rapid rate. It is estimated that people now entering employment will need extensive retraining two or three times during their working lives. Consequently, continuing part-time education throughout life is likely to increase in importance relative to full-time school education.

Looking ahead

Exactly what the impact of continuing change on individuals and society will be, is hard to gauge. We are already accustomed to rapid change. Many people still at work today were born long before jet aircraft and television became commonplace, yet they use them almost as readily as younger generations who cannot imagine a world without such inventions. Perhaps the expanding capabilities of the computer will be absorbed with similar ease. There may be a few changes in how people live, as home life has been affected by television, but the transition may be smooth.

However, most people experience jets and TV passively. They sit in front of the screen, or in the seat of a jet, and apart from simple operations, such as pressing buttons, need know nothing of what is happening. In contrast, computer usage is interactive. Computers ask questions and how they proceed next depends on the responses they receive. Learning to interact with devices that are themselves changing with time may prove much more difficult than passive acceptance.

Some idea of what the future may have in store for the next generation is provided by the wide variety of forecasts now available. By the end of the century it is expected that computers will have made a major impact on the home. Both the house and many household appliances will be computerized and interlinked. Houses will be equipped with sensors to monitor their environment continuously and to warn of danger. If a leak of water or an electrical defect occurs, the house computer will immediately inform the occupants and, if so instructed, will send a message to the local plumber or electrician.

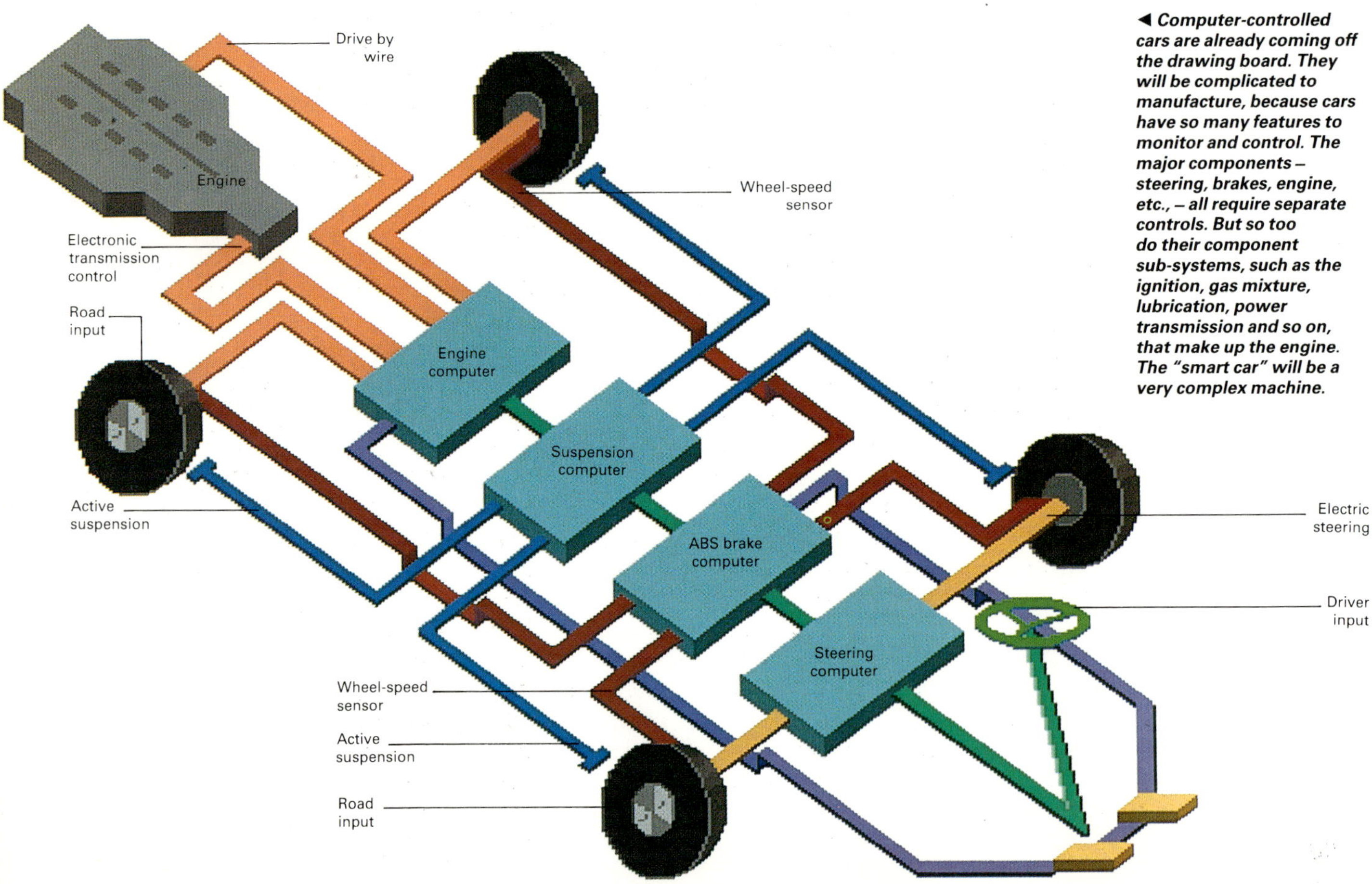

◀ ***Computer-controlled cars are already coming off the drawing board. They will be complicated to manufacture, because cars have so many features to monitor and control. The major components – steering, brakes, engine, etc., – all require separate controls. But so too do their component sub-systems, such as the ignition, gas mixture, lubrication, power transmission and so on, that make up the engine. The "smart car" will be a very complex machine.***

▲ *A robot arm offering a drink to its physically handicapped operator. One of the great attractions of information technology is the help it can give to disabled people. So long as the person can make movements of any kind – even if only with their eyes – these can be translated into instructions to the computer by means of sensors. A computer-controlled robot can help a disabled person to communicate and to do things that would otherwise be impossible.*

▲ *The small Japanese town of Higashi Ikoma has become the base for an experiment in computerized living. Its citizens are using a futuristic communication system called Hi-OVIS (Highly Interactive Optical Visual Information System) which connects their TV sets to a central computer. Each home has a keyboard like this one. The buttons along the top select TV programs. Those below are for sending and receiving messages. The small screen shows which communication channel is in use. People can use the system to talk to the center, or to each other, and can view each other simultaneously. They can call up information from the central library, and can work, shop and bank from home.*

Should the smoke and heat sensors detect a fire, the computer will alert the people in the house and the fire brigade. Other sensors, outside and inside the house, will detect the presence of an intruder (in more sophisticated ways than are presently used in most homes) and notify the police. Such a computerized system will also provide maintenance – defrosting the refrigerator, watering the house plants, and reminding the householder of routine tasks to be carried out in the house and garden. Meals will be planned with computer advice and the whole cooking sequence set beforehand.

One of the most highly computerized devices will be the car. Sensors will alert the driver to standard items, such as oil and petrol levels, and assist by, for example, setting the most efficient petrol mixture from moment to moment, or switching on the car lights as night falls. Personalized ignition, whereby the owner's voice, but no other, will start the car, is a further possibility. During the journey, the driver will receive oral instructions from the computer on which way to go. Not all communications need be from computer to human. A car's ignition might be switched on from the bedroom, allowing the car time to warm up whilst the driver dresses.

Computers will be used, above all, to communicate – for instance, with the doctor, who may increasingly become involved in advising on health problems from a distance. This vision of the future is based on developments that are already in the experimental stage. Technically, it should all be possible, but there are many who find some aspects of the vision unattractive. Is it right to concentrate so much on the home at the risk of losing some of our personal contacts? Perhaps this worry is exaggerated. Television was supposed to have a depersonalizing effect, but in reality it does not seem to have changed the range of human contacts greatly.

The total sum lost annually through computer crime in the USA is estimated to be in excess of $1 billion

What can go wrong

Of course, computers do go wrong sometimes. Will this be a major problem for a society that increasingly depends on them? The idea of a self-repairing computer, along the lines of a living organism, has often been discussed. But the highly reliable computers aboard spacecraft have shown that even present computers, properly constructed, can be adequately robust. Not all breakdowns occur within the computer. Damage by lightning might seem a remote possibility, yet half-a-dozen major computer failures a year are attributed to this cause in British businesses alone. The number of significant computer breakdowns from all causes is increasing each year, and the consequences can be serious. A survey in the USA found that 90 percent of all firms suffering a major computer failure went out of business within the next 18 months. This is some indication of the risks attached to automated homes and businesses. It takes no account, however, of what is perhaps the biggest threat, which comes from human beings.

"Hackers" are compulsive computer users, intent on exploring all the machine's possibilities. A favorite pastime is to gain entrance to a system that is closed to them – for example, one run by a finance house or by the military. Sometimes they leave a message to show that they have penetrated the system. Even if they intend no harm, they can cause damage. Students who gained access to patient records on the computer of a US medical school accidentally wiped out a large amount of data and brought part of the school's research program to a halt. Sometimes the intention is malevolent. Computer operators who have been dismissed by their firms have been known to take their revenge by deliberately trying to disable systems. A trivial, but irritating way is to insert an anonymous message in the computer files. The message might be, "I am the random glitch – catch me if you can". This is then printed out along with anything the computer produces – from letters to payslips. The subtle part is that the programmer has arranged for the message to be shifted in a totally random way to another part of the computer memory every time something is printed out. Whereas it might be possible to track down where the message came from in the computer, there is no way of knowing where it has moved to. The only way to get rid of this type of bug is to empty the whole computer memory. More destructive than this is to trip the wiping out of all memory in the computer system. This is usually done by a so-called time bomb – a hidden command that can be triggered by an unsuspecting operator long after the miscreant has left the firm.

Such unauthorized erasing of memory is an example of "computer crime", a rapidly growing area of criminal activity. Most computer crime involves money, and banking is a prime target. Criminal hackers who gain access to a bank's central computer can simply transfer minute sums of money from a large number of accounts to one they set up for themselves. The losses from any individual account are often so small that they go unnoticed. Equally, an executive might use the computer to falsify sales figures, making the firm look more attractive to prospective investors. How widespread is computer crime is hard to tell. Firms are often reluctant to prosecute those who are caught because the publicity might undermine customers' confidence in the security of their system. According to one estimate, the total sum stolen in the USA already exceeds $1 billion a year. This figure is expected to rise even further, since unlike ordinary theft, the amount of money involved in each computer crime is usually large.

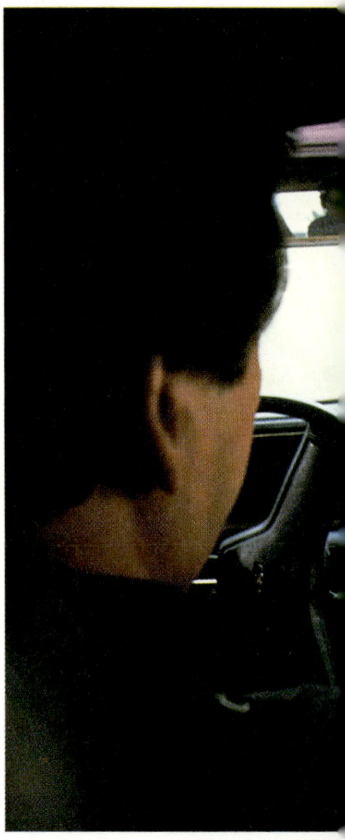

► A policeman on patrol duty calls for information from the central police computer. Police computer databases not only hold information about criminals or suspects, they can match this information against data on known crimes. Since criminals often have fixed habits, such matching can help in the detection and prevention of crime. The physical appearance of a suspect can be checked quickly before deciding on what action to take.

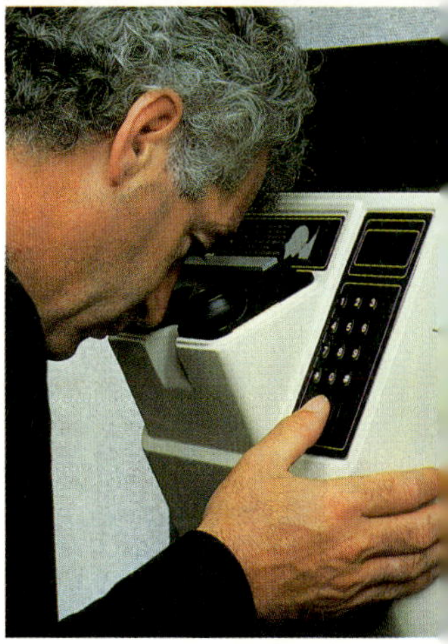

► A recent discovery is that the pattern of the blood vessels crossing the retina of the eye is unique to each individual. Even identical twins have different patterns. Just as fingerprints can identify people, so can "eyeprints". Here, a retinal pattern is being checked. Light reflected from the interior of the eye provides an image of the retina which is then compared by a computer with a database of known retinal patterns. The process is now used to control access to high-security areas in particular.

Privacy versus security

For the individual the important questions are often whether data from different databases are being combined, and how to find out about it. Not surprisingly, databases dealing with government security work are rarely made available to the general public. But something is known of surveillance techniques. For example, computers are now widely used to aid automatic tapping of specified telephone numbers. Also common is the interchange of information between databases.

Such methods are typical of the computer systems used by the police. Information on, for instance, cars seen near scenes of crimes, ways in which crimes have been committed, fingerprints, and so on, can all be brought together. In Britain the system now employed for this sort of enquiry is appropriately called HOLMES (an acronym for Home Office Large Major Enquiry System). From the police viewpoint the virtue of computers is that they have memories that are both large and long-lasting. For someone who accidentally appears on a police computer, however, this can sometimes be a problem. In a number of instances in the USA people have been listed on FBI or other police computers, who have never ever been charged with a crime. At worst, this could lead to innocent people being denied certain jobs or barred from other activities.

▼ "Digital display" – fingerprint being used instead of a signature to verify a cheque. When fingerprints had to be compared and identified by manual means, the process took a long time. Now they can be stored and analyzed by a computer, making identification much faster. The system must be able to allow for small changes in the fingerprint – for example, when the finger has been scratched.

Computers and government

At government level, the effect of computers can be decisive. The current debate in the United States over the SDI (Strategic Defense Initiative) program hinges in part on the problems presented by powerful computers. The full program may prove too complex to be carried through successfully by existing computers, even if the political will is there. Much of the fighting equipment used by today's armed forces is controlled by computers. Mortar bombs can be programmed to search for moving objects – such as tanks – whilst they fall, and to alter course slightly to explode near them. Rocket-propelled missiles have a similar targeting capability, but with greater freedom of movement.

Computers are particularly suited to army intelligence operations. One idea is to cover potential battlefields with optical fiber networks linked to underground sensors that detect any movement. This array would give continuous information on everything taking place regardless of weather or visibility. It could further be linked to mines scattered in the area which could be triggered by messages from the sensors. Unlike missiles, where the microprocessor is destroyed in the explosion, a network buried below ground level can be used repeatedly. Discussions of strategies such as these are causing a revaluation of current methods of warfare. Perhaps tanks will be less important in the future, if these new methods allow them to be knocked out quickly and cheaply.

Computers are affecting international politics in other areas besides strategic planning. In 1981, the government of Japan and Japanese industry jointly launched their drive towards the fifth generation ("intelligent") computer. Their project was seen by many other developed countries as a direct challenge. In the USA it was referred to as a "technological Pearl Harbor". The American response was rapid. Within a year, several leading US firms were trying to agree on a cooperative development package to rival the Japanese efforts. Such competition between developed countries, however, has only drawn more attention to the gap between developed and developing countries.

In North America, there is almost one telephone for each inhabitant. In Africa, there is one telephone per 60 inhabitants. It is not that developing countries have failed to recognize the importance of communications. Rather, their early emphasis was all on the mass media, especially radio. Their first priority was to disseminate essential information – about sanitation, health, agriculture and education – as widely as possible. Funding for telecommunications was therefore kept at a relatively low level. Even in many developed countries telecommunications are only now being given a high priority.

The mass media are an example of what is known as vertical communication. That is, information is transmitted between people at different levels. In the case of the media, it passes from a central source to the general public, with little feedback. Information passing between people at the same level is called horizontal communication. A telephone conversation is an example, providing good feedback between the participants.

Implementing change depends a great deal on good horizontal communication. Nearly all the everyday news people want to know falls into this category. Much of the effort and money spent on travel in developing countries would be eliminated, if there were a reliable, readily available telephone service. But the debate about means of communication is also one about control of information. Mass media can easily be controlled by governments, whereas many other forms of telecommunication cannot. The central question is, What information will circulate around the world's networks? We may be moving into an "information society", but it is still unclear how information and society can best be made to interact.

► A computerized tax center – a sight guaranteed to strike terror into even the stoutest hearts. Currently, the computers' main use is to plot an accurate path through the maze of tax regulations and so determine the tax payments to be made by individuals and corporations. In the future, such central computers may have access to a range of information on both individuals and institutions, allowing tax inspectors to unearth discrepancies between income and expenditure. Some people fear that such developments will lead to a "Big Brother" regime, as described in George Orwell's* 1984. *Such fears may be exaggerated, but centralized monitoring of citizens is becoming easier.

Glossary

Acoustics
The science of sound, dealing with its production, transmission, reflection and absorption.
Aerial
See ANTENNA
ALU
See ARITHMETIC AND LOGIC UNIT
Amplifier
A device that multiplies a signal by a constant factor.
Amplitude
The maximum deviation from its mean value of a physical property which is subject to modulation.
Amplitude modulation
Common method of encoding a carrier wave in radio transmission, with the signal modifying the amplitude, rather than the frequency of the wave.
Analog
A description of a signal that may vary continuously.
Antenna
A component in an electrical circuit that radiates or receives radio waves.
Arithmetic and logic unit
The part of a COMPUTER that makes decisions in handling information and controls the sequence of steps to be followed in solving a problem.
Artificial Intelligence
Once defined as "the science of making machines do things that would require intelligence if done by men". Intelligence created using non-living man-made microelectronic or other components.
ASCII (American Standard Code for Information Interchange)
A commonly used computer code that assigns a binary number to every letter of the alphabet, piece of punctuation etc.
Bandwidth
The difference between the upper and lower limits of the frequencies needed or available to transmit a signal.
Bar code
An electronic code, normally a pattern of printed black lines, used on shop goods to signify price, weight, etc, and read by a LASER scanner or light pen.
Binary code
Number system on the base 2, frequently used in computers, microprocessors and digitized data of all kinds.
Biochip
A concept, still in its infancy, whereby biological material would replace semiconductors as the basis of the computer chip.
Bit
Short for "binary digit", the smallest unit of information that can be stored in a computer's memory, represented by a pulse of electricity or its absence corresponding to a 1 or 0 in BINARY CODE.
Byte
A set of BITs (0s and 1s), usually eight, that represents a single character and is handled by the computer as a unit.
Central processing unit
The part of a computer that draws data from the memory, processes them in the arithmetic and logical unit and outputs or stores the results, following the instructions of the operator or program.
Computer
A device that performs calculations and stores their results, according to a program.
Conductor
A substance capable of carrying electric current.
CPU
See CENTRAL PROCESSING UNIT
Cortex
The outer surface of an organ, such as the brain (where it is the seat of the higher functions).
Database
A system of centralized information storage to which individual computer users may have access, often by telephonic links.
Data processing
All the operations performed by a computer on the information it receives.
Digitization
The conversion of an ANALOG signal into a digital one, usually in BINARY code.
Doping
The process of adding chemicals to modify the electronic properties of semiconductors during the manufacture of microchips.
Electromagnetic radiation
The form is which energy is transmitted through space or matter, using an electromagnetic field. Its wavelengths carry radio waves and infrared waves, visible light, ultraviolet, X-rays and gamma rays.
Electronics
A science dealing with SEMICONDUCTORS and devices where the motion of ELECTRONS is controlled.
Expert system
A computer program that solves problems in the same way as a human does; a key area of ARTIFICIAL INTELLIGENCE.
Feedback mechanism
A device that controls the operation of a system by detecting the effect and regulating the output automatically.
Frequency
The rate at which a wave motion completes its cycle.
Hacker
Popular name for compulsive computer user who, often working from a remote terminal, gains entry, to and sometimes interferes with, computer systems to which that person has no authorized access.
Hardware
The computer and its peripherals: printer, screen etc. See also SOFTWARE.
Information technology
The technology relating to the collection, processing, storage and transmission of information.
Integrated circuit
A structure (often a silicon chip) on which many individual electronic components are assembled.
Laser
Light Amplification by Stimulated Emission of Radiation; a device producing a very intense beam of parallel light with a precisely defined wavelength.
LCD
See LIQUID CRYSTAL DISPLAY.
Light Pen
A light-sensitive instrument, resembling a pen, that allows a computer user to select from a menu by touching the screen, or to draw on the screen.
Liquid crystal display
Form of displaying information using liquid crystals to block or allow the passage of light onto a reflective surface.
Mainframe
A large central computer, to which smaller computers and other devices may be linked.
Microchip
A complete electrical circuit built into a single piece of SEMICONDUCTOR material, usually silicon.
Microcomputer
A computer with the CENTRAL PROCESSING UNIT contained on a single silicon chip.
Microprocessor
An electronic device that receives, processes, stores and outputs information according to a preprogrammed set of instructions.
Modem
"Modulator-demodulator", a device used to convert the output of a computer into a form suitable for transmission by telephone.
Network
A system of communication links - by computer or otherwise - between members of a group or between different groups for information-handling purposes. The links are called "nodes".
Noise
Unwanted sound, current or voltage that interferes with the SIGNAL.
OCR
See OPTICAL CHARACTER RECOGNITION
Optical character recognition
Electronic memory storage method in which a computerized optical scanner identifies and records text characters.
Optical fiber
Extruded glass fiber of high purity, used to transmit a light signal; used widely for telephone systems.
Photon
A quantum of electromagnetic energy, often throught of as the particle associated with light.
Piezoelectricity
The relationship between mechanical stress and electric charge exhibited by certain crystals.
Pixel
Short for "picture element", the smallest area of the computer screen that can be individually turned "on" or "off" to build up graphics or text characters.
Program
The set of instructions to be followed by a COMPUTER or MICROPROCESSOR.
Radio
Communication between distant points using radio wave, electromagnetic radiation of a certain frequency.
Radioactivity
The spontaneous disintegration of unstable nuclei, accompanied by the emission of RADIATION of alpha particles, beta particles or gamma rays.
Reflection
The bouncing back of energy waves (eg light radiation, sound waves) from a surface.
Refraction
The change in direction of energy waves as they pass from one medium to another.
Relativity
Theory of the nature of time, space and matter, enunciated by Albert Einstein.
Remote sensing
The use of distant sensing devices (normally carried on aircraft or spacecraft) to detect features on the Earth.
Resistance
The ratio of the voltage applied to a CONDUCTOR to the current flowing through it.
Robot
Machine that does work automatically according to a PROGRAM. A robot may be able to detect limited changes in its environment and adapt its movements accordingly.
Semiconductor
A material whose electrical conductivity varies with temperature and impurity. By introducing impurities to different regions of a semiconductor, it can be modified for different electrical purposes.
Servomechanism
An automatic control device in which a command signal from a reference device uses FEEDBACK to control a higher-power output device.
Signal
The variable impulse by which information is carried through a system.
Silicon
A SEMICONDUCTOR material, the basis of the microchip, the heart of the computer.
Software
Computer programs held on magnetic tape or disk etc.; or, loosley, the magnetic storage media themselves. See also HARDWARE.
Spectrogram
Electronically produced visual pattern of bars representing variations in sound, used in speech analysis.
Television
An apparatus for communicating moving pictures by radio transmissions.
Transducer
A device for converting an input signal of another energy mode, normally electrical.
Transistor
An electronic device made of SEMICONDUCTORS used in a circuit as an amplifer, rectifer, detector or switch.
Video
See TELEVISION.
Videotape
The magnetic tape on which a VIDEO signal can be recorded.

Units of Measurement

In general the International System of Units – SI units – is used throughout this book. This system is founded upon seven empirically defined *base units* (eg ampere), which can be combined, sometimes with the assistance of two geometric *supplementary units* (eg radian) to yield the *derived units* (eg cubic meter) which together with the base units constitute a coherent set of units capable of application to all measurable physical phenomena. Some of the derived units have special names (eg volt). For the sake of convenience smaller and larger units, the multiples and submultiples of the SI units, can be formed by adding certain prefixes (eg milli-) to the names of the SI units. In any instance only one prefix can be added to the name of a unit (thus nanometer, not millimicrometer). Of the other units in common scientific use, it is recognized that several (eg hour) will continue to be used alongside the SI units, although combinations of these units with SI units (as in kilowatt hour) are discouraged. However, other units (eg angstrom unit) are redundant if the International System is fully utilized, and it is intended that these should drop out of use.

Base units

Quantity	Unit	Symbol
length	meter	m
mass	kilogram	kg
time	second	s
electric current	ampere	A
temperature	kelvin	K
luminous intensity	candela	cd
amount of substance	mole	mol

Derived units

Quantity	Name	Symbol
frequency	hertz	Hz
force	newton	N
work, energy	joule	J
power	watt	W
pressure	pascal	Pa
quantity of electricity	coulomb	C
potential difference	volt	V
electric resistance	ohm	Ω
capacitance	farad	F
conductance	siemens	S
magnetic flux	weber	Wb
flux density	tesla	T
inductance	henry	H
luminous flux	lumen	lm
illuminance	lux	lx

Supplementary units

Quantity	Name	Symbol
plane angle	radian	rad
solid angle	steradian	sr

Non-SI units in common use

Quantity	Name	Symbol
plane angle	degree	°
plane angle	minute	′
plane angle	second	″
time	minute	min
time	hour	h
time	day	d
volume	liter	l
mass	tonne	t
energy	electronvolt	eV
mass	atomic mass unit	u
length	astronomical unit	AU
length	parsec	pc

Index notation

Very large and very small numbers are often written using powers of ten. The American system in the table below names large numbers according to the number of groups of three zeros which follow 1,000 when they are expressed in numerals – eg 1 billion (bi- meaning two) is 1,000 followed by two groups of three zeros.

Name	Numeral	Value in powers of ten	SI prefix	SI symbol
one	1	10^0	—	—
ten	10	10^1	deka	da
hundred	100	10^2	hecto	h
thousand	1,000	10^3	kilo	k
million	1,000,000	10^6	mega	M
billion	1,000,000,000	10^9	giga	G
trillion	1,000,000,000,000	10^{12}	tera	T
tenth	0.1	10^{-1}	deci	d
hundredth	0.01	10^{-2}	centi	c
thousandth	0.001	10^{-3}	milli	m
millionth	0.000001	10^{-6}	micro	μ
billionth	0.000000001	10^{-9}	nano	n
trillionth	0.000000000001	10^{-12}	pico	p

Abbreviations not already given above

A	mass number
Å	angstrom unit
AC	alternating current
AF	audio frequency
asb	apostilb
atm	atmosphere
AW	atomic weight
bhp	brake horse power
bp	boiling point
Btu	British thermal unit
C°	centigrade degree
°C	degree Celsius
Cal	see Kcal
cal	calorie
ccp	cubic close-packed
CGS	centimeter-gram-second (system)
Ci	curie
dB	decibel
DC	direct current
EHF	extremely high frequency
emf	electromotive force
emu	electromagnetic unit
esu	electrostatic unit
f	femto-
fcc	face-centered cubic
FM	frequency modulation
G	universal constant of gravitation
g	gram
g	acceleration due to gavity
Gb	gilbert
gr	grain
Gs	gauss
h	Planck constant
ha	hectare
hcp	hexagonal close-packed
HF	high frequency
hp	horse power
IF	intermediate frequency
ir	infrared
k	kilo-
k	Boltzmann constant
kcal	kilocalorie
kgf	kilogram force
L	lambert
LW	long wave
ly	light year
M	mega-
mbar	millibar
MF	medium frequency
MKSA	meter-kilogram-second- ampere (system)
mp	melting point
mya	million years ago
MW	medium wave
MW	molecular weight
Mx	maxwell
$\mathcal{N}$	Avogadro number, neutron number
nmr	nuclear magnetic resonance
Oe	oersted
O.N.	oxidation number
P	poise
pH	hydrogen ion concentration
ph	phot
ppm	parts per million
R	röntgen
R	universal gas constant
°R	degrees Rankine or (Reaumur)
rad	radian
rd	rad (dose)
rpm	revolutions per minute
sb	stilb
sg	specific gravity
SHF	superhigh frequency
sr	steradian
STP	standard temperature and pressure
subl	sublimation point
UHF	ultrahigh frequency
uv	ultraviolet
VHF	very high frequency
yr	year
$\mathcal{Z}$	atomic number

Index

Page numbers in *italics* refer to illustrations, captions or side text.

A

B

C

D

E

F

G

H

I

K

Credits

Key to abbreviations: FSP Frank Spooner Pictures; MEPL Mary Evans Picture Library; NHPA Natural History Photographic Agency; OSF Oxford Scientific Films; SPL Science Photo Library; TCL Telegraph Colour Library; b bottom; bl bottom left; br bottom right; c center; cl center left; cr center right; t top; tl top left; tr top right; l left, r right.

5,6 Imagine **7** Imagine/Scientific American **8**t SPL/A. McClenaghan **8**b OSF/B. Kent **9**l SPL/Imperial College, London **9**r, **10, 11**tl, **11**tr Imagine **11**b TCL/I. Kennedy **12**l, **12**r, **13**l Imagine **13**r Splitsecond/D. Thomas **14**t Imagine **14**b OSF/S. Dalton **15**t SPL/Dr G. Bredberg **15**b Imagine **16**t NHPA/S. Dalton **16**c R. Payne/American Association for the Advancement of Science **16**b Ardea/F.Gohier **17** Format/R. Kempadoo **18** TCL **19**tl Imagine **19**tr Camera Press/T. Lanser **19**b OSF/D. Macdonald **20** SPL/D.Kryminec **21**t Imagine **21**b OSF/M. Chillmaid **22, 23**tr Imagine **23**tl OSF/R. Packwood **24**t SPL/Petit Format/B. Livingston **24**b,**25**b Imagine **25**t SPL/CNRI **26** SPL/M. Kage **27** Imagine **28** Equinox Archive **29** Imagine **30** Imagine/Scientific American **31** Logica **32** Keystone Collection **33**tl, **33**tr Imagine **33**b S. and R. Greenhill **34** Imagine **35**l Photosource **35**r MEPL **36,37** Imagine **38**t Bruce Coleman Ltd/R. Williams **38**b Magnum/Cornell Capa **39**t Bruce Coleman Ltd/M. Freeman **39**b FSP **40**b OSF/J.A.L. Cooke **40–41**t OSF/L.L. Rue **41**b Imagine **42–43** Telefocus Picture Library **44** Zefa **45** Imagine **46** Zefa **47**t Ted Spiegel **47**b Imagine **48** Rex Features **49, 50–51, 52** Imagine **52–53** SPL/Dr J. Burgess **53, 54**l Imagine/Scientific American **54–55** SPL/D. Parker **56–57**t IBM/James Kilkelly **57**tr IBM **57**bl, **57**cr, **57**br Imagine **58**l S. and R. Greenhill **58–59**t Telefocus Picture Library **58–59**b Central Office of Information **59**br SPL/H. Morgan **60**b P. Addis/New Scientist **60–61**t SPL/H. Morgan **61**b Imagine **62** Marconi **63** Imagine **64** Civil Aviation Authority **64–65**t Telefocus Picture Library **65** Planet Earth Pictures/F. Schulke **66** TCL **67** Imagine **68**t BPCC/Aldus Archive **68**b Animal Photography **69** Imagine **70** National Portrait Gallery, London **71** Library of Congress, Washington **72** Imagine **72–73** Art Directors/C. O'Rear **73** IBM/Claire Albahae **74**tl MEPL **74**tr Art Directors/W. Hodges **74–75**b Landrover **76–77**b TCL **76**t Jerry Mason **77**r TCL/J. Reardon **78** Art Directors/C. O'Rear **78–79** Rainbow/H. Morgan **80** John Schulz for PAR/NYC **82** SIC-PetT **83** Imagine/Scientific American **84**t, **84**b Rex Features **86** Imagine **87**t New Scientist **87**tc, **87**bc, **87**b, **88**l Imagine **89** Imagine/Scientific American **88–89** FSP **90–91** Rainbow/H. Morgan **91**r AAH Meditel **92**t, **92**b Pierre Mens, Press Promotion **93** London Features International Ltd., **94**b British Library **94**t Imagine **95** SPL/NASA **96**l, **96–97** Rainbow/D. McCoy **97**r Rainbow/H. Morgan **98** Imagine **99**l Rex Features **99**r Zefa **100**l The Guardian **100**r SPL/T. Povett **101** Imagine/Scientific American **102**l British Aerospace **102**r SPL/B.H. Frisch **102–103** SPL/H. Morgan **103**r Jerry Mason **104**l, **104**r Rediffusion Simulation Ltd., **105**l S. and R. Greenhill **109**r Pierre Mens, Press Promotion **106** Thinking Machines Corporation **107** IBM **108–109** Imagine **110–111**t IBM **110–111**b SPL/L. Mulvehill **111**r FSP **112** IBM – Eurocoor **113** Art Directors **114**tl, **114–115**t Rex Features **115**r Imagine **114–115**b, **116–117**t FSP **116–117**b Rainbow/D.McCoy **117**r Zefa **118**l S. and R. Greenhill **118**r, **118–119**t, **119**b FSP **120**b Imagine **120–121** FSP **121** Hi-Ovis/Marshall Cavendish Picture Library **122–123**t, **122**b, **123**b, FSP **124** Zefa

Index Barbara James and John Baines
Production Joanna Turner, Clive Sparling
Typesetting Anita Rokins
Media conversion Peter MacDonald